THE TERRORS OF THE ULTIMATE QUEST!

And the things advanced upon him! Suddenly he saw them, rushing forward in a furious throng, a mass of pale, lithe, loathsome figures. They were human, after a fashion—at least they walked or ran upright like men— but mere mockeries of humanity were they. Unclothed, they raced at him on feet bearing three large toes and heavy, horny nails. Their skinny, extended arms ended in gnarled hands with three big, dangerously curved claws. Their heads bobbled atop scrawny long necks, and those faces! The faces, grotesque caricatures of the human norm, were beyond belief; Bleek felt himself confronted by living nightmare. They had no nose save slits for nostrils, nor external ears, nor hair; they had thin mouths from which glistening, dripping fangs protruded, mouths that twitched and worked and drooled as they emitted thin, nasty squeaks; and eyes that dominated the ugly features. Their eyes were like saucers, fishy ovals spread across half the face, never blinking, staring damply at him as the things closed in. Bleek saw all this in one horrific instant, then turned tail and fled with a scream back the way he had come, dashing off of the avenue and behind a cubic structure in a feverish attempt to lose the creatures. The hideous monsters were hot on his trail, however, and more charged forth from other angles. He ran on, heedless of direction, twisting and turning between blank-walled buildings in an all-consuming effort to escape.

He ran forever, as he imagined it, pursued by a horde, of which the slightest glimpse induced lasting disgust and mortal terror. He knew not where he fled, nor did he think or care of such matters; his only thought was to get away from those freaks of life and nature . . .

The Journey of Jacob Bleek: the complete novel, plus six more tales chronicling the adventures of the daring medieval wizard.

THE JOURNEY OF JACOB BLEEK

and

The Further Adventures
of Jacob Bleek

by Jeffery Scott Sims

Published by Dyrezan Press
Collection © 2019 by Jeffery Scott Sims
ISBN: 978-0-9899322-4-0

THE JOURNEY OF JACOB BLEEK

THE FURTHER ADVENTURES OF JACOB BLEEK

RETURN FROM THE DARK LANDS

Nothing lasts forever, not even the universe if current understandings are correct. Published fiction—including popular works—are especially prone to disappearing down black holes, or being overwhelmed by entropy. I, unfortunately, am not immune. Quite a few of my published tales from receding yesteryears have become increasingly hard to find. As a rule, this is due to the publishers having sold out the relevant magazines and anthologies, or in some instances because those publishers have sadly bit the dust. One may also suspect cosmic conspiracies or evil occult influence. Whatever the case, I've arranged to bring back to the public consciousness a batch of works that have over time vanished from mortal ken.

The big deal here is the second edition of the novel *The Journey of Jacob Bleek*; not the original story of that long lasting, ominous and cunning character, but certainly the crucially central tale presenting the man, his mission and method. I feel that the novel places his many other tales in proper perspective; having read the novel, all the rest fall into place. Necessarily so, for *Journey* actually begins at the beginning of Bleek's amazing career, after brief exposition plunging the reader into a series of unfolding linked escapades, hurtling headlong toward Bleek's appointment with cosmic destiny.

The novel is complete unto itself, yet I never considered leaving it there. In fact there were earlier stories dealing with Bleek, though they didn't cohere until the book hammered out the framework. The conceit underlying subsequent tales is simple: the novel constitutes a mere sampling of its hero's exploits, with the later short pieces recounting adventures which didn't get recorded in the novel. They fill in the gaps created by Bleek's lengthy span of life, a period capable of producing an endless series of exciting and harrowing events.

So, in addition to the ten adventures provided by the novel, for this new publication I have added six more. Four of them fit the pattern of stories that serve as "missing chapters," readily linking with those of *Journey*. These are "Beyond the Crossroads," "Morstenburg," "The Crags of the Schwartzenburg," and "The Companion of Jacob Bleek," involving weird undertakings in Germanic locales and an Egyptian excursion similar to those of the first half of the novel. The remaining two were composed prior to the conceiving of Bleek's quest. The character originated as a focus of spookiness dealing with grand magic. These tales, "The Love of Jacob Bleek" and "The City at the End of Time," in retrospect appear to take place after the epic journey, when Bleek has settled down to secretive arcane delvings. Continuity isn't precise in that respect, the way of things with stories developed over several years. These two, among others, surely suggest more excitement in store for Bleek after completing his immense wanderings.

Enjoy this expanded edition of *The Journey of Jacob Bleek*. Hopefully the reader may feel the thrills of strange places, beings, creatures, and the deeds of a most unusual hero.

Jeffery Scott Sims
July 22, 2019

THE JOURNEY OF JACOB BLEEK

Prologue

Jacob Bleek—he who, in the fullness of time attained fame as the mightiest of sorcerers, the supreme master of the black and esoteric arts—in an earlier epoch of his life grew weary of his laborious and unremitting studies, yet dreamed that there was more to be learned; dreamed of marvels beyond rote spell and hex, of wonders beyond his current knowledge, or that of any man living or dead. Indeed, his bookish delvings had carried him far already at that time, beyond the reach of his fellow warlocks, to the point that other scholars and correspondents, having learned of him and his work, had come to envy him his knowledge, and even to fear him his prowess. There were things that he knew, on matters which troubled them, that they did not, despite their greater years; and there were things that he had done, achievements which he had shown them, and still wilder accomplishments of which he had boasted, and possibilities on which he had speculated, which troubled them sorely, or even terrified them. Some of the terrors which he revealed to them had been shown to be objectively true; there were firm indications of others which surpassed the former in horror; and then there were yet others, of which Bleek had only hinted or whispered, which served to damn him in the eyes of his erstwhile colleagues. Over time they had come to find this youthful zealot (for in that epoch he was still a young man, in years if not in wisdom, and had not yet attained that notoriety which dogs his memory to the present day) unpleasant, and wished to hear no more of or from him.

Bleek had also tired of his situation in life, that of the eternal student, one who scrambles for a living in the common market to sustain himself, buying or selling with loquacious and vulgar peddlers who care naught for wisdom or genius; one who shelters himself in one cheap garret attic after another, squatting squalidly until his actions or manners require him to move over to the next street and the next decrepit boarding house; one who reads crabbed text and peruses intricate diagrams until his eyes begin to permanently weaken. All his years to this point had been spent in the bustling, noisy seaside port of Bruges, into which the great ships came from far places, and caravans departed into the interior, connecting to the wide world of which he knew only by report or rumor, never having seen any of it himself. Of this life young Bleek, so he decided, would have no more to do, for he had borne with it almost since he had begun to read and turned his mind to thoughts out of the ordinary, and it appealed to him not, and also he concluded that his studies, far ranging though they were, had attained their practical limits. There was nothing more that the printed page, as it was available to an earnest youth of modest means, could teach him, and if there be other books of worth, he feared that he must seek them out, wherever they lay, rather than hope that they would ever find their way to him.

Above all, Jacob Bleek dreamed of a goal beyond that of his fellows, a desire for real knowledge and genuine power which superseded that traditionally promised by the control of magic. He had, to be sure, sampled all the delights that conventional necromancy and cabbalism could bestow. He had raised the dead and wrung from them nuggets of useful information; he had talked with glorious shades of old, and learned from them secrets locked away in forgotten chambers or lost to the centuries; he had cast signs and woven spells which conjured up demons and other curious and alarming species; he had plumbed those depths of antique lore which opened up hints of strange and distant vistas into places and times unknown and unsuspected. These things he had done, with such proficiency, dedication, and success, as to draw forth startled gasps of admiration and dismay from his contemporaries; yet these things at first satisfied him little, and finally not at all. There was more to be known, more to be mastered. There were the secrets of the Gods themselves, the Old Ones—not the false, feeble, empty gods of the pious herd, but the great and unfathomable Entities who had constructed the vast universe for Their own pleasure, and who controlled every aspect of its substance—They who knew all, and were all, all things that ever were or ever could be. No man before, however wise and however keen, had ever, to the best of his knowledge, more than guessed at Their existence, nor had divined Their nature or Their intentions; yet Bleek had deduced Their existence and Their attributes from his studies of old myths and his own cold, clear-eyed analysis of the universe as he knew it. That universe, in all its wondrous complexity, did exist, and Someone, he logically concluded, must lie behind such an intricate instrument. That universe was a cruel, callous, remorseless realm, a place of vast, merciless forces and impersonal cosmic currents, conceived not for man or for any trivial creatures, but for the purposes of the Entities who created it. They might not be friendly to the meaningless puppets They had fashioned by whim or by jest, but They were all wise, and could be approached on Their own terms. Bleek imagined himself as the only man in all of creation who could peel away the layers of utter mystery which shrouded the Old Ones, and in doing so make Them known to him, make himself known to Them, and by so doing establish harmonious contact and acquire from Them the pure wisdom and boundless domination of matter and destiny which had hitherto been the sole right of the Old Ones.

What Bleek desired, above all other attainments, was to see the world, in all its matter and motion, through the eyes of the Gods. He wanted to know as They knew, to experience omniscience, a power which must necessarily grant omnipotence. Armed with Godly vision, there would be no limit to his accomplishments and, if he so chose, to his domination over others. The universe would be thrown open to him, to use and to abuse as he saw fit for his happiness. Indeed, with such boundless sight he would be as the Gods Themselves, and perhaps no longer need to revere or fear Them.

If the grandiosity of total knowledge and supreme power would be his, Jacob Bleek must seek the Gods wherever They might be found, and along the way learn whatever more must be known by him before he came to meet Them; and this he resolved to do. The resolution grew to obsession, and the obsession engendered action. He would journey forth into the wide world, charting a course dictated solely by circumstance and discovery, until he gained his end. He laid his plans wisely. First he sold off his meager belongings, those personal effects which he could not carry on his proposed life on the road. He divested himself of said items, save for the most modest necessaries, in return for a trivial sum of coinage, though that be more than he had ever possessed before. Even so, it would do only for a start. During his travels he would have to live by his wits, and make the most of suitable opportunities that presented themselves. Such practical matters he would consider when his situation required him to do so.

The majority of his possessions consisted of books, most of them old, many of them rare, a few of considerable worth. Bleek parted with these grudgingly, beginning by selling the lesser volumes, which no longer served his intellectual needs, at the book shops. Certain editions commanded reasonable prices, which made it possible for him to provide for himself in a somewhat more respectable fashion. From the proceeds he earned sufficient wealth to purchase a pony and an extremely small but rugged wagon, which would take him and his remaining belongings farther and faster than he could otherwise have managed. He chose this method of conveyance, rather than signing on to a ship—which he had naturally considered—partly out of economy, and partly because once aboard a sailing vessel he would have little control over his own movements, and he desired the ability to travel where he would, without being at the mercy of the schedules and whims of others.

There were still more books, however, which presented him with something of a quandary. Some of the aged tomes in his collection were not safe to release to other men, whether they be men of knowledge who could make use of them, or whether they be unwary of the contents. These books contained powerful magical formulae which should not be cast about recklessly, but which were past their utility to Bleek, or which he could not afford to bear with him; so these he burned, regardless of the financial loss. That left a relative handful of volumes which, when he came to think of them, he concluded he could not live without, no matter how troublesome the burden be; so he packed them in canvas wrappings with his few retained effects, and loaded them into the little wagon.

And so, on a fine spring day, the very day of attaining his majority, at the age of one and twenty, young Jacob Bleek departed from his last settled abode in the lonely room high above the market street, and set out on his extraordinary quest. Whither his journey would take him he knew not, nor did he much care, so long as it opened to him the world, and led to the peculiar wonders he craved. He traveled east on the good road from the coast, passed by and passing the trains of tradesmen, heading in no particular direction but away from where he had been; for he had no set destination in mind. He would go where the road carried him, and know where he was going when he found the place.

Pursuing his course east for some days, Bleek entered a region of low, rolling hills, a densely wooded land dark by daylight, with few villages. He made it his custom to spend the night at traveler's inns, not sleeping in the wagon unless the courtesy of the road failed him. Through this region he made his way pleasantly enough, until he came to the banks of the big river, the mighty River Rhine, and knew he had crossed over into the domain of the Germans, though the language had been spoken for much of his trip to this point. Bleek understood the speech well, it being not so different from his own, and he having a talent for languages, one also derived mainly from study. His extensive reading had often required the command of foreign tongues, and the brooding, analytical Germans had written much through the centuries on subjects of interest to him.

For two days he made his way up river through the dank forests, seldom meeting others, now heading south toward the more populous cities which, he knew from his geography, must lie beyond the wilderness. On the first night of his southward progression he had to lay up in his wagon, for so scarce was fixed settlement that he could not find an inn to house him. In the morning, having broken fast with his scanty provisions, he continued onward.

I. The Haunted Village

That evening, very late, Jacob Bleek rode into a little village tucked off the main road (such as it was, for the surface was bad, indicative of infrequent use and care), and partly obscured from travelers by gloomy woods. The village was darker than he would have expected, though it possessed an inn, one of which he did not much like the looks, for it appeared ill maintained, and only a single yellow light flickered downstairs through the grimy, glazed window panes. It seemed to be his sole option, however, other than camping on the road again, which he hated, so he resolved without further inner debate to make the most of the situation. He tied his horse and wagon and entered the decrepit structure, pushing open the creaking oaken door. It was a musty place, lacking most of the homey touches of cleanliness and decoration that wayfarers are wont to expect, and he suspected that it was not immediately or often tenanted, but it would satisfy his basic wants if the establishment offered a meal and a bed. He rapped with his knuckles on the tarnished copper bell at the counter.

Presently the landlord appeared from upstairs, a shabby unshaven man past his prime, if truly he ever had one. The man was hardly dressed for business, and seemed surprised to find company. In truth, he started wildly, and drew back for a moment, as if he had a mind to flee from the presence of his guest.

"Lost your way in the twilight, sir?" cried the landlord, after a tense pause. "With the state of the roads in these days and times, I don't wonder." Bleek explained his presence, and requested accommodation. "That I can manage," agreed the man, "although it's rare that such is called for. So you be a traveler, for certain? Few make their way to Wetzelburg. You'll be staying only for the night, I'll reckon." Bleek assured him, with carefully controlled fervor, that such was the case. "Then I'll oblige you, to be sure. How do you travel?" Bleek told him that he owned a horse wanting attention. "So that will be done. There is an upper chamber to the right of the stairs. Make yourself at home, and I'll attend to your beast, and then see to getting something prepared to fill your belly. My wife can cook up something in no time. Welcome sir; Johann Seidel welcomes you, in the name of our village, and I'll see your money, please."

Bleek fetched his leather travel bag and climbed to his room, which proved, after he lit the lamp, to be no more than he expected; still, he had lived in worse. Shortly the proprietor returned with a bowl of water for shaving and cleaning, and a jug of same for drinking. "Come down as you will," announced Seidel, "for your supper awaits." In no time at all Bleek took advantage of the offer, for he had eaten little throughout the course of a long day. The woman of the house peeped from the kitchen once, not to show herself again (not for the duration of his stay, as it happened), nor did her husband make any effort to arrange an introduction. A dish of stew and stein of beer had been laid at one of the three rough-hewn oaken tables of the dimly lit dining hall. He ate with gusto, though the quality of the cuisine was nothing to impress. He thought it the leftovers of his host's own meal. The repast did serve to fill, and that contented for the moment.

Throughout the simple feast Bleek detected that Seidel eyed him strangely and furtively. Good Johann busied himself by polishing jars and utensils in sore need of attention, yet he seemed greatly interested in, and perhaps perplexed by, his silent guest. After Bleek had cleaned his plate, and motioned for a refill of his stein, the visitor deigned to engage the man in small talk, in order that the fellow might be drawn out, and be brought to speak what was on his mind, for something there surely was. The landlord's agitation increased by the moment, and eventually he could not contain himself.

"Truly, you be a live man?" he cried. Bleek found this an unusual question, and said as much. "So you would, and should, say, sir," replied his host, "and it's my place to receive no less from you, but I tell you that in these parts it's a genuine consideration—I don't expect to convince the wife, as it is, which is why she won't come out—and an honest and decent, God fearing man can be none too cautious with strangers, and that be the fact, and there, I've said it." The man had actually said very little to the point, so Bleek pressed him, and found him nervously voluble. "In this village, sir," continued Seidel, "the formerly happy village of Weztelburg, there be people who aren't quite people, who walk about when they shouldn't, if they really walk at all, and who pay visits that aren't called for nor welcome. They were men once upon a time, like you and I, but they're something more or less than that now, and they keep coming back, and we of the village can't abide it.

"They're attracted by the lights, you see. They only come by night, and they're drawn like moths to the light, so we here don't keep many fires or lamps burning. I'll light another, if you insist. No? Thank you, sir. It's more than I can stand to have them creeping around, and peering through the windows, and trying to get inside. It can be a bad time when they do. I don't mean to scare you, but we've had fine citizens, and their women and children, go missing after such a visit; so, it doesn't pay to take chances.

"Perhaps I've said too much," Seidel mumbled, after a long silence. "I don't mean to frighten off good business, for the Lord knows I can use it. Pity us, sir, but don't worry yourself. Keep to your room, and forego the light, and you should have no trouble. Such a story must sound foolish enough to a man of your sort." On the contrary—of course—the tale mightily interested Jacob Bleek, who would pass up no opportunity to increase his store of knowledge on such matters. He explained to the fellow that he was no common tradesman, as perhaps had been surmised, but rather a wandering scholar, a man of deep ideas and fulsome education, who had made it part of his line of study to investigate occurrences of precisely this sort. "I knew there was something exceptional about you," Seidel said heartily. "You look like a man who thinks for a living, though I'd have guessed rather young for such a noble calling." Bleek assured him that it was so, and that in his own circles he was considered a man who did as well as thought, and that he was in possession of certain powers and special influences which, in the right circumstances, could be brought to bear on such a case as this.

"That be music to my ears," cried the landlord. "Wetzelburg be haunted—that's the long and short of it—and none here knows what to do about it. Our minister gave up on us long ago, and fled the town, and since his day there's been no one to look into the bedevilment nor do anything toward putting it down. But a clever man, a reading man—one who knows all about mysteries and secret things—that man is in a position to do a world of good for folks around here. Maybe you have some words or potions (that have been approved by the church, I'll reckon) that will do the job and make things right again."

Bleek promised nothing, except to casually announce that he might not be so entirely inclined to continue his travels in the morning as he had previously intended. If he were assured of adequate lodgings for the duration, it could serve his own purposes to stay on for a period, and acquaint himself further with the misfortunes of Weztelburg. Seidel hesitated only for the moment before accepting the proposal, offering his accommodations to the esteemed visitor, and adding that it would be a blessing if the troubles ceased, and business picked up. Bleek asked several more questions about the nature of the strange happenings in the village, but derived little more useful information from his host. Having reached this stage, the man seemed reluctant to speak concerning the details or history of the manifestations.

Bleek spent the night in a bed which fulfilled its promise, being not much less suitable for the task than others he had enjoyed; and when the sun had risen above the treetops he descended for breakfast, which Seidel did seem pleased to provide (after his guest renewed his desire to investigate the mystery), and then went forth into the lonely village of Weztelburg in order to learn something of the place and its inhabitants. He found it a dreary town, lacking in charm, in industry, and in the sounds of activity and life. It was too tired, too quiet, too furtive for his tastes, at least from the standpoint of a traveler; for these indications suggested to him that something was going on, beyond the concerns of his landlord, which truly did affect the entire village. The cottages were unkempt, the lanes rutted and holed. Bleek noted that the citizenry were not early risers, or they chose to delay their morning business well beyond the dawn. Another burg of this sort he might have deemed sleepy; this one, he mused, appeared to be hiding.

As he, with apparent indifference, strolled the streets, he began to meet and greet the first people to stir from their homes. All initially reacted strangely to his presence, and none were eager to commence conversation. Bleek, as he passed, forced his words upon them. The few tradesmen invited him into their shops or offered services he did not require; he asked the questions of an ephemeral visitor, and they replied guardedly. He hailed housewives outside of their cottages, women who jumped and blinked at him, and only then remembered standard courtesy. He spotted small children peering fearfully at him from behind windows. He observed at a remove—making note of the location—the village cemetery, which lay in a damp hollow by the edge of the forest, with the spire of the closed and tottering church looming nearby. Bleek would go there, to learn what he could (and to amuse himself, if he learned nothing, for such places always sparked his interest), but first he intended to hear the voices of the village folk, to the extent that they could be encouraged to speak.

He stopped a woman on the street, an elderly crone carrying a straw bag full of groceries, and accosted her bluntly. What manner of town was this, he demanded, with no church, and silent, solitary ways? He pretended to complain of his poor welcome. The woman made a superstitious sign of deliverance—one which Bleek knew to be absolutely useless, but which the vulgar placed great store by—and begged him to spare her if he be a "shade". He wondered aloud if spirits walk by daylight, and she checked herself, and granted his humanity, begging his pardon, and further pointing out what he already knew, that few living visitors appeared in Wetzelburg.

"I thought for a moment," she admitted, "that you be one who walks without proper and natural leave, as if you had much on your mind, when there should be naught on or in your mind. I see my mistake, and apologize for the insult, but I've been plagued much by shades, which are more solid than I like, and will pester a body so. Not by the light of the sun, I realize, and there be my error, though I'm sure of little these days. For many years I've gone abroad in fear, and I dare say that won't change soon."

Bleek asked about the source of her terror. "Them who creep from their graves, and make misery for the living, when they should lie quiet," she replied. "Evil men, all of them, and their women and children too. Dead, each one of them, but hating the living so much that they come back to haunt and torment, to threaten, and sometimes, when the cruel desire strikes them, to lie in wait and snatch away warm bodies, for no decent purpose, I'll be bound. It does happen that way on occasion; such a fate took my sister last year, when the foolish woman insisted on drawing water from the well by night, a time when thirst should have been the least of her concerns. They got her, and I've seen her no more, nor wish to, knowing where she must be now."

Bleek established that she meant what she said, and she willingly added many convincing circumstantial details of her sister's disappearance, but the old woman could not be brought to speak further concerning the nature of those who stalked the village by night, and she grew quarrelsome by degrees, and finally warmly resentful, as if he were interrogating her upon a point which it was not good taste to pursue. He released her therefore, and let her pass on her way, and he continued on, and accosted still others, and from some he derived similar tales, but all their stories lacked the whys and wherefores of the business, and Bleek came to realize that he faced a conspiracy of silence, or fear, or something otherwise, which held their tongues and sealed their lips on the critical point. For the wizard knew, being a scholar and a man devoted to digging deep into weighty matters, that knowledge of cause will always lead more quickly to a solution, than a recitation of effects.

He returned to Seidel's house for his supper, dropping hints to his landlord that he was gaining ground in fathoming the mystery, and having suggested as much, was well fed. His host was no more willing to add to his testimony than before, so Bleek genially forbade demanding an answer, yet he had now begun to suspect that there was much else these people could tell, if they had minds to do so, and since they clearly did not it followed, by Bleek's reasoning, that they had sound personal reasons for not telling all. He concluded this, noted the provisional fact, and considered future plans. In his room that night, by the light of his single tiny lamp (which cast no glow through his tightly shuttered window), he perused such books as he retained, and recalled others, pondering those chapters which bore upon similar occurrences. A theory came to him, which he would test when he was ready.

Before taking to his bed Bleek peered between his shutters into the dark street below. It was impossible to see much, and he could be sure of less, but for a moment—just a brief instant—he thought he spied a human form moving slowly down the street, moving in an oddly unnatural manner. He shortly lost the figure, and was not eager to derive conclusions from so trivial an experience, yet he had seen something there, and he knew by now that none of the proper townsfolk would dare wander far abroad after hours, so he wondered if he might have seen something extraordinary. The thought pleased him; the phenomenon was quite active, still awaiting his verdict.

On the next morning useful Johann plied him with food and drink, and bragged of his care of his guest's horse, and insisted on sage actions and remedies. "Must this go on?" cried the poor man, piteously, turning to the others present as if looking for their agreement. These others were a group of frowning, unpleasantly visaged fellows sitting together at a corner table, men who eyed the stranger watchfully and listened carefully, yet said nothing. "You know our dreadful condition, and with your wisdom—which surely promises a deal—can't you rid us of the misery? Are you indeed the man for whom we've been waiting, ever since the minister deserted us?" The guest assured his host that he was such a man, was the man indeed, and would act with dispatch when the time was right. He cautioned Seidel against the taking of hasty measures; the operations of the higher, esoteric arts were complicated, tricky, even dangerous when not coupled with forethought; if he acted unwisely, prior to completing his research, he risked harming those who least deserved it, an outcome which Seidel would surely reject; and he boasted, in an offhand fashion, of his developing schemes, which he thought might lead soon to a final conclusion to the unhappy business, but only if his plans were sound and carefully thought out. The landlord seemed mollified for the moment, though he muttered under his breath at the cost of good food and drink, and feed for a healthy animal, and appeared inclined to discuss the issue, until Bleek announced that he must go forth once more, and finish his preliminary study of the situation, which should not be delayed on any account, for his duty to his fine host called him, and he would not rest this day until he was certain in his mind what he ought to do. That cheered Seidel greatly (and apparently the other men too, for they whispered with animation among themselves), and he bade his lodger undertake the furtherance of his mission at once, and on that note they parted.

Jacob Bleek set out, under a grim gray sky, walking staff in hand, with one goal in mind, this being the village churchyard with its cemetery. Along his route through town certain worthies thought to accost him, or made as if to do so, but none got beyond mumbling a few words of greeting, or the beginnings of a question. One keen glance at his cold, impassive face tended to drive them away. The cemetery lay, as he had earlier noted, at the end of a long lane which extended to the point where the overgrown trees of the dark forest first began to grow forbiddingly thick. It might always have been an isolated place, but now it seemed divorced from the community, as if shunned. He had seen no one passing that way before, and he saw none doing so this day. The villagers, he gathered, cared not for this sacred seat of their worship, or this hallowed shrine to their dead.

He made his way to the low stone wall which bordered the property, a barrier poorly maintained if at all, and peered within. There stood the crumbling wooden church, its windows broken out, a portion of its roof sagging, at the end of a weedy path, the surrounding grounds lush with wild shrubs and briers. The graveyard extended to the left of the building, sloping downward toward the trees beyond, and circled around to the back. He observed a variety of lichenous monuments, most of granite, a few of marble, and more wooden crosses above low earthen mounds. A number of the crosses, and a couple of the finer monuments, lay flat or teetering. He sought the iron gate, which proved to be rusted shut, though unchained—in fact, he spied the chain broken on the ground, partly hidden by weeds—so he leaped the wall without further ado and entered the compound.

The door of the church stood shut, but hung from loose, creaking hinges, and it was but a moment's work to force it open. Bleek passed into the gloomy sanctuary, finding about what he had expected: a small chamber with a few benches, as befitted a small community, and a raised pew at the end, attained by a short flight of steps. This he saw, along with the signs of creeping decay, in the form of heavy dust, and thick cobwebs, and broken or rotten wooden furnishings, and jagged shards of colored glass beneath the mostly vacant sockets of windows. The Holy Crucifix, of grimy bronze, lay on the floor in the dust, cracked and minus one agonized arm. One could conclude that formal religious service played no current role in these people's lives, as he had already hazarded to guess; for, so he had found from his studies and prior observation of men, the crudely pious tend not to act upon their supposedly better impulses, unless they be led by an approved and properly sanctioned minister. He was gone, and none had taken his place, and thus the temple had been abandoned by all.

Surely, however, there must be more to the story than that, thought Bleek. Simple logic carried the wizard only so far in the analysis of the mystery. There must be more to be learned. On one bare wall, stripped of whatever ornamentation it had ever possessed, he detected writing scrawled large on the dingy surface. He approached, attempting to puzzle out the meaning in the dim light. The message, perhaps written with charcoal or daubed with a finger, must have been difficult to read at the best of times, for it was old, and the actions of time and dampness had been long at it, but he could decipher enough to know that it was composed in the best educated High German, of a sort certainly uncommon in these parts. A farewell, perhaps, from the departed minister? Bleek fancied that it was a sort of general condemnation, although of what he could not know. One word, written in bold Gothic strokes, especially stood out from its spidery neighbors, and that word was SHRECKEN.

That amused him; indeed, the more the sorcerer delved into the mystery, the more he derived necessary entertainment from it. The citizens of Weztelburg knew more than they told; there was something which, for their own reasons, they chose not to tell; their calculated secrecy increased his desire to expose the secret. Their minister had left them to their dismal fate, and was gone; yet might he still speak? Bleek picked his way past debris into the inner office, where records could still exist. After familiarizing himself with the contents of that room, it seemed to him that all of the church and parish paperwork remained. There were numerous ledgers, one containing attendance rolls, another financial statements, still another lists of weekly sermon themes, the latter with copious theological notes. All were written in the same precise, educated hand. He supposed that the minister, in his panic, might have fled without taking any of these records of his office; that was possible, though curious, for wherever he had gone the man would have to answer to superiors. A final note in the sermon book caught Bleek's eye, a reference to Sodom and Gomorrah, and the theme of betrayal of hospitality. It bore a date of six years before. A connecting door lead from the office into the minister's private quarters, which still contained furniture in a sad state, much knocked about and broken, and many personal belongings and items of private value. The man, whose name was Laninger, had taken little or nothing with him when he abandoned his parishioners.

Having returned to the office, Bleek located one other ledger, tucked into an alcove behind the desk. Examination revealed it to be a sort of casual parish diary, containing tersely written entries about events of village life which might interest a local minister. There were references to births, marriages, and deaths; holy days, and the abundance or sparseness of offerings at such times; the organization of festivals; the seasonal dispensation of charity, a social function which apparently had operated at a primitive level. There were, in addition, certain cryptic entries toward the end of the document which struck the wizard as potentially pertinent.

They gave a sense of having been written by a man who was not quite sure of his facts, yet who wrestled with terrible doubts and suspicions. The first entry of this kind read simply: "Tradesmen gone, with their people, all twelve; wagons and horses remain. How did they leave?" The second stated: "Much coinage, of good quality, circulating in the village. Problem of wealth solved. Source?" Minister Laninger—for so Bleek presumed the author to be of all these writings, since this village was not likely to possess another scribe—seemed to be pursuing a mystery of his own. "I fear the best elements of the village are involved," ran another passage.

There followed a lengthier entry which told much. "Seidel and his committee came to me this morning to complain of the ongoing disturbances, which they aver are true, and growing intolerable. He swears that there are unmarked graves in the forest from which the visitations emanate, many such graves. The men demand that the remains be taken up at once and transferred to the cemetery, and that I grant the souls proper rights, and that this will conclude the trouble. I agree, for the sake of the souls, though I wonder as to the sanctity and efficacy of the action. Good God! What have they done—these, my neighbors—and what will become of us all?"

A few more followed:

"Last rites performed. This desecrates the yard."

"I have seen one with my own eyes. They still walk."

"The conspirators require further action on my part. Want me to curse the shades in the name of God. This I will not do. Heated words from Seidel, their leader, when I told him so. Threatened to complain to the district and report my suspicions. Seidel took it badly. Threatened in turn. Should have kept my mouth shut."

The final entry read simply: "Terrible row tonight with these, whom I once called my people. Will depart for Heidelberg in the morning. They must answer to God and man, or there shall be no peace in Wetzelburg." That was all. If the minister departed, as he proposed, and the townsfolk claimed, then he had chosen to leave without his records, as well as certain personal effects which one would have expected him to take. That being the case, Laninger must have been in a great hurry. It was interesting, also, that his intended report to Heidelberg had led to no apparent consequences in the village. As these people told it, he merely left in order to get away, not being able to stand the constant strain and fearful nature of the situation, and had never returned.

Other ideas, most fascinating ideas, occurred to Bleek, yet he chose to hold them in abeyance for the moment. He collected a few of the papers for his files, tearing them from the ledgers where necessary, stuffed them into the inner pockets of his cloak, and exited the ruin of the church. Straight away he entered the grounds of the cemetery, treading quietly among the monuments, stones, and wooden markers. Much here was quite old, and might have held his interest in other circumstances, but he was determined to concentrate on his task. He noticed the lack of fresh flowers or ornaments of devotion on the newer graves; clearly, it seemed to him, no villager came here anymore, not even to honor their dear departed. Bodies must still be interred—for there were burials of recent date—but otherwise the folk stayed away.

Jacob Bleek found what he sought. Already he had guessed much, and was seeking certain indications that would correspond with the story told through the papers of the missing minister, and thereby verify a theory; and there they were. Somewhat separated from the standard grave sites, off in a little shaded corner of their own, where the great dark trees overhung the cemetery wall, he came upon a closely grouped set of thirteen burials, mere mounds of packed earth, as might be provided for the lowest and most vulgar of the deceased. Cheap wooden crosses had once been fixed onto the mounds, but they all lay flat now, and broken or scattered. Bleek picked up a fairly complete specimen, turning it over in his fingers as he examined it. The crudely fashioned symbol bore no trace of name, dates, or any other customary notation. That did not surprise him. He had deduced as much before he saw it, and a survey of other fragments reinforced his conclusions.

The sorcerer had it in his power to take action then and there, and in so doing complete his side of the bargain, according to the compact he had agreed to with Seidel, his congenial host. He had a fair idea what was called for, how to go about it, what could be learned by him, and what the probable consequences would be. All this he knew, and was quite capable of proceeding immediately, yet he chose not to do so. Although not required for a man such as himself, Bleek preferred to invoke the supernatural agencies by night—it was customary, and like many of his colleagues he suspected that the dark powers gained potency when wreathed in darkness—and, also, he desired to enjoy the unlimited hospitality of the inn for the rest of the day. He suspected, for the best of reasons, that said hospitality would be moot on the morrow, and that he had better make the most of it now.

So he returned to the inn, fending off his host's probing questions, assuring the man that all was in order and that the great moment for action was nearly at hand; and having put off Seidel for the time being, Bleek settled himself into contented inactivity, savoring the great feast that he cajoled Seidel into creating for him. He ate and drank of the best that the village had to offer, demanding more and better at each course. The landlord of the Wetzelburg Inn acquiesced gamely, though on occasions he insisted on intruding with further questions or pleas for information. "Far be it from me to ask after your secrets," the man observed at one point, going on to say, "but there be other folk here, the town fathers, if you will, who are keen to know of your plans, and what they will mean for us, and how we will all be the better for your business. I've advised them not to pester you, nor do I think they're inclined to do so, you being a man of magics and mysteries and such matters, but their nerves are sorely fretted by what we've undergone during these strange days, and they'd like to hear that you'll put an end to it." Bleek promised him, on a sacred oath, that the unpleasantness plaguing the village would be resolved within the span of another twenty-four hours; that before daybreak, if certain notions were borne out, and all went well, then an undeniable outcome would be obtained, and the curse permanently lifted. At this Seidel radiated joy, and redoubled his attentions to his guest, and shortly left to pass word to his neighbors that marvelous events were close at hand.

With the ever dreadful fall of night all forms of outward society ceased, and the good folk of the village withdrew indoors, and they pulled down their shutters and barred the windows, and they waited expectantly, none daring to stir abroad. No one blessed with a vestige of sanity would have chosen to go forth on this night; and yet, there was movement in the village. The door of the inn opened briefly, then closed behind Jacob Bleek, who trod alone through the desolate and forlorn streets of Wetzelburg. He went well wrapped against the bracing chill and brisk wind of evening, carrying on his person a small notebook inscribed in his hand, two glass vials of special chemicals, and a small earthenware pot or jar, tightly covered, which contained a curious, evil smelling paste which he had concocted out of his supplies that afternoon. These items he carried in a bag over his shoulder, like an itinerant peddler transporting his wares. Perhaps some of the villagers peeped from their darkened windows and watched him go; certainly Seidel did so, with the fondest of hopes and even calls of encouragement. Bleek smiled to himself, advancing serenely and confidently through the streets, then down the long lane which led to the church. He took no lantern with him, for the moon succeeded in piercing the ragged clouds, a lamp unto his feet to light his way and render possible all necessary endeavors without artificial aid, which he thought fitting.

Entering the churchyard, he made his way through the gloom—which seemed to gather more thickly around him, perhaps due to the pressing trees—to the realm of the dead, and there he set up shop, as it were. He consulted his book one last time, though he knew its contents well, and laid out his materials on a toppled stone fairly near the grouping of anonymous graves. He unsealed the earthenware jar, and the odor which arose from its contents was not to be described; it would have staggered an ordinary man, though Bleek did not react in any visible manner. He was accustomed to such ointments as this, and he knew well of what ingredients it was composed, and how they had been obtained, for he had acquired them himself in earlier times and kept them ready for use. The secret of the pasty brown substance was known only to he and a few other worthy scholars of the world, and perhaps to one other: he who had perished, oddly and frightfully, so that essential extracts could be removed from what was left of his mortal frame. Bleek no longer recalled the fellow's name, if he ever knew or cared, but he thanked the man now for what he had unwillingly contributed to the wizard's education and store of knowledge. The two vials contained unusual chemical solutions, composed of several rare elements, including uncommon herbs derived from far lands, which functioned as catalysts when combined properly with one another and with other, more powerful potions, such as that within the jar. From each vial Bleek measured a few drops into a thimble cup, and these he poured into the jar, and when this operation was concluded a reaction occurred, a hissing and a steaming of the interacting substances, and with that a transformation took place, and the sum of the disparate elements became far greater than that of the separate parts. Working in unison, they became a new and radically different element, one which could never—nor ought ever—occur on the earth, but having been cunningly fashioned by learned mind and trained hand, was capable of the most extraordinary possibilities.

Having stirred the contents of the jar to the consistency of thin gruel,

THE JOURNEY OF JACOB BLEEK

Jacob Bleek walked among the unmarked graves, dipping his free hand into the container and sprinkling the solution from his fingertips over the low mounds. As he did this he recited words from his book, potent words he had once copied from the infamous *Incantations of Power* by Narcassus, formulated during the intellectual heights of antiquity, words which served to open that door which ignorant folk consider forever closed, and which many of the wise consider best closed. The mighty words of the pure, pagan Greek tripped from his tongue, in an apparently careless or artless manner, for such syllables required no false solemnity or other affectation. In combination with the sinister mixture, they were quite able to achieve the goal, even if he had laughed or sung them.

The breeze grew chillier, mounting in intensity. It rushed and swirled around Bleek as he finished his incantation and stood motionless before the silent graves, and it flapped his cloak about his legs. Then the wind died; it stopped of a sudden, as if driven away from the scene by a new and contrary power, and then the expectant mage discerned the first hints of motion. Something stirred in that solitude, pale vapors which streamed from the mounds and coiled above them, coalescing slowly. Thirteen ethereal masses hovered before his eyes, appearing to solidify and take on recognizable shape, and presently there stood before him the well defined images (perhaps a little hazy about the edges, but very little) of thirteen human beings, grown men and women, as well as the smaller forms of children. These were the shades of the departed, and Bleek could not help but note that one of them stood somewhat apart from the others, and appeared to wear the vestments of a country clergyman.

It was not he, however, who spoke for the group, but the spirit to the forefront, a tall, heavily built man or being, with a horribly pale and white face framed by a black, goatish beard. This grave entity said thusly to Bleek, "Why have you called us up, when we are ever willing to come of our own choosing?" The wizard explained his business, although not as he would have done to Seidel or his compatriots; he made clear that he came and acted with no hostile intent toward the tormented souls of the deceased; that he desired only information from them; that he might possess something to offer in return for such knowledge as they were willing to impart. "Then I shall favor you," quoth the ghostly spokesman, "and tell all to you."

The story that he—who, so he informed, once bore the name of Schmundt—had to tell surprised Bleek not, for in his cleverness and from his diligence in research he had already deduced most of the secrets underlying the haunting of Wetzelburg. "We came to this village and stopped for the night, traders seeking lodgings and the hospitality of the road, as is the custom in every land. Our labors took us far, and consumed months of our lives, so we always traveled with our loved ones, whose company was a delight to us. We had come from the south, up the river, and in that southern region we had prospered exceedingly, and now we were making our way home, far to the north of this place, in order to make merry with the treasures we had accrued. This we would have done, by rights, save that the cruel and merciless inhabitants of this village, stricken by poverty, thought to relieve us of our gains. We expostulated; we struggled; we fought them, and the gang (for so I deem them) slew us, with our women and children, heartlessly destroying all so that the fruits of theft could be enjoyed without the annoyance of talkative witnesses. Having torn and rent our bodies, they committed the further insult of concealing our ruined remains in unconsecrated, unhallowed ground, thereby antagonizing our spirits, which thirsted for vengeance. This we craved, and after our feeble fashion we began to trouble them according to our weak powers, making appearances to them in unlikely places and speaking to them at times ill chosen for their sensibilities. They were seized with fear, but rather than make amends before God and his instruments on earth, as was their holy duty, they attempted to placate us by removing our rotten bits and pieces to the sacred ground of the church, which might have satisfied us in the beginning, but having grown greedy with a desire for justice—driven by the need for vengeance, as their greed for gold had driven them—we laid off them not, but rather redoubled our efforts, and sought new means of ripping happiness from their lives. It was at this time that their minister joined us, a godly man who wished justice for us, and whom they foully murdered for his godliness. Since then he has been with us, searching for retribution.

"It goes on. We are weak, but we terrify. We can not touch them, but we distress them, and at times, by our very presence, we are able to drive isolated individuals, run them like sheep and force them into the fastness of the forest, where they perish alone. This we do. We would do more, if we could. We dream of ending the matter. Nothing more remains to us. We walk, until the deed be done."

Jacob Bleek stated that he understood the situation, and explained to the weird presences that he had been delegated the task—for which he had received something by way of compensation—of ending the haunting once and for all, and that he was of a mind to do just that; that he knew of a means by which said task could be equitably carried through, and that he thought the time ripe for a closing to this chapter of affairs, which pleased the spirits in no way more than it pleased the villagers. Bleek pointed out, to those who heard his words without fleshly ears, an additional property of the potion he had mixed for this occasion, and offered to say one more spell, similar to yet greater than the one he had previously recited. This particular devising of magic, he allowed, would subsist for only the single night, so he advised them to act quickly if they would act at all—how they utilized the opportunity, after all, was entirely their own business—and afterward, do what they may, he urged them to rest quietly in their graves, as was the custom for such as themselves, and by no means so unhappy a state, he supposed, as that in which they currently found themselves. Schmundt agreed to the proposition, and the rest indicated by signs that they too accepted the terms, including the minister once called Laninger, who seemed rather eager to commence with the scheme.

So Bleek spoke more words, the words he had promised, effective only while the mysterious potion retained its strength; and something more happened then. The spooky pale forms faded away in smoky wisps back into the ground, but no sooner had they vanished wholly from sight than the packed earth of the several mounds began to heave, and fissures began to appear on those surfaces, connoting a considerable commotion beneath. At this the wizard knew that his latter spell had succeeded, and that no more of a contribution was required from him, so he departed from the cemetery and the churchyard, and hurried back through the night to his lodgings, where he would make ready for the last night of his stay among the fine folk of Wetzelburg.

Upon his return to the inn Bleek was met by Seidel and a council of his fellows, the village fathers, no doubt, men of an aspect like unto his host, including those who had sat by silently at breakfast. With craven, fawning manners they plied him with questions, asking after his mission, demanding to know whether they could return safely to their homes, whether their streets could be strolled without dread as in the far off days of yore. Bleek said to them, with a grin of unreadable mirth, that he had instituted a purgation, and that he suspected all would soon be quiet in Wetzelburg, that they need never again fear, when this night be done, the specter of troubled shades. They rejoiced, and cried out in merriment, and the host insisted upon opening up his stock of the best he had to provide to his compatriots and his guest, and the bottles were passed about, the wine flowing freely and sloppily from cups to lips. Bleek did not partake, nor did he join them, but rather hastened upstairs, leaving them to their pleasure, and made for his room, where he chalked a complicated geometrical sign on the outer side of the door, which he then tightly shut and locked, and within he mumbled more words of power to himself, and then settled himself down to wait.

For the space of an hour the stupid noises of carousing filtered up from below, while Bleek quietly devoted himself to reading. His studies continued to absorb him even when the noises below altered abruptly, and he heard, with one part of his attention, the sounds of muted muttering and gasps of astonishment. Then came a great rending of wood and metal, as if of a door torn from its hinges, and a crashing and a commotion, and an instantaneous outburst of shrieks exploding from terrified throats. He heard from below the sounds of seemingly endless chaos and destruction, always punctuated by screams and pleas for mercy, and footsteps thumping rapidly up the stairs and down the hall past his door, accompanied by still more cries of mortal anguish. Then he heard a heavier tread clumping toward his door, a pause, and then powerful knocks upon the sturdy panels, followed by a harsh, inhuman voice demanding entry. The sorcerer looked up then, and called out firmly, with steady tones, beseeching the visitor to pay heed to the sign inscribed upon the door. He received no reply, but presently the heavy steps trod on, and what walked beyond the door disturbed him not.

When the ruckus at the inn had died down, and all seemed still, he stepped to the window, not choosing to peer out, but rather listening. In the distance, from other parts of the village, he detected more cries, shouts, and screams, rising faintly to his ears, and intensifying and multiplying as the minutes passed. How long it continued he could not say, but in time the incredible noises died down, and then all was quiet in the night, as silent as the grave. Then he closed his book and betook himself to bed, extinguishing his single lamp, and presently knew no more.

In the morning, after the sun had risen well above the tops of the trees surrounding the village, Jacob Bleek awoke, and gathered to himself his few belongings, and descended to take his leave. He paid no attention to the evidences of the night's disorders which he saw all about him, though those evidences were many, offering a multitude of stark images which would craze the brain of the faint of heart. He picked his way to the bar and, without bothering to ring the copper bell, helped himself to the viands there—considering them as a form of final payment for services rendered—and then departed the inn to take his pony and cart in harness. And he rode through the town, which now seemed as silent and empty by day as it had once by night, and shabbier as well, as if a lengthy festival had just ended, and the townsfolk, in the aftermath of their merriment, not having troubled themselves to clear away the mess. And nothing moved amidst the desolation; nor, he suspected, would anything move there again.

His work was done, and as he rode away from the scene, onto the route which would take him back to the big river, he thought of the work he had performed there, and what he had accomplished for all the parties concerned, and he found it good. The end had been achieved, and in addition he had once more exercised his unique abilities, testing theories and honing skills which he would fain allow to lie dormant in his mind. No one came forth to thank him for his efforts, or to congratulate him on his success, nor did he expect such—indeed, it would have startled him exceedingly—but the wizard felt warmly in his breast, and Jacob Bleek knew that the fine folk of the fair village of Wetzelburg would be troubled no more.

II. The Error of Helvetius

Jacob Bleek continued his journey up the great river Rhine, reaching at last the more civilized and populated regions to the south, and from there he made his way to a long desired goal, the famous city of Heidelberg, site of the renowned university, where the wonders of the arts and sciences reigned supreme. In this city he chose to establish residence, for he wished to install himself at that place of learning, where he hoped to find men not unlike himself, clever men of intellect and daring who would understand him, with whom he could cooperate in tearing asunder the veils of ignorance and plumbing the depths of the cosmic secrets which he had dedicated his life to fathoming.

This he did, and for the first time since childhood Bleek felt something akin to happiness. There was much about Heidelberg to attract him, a city so different from the provincial backwater (as he termed it) where he had spent his youth. Here he discovered evidence of a society that stimulated the mind, a special world where ideas and concepts formed the established coinage, where a man was judged rich to the extent that he was deemed wise. With his first step onto the grounds of the university he felt at home, as he beheld the storied citadels of knowledge—like a fabulous cathedral, the focus of all faith—and the busy, earnest swarm of professors, masters, and students who dwelt there, the worshippers at the hallowed shrine. These, he knew, were his people, and among them he would find acceptance, perhaps even friendship, as well as that knowledge and power which he craved.

It was no easy matter to present himself there as more than a sight-seeing tourist, for he arrived without formal references. He possessed no credentials by which he could gain ready admission to the cloister: he knew no one, no one knew him; his education, while deep and profound, had followed none of the standard rules which the professional is bound by courtesy to respect; his training had been obscure and secretive, of necessity, and despite his attainments he had acquainted himself with few persons of eminence, and most of those only by correspondence. His initial introduction, as a result, created no shock waves, nor even a great stir of interest, and one might have wondered whether his assault upon those academic walls stood any chance of success. Bleek, however, was an astute fellow, and determined to batter in those walls, and such intellectual engines as he possessed he employed to best advantage in order to prosecute his siege.

Having taken cheap lodgings as near to the university as practicable (for he was in no position to live on the grounds), he began attending the open air gatherings on the square, where brilliant scholars expounded, for their pleasure, to all who would hear. Bleek introduced himself by the quality and variety of his questions, in which he managed to drop certain names or arcane allusions which, he presumed, might catch the ear and foster the interest of those who shared his pursuits. From the startled glances and hesitant responses he drew from some of the speakers, he guessed that he had succeeded. The students and other members of the crowd mumbled and muttered in puzzlement among themselves, but there were lecturers who paused and noted him with curiosity, and who occasionally answered his questions with questions of their own, which they were not wont to do.

The same practice he followed in the class rooms, slipping unbidden into the back of the halls and breaking into professorial talks when he could do so to good effect. There were those who doubted his eligibility to attend, and bade him leave, but there were others, those few, who wondered about this odd young fellow, and bade him stay. Whenever he could he stated his name, that it become known and bandied about, so that they would marvel at a man rather than at a meaningless face. Bleek assured himself that in time the barrier dividing him from these men would break down, and then all doors would open to him. He was willing to devote as much time as it took, however long, to achieve his immediate goal.

As it transpired, his acceptance came about in a rather direct fashion, and developed more quickly than he had counted upon. During an otherwise convivial classroom session, in which the lecturer had expounded upon the many uses of organic acids, as they might be applied to living, diseased, and dead human tissues, Bleek had contrived to introduce an insidiously clever comment into the proceedings, a seemingly casual reference which pulled up short the speaker, causing considerable commotion among the students; something about employing the requisite combinations of acids, along with certain exotic substances, in order to alter the state of the tissues in an unusually questionable direction. The professor hotly demanded the source of the young man's knowledge. Bleek calmly alluded to his own private studies, which drew a smirking sneer, and further made mention of his old teacher from earlier times, whom he identified. Bleek himself was rather taken aback by the result, for it developed that the name of Huysman meant something to the present speaker. That dead worthy had certainly impressed and influenced his pupil, but only now did Bleek begin to realize that he had been taught the fundamentals of the esoteric arts by a master, one once widely recognized in his own formidable circles. The professor, who shortly introduced himself as Matthias, had known Huysman well—in fact, the latter gentleman had taught for a period at the university, until he had been ostracized and driven from the land for being too public about his research—and instantly warmed to any student of that departed wizard. No sooner had the lecture concluded than Matthias beckoned Bleek to him, and they held a long discussion on the young scholar's background, attainments, and goals.

Matthias may not have cared for all that he heard (and he felt it necessary to warn Bleek against to great an openness in the expression of his ideas), but he recognized intellectual quality when he heard it, and he determined to ease the way of this visitor into scholastic society.

In no time at all Jacob Bleek had been presented to the relevant staff of the university, those who possessed a quietly acknowledged or covert interest in studies that must, given the time and place, remain somewhat secretive. On the strength of Matthias' estimation, they were at least willing to accept the young man as a serious student, if not as an equal. Bleek still had to prove himself worthy of entering into their inner councils, but he knew now that he would not be shut out a priori. He was granted lodgings on the university grounds, a tiny room smaller than his chamber in Bruges, yet which satisfied by bringing him into the thick of things. He even received a trivial stipend, one almost sufficient to hold body and soul together. It would serve, for the moment; Bleek had big plans, and he was right where he wanted to be.

He found himself dwelling among an unofficial conclave of masters and full professors, wise men who ostensibly specialized in the various approved schools of natural philosophy while actually devoting their thoughts, behind closed doors and at late hours, to matters alchemical, magical, and necromantic. Few students were privy to these studies, and no one outside the cloister was ever supposed to learn of such mystical delvings. In an era when men might suffer the loss of liberty or life for daring to ask the wrong questions, it was especially important that no hints of the derived answers should ever leak out. Bleek accepted the conditions, for they were his own as well—when embarked upon great projects, he had no wish to be disturbed by the commonplace mortifications of little minds—and he would have granted any terms that allowed him to remain, and to work.

It may be disputed how much Bleek actually learned during his residence in Heidelberg. He came to that city bearing great insights and the beginnings of profound experiences, and there were no general subjects of furtive lore that were altogether unfamiliar to him. Surely he lacked certain elements of training, and particular knowledge of procedures, which he could only acquire by living among and working regularly with men such as these. This he now did, and for a period he felt as if he had found his place in the world, that there he might choose to live long and grow elderly and respected among his peers, gaining and sharing the secrets of the universe that obsessed him. With his new colleagues he debated and argued, deduced and induced, pursued failures to their dead ends, and chased successes to their possible limits and beyond. All of this, carried out under the cover of an upstanding university, pleased him enormously, filling his days with contented study, and his nights with fruitful experimentation.

With Matthias he could discourse freely on any topic, and they held many long conversations concerning Bleek's search for the Old Ones, and what he desired of Them. The older wizard did not profess to know much about the great Gods of all time and space, but what little he had deduced about Them led him to question any attempt to find Them. They must be, he said, unimaginably powerful beings, pure Force with Mind, who saw mankind as instruments of amusement at best, which They would as soon crush as coddle. He would not be categorical, but he could see no benefit in treating with Them; it was best to leave the ultimate powers alone, lest They become too interested in oneself; there were twice-told tales, and hints derived from the papers of ancient mages, which indicated that such attention could lead to frightful personal danger. Bleek demurred, of course, arguing vociferously, yet their debate remained friendly, engaging, and stimulating. These were heady days for him.

Yet this phase of his life was not meant to last, and the seeds of discord were sown early, from his dealings with a certain man, one of the premier scholars of the entire age, and a formidable star of Heidelberg. This notable gentleman styled himself Helvetius—though he were born to the name of Herman—and as a full professor of mathematics he was avowedly entitled to much honor. He bore other credentials, of a less forthright nature, which among this secret society of the elect, into which Bleek had inserted himself, served to raise him up on a unique pedestal. Helvetius was, as all of his contemporaries averred, the ultimate sorcerer, the mages' mage, the most illustrious seeker after and subduer of cosmic mysteries. There was nothing he did not know of the black arts; or, if perchance, one theorized a gap in his knowledge, it was considered a certainty than none other could make up the lack. What Helvetius, hoary with age and wisdom, knew filled volumes; what he might not know was most likely beyond all mortal ken.

He dabbled in everything and, when disputes arose among his colleagues, his word was the last word. Nay, more; it was law, and none dared oppose him, for fear of risking reputation, and being made to look foolish before him, and in the eyes of others. Helvetius was indeed a powerful wizard, and he knew it in his heart, and he behaved accordingly. As a result he was more respected than liked, more fawned upon than befriended. This suited him, as it accorded with his character—perhaps he would have had it no other way—and he allowed no lesser lights to dim his brilliance, tolerated no other mind to cast shadows upon his learning.

Had Bleek been granted the boon of acting solely according to his own interests, this was precisely the sort of man he would have chosen as a mentor; for he craved the education this Helvetius could afford him, while caring naught for the human dimension, the common emotions and vulgar feelings which seemed to him to animate the rest of the world. Helvetius might be overbearing—what of it?—he might be jealous of his fellows' esteem—what meant that to the youth?—he might be cold and callous, indifferent to the wants of others—it might be that Bleek himself could give lessons along those lines. The new man was willing, even eager, to serve as an humble acolyte, if by stooping he could eventually climb to the heights he sought.

Being who they were, however, it seemed impossible that they could associate with anything approaching amity. Certainly they failed to do so. Conflicts arose and festered between them. Helvetius shunned arguments, considering them beneath him, and took it ill if Bleek, as was his wont, pressed fresh ideas upon the older man. Helvetius knew all the best ideas— he often proclaimed such himself—and was more disposed to lecturing than debating. The beardless Bleek, after his quiet fashion, could be most insistent when driving home a point, and if he drove too hard, the gray-bearded Helvetius would more surely retort with mockery, insults, and sarcasm than with a devastating datum. This gave the older man a malicious glee, while satisfying his erstwhile pupil not at all. Bleek did not let up, of course, for such was not in his nature, and increasingly Helvetius would not budge, never giving an inch when he thought that to do so would benefit his tormentor. Eventually the professor conceived a veritable dislike, or even a hatred, for his latest colleague, and he began to find delight in cutting the other to the quick, or stymieing Bleek's efforts to improve his skills.

Still, the latter continued upon his chosen path, seeking enlightenment, meeting resistance. During one talk, delivered in his chambers to only a handful of keener students, Helvetius expounded upon the principles of calling dead spirits for the purpose of acquiring lost information, and he posited a method for reducing certain active crystals (critical ingredients in a powerful solution bearing tremendous effects) into a usable liquid form. Bleek, who had appeared without invitation, mildly countered by mentioning a report he had read in the *Forbidden Transformations* of Lestronius, which advocated the separation of the salt crystals from the metallic crystals, an operation which served to enhance the desired awesome effect. Helvetius snorted that he held no truck with hearsay, that he advanced ideas which had stood the test of his own secret laboratory. As the speaker went on Bleek coughed, and allowed that he had, during his previous career, dabbled with his proposed procedure, and had garnered results which he considered other than trivial. Helvetius laughed coldly, demanding a demonstration at the earliest possible moment—in fact, setting a deadline which he thought insurmountable, for he insisted that those assembled be available for judging the claim—at which point his irksome colleague produced a flask from beneath his cloak, a flask containing a pearly, shimmering fluid quite unlike the substance the older sorcerer had brought for display. This, said Bleek, was the separated crystal solution, and in combination with the other materials, and the standard invocation, must loosen disembodied tongues. Somewhat shaken, Helvetius had loudly insisted that the gathering form an impromptu coven for a séance on the spot, in order to test the presumed potency of the solution. They did so, and there was much grinning and nudging among the others, for they felt confident that no one could get the better of their master, and they looked forward to seeing Bleek (who was not at all a popular fellow among the students) crawl away in disgrace. They mixed the full potion according to the recipe of Lestronius, adding the necessary bits of things dead, the things never alive, and a couple of morsels perhaps not quite dead, and boiled these things in a heavy iron kettle while Helvetius chanted from his great personal book of spells. This being a quick study, the wizard called randomly into the foul air, asking for nothing more than a sign. The rest, including Bleek, chanted in unison, in antiphonal response to the words of their leader. Something did happen then: the reeking fumes from the boiling mass in the pot coalesced, writhed in the air of the close room, and formed a dense ball with a hole in the center, a hole which seemed to stretch back into black infinity, and from out of that smoke-wreathed tunnel there did issue a voice, a low, disturbing muttering, and then another like voice, and still another, until soon it was as if Pandemonium had intruded into that place, and a chorus of baleful whispers ensued. Not much information of utility could be gathered from such a confused oral display— and Helvetius made the most of that fact later—but the students busied themselves taking notes as best they might, and all privately allowed, when discussing the occurrence afterward, among themselves, that Bleek, with remarkably little effort, had made something extraordinary happen, not least of which part was the total nonplusing of Helvetius, who found himself utterly unable to react throughout the event. After the potion had boiled away, and the strange cloud dissipated and the weird voices had muted, Bleek considerately answered those questions put to him by his fellows, but it was not long before Helvetius cited the lateness of the hour, and drove his guests, as well as the annoying young warlock, from his rooms.

Developments of this kind occurred often enough to cause the older gentleman to seethe with barely contained rage whenever he encountered the young man, whom he had come to style "the interloper". The new situation galled him; he could detect that Bleek, even if not liked, was gathering to himself the grudging respect of those who understood the mysterious arts, and in very little time they ceased to treat him as a student, but accepted him as a peer, and an important one, at that. As if that were not bad enough, full professors, led by Matthias, willingly consorted and consulted with Jacob Bleek, that nobody, whose special knowledge and sharp wits they found helpful in their own studies. One may ask, why should this dredge up difficulties and black thoughts? For Helvetius remained the grand old man among the wizards of Heidelberg, and might have done so for all his natural years to come; and yet the situation contented him not, and he fretted, and every slight, real or imagined, twisted and knotted in his mind, until such time as he could no longer think clearly or behave properly, but flew into sudden furies without ostensible cause, and his daily bread sank like mouthfuls of stone into his belly, and his daily wine tasted like vinegar to his tongue, and he paced wearily at odd hours, scowling at nothing and no one.

One thing particularly infuriated him: Bleek pretended to a mastery of the summoning and control of demons and other underworld entities—so Helvetius told it, for in truth the visiting wizard owned only to a burning interest in the subject, and a desire to learn much more along those lines— which happened to be the professor's chosen preserve, a matter into which he had delved over decades, and considered himself the absolute authority. What could be done, and not, and what could be undone, and not, involving the most ill-reputed of infernal powers, were topics in which Helvetius would not bow to any other man, nor grant any equality of ability. In his time the great master had ransacked the forbidden works of the library, studied crumbling manuscripts and fading palimpsests on parchment, and in his estimation had gained a unique understanding of these works, ancient and modern, and the beings on which they reported. He had read, and absorbed, the peculiar writings of Thutmoses the Egyptian, the martyred seer of fabled Karnak; he could recite by rote certain important passages from four separate books transcribed by Artocris the Greek, whose unhallowed theories terrorized even the most dedicated of covert scholars; and he himself had translated, from tattered fragments, the hitherto unbreakable cypher of Belisarius Augustus, and drawn forth from those well protected words secrets of unsurpassable evil and delight. From these and other sources, claimed Helvetius, he had learned what mortal man could of books and from the thoughts of others; and, in addition, he had pushed his own personal experimentation to heights unforeseen by the Classical titans and giants of yesteryear. Through his unending labors he had conspired to call up beings unaccustomed to doing the bidding of man, creatures that would gladly harm or kill any man who annoyed them. He had called them, and they had come; he had gazed upon their faces (such as had faces) and he had lived to make formal record in his comprehensive notes; he had, in special instances, demanded favors of the lesser horrors, and they had, however sourly, complied. Without any resort to fawning he had demanded favors, and bellowing against the indignity they had granted him boons, which in two notable cases—so it was rumored, and never quite denied—had removed perceived enemies of Helvetius from the known world.

All of this knowledge and power belonged to him—it was his exclusive intellectual property—and to have this pallid, lusterless peddler of conjurer's tricks, this Bleek, without approved antecedents or vetted education (he did not grant to long forgotten Huysman, whom he recalled now with distaste, anything but mere technical proficiency, a man without imagination or prudence), stumbling into the university and setting up shop as a fellow worthy of consideration, and daring to seize for himself this sacred line of research; that indeed passed all bounds, and identified the fool beyond all doubt as an intended foe, to be toppled or overcome by any means that suggested themselves. Helvetius decided that he could not allow his opponent to succeed. He owed it to himself, and to his colleagues, and to the university, all possessing reputations, public or otherwise, which must be maintained and guarded. This Bleek, he reasoned, was a tragic influence upon them all, and therefore he must go.

He had already discovered, however, that ostracism and snide remarks served him little. Bleek was a distressingly resilient young man, and in his own subdued manner gave quite as well as he got; at least, that seemed to be the opinion of others, based on comments that had reached the ears of Helvetius by unfortunate chance. No one dared tell him to his face, but a few idiots truly believed that Bleek had scored points against him. If Bleek believed that—and of course he did, regardless of the truth—then he would not go voluntarily, but stay, and persist in his machinations. Subtlety would not work with such an oaf; very good, then, decisive action was called for. That sniveling puppy must be driven from the precincts by a devastating public humiliation, one so crushing and final that his pretense to reputation could never survive the blow, nor vanity allow him to remain to sip the bitter dregs of defeat.

So thinking, Helvetius commenced his campaign to lure his adversary to his doom. He began by introducing the monumental subject of the invocation of dangerous demons into his lectures and private talks, letting on that he was working upon new theories that could soon bear fruit, and lead to unexpected practical results. He was pondering, as he insinuated, fresh formulae of power that would not only call up dire beings of spiritual immensity, but grant greater, more reliable control over them, such that a human master could ask—nay, demand—favor of the most ferocious entities, those whom even Helvetius had hitherto shunned, and those beings would have no choice but to comply. The possibilities were infinite, he claimed; already his imagination soared, while he wracked his brain over last details, and he looked soon to a public experiment (by which he meant an exceedingly private one, solely for the benefit of his trustworthy colleagues) which would verify the claim, and establish the fact of his omnipotence over that unnatural kingdom.

His fellows knew not what to think, for under any circumstances such talk troubled them, and even hearing it from Helvetius, who ought to know of what he spoke, alarmed them greatly. They remonstrated with the professor, arguing that he dared too much, pointing out that there were limits which could not be safely or sanely pressed, and chasms of knowledge which could not be so easily spanned. Most of them knew something about the matter at hand; Matthias had once discoursed with Abemoth, the fourth level deceiver, and Wendegar had called up and suffered at the claws of the detestable Dreelfai, and Ludovico, in his younger days, had recklessly raised the notorious Lord of the Worms, and Ludovico still walked with a limp for his pains. Terrible as they were, all these entities were minor potentates of inferior principalities, compared to those Helvetius spoke of now. That he could accomplish magnificent things they did not deny—for did not his past achievements support his increasing claims to confidence?—but they urged him to rein in his ambition, lest the lust for power and glory carry him over the precipice into perdition. Helvetius laughed, allowed their concerns, made some mention of future restraint, and then went on dropping his impressive hints.

Throughout this period Bleek had little apropos to say, preferring, as he said, to await deeds rather than accept words. This angered Helvetius, who sought a response which he could turn about and employ as a cutting weapon in debate, in order to gain a verbal advantage before he made his move. Bleek would not rise to the bait, so the insidious campaign against him (although no one knew it to be such) continued. Helvetius now suffered apparent slips of the tongue, in which his claims mounted to heights of extravagance; these remarks routinely alighted upon topics known to be dear to Bleek, and there were those who wondered why the young scholar exhibited so little interest, and received the reports with indifference. In due course Helvetius sent out certain students of his, gentleman of good family without fortune who owed him for largesse, to accost Bleek and draw him out. This portion of the plan seemingly bore fruit, for one day, while being harangued by this crowd, Bleek suddenly discarded his reserve, and proclaimed to all present that an unnamed but well known professor of the university, in striving to enhance his stultified reputation, had proved much indeed, if idle chatter be proof, and if any disagreed with that conclusion, then it must only suggest to the wise that the worthy old gentleman had finally slid into his dotage.

This utterance, thought Helvetius, to whom the news was hastily and gladly conveyed, played perfectly into his hands, for now he could attack with abandon, while seeming to counter-attack, in defense of his honor and academic standing. He shortly convened a lecture devoted to the subject of the more virulent demonic forces, ensured that a big group would attend, and saw to it that Bleek received notice of the event, which was guaranteed to be the most forthcoming talk yet dealing with the weighty question. The interested parties congregated in a disused hall some hours after the evening bell, when all the clocks of the town had struck midnight, and when Helvetius arrived he noted with savage glee that Bleek had shown.

The grand old wizard, this night dressed in a startling crimson cloak embroidered with conventional designs of the constellations and obscure geometrical symbols, once more advanced his professed discoveries, which he assured the modest throng would enable him to hold sway over frightful monstrosities of the unseen world, force them to obey his whims, and thereby make him a legend in the annals of the black arts. This he had accomplished, he told them, and this he was prepared to prove to their satisfaction, at the proper time and place, which must be chosen according to the requirements of the experiment, as well as to their convenience. His statements generated an excitement among the gathering, and there were approving comments, along with friendly words of caution, and the beginnings of lively discussion, and even scattered applause. Few there were who would dare attempt such a program, or participate themselves, but all present would happily attend and watch while the master performed. Helvetius ignored the generous buzz of approbation, however, and launched into a new and startling discourse, which served to alter the situation in dramatic fashion.

"It would please me to assume," he began, "that all of you—the fraternity of the wise, the disciples of boundless and everlasting Truth—stand behind me, and wish me well, harken to my success, and honor my achievements, which you shall soon observe for yourselves. That would make me proud indeed, in my humble fashion, to accept the unity of your intellectual support. Unfortunately, and distressing to relate, and sad to admit to my poor heart, it has come to my attention that one among you does not hold with the rest, but rather stands against you, against me and my difficult labors. I can scarcely credit the notion—so ignoble, so wounding to my feelings—that I should, in essence, be accused of charlatanry, by any member of this body, but such is the case, and as much as it displeases me to do so, I must address the point, though in the process it cause me unendurable agony of mind.

"There be one among you who elects to doubt me, to question the plain facts, to assail the verities I expound, to which I have devoted my life. This man comes to us as a visitor, an unknown quantity without papers of accreditation, without references or good name, without evidence of accomplishment, offering instead merely his attestations of desire to learn our secrets and, I suppose, profit by them, perhaps without any strenuous effort on his part. This young man—an uneducated youth, and no more than that, whatever others may believe out of charity—dares beard me without just cause, operating, I believe, under the false impression that by seeking to diminish my established name he could correspondingly magnify his own.

His name lacks value; so are his ideas fetid and empty of content; will you blame me or accuse me of hyperbole if I feel the need to speak on this occasion, in order to repel his base and mean spirited charges?"

The fierce gaze of Helvetius swept the room searchingly, drawing out the moment until that gaze paused and lingered on its quarry. "I refer," he continued, "to Jacob Bleek, a rising star I hear, an important fellow; certainly important in his own mind, and possibly capable enough when it comes to self-promotion, although one must question other aspects of his character and qualifications. Ah, here he is now, the man of the hour, the champion of our times, come to lead us all down the right path. Would you care to step up to the podium, my good friend, and take my place?"

Bleek barely shook his head, an even, precise movement like a metronome, but said nothing. Helvetius smirked, then feigned a crestfallen demeanor. "But, good sir, my dear little Jacobus"—for so Helvetius was known to refer to his rival when he was absent (though there was nothing objectively little about Bleek, in stature or mind), thinking it a belittlement, and now did so to his face, for the old wizard no longer recognized the need for even the illusion of civility—"clever little Jacobus, you must address us, or afford some opportunity to satisfy us. Really, sir, you have passed the limit, and I will not accept less than a full accounting, and I am happily convinced that I speak for this entire body. Tell me then, before this assembly, who is the keener mage, which of us is the master of magic; is it you or I?"

Bleek allowed, without trace of emotion clouding his face or tingeing his manner, that he considered himself the superior on matters of note. At that Helvetius threw up his hands in a gesture of helplessness, and stared wildly about him, as if powerless to avoid an unpleasantness from which he would have chosen to shield his colleagues, and then he spoke the following, with what seemed genuine sorrow: "Far be it from me to argue the point when, as philosophers all, we are aware that weighty disputes are capable of resolution by other more direct, and decisive means. Perhaps you have learned something, Jacobus, since you came here, and perhaps you are still able to learn from experience—that the future will show—but I propose a test of comparative abilities, a modest presentation of sorceries, as it were, to establish before all our current standing within the secret society."

This caused a great tumult among the gathered worthies, a few of whom knew what it was all about, others of whom knew nothing of the personal stakes; but all, even the doubters, could expect a fine display of magic spectacle. They knew the power of mighty Helvetius, and however lopsided such a contest should prove, it must impress. A few might question the apparent inequality, and Matthias, at the least, might wonder which way the inequality tipped between the two men, but no one chose to condemn the offer. Their caution would have proved fruitless in any case, for Bleek, with few words and a complete lack of boasting, acknowledged and accepted the offer.

"Sir, you gladden my heart!" crowed Helvetius. "Be it so. There only remains the setting of parameters, on which I trust we may quickly agree. I have discoursed at length on my latest research and discoveries concerning that outer world, forbidden to most mortals, that plane of existence where the most monstrous of demons hold sway and lurk in wait for the unwary and the foolish. I propose to dabble yet again at the boundaries of that world, secure in the knowledge that my wisdom and competence shall sustain me, come what may. Perhaps, dear Jacobus, you will elect to accompany me, and reveal to your esteemed friends what you can achieve in that realm?" Bleek nodded once, otherwise standing motionless and silent. Helvetius nodded back, a frenetic bobbing of his gray head, and said, "You agree? Very good; already we progress. And have no fear, my son, for we all realize that it is merely your manners which stop your throat, and not dread. For the information of all, however, let me make clear that my latest work involves contact with the worst of entities, those maddened by hatred for the sweetness of life, and craving all that is evil. I have endeavored to master my formulae, and perfect my material agents, and in the process—so I flatter myself—I can tame certain beings who, throughout the ages, have been renowned for their uncooperative, and even threatening, attitudes. I stand on the verge of my greatest achievement yet, for I propose to call up, now, the formidable spectre of Baalademus, He Who Walks Between the Two Worlds, but who opens the celestial doors only unto the Land of Death. Ah, I see from your faces that you know the name, and it troubles you. I feel no fear, for I have prepared myself long and truly. So what say you, little Jacobus? I see that you do not react to the name. Are you ready to confront and control the fabled powers of Baalademus?"

Jacob Bleek said that he was, and with those words everything began to happen according to the well laid plans of Helvetius, who basked in the pleasure of the moment, knowing that the final trap had been sprung. For he, with all his brilliance and study, had just barely learned how to call up that hideous entity, and would scarcely be able to invoke its terrestrial form before sending it away again, for fear of his life. Bleek, it stood to reason, would stand no chance at all, and—who knew?—might, during the ceremonies, act in such an idiotic manner as to remove himself from the equation, and perhaps from this world, permanently.

All present now retired, at the friendly urging of their host, to a sheltered alcove of the alchemical hall, where every necessary substance was kept that a keen magician would need. Helvetius and Bleek went side by side, as if bosom friends and allies, surrounded by the others, who carried lighted candles of several colors, at a respectful distance. In the chamber where the pair would operate their audience took seats along the walls of the room, well away from the massive five-sided table where the incredible rites were to be performed. This table was laid with beakers, burners, kettles, mortars and pestles, all pre-arranged by Helvetius. Large, stout cabinets contained the solutions, metals, and minerals they would require. Lamps were lit, and both men got to work right away, and as they busied themselves a remarkable thing happened. Jacob Bleek, normally so quiet, so mild, so self-contained, grew querulous or otherwise talkative, as if battling an attack of nerves, and he thrust himself forward, insisting on taking the lead in the preparations, and handling the materials himself, averring that he was the more knowledgeable of the ingredients required to effect the spell, and could deal with all of it himself, without the aid of his senior. This boastful manner surprised many, and amused Helvetius, who recognized the patter of the unsteady amateur when he heard it. Furthermore, Bleek impressed the gathering as being clumsy in his actions, as if he struggled with inner thoughts while he worked, and could not fully concentrate on the task at hand. This cheered Helvetius still more, who observed only enough to know that the preparations, in accordance with his interjected advice, developed properly. The younger man heatedly disdained the advice, but seemed to follow it faithfully nonetheless.

At such signs of hotheaded recklessness Helvetius felt at ease—surely this moronic youth could never prove his equal—yet even he was staggered and given pause when, in a fit of wild-eyed bravado, Bleek now insisted on continuing his lead, and undertaking the prerequisite spell first. It would be he who first called forth the mighty Baalademus, and he who would experience the initial effects of that demon's fury and rage. At this Matthias thought to step in, and he rose and cried out, but Helvetius condescendingly waved him back into his seat, and demanded no further interruptions, pronouncing them dangerous from this point onward. Also, he slyly demanded respect for the decision of his "noble colleague", and stated on his personal authority that he would brook no interference until Bleek had, through his own actions, made his case before the assembly.

When all was ready, potions prepared and boiling, books open to the desired pages, and notes scattered upon the table, Bleek stepped forth and made as if to start, then appeared to think better of it, and to consult the master in a low voice. The spectators heard naught, but Helvetius grinned cruelly, and whispered something quiet yet harsh in response, and then the young wizard did commence with an appearance of haste. Indeed, he seemed to rush through the ceremony, as if it be something unpleasant he wished to put behind him, while at the same time appearing to hesitate at every step, as if unsure of himself, and out of his depth. He abruptly mixed the mysterious chemicals (almost turning over a clay pot containing jellied bitumen) which combined to form the elixir of power, a foaming mess which hissed steam and spat sparks of blue, then began to gabble the monstrous words which would react with the solution in order to obtain the result. He spoke them in a nearly incomprehensible fashion, racing through a mouthful, then halting to scan his notes with a finger, then fluttering the brittle pages of a book as he moved on. He recited the spell so poorly, and with such annoying episodes of inaudible mumbling, that Helvetius had to rebuke him aloud, though that was frowned upon during magical business of any variety, as promoting discord among the powers which enable wizards to communicate with the outer spheres. It served in this case, however, for Bleek accepted the admonishment with seeming gratitude, and shortly spoke with increased clarity, raising his voice and enunciating the individual syllables with greater precision, so that midway through the most critical word the listeners heard clearly the fragment "—demus," and from that point onward they had no trouble following the repellent chant. Bleek, however, now seemed to stumble into still more difficulty, though he was past the hardest part, all that remained being mere formality. He mopped his brow, loosened the collar about his neck, leaned upon the table and gasped for breath. His voice failed him once again, and then he pushed himself away from the table and, in miserable tones, muttered that he could not go on, and that Helvetius would have to take over for him, if his eminency would be so charitable.

The mighty wizard and professor strode forward, brushing Bleek aside, and without the pause of a second took up the spell in midstream, continuing as if there had been no break, and as if he had led the way from the first. The younger mage drew back, sporting an expression of chagrin and shame, and took himself over by the door, where he was immediately lost to sight, being no longer of any interest, for all eyes were on Helvetius, who approached the fateful moment of resolution. That sorcerer continued speaking in a ringing voice, and with grand gestures, a fine recitation, for he knew the words by heart, and had no need of notes or recourse to passages in books. He reached the end of the litany: "Come, come O great one—I set my foot on thy neck—do as I bid, whatever that shall be"—and swung about to face his audience, arms raised in triumph, as a lurid red light flamed from the fulminating contents of the kettle.

The back of the room seemed to disappear from sight or existence, replaced by a wall of inky black; not mere darkness, the absence of light, but a dense, encroaching blackness that reached out tenebrous tentacles and made as if to smother the flaring illumination of the lamps. From far within the black mass there seethed scintillating specks of painfully bright colors, which winked and flashed and seared the eyes and burned into the brain. The colors coalesced, attained a form, assumed a solidity, and then became more than mass or shape, but a thing, a thing that lived and moved into the room, though such a thing should never live nor move on this earth nor on any other world. There were chokes and cries, even a scream, from the assembly, and all leapt from their chairs and pressed against the wall behind them. They did not flee, of course—for these were not silly children or ignorant peasants, but educated devotees of the esoteric arts—but they knew fear, for this was something beyond their ken and their powers, and they above all men could appreciate the grave danger they faced, a danger held at bay solely by the power of the gigantic human will before them.

Helvetius observed his inferiors cringing away from the monstrosity behind him, and turned easily to face the unholy being from the nethermost pits. And then, contrary to all expectations, he did that which maddened the throng with horror, and did indeed instigate a stampede among those others, who shortly fled shrieking into the night. For the great, the insurmountable Helvetius, the heralded mage of Heidelberg, shrieked in terror like a beast caught in an iron trap, and shouted in a tremulous voice that echoed through dimensions other than those of the room, "Who be you? What be you? From whence dost thou come?" And an answer came from that grotesque and loathsome and unendurable thing from beyond: "I am Astrodemus, Master of the Starfire, He who sets the suns alight in their time, and destroys them in time as it amuses Him, along with their many worlds. Art thou the insect who dares call to Me, and fain would dictate to Me?" Helvetius never replied, for at that moment a beam of intense light—of hard and crystalline light, if such a thing can be imagined—shot forth from the creature, and a blinding blaze filled the room. When the brilliance subsided Astrodemus and all the magical mirage associated with Him had gone, and though the accouterments of the chamber seemed untouched, there was nothing but the most foul traces remaining of the man who had styled himself Helvetius.

The wizards of Heidelberg, during the following days, puzzled over the problem, and arrived at mutual conclusions concerning the mistake their colleague had made which led to his unfortunate annihilation. They helped themselves to the notes of Jacob Bleek which had remained behind, and were able to glean the magnitude of the error of Helvetius. The latter magician had seriously underestimated the former who, it now appeared, had cunningly taken charge of the experiment for the sole purpose of inducing this result. Bleek, concealing his words as he might, had not invoked Baalademus, nor had he ever intended to do so. Rather, he had slipped into his chant the name of a far more dire entity, one that even Helvetius would never have dared to summon, knowing as he did that success must be immediately fatal to the wizard who so foolishly called. Bleek had contrived to direct the spell toward the inconceivably deadly Astrodemus, then had deliberately faltered, thus allowing his elder to complete the task, and accept the hideous consequences.

In fact the error of Helvetius had gone deeper than that, for all of Bleek's actions during this period had been shammed. His indecision, his clumsiness, his apparent fear of failure, had all been a show presented for the benefit (if that be the right word) of his tormentor, in order to draw him into the contest and propel him willingly to his doom. Helvetius, in his pride and anger, had never understood what was being done to him and, as it transpired, had never stood a chance against his chosen foe. Thus ended the life of Helvetius.

Bleek, as it subsequently turned out, had absented himself from the room before the climactic event; for whatever his faults, he knew his limits, and while he claimed the prowess to summon such a being, he did not yet pretend to the power necessary to control it, and quite reasonably desired to avoid its wrath. The young sorcerer had planned well, and had taken steps in advance to ensure that he faced no retribution, from any source, for his deeds. When the gentlemen of the black arts came looking for him, intending to bring him up on secret charges and punish him, they found him gone, with signs in his room of hasty departure, and nothing of value remaining. Clearly he had fled the university that night with his meager possessions, as well as two old and rare books of mystery from the library, irreplaceable volumes which were sorely missed.

The great wizards of the University of Heidelberg never saw him again, although they may have heard of him in after years, when accounts of the man, his wanderings, and his achievements spread, and his legend began to grow. They never forgot, however, those incredible days when Jacob Bleek came to them, and sojourned among them, and passed from them; and they long remembered the error of the grand master Helvetius, how it came about, and what it cost him.

III. At the Court of the Graf Von Waldorff

Jacob Bleek having fled precipitately from the wizards of Heidelberg, he desired to place much distance quickly between himself and those powerful and dangerous men, so he journeyed towards the dawn, across the expanse of Germany, down to and along the Danube, and so into the eastern marches bordering the kingdom of Austria. While traversing that region his money gave out, and Bleek was forced to fall back on the profession open to all sharp-minded itinerants: that of the nostrum peddler, the purveyor of bodily health and mental satisfaction. Even with the modest resources at hand he was able to offer considerable numbers of impressive looking and foul tasting potions to please the needy and the gullible, and it did not hurt his career that, being a clever sorcerer who had trained or dabbled in many disciplines, he actually knew a thing or two about the subject, and that certain of his exotic prescriptions were sufficiently efficacious that a patient might expect to derive some benefit. By selling his wagon and pony Bleek was able to raise enough capital to set up a shop of sorts, and in no time at all he had begun to attract a clientele, who swore by his services and were willing to part with the pittances they had saved after their oppressive taxes.

Bleek's new residence lay in the obscure village of Anheit, a rather sad, dreary place far from the crossroads of commerce and trade. Well enough it was for a man to lose himself for a while, but he had no intention of making it other than a temporary abode, where he could enrich himself to the extent of accumulating funds to pay for his next course of travel. For a time, indeed, his extemporized mode of life appeared to serve his ends, as the pathetic sufferers of the locale, bearing their ailments and their slender coinage, trooped to his door in pursuit of their lost and forgotten well being. There were those who actually did experience a lessening of their unwanted symptoms and pains. Bleek knew his medicinal herbs, and he knew the human body—midnight studies, from past years, of stolen cadavers had taught him much that would impress the practicing physician—and in general the requirements of the peasants were easy to meet, and challenged little his abilities. He also enjoyed the opportunity to undertake sly experiments upon the living frames of his wards, tempting them with fabulous cures when, in actuality, he sought knowledge of the effects of strange concoctions that he had devised as a result of his research. In these cases the medical benefits to the victims proved slight, but Bleek acquired an interesting corpus of information concerning the actions of rare drugs upon the bodies and minds of his subjects. Few of his patients died outright due to his ministrations—dreadful seizures or sudden insanity were the rule— and in these, and other awkward cases, he could always blame improper conjunctions of the planets, or bad air, or even the evil hearts of those unfortunates, which supposedly interfered with his virtuous remedies. The simple villagers accepted his explanations, in return for the overall public good that he brought to them.

Bleek, of course, being Bleek, could not rest at that, but must advance his cause in other ways, casually allowing it to be known that he had much more to offer those able to afford it, marvels which extended far beyond the common mysteries of medicine. It was not long before the good folks of Anheit recognized the residence of a sorcerer within their midst and, while some were gravely troubled, others thought to profit by the fruits of his unearthly powers. These people, many men but more women, would creep forward in odd hours seeking spells rather than drugs, and if their desires amused Bleek then he would act, seemingly on their behalf. They came to him craving love, or revenge, or wisdom, and in response to their needs—if the price be right—he would chant, incant, or recite special words, while he mixed and simmered his elixirs, and when he did these things something was sure to come of his efforts. The boon granted was, occasionally, that which was asked, and there were several happy customers of his wizardry, who could brag to their fellows of his magical prowess and thereby spread the word to others willing to pay. More often than not, however, the beneficiaries of his dark scholarship held their tongues, for the consequences of his sorcery tended to be untoward, unexpected, or counterproductive— and when not dangerous, at least embarrassing—for Jacob Bleek served no one but himself, and dispensed his charms solely for his own purposes, thinking of the villagers as no more than mice, to be used as he saw fit, in order to test his notions and gauge the results, thereby adding greatly to his store of arcane lore.

Not so wise and cunning as he later became, Bleek had fashioned a state of affairs for himself which could not continue forever, and in the fullness of time great tribulations stole upon him. How it happened he never knew, for he was never in a position to learn, nor did anyone ever care to tell him. Perhaps Maria, the lame old woman, complained that his treatment of her bad leg availed her little, while allowing demons into her heart; for he had used her in a sleeping state as a living mouth for local spirits, who provided him with helpful information concerning Anheit and its citizens past and present, but who unfortunately lingered to torment the hag during her waking moments. It might have been Erwin the baker, who complained of pains in his chest, and then failed to fully appreciate the cure; for Bleek had solved the problem by endowing the man's tumor with a strange life of its own, and when, one night, the thing actually managed to burrow out of Erwin's body, it had not only left disgusting traces before it had gone, but had first stopped to eat the baker's dog. Or was it Sennhild, the teenage lass in love, who sought a potion of reciprocation? Bleek's subtle ointment had worked on her intended young man, but something added to the mix as a casual test—an experimental derivative, made up from the crushed bodies of corpse beetles—had induced such foul physical mutations in her beloved as to make him abhorrent to her. Perhaps it was one of these, or another, or merely an informant, an officious busybody of the sort who always suspected, with or without due cause, the worst of his fellow man.

Whatever the case, one morning Bleek found himself accosted in his shop by armed men who came in the name of the law to arrest him for sorcery, witchcraft, and practicing medicine without license. They took him roughly away from that place, before onlookers who raised no hand on his behalf—though several of them were his best customers—and roughly chained him, wrapping a black hood about his head, and roughly threw him into the back of a wagon, and roughly drove him to another place, where they removed the hood and roughly hurled him into a dungeon. There, after a period without food or drink or light, a bailiff and a priest came to him, and the former assumed jurisdiction in the name of the local authority, solemnly read out the charges, and indicated the magnitude and variety of the corporal punishments in store for the prisoner; after which the latter cursed Bleek's soul, and assured him of eternal damnation in the next world, once this world should have had its way with him. Only then did guards carry in a meager sustenance, and then the great iron door of the cell closed with a reverberating clang.

Jacob Bleek was infinitely distressed by his predicament. Trapped in a dank, dark stone chamber beneath an unknown building, with no amenities of any kind, save for a moldy straw mat on the floor; at the mercy of cold-hearted enemies, with no friends or supporters worthy of consideration; separated from his belongings, including the charms and potions that might have served in his defense. However he chose to view the matter, his prospects did not look good. In due course, perhaps very quickly indeed, he would be hauled before a provincial court of some kind, and verdict would be rendered, and he would be done away with, following the most cruel tortures that the basely inventive minds of the ignorant could devise. There was nothing he could do for the moment to remedy his circumstances. He must wait, and hope, and make the most of subsequent developments, if possibilities in his favor should arise.

He could not have said how long he remained in that black hole, for time meant nothing there. It might have been hours, might have been days; in the absence of incident, he could not truly judge. Surely it seemed an endless span. The moment came, however, when the massive door drew back, and Jacob Bleek blinked against the searing light of a torch, and three gruff men entered bearing food and a basin of water, and they commanded him to eat, to drink, to clean himself, and to prepare himself for his fate, as he had been summoned, and his supreme moment was at hand. Bleek did as they bade him, and then they led him from the cell, down a grimy, soot-blackened corridor past other padlocked chambers, up a spiraling flight of narrow wooden stairs that creaked beneath his boots, and so into the open air and sunlight, which he had begun to despair of ever beholding again. The stark radiance agonized his eyes, yet he welcomed it.

He departed from the small brick structure which served as the portal to the underworld of the jail, and found himself facing a very different edifice across a broad, grassy courtyard. This was a grand house, clearly the residence of a grand man, a man of power in the district, though there was more wood than stone in its construction, and though it had seen better days, exhibiting signs of disrepair and decay. The ornate front door and presentation porch faced him, but Bleek was hurriedly marched to a side entrance, and forced through a series of passages leading past the small and miserable servant quarters. Beyond those he found himself within chambers bearing evidence of some luxury and modest excess: worn rugs and tattered tapestries, with ornaments and fittings meant to pass for gold, though they were only brass. Thus he was led into the great hall, where weighty matters were adjudged.

This broad, high ceilinged room impressed more than the others, for it possessed still more of the trappings of greatness. The walls and floors, as could be seen around the carpets and hangings, were built of pinkish-gray flags of granite. Expansive windows with clear panes opened in the side walls, with the curtains drawn back allowing plenty of natural illumination. There were two marble statues, white, one of a sage man, another of a beautiful woman, in classical pose and dress. A handful of figurines, perched on enameled stands of intricately carved wood, appeared to be real gold, although their workmanship suggested plating rather than true depth. Four guards in colorful uniforms, armed with ceremonial halberds, stood in the corners of the hall. At the far end rose a dais, and atop that stood a robed gentleman of many years and a heavy ornamental chair of stained oak inlaid with silver, and atop that chair—not quite a throne, but close—sat a man.

One of Bleek's attendants went forth to bow and whisper to the standing worthy, who then stooped to whisper to the seated man. The latter motioned lazily, and the attendant ordered Bleek to approach. He did so, alone, for the three who had accompanied him drew away and left the hall, and he faced the formidable personage in the seat of power. This was a large man, well-muscled though tending to corpulence, well dressed, with rings on his fingers, and wearing over his showy attire a cloak of blue with white stripes running down from the shoulders, a mark of office. His face was flabby and unshaven, his grizzled whiskers enclosing a grim mouth, while above it protruded a bulbous, red-veined nose. His eyes were both dull and keen;

curiously lifeless, yet eager, as if for game or sport.

The standing man spoke harshly: "Bow to the Graf Von Waldorff, who sits in judgment upon you this day." Bleek did so, and the seated man laconically acknowledged the prisoner with a tired wave of his hand. "I am Gustavus," continued the speaker, "priest of the True Church and counsel to the Graf, before whom you will plead your case. I shall present the evidence against you, while he, in his majestic wisdom and mercy, shall rule wisely, and make known to you your fate. You answer to the name of Jacob Bleek; speak if it be so."

Jacob Bleek meekly admitted that it was so. "Then know, sinner," cried Gustavus, "that you stand accused of foul sorcery, base wizardry, and ungodly dabblings with evil powers emanating from the blackest pits of Hell. There are laws in this country against those who would infect our land with such loathsome abominations. These laws have been devised by the highest of minds, both secular and spiritual, and they carry frightful penalties for those who have willingly sold their God-given souls to the ultimate depravity. The penalties are unendurable pain and ghastly death. When we are finished with your torment, you shall be drawn and quartered by the Graf's own steeds. This fate awaits you... if you are guilty, that is. I urge you to confess now."

Given the foregoing presentation, Bleek saw no benefit to confessing, and respectfully submitted that he was innocent. The Graf yawned, and at this point deigned to speak. "Gustavus, point out to this fellow the unpleasant ramifications of his plea of innocence."

"Very good, my lord, an excellent and thoughtful suggestion from a well seasoned mind. Culprit, verily I say unto you, that the plea you stupidly insinuate into our ears shields you not from just retribution. If you do not confess of your own free will as an honest citizen should, then you will be returned to the dungeons for interrogation. There you will be racked, and pummeled, and torn, and ripped; and you will be questioned, and questioned, and questioned again, until such time as you decide to speak openly. When that time comes—after all of that—then the aforesaid penalties will apply, without amelioration. So, you see, it is very much in your best interests to confess now, so that we get to business without delay."

"That makes sense to me," said the Graf. "I wish to join the hunt as soon as possible. My hounds and retainers await, and I am loathe to waste more of my life on this trivial affair."

All of this put Bleek in something of a quandary, for he could not help but notice (clever fellow that he was) that he was being offered only a set of terribly poor options, all leading to disagreeable results, none of which satisfied him. It seemed to him that he had reached the end of his road, and this distressed him exceedingly, for there was so much of that road still to travel; so much he still had to learn, so much still to accomplish. His education was not complete, and as for his attainments! There was a deal to do before he established himself as the greatest of all sorcerers, much less probe and uncover the final secrets of this big universe, and achieve the power and wisdom that only the mysterious Gods of creation and existence could bestow. Dismay clawed at his throat; he felt gravel in his gut at the thought of all the lost possibilities, should his span of life close now. Grasping at straws, he opined that a man of his parts might prove useful to the Graf.

"I seriously doubt it," drawled that worthy. "I've heard something of your crimes—frolicking with the peasants, and fixing their bones, and peddling charms, and what not. I happen to be in fine health; what's more, I hate doctors of physick, and a second-rate mage, so I'm informed, makes for the worst sort of doctor. No, keep your instruments, your spells, and your experiments, away from me. I shall not allow you to do with my body as you will. I dwell within it as a favored tenant, and I will not risk eviction."

Bleek pointed out—while still strenuously denying the charges—that he possessed other skills. The Graf, for instance, must have enemies, as did every important man; surely a supposed wizard, if Bleek were such a creature, could devise fruitful and amusing weapons against the foes of a noble lord. "And range them against me in turn," noted the Graf. "I am no kind of fool, certainly not that kind. I could not sleep easily in my bed while you tarried near. I handle my enemies by my own means—the rack, the lash, the sword—methods I tend to find effective, and which are sanctioned by the Holy Fathers.

"You see, unfortunate Bleek, that you have nothing to offer me. Health I have, and those who oppose or annoy me I trample underfoot. It is a pity that you can not do more with your books and your potions. Were you a proper alchemist, practiced in such arts, then you might prove a boon to me indeed; but then, were you such a scholar, you would not be hiding in Anheit, wasting yourself on those of no account or rank."

Bleek asserted that he was privy to many marvels along those lines and, given access to his books and materials, must be able to work to the benefit of a merciful lord. "I doubt it much," came the languid reply. "Your appearance, your station in life, do not impress. Besides, your belongings have been confiscated, according to law, and now are my property. If found guilty, that constitutes your fine. If found innocent—ha! that's a rare jest, eh, Gustavus?—if found not guilty, whatever pittance I accrue from your wares shall pay your court fees. Therefore, put aside your dreams, and submit to my justice."

"Yes, we have heard quite enough from the prisoner," said Gustavus crushingly. "He can not talk his way out of his predicament, nor is he in a position to buy his freedom." "Correct, my venerable counselor. If the accused had real assets, or could change lead into gold, then we would have a subject worth discussing between us." "So we would, my lord, but as that is not the case--"

Of a sudden Bleek broke in desperately, asking if the Graf were keen for gold. "I am, as is any man, when he can get it, or when he can't, for that matter. I reign over a poor district in a rich province, and that fact has been known to rankle. Wring the peasants as I may, my means often fail me, and I am unable to live always according to my desserts. It is a perennial problem, one which has called forth from me many a railing against unjust fate. Also, I have a wife whose family failed to deliver the entirety of her dowry as contracted, and I possess a comely but quarrelsome mistress who has spent that much and demands more. Why, knave, do you conceal from us a pot of gold? If so, Bleek, your future may not look so dire." The prisoner noted that, among the countless arts reputed (as he put it) to wizards, was the ability to manufacture the heavenly metal from base substances, or to otherwise produce it in quantities where little had existed before. This intrigued his lordship more than any aspect of the proceedings thus far.

"You play us false, vile one," said Gustavus, with a hint of caution in his voice. "If you can make gold from rubbish, as a potter creates an urn from masses of clay, then wherefore your situation, your cheap lodgings and miserly equipage? This is nonsense. The Graf's time is precious, and you shall not burn it as we burn the candle of your life."

Bleek, thinking quickly, invented for his persecutors the notion of a sorcerer's sabbatical, a period during which the dark scholar forsook all but the necessaries of life in order to clear his mind of worldly matters and devote himself to study. He suggested that he might have recently embarked upon such a course, and that his recent conditions gave no clue as to his magical pecuniary wisdom. "You talk in circles," snapped the Graf, "and my head spins without wine. Say on bluntly, and tell me true: do you know the alchemical secret of creating gold? Does that lie within your power?"

Bleek, with a feigned sigh, and an air of making a clean breast of the matter, granted that much they suspected about him was fairly accurate, and that he had mastered the secret, and with the right materials and support was in a position to prove it. Von Waldorff and Gustavus put their heads together and conferred quietly for some time, appearing to go back and forth between doubt and desire, until finally the Graf waved aside his counselor and said, "In the name of holy justice, it would plague me terribly to condemn an innocent man due to unseemly haste. While I reconsider the evidence in your case, I feel it becoming to suspend verdict and sentence. During the period of the postponement, I would turn my brain to other matters, quite unrelated to the charges against you. This evening, Jacob Bleek, you shall dine with me. That is all." With that the Graf called for the three attendants, who had stood within earshot beyond the door of the hall, and they led the accused back to his temporary abode in the dungeon.

There he remained in the darkness and the dampness, without ability to track the passage of time, alone with his thoughts, which turned first in this direction, and then in that, according to the hopefulness or the morbidity of his mind. It seemed that he did have a chance to avoid, or at least put off, a senseless death; had not the Graf spoken thusly? On the other hand, Von Waldorff was a man of vague and conflicting humors, and the joys of the hunt might serve to distract him from his proposed dinner guest, who could be left to rot in misery, until such time as casual remembrance led to a snap decision in favor of execution. There were many possibilities facing Bleek; most were undesirable, and in the best of circumstances there remained the problem of utilizing his cleverness to save himself from these witless barbarians.

And yet the iron door of the cell did open in due course, and guards bore to him water and commanded him to wash, and provided him from his own stolen stock with a fresh suit of clothing, which he donned. Thus made presentable, he was conveyed again to the great house, and presently found himself in the dining hall, a fair room with antlered heads of stags adorning the walls, and a big oaken table at the head of which sat the Graf Von Waldorff, with his chief henchman Gustavus at his right hand. The Graf bade him sit at his left, and dine. They had already begun their repast. The food was venison and little more, but it was good, and there was much of it, and Bleek ate wolfishly to make up for the meals he had missed.

When it suited him the Graf belched and said, "I crave gold, in quantities I can't shear from my stubborn flock. You say you know the secret of making it. Faithful Gustavus calls you a liar. If I must choose between the two of you, then you die, Bleek."

"It is well known among the educated," mumbled Gustavus around his mouthful of flesh, "that alchemists have endeavored without success to extract that secret since the age of the Babylonians. I have consulted the manuscripts. Fabled Hammurabi himself commanded his heathen wizards to supply him, but they failed him utterly, and he slew them to a man, along with their women, their children, and their asses. None since have achieved the goal, though many have promised. Now you promise, when your life hangs in the balance. I say you play us false, in order to buy a few more hours of breath."

Jacob Bleek strenuously rejected that analysis, begging them to believe and have faith in his learning and training. The long sought secret had been broken, he assured them, quite some years before, by the very best of sorcerers, one who chose to keep the secret for himself and a few select colleagues, lest the arts involved become well known to the world, and all and sundry took to producing wealth, thereby trivializing its value; for where there is abundance of supply, there is lesser value. Did that not follow? What would they give for a bushel of hay? Gustavus acknowledged the point but, said he, "These are mere words, and words from a condemned man are as cheap as grass. I implore you for proofs, as you value your life."

Bleek allowed, in the name of fair play, that a demonstration would be necessary, and made clear that he was ready to provide same, if they could give him the raw materials he required, for he came not to their enchanting realm prepared for such business. Certain notes of his, written in a mysterious script to defeat prying eyes, were needed, as well as the essential elements. Gustavus sneered, "We do not store magician's tricks in our barns," and the Graf moodily mused, "I can not send over the earth for odd chemicals and powders, nor have I the patience; so, if what you need isn't attainable here, then you must seek it in the afterlife, for that is where you shall surely go."

Bleek assured that everything of importance could be obtained locally, providing that his gracious host could produce a large amount of lead. "That dirty mineral exists here," said the Graf, "sufficient to build a mountain, if that I sought. You shall have your lead, and it will cost me nothing. If need be, I'll put together a mining gang of my prisoners and tax debtors. Now, what else must Gustavus catalogue for your demonstration?" Bleek listed the substances, and made mention of the processes employed to work the miracle. The counselor, after some consideration, allowed that the substances could be had, and the processes arranged, and forthwith the Graf ordered it done. "Show me gold," he declaimed, "where none existed before, and you shall have your life, your property, and my good will. I lend you an apartment for your residence, and a shed for your labors. Live at ease, O wizard, while you please me."

The Graf Von Waldorff, for the time being, proved as good as his word. Bleek no longer felt himself a prisoner (though he knew very well that he remained so), and he was given the space to work and, after some delay, every necessary item for which he asked. Within a matter of days he was ready to begin, and what he initially had in mind should not take long. He could not, however, rest easy in his mind, for his situation was most precarious, and could only become more so the longer he stayed. He had promised much, and hinted at more, but there were limits to what he could offer the rapacious Graf.

As far as it went, Bleek had told the truth to his captor. Unknown to laymen and the secular powers of the world, the mysteries of alchemy had indeed been made to give up the secret of transforming lead into gold, a fact well known for centuries to the highest circle of sorcerers. None other than the legendary dark scholar Porfidias of Toledo had exposed the way to the answer during the grim age of barbarism, when all the continent was shrouded in gloom and misery, and the lights of learning flickered feebly like solitary candles scattered thinly across a vast, benighted plain. Porfidias, he of the fabled brain, had, like a proper researcher, sought not gold or other tangible reward, but knowledge, in the purest possible form. He had turned his intellectual delvings to the study of the nature of entity, the ultimate composition of all material things, and sought to understand the secrets locked within the very fabric of the universe. Operating without preconceptions—so unlike the esteemed philosophers of the ancients—he had begun by asking himself the obvious questions: What is matter? Why do different materials possess singular properties? Why do they tend to keep their properties, until acted upon by the forces of the world, such as heat and light? When properties were altered, what patterns could be discerned? How could one control the processes of alteration, and make of them useful tools for deliberate transformation?

Wonderful Porfidias, a hero to all his spiritual kin, asked the age-old questions, but unlike his forebears, found the answers. He conceived the unusual notion that all entity within the cosmos was founded upon the minute vibrations of invisible particles, the simplest substratum of reality. The types of particles were few in number—in theory, he proposed that there might be only one type—but differential rates of vibration lent to them distinctive properties, and thereby made possible all the various elements and combinations of matter. He hypothesized that energy could be brought to bear upon these particles, which would serve to excite them, raising their vibratory rate from one level to the next, and in so doing transform one element into another. The idea, after its own fashion, was rather simple, for had not common men always understood the basic formulation? Apply heat to common wood, and the result was charcoal, a substance of a wholly different nature. Boil water, and it transforms from liquid to vapor. Might it not, therefore, be likely that processes existed which could dig deeper beneath the foundations of existence, and utterly change the natural states of the seemingly permanent, bedrock elements?

This Porfidias set out to establish, and establish it he did. Starting from the known principles of alchemy, as they were dimly understood in his day, he expanded his already vast knowledge through a careful and consistent program of controlled experimentation. He employed fire from monstrous cauldrons, generating incredible heat; he focused rare beams of searing light, via titanic mirrors, from the sun's seemingly gentle radiance; he brought to bear special acids of horrific power, and sought new formulations of grotesquely caustic alkalis. These sources of energy he used, as well as others drawn from the lore of wizardry, in order to test their effects upon one element after another. The campaign took years—it consumed his entire abilities and his every waking moment—and some authorities claim it ate up his life, for legend records that he died tragically, broken in body long before his just span, devoured by pustulating sores and rampaging tumors.

Yet before he died, he succeeded, and he passed on his discovery to the elect. Among his many findings was the revelation that certain, apparently worthless, minerals contain locked within themselves usable power to an inconceivable, almost infinite degree. He learned, to his own surprise, that the hidden fabric, the inner structure, of these stones vibrated at a level far beyond that of any previously recognized energy source. It was a difficult power to master; he lost one laboratory to a fiery explosion, a disaster which annihilated his assistants and scarred him for life, and which may have been a factor in his ultimate demise; but he persevered, and he learned, and came the day that he manufactured a fresh element with all the properties he desired. This substance, a combination of cunningly refined pitchblende and other strange ingredients, met every specification he had originally theorized. Its energy potential was beyond guessing; small amounts could be worked, shaped, and employed with other elements; and its effects upon them were marvelous. His magic mineral, the likes of which no man had seen before, served to alter the vibratory rates of other substances, and—this being the critical point—transform one fundamental substance into another.

Porfidias tested his process in a wise and methodical fashion, trying it out step by step on simple and common elements, but one can be sure that he dreamed of the grand goal, one which he did, in the end, achieve. He found that heavy lead possessed similar vibrations to that of gold. That pleased him much. He discovered that his alchemical stone could excite lead as it did other elements, and make startling changes to its observable properties. That pleased him still more. He learned, finally, that the transformation could be directed, and with much effort and big expenditure of energy he could make lead into something it was formerly not: slightly heavier still, of a different consistency, a different color. The result was gold. It did not resemble gold, or pass for gold; it was gold, the real thing, in all its beauty, right down to its essence. Porfidias had manufactured gold.

The great secret revealed at last, Porfidias must have died a happy man despite his horrid ailments, though he never benefited from the discovery; for he sought not wealth but knowledge, and that he acquired, beyond that of any scholar before him. His work paved the way for researches by other wise men, the best alchemists and the most devoted mages, who continued his experiments in hopes of perfecting his methods and garnering for themselves all the wealth and influence that copious quantities of gold can bestow on mortal man. Alas, this true and valid discovery, which they expected to shake the earth, availed them not, and in all the years to come there was much bitterness and gnashing of teeth over the increasingly apparent limitations of the Porfidian process, which made many a student of esoteric lore wiser, while never serving one whit to enrich him.

Herein lay the problem confronting Jacob Bleek. He could manufacture gold for his jailor—given all the necessary materials—for he knew the process, having once dabbled in that way, and saw no serious difficulties in arranging the promised demonstration. The result, however, would never satisfy the Graf, nor increase his wealth to any degree whatsoever. There was a fundamental flaw, not in the superb process, but in wonderful Nature herself, who delights in her tricks upon greedy men, and loves to play cruel jokes on them. So, in this case, she taught man morality as follows: the method of Porfidias could not pay for itself. It did not create wealth; rather, it expended wealth, in enormous quantities, and left the eager manufacturer poorer than when he began. He could get gold, sure enough—from the standpoint of the unwary, gold from practically nothing—but the process was so expensive that the manufacturing cost many times the result. In order to gain ten marks of gold, an amount of materials and energy must be expended amounting to hundreds or thousands of marks. There was no way around this problem. The process could not be tinkered with or perfected—it already was perfect—nor were there savings in volume, as a merchant might imagine. Scores of great minds had tackled this dilemma, in every case first with hope, then with dismay, and finally with despair. There was no way to make it work. The universe has its rules, which can be used, bent, or even ignored at some risk, but never broken.

The Graf would get his demonstration, and he would hold that frightfully dear gold in his pudgy hands, but what then? He would crave more and more, he would demand, he would threaten, and eventually, when the hopelessness of the scheme became apparent, his cruel rage would exhaust itself upon the mortal frame of his captive wizard. Jacob Bleek cared not for that scenario, which bought him only time rather than freedom. He could not fool Von Waldorff indefinitely—Gustavus was clever enough to see through the sham soon enough—so Bleek must plan ahead, think of what must be done beyond the test, before the hammer of doom fell.

He made the gold. He mixed his chemicals. He refined his pitchblende, extracting from it minutes quantities of the wildly vibrating ore that acted on other metals and changed them into something new. Slavish workmen, laboring under his direction, fashioned a gigantic sealed cauldron, into which he placed the mysterious source of power, along with a handful of lead. He heated the contents to the point that kettles of water boiled at a rod's distance. He governed the operation with mineral additives such as iron and graphite, which were common in the surrounding hills. He controlled every step, as the surging force beat itself upon the lead, and excited the vibrations of that dead, gray lump. Then, through a massive pipe of steel, he flushed in a rapid stream of chilled water, a cascade of sudden coolness into the tank which instantaneously geysered, blowing off the top, shattering the roof of the shed, and killing a workman assigned to the task. Bleek, who had observed from a distance, advanced after the outburst had subsided, picked up the pieces, and recovered the contents of the chamber. He was able to present to his master, exactly as predicted by theory, a handful of pure gold, of slightly less volume, but precisely the same weight, as the original lead.

The Graf was overjoyed, for he could not doubt that Bleek had promised truly, and had fashioned the gold from lead. His spies, at the behest of Gustavus, had kept a constant watch on the prisoner, in order to guarantee that he did not smuggle in native gold via secretive means, and attempt through cunning what could not be done by wisdom. The demonstration was a profound success, and for the moment served Bleek's purpose beautifully. He found himself the man of the hour, hailed as the greatest wizard of all time; an honored guest and respected citizen, to be feted and lavished with gifts and rewards. Whatever boon the Graf could bestow belonged now to Bleek, and he was assured by his grateful host that this situation should long continue, and that he should forever lack for nothing, so long as the flow of gold should continue.

Of course it was not long (only a few days, in fact) before Gustavus grew querulous, and made known his concerns to the Graf. The Porfidian method worked—this he could not deny, for he held the fruits in his own hands, and the results struck him dumb with amazement—but came time to square accounts, and what the counselor learned distressed him and raised doubts in his suspicious mind. A triumph for the ages, he agreed; yet where, he asked, lay the gain? It had been an expensive business, he noted, far more so than he had dreamed possible. At this rate, the district must be taxed into oblivion, in order to generate a ridiculously small sum of coinage. At first the Graf ignored what he deemed irrelevant carping, but he began to pay heed when he perused the bills for himself, and he angrily summoned Bleek to his presence.

That sorcerer had, naturally, prepared for this moment, and was ready with quick answers when hard questions were put to him. Of course, he granted, the recent test had generated no real income, nor had that been its intention, which was merely to make the point that the making of gold was feasible, thereby establishing the principle. That was the original method devised by the masters of the esoteric, and excellent it was for proving the case; now, however, they must move beyond this level, as had the great scholars of yesterday, and advance to the next method, which would answer for all purposes. The Graf bade him say on. Bleek—fawning and craven, all soap, oil, and honey—bragged of the ultimate means for creating wealth, a technique developed by veritable committees of wizards, and one which could not fail. Expensive it might be to make gold from lead, or any other disreputable substance, but profitable beyond imagining it was to make gold from gold.

He explained the matter thusly: there was an alternative process, known only to the wisest of mages, a deep, dark secret shared only among the inner circle, who trusted it not to lesser lights, much less to the unanointed. This process had been invented utilizing the concepts of conventional crop raising, according to notions well understood by any farmer. If one desires a field of corn, one must begin with a seed. A single seed will do, for in time it grows into a mature plant, which bears seeds of its own. The seeds may be collected, sown and fertilized, and eventually the field is there, ready for harvest, and all from a single kernel.

"You ask me to sow gold?" growled the Graf. "Tell me truly, Gustavus, is he the lunatic, or am I?" "Certainly not you, my lord," replied his clever counselor. "I assume there is more to the tale, and so withhold judgment, for a fleeting moment." "He had better be fleet, indeed." Bleek laughed as if at himself and profusely apologized for his puerile analogy. No, the actual process was quite different from the lowly farming, which was the proper lot of the peasant, and would require several items of a mysterious nature, which must be mixed into exactly the right potion, with the exact right spells chanted in exactly the right cadence—this was the ultimate in sorcery, after all—and yet the comparison was still apt. Bleek knew how to prepare seed gold, a measured quantity, and create from that many times the amount of magical, though absolutely genuine, gold. The process was constrained only by the initial amount of the precious metal. The more he had available to instigate the procedure, the more he could provide in the end.

"Being so, then take my ring, wizard," cried the Graf, and he threw it for Bleek to catch. "'Tis an heirloom, long in my family, but that counts for naught, if you tell the truth. Melt it down to slag, if that will make me rich." His prisoner averred, as if forced to admit to an unpleasant fact, that the process, while amazing in its results, was not that effective. Quite a bit more gold was necessary than could be extracted from a ring. "Curse you, knave!" shouted the Graf. "If it is not one thing with you, then it is another. If I could pluck gold from the trees, then I would have no need of you, and your flesh would soon know it. What do you want of me, that I have?" Bleek meekly suggested that a copious bag, perhaps a ten-weight, would suffice, and in return a score of such bags he would create. That would constitute true wealth, of the sort to make his host a grand name for leagues beyond the district.

"The image in my mind of such a future pleases me tremendously," observed the Graf. "What means have we to fill such a bag, my Gustavus?"

"It is a sore task," muttered the latter. "A ten-weight of gold, under current conditions, will strip you bare. All coinage must be called in, and the plate melted down as well. There will be nothing left." But the reward, cried Bleek; think of the reward! "The peasants are hostile enough," warned Gustavus; "They will screech like unruly children." "They are nothing but," sneered the Graf. "Even they will derive benefit from this, as I reckon. Gustavus, the gold; gather the gold, all of it, and our friend will do this thing, under our watchful eye, and I will be happy."

Thus it was to be. Jacob Bleek explained in detail the requisite steps of the preparation, which involved many weeks of work on his part; as it happened, just time enough to gather all of the seed gold. The peasants did howl, and muttered threats and oaths into their sleeves, but they paid. The Graf and his club-wielding henchmen saw to that. Gustavus ordered the melting of plate, and at Bleek's behest sent out for the distressingly costly materials needed for the process. No clever alchemy this, the wizard pointed out, but genuine magic, trafficking with the celestial (or perhaps darker) spheres, the recourse to elixirs and morbid chants of unknown tongue. Only this could give his lordship what he craved. Gustavus, who was inclined to obstinacy, accepted the accruing costs at the bidding of his master, who now had scarce patience with financial critique, such was his eagerness to acquire a treasure. During those days he saw the world filtered through gold-colored dreams.

The herbs, spices, minerals, and fragments of unusual or unclean dead things arrived, how procured Bleek knew or cared not. He kept himself secretively busy in the shed, appearing at meals to boast of his endeavors. The Graf had the golden ten-weight ready now, in a strong, coarse bag of burlap. No more delay would be tolerated. It was time to commence. At this stage Bleek took Gustavus, so he claimed, into his full confidence, laying out precisely what would happen, requesting the aid of the counselor and the presence of the Graf at the great ceremony. They agreed to this, in fact insisted upon it. Bleek warned that witnesses must be kept to a minimum, for foolish onlookers could spoil the spell. The Graf acknowledged the difficulty, but demanded two guards for the gold. Bleek accepted this, after laborious and ostentatious consultation of astrological charts.

Came the day, or rather the night—for it was the quiet, still period of utter darkness after midnight, under a starless and moonless sky—and Bleek called them into his magician's workshop: the Graf Von Waldorff, Gustavus the counselor, and the two hulking guards with the bag of gold. There they found strange torches burning with a murky violet light, and a big iron kettle boiling briskly, and wooden trestles laid out with packages, bags, and urns of weird and unwholesome ingredients. Bleek himself took center stage by the noisy pot, exclaiming and waving his arms like the grand master at a country carnival as he bade them make ready for the extraordinary moment to come. He fussed among the scattered magical substances, adding a pinch of this or that to the pot. He asked for the gold, and set it on a trestle near him while he stirred the oily, stinking solution with a large wooden stick. Then he demanded that all eyes fasten upon the kettle; he seized the bag in both hands and shrieked a chant that staggered and frightened his audience, though they recognized not the words; and then in one wild motion he hurled the bag into the pot and sprang away with a dreadful cry. In that instant the simmering steam from the pot converted into black, belching smoke of hideous odor, an opaque, impenetrable cloud of damp, clinging, noxious vapor that clogged the throat and obscured all sight.

From the pot there burst forth through the stifling gloom a greenish flash, and the smoke grew denser and more sickening still, and the Graf roared with surprise and fear, and the two guards—faithful to their charge, to the last—rushed forward, only to die in mid-stride. Their master, with Gustavus, held back at first, but sprang forward in turn once they could see, and found that Bleek had vanished from the room, though they had stood before the only entrance. "What manner of deviltry be this?" screamed the Graf; "Wizardry, I fear," shouted back the other. Truly spoke Gustavus, for their captive mage had gone like smoke through the smoke, and they would never see him again in this world. They discovered also, when they fished into the pot, that it contained only a well boiled burlap bag of lead among the ooze, while the actual bag of gold had disappeared with he whom they now styled thief.

Indeed the precious gold had gone, for Jacob Bleek had planned his escape well. Magic he had made, but only of a kind to transport himself a short remove from that place, along with the bag of gold, which he had switched for lead. His preparations had been lengthy and difficult, and it was only due to the avarice of his captors that he was granted the necessary time and materials for his spell of salvation. He returned to this sphere in the woods above the Graf's estate, and immediately absconded without his belongings, knowing that the stolen gold he carried away with him would more than recoup his fortunes, and allow him, when feasible, to acquire once more those items of sorcery that constituted his stock in trade.

There was, sad to relate for several of those concerned, no spell for multiplying gold, certainly nothing known to the fraternity of the mage. Had there been, the wizards of this world would long ago have made themselves the grandees of all the kingdoms. It was not meant to be, and they have ever tended to be a poor lot, scraping by as they may in order to maintain themselves and further their researches. They tend also, however, to be a clever bunch, and Bleek could lie with the best of them, when his life lay in jeopardy. He told his tales of the marvelous and the ridiculous, and they succeeded in their objective. He fled joyously for far places where he could once again practice and seek and learn, and so closed another adventure in his life. A narrow escape, perhaps, but there would be others, for Bleek was the sort of man to gain in wisdom while shunning caution, if it served his purpose; and what wizard would embrace caution, so long as there were strange truths remaining to be discovered?

The fates of the Graf and Gustavus were not so pleasant. Better for them that they had rushed forward with the guards and perished on the instant, for only misery befell them thereafter. Bleek had employed the last of his pitchblende derivative in the belching pot, and his surviving dupes paid the price for tarrying there too long. Gustavus lingered for weeks, a sick man, prey to an insidious illness that took away his appetite, his strength, and even his hair, and in the end made away with his life. The great Graf, that man of assured power, proved less fortunate still. His face and hands were scarred by something in that hot cloud and burning solution, so that he was ever after an object of laughter and derision in the whispers of his subjects in Anheit and the surrounding district, and out of his pride he lived thereafter in isolation. Furthermore, he contracted a chronic disease which wasted his body and wracked him with excruciating pain, making him useless as a lord, and hardly more as a man. He had no heirs at the time, a fact which wrecked his prospects beyond retrieval, for when, some years later, a son were born to him, the child was a monstrosity, a foul and pathetic thing, which withered grotesquely as it aged, and expired long before attaining its majority. Thus was the final revenge of the departed Jacob Bleek; and when, at long last, after seeming ages of agony and despair, the Graf died, so too did the House of Von Waldorff die with him.

IV. The Hermit's Curse

In the course of his roamings Jacob Bleek made his way into the Kingdom of Poland, where the business of garnering to himself all the magical lore of the world—and making use of those secrets to unlock the still stranger mysteries of the universe—eventually drew him to the great city of Cracow, the citadel of learning in the east. This was a grand city, ancient and ornate, prosperous and proud, daring to style itself a second Rome. While the objective visitor might have questioned that designation, it remained the case that Cracow truly boasted of a number of the higher qualities of civilization. Its architecture, massive yet delicate, oddly elegant in its towering and linear garishness, appealed to the eye, and was reputed to be unsurpassed for a hundred leagues. The dense, bustling center of the city thronged with merchants and travelers from all parts, many of them from lands beyond the known rim of the world, who carried with them strange tidings and evocative ideas. The university was new, yet already possessed keen minds of renown, men with whom a thoughtful and dedicated wizard might deal as equals. Here Bleek, presently well situated so far as material assets were concerned—for the Graf's gold, which had already carried him far, would keep him happy throughout a long life, if he managed wisely his riches—chose to make his home for a considerable period, where he could settle peaceably and learn to his heart's content.

Bleek took up residence in the Jewish quarter, and this is a place which must needs be described, for he had not seen the like before, nor experienced the notion of such a kingdom within a kingdom. The *Ghetto*, as it was called, occupied a broad tract somewhat removed from the center of the city, in the most ancient portion of town, where the exterior architecture had remained rude and crude, in some respects a holdover from barbarous times. The Jews, long ago driven from their homeland during misty antiquity, had settled there in great numbers during the dark epochs, and had brought with them all of their peculiar folk ways and traditions. Through their native industriousness they had become important elements of local society, but they chose not to wholly integrate themselves into Polish life, preferring always to maintain their identity as a people, wherever they should live. This attitude engendered suspicion, and even hatred, on the part of the Poles who, for this reason, and due to the vicious influences of baleful superstition, plagued the newcomers exceedingly. Thus the Jews had, long ago, erected the great stone wall that now encircled the Ghetto, and which cut it off from the rest of Cracow, egress and regress being achieved through only three gates, and that only when needful. Most of the Jews seemed to Bleek to be men of business, bankers and merchants, yet they were able to maintain themselves within their citadel by employing factors, hired Christians who went out into the city and the world to transact for them. It was a curious system, but it worked, and all involved prospered.

The interior of the Ghetto consisted of an old-fashioned tangle of narrow lanes upon which fronted an endless array of shabby shops and dwellings. The population within the walls was enormous, but one might not deduce that, for except in the vicinity of the market square one never saw throngs. The inhabitants tended to keep themselves within doors, and through this means and others went out of their ways not to draw attention to themselves. Despite their success, they were strangers in a foreign, and occasionally hostile, land. The grim aspect of the Ghetto, its drab functionalism, its gray slabs and crumbling mortar, were the main features which caught the eye of the casual visitor or wandering passerby. Superficial appearances were deceiving, however, for the Jews, while presenting to the outer world a bland prospect, devoted themselves to enhancing the cheerfulness and splendor of their interiors. The homes of their best men were replete with fine furnishings and costly decorations drawn from every land with which they traded, and via their convivial family life within doors they more than compensated for the apparent lack of public display and activity. Their society, hidden away from prying eyes, teemed with joy and merriment.

Here Bleek dwelt, on the second floor of an ugly and poorly plastered building, yet in a spacious apartment containing all the necessaries of decent living and rather more. He treated himself well, for he could do so—a man with money need lack for nothing in this place—and because it impressed his neighbors, to whom he gave reason enough to look askance upon his presence, beyond the fact that he was not of their kind, but a stranger who chose to live where outsiders seldom ventured. For in his rooms Bleek carried on his studies and his experiments, and those who lived near must often have wondered what sort of odd doings were taking place on the other side of his habitually locked door.

When not rapt with his labors, Bleek spent a good portion of his free time in the markets, for there he found much to please him. Books were to be had, books of all varieties, for those of the Ghetto were a reading people, and many a merchant waxed wealthy catering to their tastes. The tastes of the sorcerer were narrow, but they could be satisfied here. He managed to reacquire a number of volumes which he had formerly owned or had at his command, and built up his library still more with rare tomes of mystic import and magical treatises, many of which were unknown or unavailable in the west. Now he was the proud owner of Boris Revetsky's groundbreaking *Fathoming of the Elder Secrets*, and the wild *Dialogues On Devils* of Vegellius, and the useful but repulsive *Esoteric Morbidities* of Axion the Younger, a massive work composed shortly before the author's execution. In addition to books Bleek found in the sellers' stalls every useful variety of herb, mineral, crystal, or powder which a magician of the highest class could desire. The profusion of strange items seemed to indicate a burgeoning trade in such materials, which confirmed for him what he already suspected, that there was a great deal of covert and mysterious wizardry being carried out within the Jewish wall.

At his favorite haunts in the busy markets Bleek often rubbed shoulders with impressively taciturn, bearded gentlemen engaged in purchases similar to his own. Never would they speak to him—an obvious foreigner—nor offer any indication, even during their transactions, as to what they were doing with themselves, but Bleek thought they must be Cabalists, the fabled and unapproachably secretive practitioners of ancient Jewish magic. For centuries, as he understood the matter, they had been conducting researches and experiments of their own, an esoteric tradition quite divorced from, yet comparable to, the mainstream of European sorcery. There were rumors that the Jews, in certain respects, were more advanced than their Gentile peers, but it had proved ever impossible to pin down or verify such allegations, though what had leaked out of their secretive circles was fascinating enough. Now Bleek dwelt among them, a circumstance from which he had hoped much, yet up to this point he had been unable to dent, much less break down, their fastidiously constructed wall of reserve.

It was in one of the markets, however, the grand one in Poniatowski Square, at a stall devoted to peculiar Persian commodities, that Jacob Bleek finally made his great breakthrough. This occurred of an afternoon, of a cloudless day, of an unseasonably warm autumn, when Bleek had many purchases to make, and he craved drink. At the corner stood a wine shop, and the mage repaired to that place, only to find that a multitude of customers had conceived the same idea ahead of him, and they had cleaned out the shop to its last dregs. This frustrated him, to be left standing with coin in his hand, and no place in sight to spend it. So, in his annoyance, he did that which he normally avoided, which was to make a public magic which was foolish and unnecessary, bringing little gain and attended with much risk. It was an old trick, but one popular with neophytes. He seized a jug, scarcely damp with the juice of the wine, added a quantity of water, mixed into it an extract with which magicians are known to amuse themselves, and pronounced under his breath the age-old words. On the instant the contents of the jug became perfectly passable wine, of no recognized vintage to be sure, yet suitable for the purpose. This he quaffed, and refreshed himself, and would have gone about his business, perhaps taking himself to task later, when he was disturbed by an outburst of jolly laughter.

Bleek turned to face an aged Hebrew, a bald gentleman with bright black eyes and a long, curly white beard, eminent in appearance and dress. He was a big man, wearing flowing dark green robes of the best quality, bearing an ancient tome under his arm, and it was indeed he who had laughed and who continued to chuckle merrily. Presently the stranger said, "Forgive me, honored sir, for I laugh not at you, a guest of my people, but at my own thoughts and remembrances. It is long since I have seen that trick, one I recall from earlier and happier days of youth. I have always thought it a magnificent jest that there are those in this world who would take it so seriously. I, of course, know you not for a god, but a fellow mage. I observed all and understood what I saw, but fear not, young man, for it is not my way to reveal secrets. In the future, however, I advise discretion." Then he chuckled again. Bleek, at last, made his introductions, and bade the man tell of himself. "I am Josiah, once of the Elders, and still a personage respected in these parts. More importantly, I am one of the elect, long a devotee to the sacred Order of the Cabala. Thou art familiar with that body, I presume?" Bleek allowed that he had heard of it, at which Josiah retorted, "If you be worth your salt, then you will have heard a deal about it. Tell me, Jacob—a fine name, that, for a fine fellow, I'll be bound—to which school do you belong?" Bleek explained, simply, that he belonged to no school of the esoteric, but sought only truth, in its deepest and most fantastical forms. "An intriguing response, sir, one which suggests much, yet reveals little. Put aside these Persian trinkets; I have better available. Accompany me, if you so choose, to my house, and tell me more."

Bleek chose so, for this seemed the sort of acquaintance he desired and needed, and they left the crowds and the markets behind, and walked down unnamed and twisting side lanes into the oldest and most crumbling section of the Ghetto. Here, amidst tottering apartments and boarded up dwellings, they came to the large house of Josiah, a low but sprawling structure at the end of a lane which terminated at his door. The exterior was as unsightly as anything else in the vicinity, but upon entrance Bleek found himself in another world. The house was built on the antique Grecian pattern, in the form of a square surrounding an extensive courtyard of fountains and trees, shrubs and flowering plants. Amongst this garden roamed a lithe, black, female feline, a watchful creature who answered to or ignored, as her kind chose, the name of Sarah. She seemed to be the only other tenant of the place. The halls and rooms were untidy and dusty, but lushly decorated and richly furnished. Josiah bade his guest be seated within a chamber lined with books, while he poured wine, of the color of veinish blood, into tinkling crystalline goblets. "This refreshment must increase your joy," said the host. "I did not conjure it myself, I assure you, but acquired it from the best dealer, and paid him well for the privilege. There is much of goodness in this world that I lack, but of wealth I have a surfeit, and I use it as it suits me, and now as it blesses you."

So they drank, and Sarah joined them, leaping up and settling into Josiah's lap, and the men spoke, and over the course of the conversation Bleek told much of himself, for it had been long that he could discourse with another man as equals are wont to do. The situation pleased him well enough, and the really excellent wine sufficiently put him at his ease, that he related more of his inner thoughts than he had thought to do, in his stimulated loquaciousness revealing the course of his studies over the years, and his goals for the future. Bleek spoke of magic, and garrulously described his adventures among the fools and knaves of many lands. He even went so far as to mention his quest, that which had become his entire reason for being: his great desire to meet the Gods of the universe, the makers and destroyers of all things, and to extort from Them Their infinite secrets, which would raise him to the highest rank among wizards, and grant him ultimate power and wisdom. Josiah, who had listened contentedly to the story, balked at this. "I know nothing directly of these Gods of yours, for I care only for the One, little though He may care for me; but I dread to hear of such a quest, which shall surely bring you naught in the end. Once I read something of these so-called Old Ones, a curious passage in a tome composed by a wonderful scholar of the far north in olden times. He wrote of these Old Ones, and Their total power over all creation, and he recorded myths concerning Their Supreme Ruler, stories that astounded and frightened me. This Entity—whom the scribe dared name, though I shall not—was a God without love, without kindness, without compassion. I would have nothing to do with such a concept, and I destroyed the book. Put your quest aside, as you value your life, health, and sanity. I have dreamed of great deeds in my time, as thou dost now, but I have learned that one inevitably wakes from dreams. Your task, I think, is doomed to failure, and I suspect it is for the best. I shudder to think of the consequences of success." Bleek remonstrated, though he did not press his point, for he was feeling too agreeable, and he knew such argument to be useless. He could not convince his host, and he could not be swayed from his mission.

Nor did he learn much more of Josiah's history at the time. Bleek gathered, mainly from observation, that the man dwelt alone, save for Sarah, the perfect companion for such a retiring and reclusive fellow; living without family or even servants, the latter fact seeming remarkable, as Josiah was in a position to maintain a large household. That worthy gentleman proved singularly uncommunicative at first, and they parted that night with little more than a casual invitation for unspecified meetings. As it transpired, their next *tête-à-tête* took place later that week, after Bleek received a courteously phrased written request for his company. Bleek honored that request, and still others to come, until finally such gatherings on their part were a regular aspect of their lives, and over the course of many such meetings the youthful wizard learned the complete history of his new-found colleague.

Josiah was a mighty sorcerer, one of the greatest and farthest seeking of them all, who had once penned treatises of incredible clarity and daring under the pseudonym of Josephus Magnus. Bleek immediately recognized the name, and knew with certainty that he had befriended no common delver into mystery, but one of the masters, a man who had moved and shaken the rarefied circles of wizardry, and often left his mark at the forefront of the wildest discoveries. As the king of the Cabalists, Josiah had gathered to himself all the findings of Jewish magical lore, and carried that knowledge to a vastly higher degree. He had managed all this while maintaining himself in good standing with his people, who had revered his wisdom and honored him for years with the most respected seat among their councils. By any standards he had fared well, and a future of happiness and esteem should have been his due for the rest of his days. Something had happened, however, long ago, which had changed his life forever, and driven him into self-imposed seclusion as a hermit dwelling alone and quietly in the midst of a bustling city.

Bleek had come to realize that some secret sorrow gnawed at the heart of Josiah, but he presumed not to ask of it until his host felt easy enough in mind to unburden himself. Thus, in time, Bleek heard of the tragedy. Unlike most mages—at least those with whom Bleek had dealt, most of whom seemed rather like himself—Josiah had been a benevolent, warm-hearted sort, a man of the world, and in earlier times had conceived a fine love for a beauteous young woman. She was Ruth, the fairest daughter of the Hebrew tribes, with the manners of a princess of old, and the education and intellect of a scholar. She he loved, and she he wed, and she lived with him through all the days of his rise to power, fame, and glory. Josiah's happiness was complete; she was a material aid in his rise, for she helped him with his studies and work, and proved in every way a suitable partner for such a man. Theirs was a life of which most men can only dream or, knowing not that the world affords such possibilities, sadly fail to dream.

Josiah showed Bleek a painting of Ruth, composed from life by a great Polish artist, the only image the old man possessed of her outside of his memory. Hidden within a draped alcove of what had once been her room, it presented a picture, somewhat dusty now and worn by time, of quiet and contented feminine charm, cloaked in what most men would grant to be stunning beauty. Based on what he saw and had heard of this woman, Bleek had to admit—though he was not accustomed to giving credence to such matters—that his host had done very well for himself, and had his life not taken an unfortunate turn, would have been counted, even by the wise and noble Solon of yore, a happy man.

There had come, however, an ugly era in the tranquil domestic life of the Jewish warlock. It was a time of troubles and discontent in the Polish kingdom, of famine and political discord, and the Gentile rulers were wroth, and the Gentile peasants unruly and afraid. In their fear and anger they turned upon the strangers amongst them, the Jews, those people ever mysterious and alien, ever called upon to justify their fortunes and their lives when the brains of their neighbors burned hot and mad with the fever of rage. The blind and furious Poles, knowing not where to turn, but desiring to lash out at someone or anyone, instigated a ferocious pogrom, with the acquiescence of their masters, and surged crazily into the Ghetto. Then came fire and looting, the plundering of temples, the breaking of doors in private homes, and outrages in the streets. Jews were beaten in fury, or for amusement, and there were frenzied killings at random. No one was safe, not even the high and the mighty. Josiah escaped the ravages of the mob, but his dear Ruth proved not so fortunate. As the crime developed, it appeared that they targeted her especially, for her status and reputation were vaguely and imperfectly known to them. She would have denied the rioters entry into her home; on the instant someone in the heated crowd raised the frightful cry of "witch", and after that there was no holding them. They seized upon her person, and dragged her into the street, and gathered together a heap of combustible debris, and on that spot, as they danced and shouted insanely, they incinerated her mortal frame.

"Since that terrible day," said Josiah, "I have been cursed by a wearisome melancholy, and a distaste for this world, which still offers much to me but, alas, not that which I covet most. I live on memories of olden times, I feed on nostalgia, I drink of curious dreams. Nothing animates me now but the fond hope that one day I shall be reunited with my dear, departed wife." Bleek shrugged and noted that, according to the conventional wisdom, that reunion would come in due course, for Josiah was an old man, and at his appointed time he must leave this world, and if pleasing fables be true he should meet his love again. At this the Jew barked a harsh laugh and exclaimed, "Blast you, sir, and damn you to hell as a stupid Gentile, if you think I dream only of seeking Ruth in that final mystery beyond the darkness. I speak not as a sad old man, but as a determined sorcerer, who has devoted his years to the study of supernature. I have power at my command, and a brain that never rests. My mind is strong, as fiery hot and icy cold as in the days of my youth. I intend to master fate, rather than succumb to it. I want my precious Ruth back, and I want her alive and whole, as I knew her when life was sweet."

This statement perplexed Bleek, for he had some ideas concerning the magnitude of the task Josiah had set himself. Further adroit questioning drew an expanded response from his host. "I am convinced that there exists a way to bring her back to the full flower of life, with mind and personality intact. I have debated with myself various methods, none of which fully satisfy me. I lack a piece of critical information, though I know not what I lack. You have intimated that you know something of the subject. Cunning Jacob, your knowledge can be useful to me. Let us pool our learning, and together achieve this goal." Bleek mused aloud upon the difficulties they would face, and the length of time the research might take, and he wondered with studied discontent what would become of his own work. "I offer you a princely project," sneered Josiah, "and yet you press me to sweeten the deal? So be it; you are no fool, and I can appreciate that. Nay, I count on it.

"Then hear you me, Jacob, and behold what I offer you in return for your full and devoted services. In decades past, when the joys of life lured me on, I spent much care and toil on the attractive concept of human longevity, seeking to burst the bounds of the mortal span, and to extend by sorcery the cruel limitation of years which are naturally granted to us. I desired happiness on this earth forever, for my Ruth and myself, and though it could not protect her from the ferocity of ignorance, I tell you that I succeeded. Gaze upon my face, young man, guess my age as you will, and multiply that figure by three, and you will not deviate far from the truth. I matured in proper time, but since then the years have fled from me as if on wings, yet they assail me not. I do not claim immortality, for I can be killed, nor can I locate for certain the boundary stones of my longevity, which I suppose have merely been shifted rather than broken down to dust; but verily I say to you that my spell works and sustains me in life and health. Think upon that, Jacob, and dream of what you may accomplish with—at the very least—an extraordinary addition to your own span. If I swear to give you that, will you condescend to begrudge me a little of your time?"

They made the deal on the spot. Josiah was happy to get the preliminaries over with, while Jacob Bleek lusted after the dangled prize. So the elder wizard prepared his associate, explaining to him the processes involved and patiently teaching him—from out of a series of crumbling parchment scrolls bearing weird cabalistic symbols—the curiously ominous and complex foreign words he must recite at the appointed time; uncouth syllables and noxious bursts of sound, not Hebrew or any recognized language that ever rolled off the tongue of man. Josiah spent many nights fabricating the secret elixir which Bleek must drink when the invocation had been performed, and then Bleek did drink, and he sensed a tide of fire washing through his body, and a giddiness which bubbled up and exploded within his head. In the end he lay gasping, while Josiah told him that the magic had been done to him, that it had succeeded and that all was well. Afterward the young mage felt the same as ever; he realized that, objectively speaking, there were no physical signs to assure him, nor would there be for many a year; that he must accept the word of his host—a word he trusted absolutely, having come to know the man and his talents—and since this was sufficient, Bleek considered the bargain sealed, and undertook to do what was expected of him.

Bleek foresaw many dangers in their attempt to re-animate the long dead woman. The possibility of failure was vast, and there were similarly great perils attendant on success. He understood the problem well, perhaps—as Josiah suspected—better than any man alive, but he had never approached the matter with any emotional or personal concern for the chosen specimen. To Bleek the dead were no more than tools to be used, or founts of information, to be drained and discarded as he saw fit. To bring back the departed to full life, with tenderness and due regard for the sensibilities of the fragile subject, was an aspect of the problem which had simply never crossed his mind before. Off hand, the clever Bleek knew of three proven methods of resurrection, all of them fraught with potential or inherent pitfalls. These were the calling of the spirit, the revitalization of the corpse, and the mental transference of the target mind into a new host.

1. The calling of the spirit was simple, easy, and reliable, and Bleek considered himself a past master of this technique, to the point that the procedure tended to bore him. There were tried and true spells which, with the right material support, could unfailingly connect one with the nebulous remnants of the dead mind, draw it forth from the black hole of eternity into which it had plunged, and allow one to converse with that mind, for a short period or long, very much as if the embodied person were present. Bleek had often found this helpful in his work, but it would never do for Josiah, who longed to hold his lost wife in his arms once again, and make merry with her as a man and his woman are wont to do. He had no use for a sad ghost, and despite his loneliness had refrained throughout the years from conjuring her in that fashion. The calling of the spirit would not serve.

2. It was known to a certain rarefied class of wizard—a class to which both Bleek and Josiah belonged—how to prepare the bodily remains of the deceased, so that life could be re-infused into those tissues and membranes, at least for a period, so that the corporeal structure could become once more animate. If the corpse be fresh it was even possible, more often in theory than in fact, to awaken the dead mind to a form akin to its living state, and thereby have the subject alive and aware to a degree crudely resembling its original condition. This method worked best in the short term as opposed to the long; there were issues of gradual degradation and eventual lapsing into the former condition of morbidity. Regardless of the chances of success, this technique did not apply to the case which consumed Josiah's soul. The body of his wife had been hatefully destroyed, the husband retaining no more than a mass of ashes and a grotesque collection of charred bones, which he had lovingly kept all this time in an underground crypt beneath the central fountain of his enclosed garden. To attempt re-animation from that wretched stuff would lead only to awkward, if not loathsome, results.

3. There were recorded cases of spirits being called from the void, captured, and thrust into a new physical tenancy, in the form of a hapless subject who unwillingly donated his body and his life to the cause of esoterical research. Bleek knew of these cases, and had once experimented along those lines, only to give up the method as impractical, one which engendered needless difficulties without adequate gain. Human souls, as it

transpired, were resistant to being introduced into other hosts (as opposed to demons and other aggressive spirits, who longed for such opportunities, and sought them out with relish, though only for their own foul ends), and even when forced in, could not always be made to stay, except via the harshest measures. Furthermore, there was the invariable and lingering problem of the original spirit, the rightful possessor of the body, who tended to return unbidden and battle tenaciously for occupancy. That annoyance could be circumvented by first killing the host, but that, naturally, lead straight to the problems which inevitably derived from re-animation. It was an excellent idea in principle, but Bleek knew too well what would happen, and the dismal consequences that must ensue. In addition, Josiah was sentimental concerning the radiant beauty of his Ruth, and must needs have her back as he had known her, in body as well as in mind.

Bleek presented these points to Josiah, with some attempt at circumspection and tact, only to find his fears confirmed, that the man would not settle for any of the stated options. "This curse of loneliness and melancholy," said the Jew, "has loomed over me like a plague of Moses for the majority of my life, a curse I must break; and I will not accept half measures that offer no more than a cheap counterfeit of my beloved. Exercise your brain, good sir, and point the way to the answer, and I shall follow your lead with all the skills at my command. Expense is no consideration, nor is labor, nor danger. Do what thou must, in order to achieve my goal."

Bleek agreed, and consulted the accumulated lore of his thoughts, his books, and his own manuscript notes. He perused the incredible library of Josiah, the finest collection he had ever beheld, seeking indications and clues. What he sought, he eventually concluded, was a method of combining the second and third methods into one homogeneous whole: to reconstitute the ruined physical shell as if it were a new one, and to call the departed spirit into that fresh structure, and integrate them, body and soul, as a healthy living being was meant to be. Nothing quite like this, as far as Bleek could discover, had ever been attempted before; if it had, the procedure had most likely failed, and the experimenter had chosen to withhold his embarrassment from the world.

Jacob Bleek found the way, in time, but it was not a simple method. There was no single spell or concoction that would turn the trick; the undertakings that would recompose the body were wholly different from those which reinvigorated the spirit. Firstly, there was the burning question of how to revivify a corpse which had been so savagely handled, to restore it to completeness from the ghastly shreds which now existed. How to do this, with a reasonable surety of success? Bleek had gleaned obscure references to a vaguely known, scarcely comprehended denizen of the outer darkness, that twilight world beyond this one, a land existing within a framework of time and space unique to itself, which only sorcerers and fools dare to fathom. This entity, called Mordoran in the sole entry which dared name it, had once upon a time, in centuries past, approached or been summoned by the ancient sorcerial master Artocris. Bleek had long studied that man's exploits, but was hitherto unfamiliar with the tale; Josiah's awesome collection of priceless works paid dividends now. Artocris had spoken to the creature, or demon, or mystical force, and inquired of its nature and properties. Sayeth Mordoran: "I am that which amuseth itself in the Ultimate Night, by jesting with Fate, and playing games with Chance. For pleasure I bend and twist the Laws that govern all things, as no man may do . Ask of me the impossible, satisfy me in turn, and if it be within my power I shall grant thee one boon, and one only, which can not be. Ponder before thou asks, for I shall act quickly, and what I do I am loath to reverse." The wise Artocris thought long upon the matter, and in his wisdom chose to ask for nothing, deeming safety, in this instance, superior to desire. "I shall not test thee, mighty demon from beyond the spheres," quoth the wizard of old, "lest I be tested, and found wanting, and lose all as I gain little. Depart from me, and speak not to me again." Such was the story; no more than that, but what possibilities it opened! Such a being, for some unspecified price, must control sufficient power to rebuild the nasty wreck of Ruth, and so prepare the husk for spiritual occupancy.

If they could get that far, Bleek foresaw no trouble in capturing the wandering ghost of the female and stuffing her back into her restored body. He laid out his proposal to Josiah, who accepted, but not at first, and then with a shudder. The old man knew the story—there was not much he had missed over the years—but it had appalled him, for he respected the cautiousness of wise Artocris, and dreaded dealing with an entity that the great one of yore had shunned. What of the demanded fee? What form and magnitude might it take? As the old saying goes—one taken literally by mages who know of such things—the devil was in the details. "Must we sell our miserable souls in order to recover that blessed one?" he wailed. The subtle Bleek wondered aloud if the objective justified such risks, and hesitantly recommended abandoning the project, at which Josiah vigorously remonstrated. "Anything for my love," he cried. It was decided: they would explore the possibility.

Their research, their preparations, leading up to the attempted contact, consumed weeks, and would be of interest only to the most erudite scholars of the mystic arts. They learned spells, refined incantations, boiled and stewed strange substances. They tried out words of power, got them wrong, tried again, finally saw daylight, even if it was a light leading directly to darkness. Came a somber night, and a disembodied voice spoke over their huddled shoulders, and said to them, "Bring me three." Being who they were, and knowing who spoke, they understood what was required of them.

By now Josiah, driven by hope and desire, had grown reckless, and he hesitated not, but drew Bleek with him into this gruesome enterprise, insisting only that they go beyond the walls of the Ghetto for their prey. Bleek argued the point, dreading to arouse the surrounding Gentile population against them, but his hoary companion would not brook sacrificing his own, and furthermore had harbored throughout the grim years, since Ruth's murder, a fierce though indefinite longing for just vengeance. So they stole out of the Jewish quarter three times on three separate nights, and three times they fastened upon three unwary victims, and incapacitated them, and dragged them back to the crypt beneath the fountain in the garden of Josiah , and there performed three unhallowed ceremonies, and a door opened three times, a door in the fabric of the world, and three times the victims were conveyed, in some unguessable fashion, beyond that door, never to be seen again. When the third offering had been presented, and had gone screaming into the pure blackness of the nowhere realm, they retired, exhausted and fretful, to await the events of the coming night.

And Mordoran did return that next night, after they had pleaded with him to appear in the crypt which sheltered the remains of Ruth; and this time he showed a face, from which the two wizards cowered in terror. And Mordoran laughed and said hollowly unto them, "Thou hast humored me, which I find good, and it humors me more to appease your humors. What dost thou crave? Think long, then ask of he who can give."

And Josiah said, with quavering voice, "Mordoran, I wish a boon. August one, gaze long on these miserable remnants scattered upon this dais of onyx, the remnants of she I loved, and see with thy inner eye how she once appeared, when she was humanly fashioned, and restore her, as only thou canst, to her fair and unblemished form. I ask of thee as little as I can, for it is naught but a miracle that I seek." The face of Mordoran, which should never be seen by mortal eyes, emitted another laugh and twisted into a smile—one frightful to see, so that the two men cringed and felt unclean in the presence of such foul mirth—and came the words, "What do you intend with the reshaped corpse?" Josiah told Him, as best he could, what they planned to do, and what it meant to him, and how he would shower the name of Mordoran with epithets of gratitude. With yet another laugh the dark force cried, "It is good. So be it. I restore her to perfection. Do with the result as thou wilt."

The vile face vanished. Darkness descended upon the chamber. The twin torches flanking the dais were obscured, whether by a cloud or a tangible form the witnesses could not tell. Sight failed them, all senses ceased to function. They saw, heard, felt, nothing. When sensation returned, inky night lingered for a time over the dais, a darkness which the rays from the sputtering torches could not pierce. Then full vision resumed, and the chamber was as it had been, except that now the dais was occupied.

Bleek beheld the nude, motionless form of a young woman, and even he—who thought little of such matters—had to grant that she was the picture of loveliness, of the sort that artists dream but never capture. Indeed, he had seen the painting of Ruth, Josiah's prized possession, but it had not prepared him for this fleshly spectacle. The artist's inspiration had faltered when confronted by this reality. No wonder that the elder sorcerer's first reaction was to cry out and drape himself over the fresh and unmarred body, and sob happily to himself, calling the name of his dead wife over and over. When he had composed himself he rose, nodded grimly to Bleek, and said, "Now it is our turn."

Bleek felt of the body, though Josiah frowned and cursed his impudence. The young wizard judged that, while this was still death in their presence, the body was wholly restored, the salvage complete. The skin, soft and yielding, even radiated a feeble warmth. This was the framework of life, and required only the breath of the soul to re-animate it. Bleek allowed that he was satisfied thus far, and with that they got down to the strange business of calling back the lost spirit.

The procedure was simple. Both of them knew the words, the gestures, the intonations which harkened to those in the shadowy land of the dead, located the fading ghost of interest, and drew it to Earth. Each was able to play a role, though either would have sufficed. The body of Ruth was prepared by Josiah with ointments derived from rifled Egyptian tombs, while Bleek chanted the spell which fastened upon the spirit of Ruth. A sickening stench rose with the green and red and yellow vapors which poured up from the four urns marking the corners of the dais where lay the still body. The husband then took over the invocation, explaining in his own ancient tongue that her healthy body awaited her return, and ending with a shout as he ordered the mystic powers to take hold of her gently and convey her soul back into its proper home. The colored vapors mingled, thickened, belching forth of a sudden. Josiah fell silent. He and Jacob Bleek peered expectantly through the murk. The dank gases thinned.

The body moved! The twitch of an alabaster limb, the flicker of a dark eyelash, told them that an ethereal presence had been transfused into the flesh. The fair shape writhed, hands groped feebly at air. The ruby lips parted slightly, and from them issued a low moan. The essence of Ruth had returned to her body. "Before she wakes fully," said Josiah, "let us deliver her from the crypt, the place of death, and convey her to her room, the place of life." He brought forth costly raiment, identical to that dress portrayed in her picture, and clothed her, and the two men then carried her from that gloomy chamber, and took her to her bed in the finest room of the house. There she came, by degrees, to awareness of her self and her surroundings.

When Ruth's eyes had opened Josiah commanded that Bleek fetch hot soup, for she might require nourishment. The younger wizard performed his mundane task, returning in a few minutes with a laden tray. Short as had been the passage of time, he sensed that the atmosphere of the occasion had changed, and that all was not entirely well in the house of Josiah. The husband seemed pensive, troubled; the patient—wide awake now—in the throes of some insidious disturbance.

Ruth lay upright on soft, fluffy pillows. As yet, it developed, she had not spoken, but her eyes were wide and round, with much of the whites visible, and she gazed strangely about the room, at Josiah, and now at the stranger. When the latter entered the chamber she turned her head with a jerk, and her flowing tresses shook violently. She looked back at Josiah, who smiled to reassure her, and he whispered comforting words. She stared at him, as if in wonder.

"Is it really you?" Those were her first words to her elderly husband. "It is I," replied he. "Be not surprised, though I have changed somewhat, for more years than you can imagine have passed; but it is I, who have ever loved you, and now have called you back to my side. This man is my companion and assistant, and with his aid I have rescued you from an evil and unnecessary fate. Have no fear, for all is well now, and soon all shall be as it was." And he smiled again, a loving, comforting smile, and he took the tray bearing the bowl of soup and would have pressed it upon her. Ruth did not return the smile, however, but looked away, straight ahead, and stared at nothing as she seemed to retreat into herself.

She sighed, she gasped, and she said, "This is life, then? I was alive once, and I live now, but before this—there was another time, and another place— an intervening state, which was the end." Josiah implored her not to speak so, telling her, "It was not the end, merely an unsatisfactory interlude. That will be forgotten in time, discarded in the dust of stale history. You live, and I live, against every rule of nature we are re-united, and we shall be together forevermore. My curse of despair is lifted at last!" Here he left her side for a brief moment, turned to the curtained alcove and withdrew the concealing fabrics, revealing her aging painting. "As in the old days—which were only a moment ago to you, but an eternity for me—our joy shall reign supreme."

And Ruth laughed, a terrible laugh to hear, for it sprang unbidden from unfathomed bitterness and unforeseen distress; and her eyes widened more, and the pupils contracts to tiny points of black. She practically screamed the laugh as she leaped from her comfortable bed, paused, standing awkwardly, then lunged toward the picture. "This—you saved this—the image of my joy in life—the image of my dead happiness in life. This lives!" Then she tore at the picture with clawed fingers, and the old, flaking paint came off in strips. She laughed still as she destroyed it, but when Josiah moved to intervene she backed into a corner and confronted him with twisted, writhing features.

"You would bring me back," she cried, "and have all as it was. We will be together again, and speak of your work, sharing thoughts, holding hands, embracing as only the living can. All this to be mine again! Dear husband, there is much of which I can speak. I will tell you of flame, I will tell you of flesh crisping in the holocaust, of agonies beyond the mortal conception of agony. All this I will give to you, and yet this is but the beginning.

"These eyes of mine, or what lies behind them, have seen into the realm of the dead. That was my realm, a land where each second is a forever, where horror is the bread of existence, and despair the wine. You can not conceive—nothing you have read in books, or documents, or scripture, can prepare you for my tale—and I may lack the words to tell you. Our life together, compared to my life in death, is naught but a fleeting, fading memory, a hopeless moment ripped from the ages of infernal ghastliness. I say to you that I have always been dead; that I am dead still. In every sense that counts, there is no returning from that world. The fear, the torment, the sickness and disgust, reign in my bosom. It is within me; it saturates my flesh, it beats upon my mind, bruising and crushing my brain. There is no escape from that knowledge! For your sake, dear, doomed Josiah, and for my own, you would have done better to have left me there, for this taste of life brings only madness. How could it be otherwise, when I must always dread that to which I must eventually return. No matter how many years your arts may grant, I know my fate. It is the fate of all men, and it is intolerable and unspeakable."

At that her voice broke, and Ruth fell limply into a heap, and when Josiah rushed to take hold of her and lift her from the floor she began to shriek mindlessly, and she struggled wildly in his grasp. He begged for help from his assistant, so Bleek unwillingly joined the fray, and the two men managed to force that crazed thing onto the bed, jarring the tray and overturning the soup in the process. She continued to struggle until her strength gave out, continued to shriek until her tongue failed. Then they bound her to the bed. She passed into unconsciousness, but before dawn she was awake, screaming and struggling again, her mad eyes distended, unseeing; and nevermore did Bleek hear an intelligible word from her foam-flecked lips.

Bleek had feared this, and dreaded it. What she had experienced, at death and beyond—what her eyes had seen beyond the black veil, what she had found there—was not meet for the living, for no mortal mind can fully conceive of or accept such knowledge. Even Jacob Bleek, who had plumbed such abject depths in his time, understood only a fragment of what she had known in its entirety, and what he merely suspected was sufficient to deny him sleep on certain thoughtful nights. Josiah, he presumed—the hopeless, wonderful, loving Josiah—had guessed little and thought less of the problem, and so, with the finest of intentions, had committed this tragic act, which boded ill for himself and his love. And yet, Bleek mused, this Josiah was a wise man. He would see reason, do his sad duty, that which must be done: erase the results of this cruel experiment. Somewhere, it occurred to Bleek, beyond the crystal spheres of space or deep within the blackest pit of Hell, Mordoran must be laughing again.

Jacob Bleek, that clever sorcerer (perhaps too clever at times by half), was in for a shock. Came the morning, which should have been a time for reflection and consultation, when the fierce countenance of Josiah came upon him, and that mighty wizard, driven to distraction or, perhaps, madness himself, rounded upon Bleek and denounced him as an intruder, a troublemaker, and a conniving, spiteful demon. "This is your doing!" roared the old man, who had lived long and might, if he be correct, live for long ages yet. "My only mistake was to rely on your wisdom and goodness. It is the wisdom of foul cunning, and the feigned goodness of sneering evil. You did this to me! I asked you to lift my curse, and you lay another. What you have delivered me is nothing more than an animal, a monster in human shape." Bleek tried to protest—after all, it had really not been quite like that—but Josiah would hear none of his pleas. "I damn thee, Jacob!" shouted that shattered man, "I transfer my curse to you. Do you understand what I say? You are cursed, as I have been. Go where thou wilt, learn what can be learned, I demand that your quest fail you in the end. Never shall you find what you seek, though you journey throughout the eons until the doom of all things. Go now—leave my house, remove thy stain from this place— and embark once more, with my curse hanging over thee, on that journey that shall lead only to heartbreak and oblivion!"

Bleek fled the house of Josiah, and never crossed the path of that enraged wizard again. Shortly thereafter Bleek left Cracow for good, and he breathed somewhat easier with each league that separated him from the man who had once called him friend. He did set out once more upon his quest, for nothing could shake his determination, but now he traveled with a heavier heart than once he had been wont to do. Bleek had no choice but to face and to ponder one of the less pleasant aspects of the mystical, magical life, and at odd moments throughout his journey it would come back to haunt him. The curse of a powerful being such as Josiah, however unjust its laying, was not to be taken lightly.

V. The Countess Kronnberg

There was once a village, hard by the marches of the Magyars, a village known to its inhabitants as Istrakyager, though it was called something different by the census takers of the king. They saw it seldom, perhaps once every ten years, when the royal coffers ran low, otherwise having no use for the place. Other outsiders saw it more often, perhaps, though still but seldom, for the village was far into the wild lands, where honest travelers had little reason to go. There was nothing of consequence to attract them in that lonely land, while there was much that might tend to repel. A near unbroken forest of tall pines cloaked the region, great old trees like ranks of silent sentinels standing to attention in honor of an unknown lord, waiting expectantly on the steep slopes and rugged crowns of the endless hills. Surely something lived out there in the murky woods, though no trustworthy report of man confirmed this, for there were few who dared to pass under and between those serried ranks. A road, if it may be referred to as such, twisted for many leagues among the bases of the forbidding hills, pressed closely by the lowering pines, winding from the north and then following straight away a tiny clear stream, nameless, which flowed through the village.

Istrakyager was an olden name, dating from the vanished age of the pagans, an age not so far distant in time in that part of the world. Because the word was pagan the king's men did not speak or write it—the name was found on no map—but the villagers employed it, as for them very little had changed over the centuries. Life continued, for the local folk, much as it did in the lost days; they retained many of the old traditions, old dreams, old fears; and if foreigners (meaning everyone who did not abide by the old ways) cared not for that, those who dwelt in Istrakyager cared not for them. The folk seldom left their village save, rarely, to carry trade goods to distant markets. In the flat green bottom lands along the creek they grew the food they needed, and being hardy, skilled folk, they could make most else they required. So they stayed, and the infrequent travelers did not come as a rule other than to pass through, hoping to be long gone by the fall of night; for there was nothing to lead them there, and if by uncommon chance they must break their journey at Istrakyager, there were few who would bid them remain.

Jacob Bleek, driving alone in a carriage piled with his possessions, emerged from the dark forest late on a chill afternoon and headed south by the little stream which gurgled as it splashed over the rocks, and sparkled as it sprayed in the sunlight. As the trees receded he beheld pasture and crop land, and beyond that he spied the village. He knew not the place nor its name, but the day had been long, and the road cruel, and he was keen at that hour to find some place like it, where he might find hospitality before the sun sank behind the next dark hill. He continued along the road, which was rather better here—more, at least, than an uncomfortable rutted track—crossed the water on a creaking arched bridge, and so entered the town.

He had seen men in the fields, farmers already heading for home, but he had not hailed them, nor they him. Upon entering the village he came across others, including the shawled women, who nodded politely as he passed, then went back to their concerns. In its ostensible form the place was like other habitations he had seen; he ought to be able to count on available lodgings, though he refused to speculate on the quality of accommodations and service. As an old hand at travel, the dedicated journeyman had long ago learned to take what he could get.

There was a church, a well maintained structure in the eastern fashion, which he had not heretofore seen in those parts; a shop, another, and yet another, which were already closed for the day; and there was the tavern, clean, very small, not an establishment accustomed to big business. Bleek pulled up in front of the shut door, dismounted, tied his horses, and approached. A knock at the door produced, after a considerable pause, the owner, a burly, heavily bearded man in his last youth, who solicitously bade his guest be welcome and enter.

The host, a well behaved and mannered fellow despite his rough appearance, introduced himself as Radetsky, thanked his guest for honoring with his presence the humble village of Istrakyager, and urged him to make himself at home. Radetsky averred that his tavern did serve as the inn as well, cautioning that resources were few, as travelers were few, but offering assurance that whatever could please Bleek, if it be available, was at his command. The weary wizard thanked him for his courtesy, requested care for his steeds, a sharp eye for his goods, and food, drink, and shelter. All this was promised, and would be performed or provided with alacrity. The lady of the house, a friendly, younger woman named Maria, insisted on presenting herself in her apron, then dashed away to prepare his dinner.

As Bleek ate his simple but satisfying meal of hot, peppery sausage and coarse brown bread with fresh-churned butter, other patrons arrived and joined him in the dining hall, taking up seats at the other tables. These were obviously locals, just out of their fields, a clientele which explained the ability of Radetsky's inn to operate profitably without frequent visitors from outside. These were tough-looking youths—although pleasant enough, in their wary fashion—who most likely had no women at home to care for them. They greeted Bleek with a nod or word as they entered, without endeavoring to infringe upon his solitude. The host was rather different. After seeing to the sorcerer's bags, and helping his wife serve his other guests, he took to hovering about Bleek and asking impudent questions in an open and engaging manner. "Had a long day on the road, sir?" he would say, and

"Rode in from the north, did you, sir?" or "Perilous roads for a pleasure jaunt, upon my soul." Bleek was polite but noncommittal; he had no designs on this place, and his natural reticence had been enhanced over the years as he had learned the necessity for and wisdom of judicious silence. It mattered not to him who they were, nor who he was to them; on that basis he could do business with them of an evening, and all concerned should be content.

As he sat with composure at his table, digesting his meal, Bleek did ask casually of his host about the locale, but derived very little more information than he might have deduced, had he been so inclined to trouble himself. Istrakyager was an old village in an old land, which kept to itself in the main, with the acquiescence of the world beyond, and no one thereabouts had much cause for complaint on that score. Only now did Bleek hear the name of the village, and it did intrigue him a little, for the root of the word reminded him of a word he knew, in a context other than geographical; and he airily made mention, as if due to a slip, of the extremely ancient term "Istrakion," which he would expect only the most cloistered of scholars to know. It was a name, with dreadfully old connotations, which he assumed long forgotten by ordinary folk; yet it seemed that he might have been somewhat mistaken, for Radetsky's eyes flashed with cheerful surprise, and a few of the other men turned Bleek's way inquiringly, and gazed upon the newcomer with greater interest and respect. Even Maria, who was making her rounds with a jug of ale, paused as if in thought. The landlord laughed merrily and cried, "That is a name I haven't heard since my grandam, gone all these years, last sat me on her knee. She was fond of stories from the elder times, she was, and I lapped them up in my day, though my dear father warned me against them. I asked the minister about that name once, but he knew nothing of it, or wouldn't tell me. I've often wondered. Are you a man who knows of such things?"

Bleek jovially assured him that he was not, that he had heard the term in passing during his travels in the wide world, but that it signified no more to him than it did to the undoubtedly learned minister of Istrakyager. That marked the end of the discussion, and shortly Radetsky went on his way, tending to his many customers; but Bleek was left to chuckle to himself, and ponder with amusement on the nature of stray survivals from the lore of yore, and to think of what odd ideas might still be taught to these people around their hearths or even from the pulpit; ideas they might retain dimly in their hearts, though they no longer acknowledged the dark, legendary sources in their minds. Were he a different man, with different ambitions, these fine folks might, he thought, constitute a worthy line of study.

He had been allotted the garret room under the peaked roof, the most difficult to reach but, as Radetsky informed him, the only room with a wide window that looked down upon the expanse of the town. So it did, although local pride had rather magnified the boon. By this time it was quite dark, with precious little to see save the somber, angular shapes of structures with their flickering interior lights, and a vanishing hint of hills rising behind, now wreathed in mist. That was all, little enough for a traveler like Bleek, who had seen so much from so many windows in his day. Beside that, he was very tired, and desired only rest and sleep, from which he imagined nothing short of a pitched battle outside his window would rouse him. The chamber itself was common in every way, rude and small, yet thoroughly up to its assigned task, and bearing a hint of a woman's touch in the flowers that graced the bed table. He arranged his effects, doused the lamp, and immediately fell into deep slumber.

It was, then, with considerable dismay that he found himself aroused from unconsciousness at an hour which felt—which he sensed was—far too early to have sufficiently revivified his weary mind and body. He knew not the hour, nor could he hazard a guess at the time, except by noting that his chamber was still pitch dark, and that there was no sound of activity either within the inn or anywhere within earshot, and that he still fought against the demands of sleep which continued to fog his brain. He deduced, therefore, on these grounds, that the hour was disconcertingly early, that there was no justification for wakefulness, and that his peace of mind would best be served by rolling back over and losing himself in sleep once more. An excellent plan of campaign, no doubt, but one which failed him now. He could not evade the impression that something had jarred him into untimely awareness—a voice, he thought, had spoken to him—and as he sighed and pondered the matter more, so too did slumber inch out of reach until he knew that it had eluded him for the nonce.

With a snort of disgust he threw aside his tattered blanket, sat up, the joints of the hard bed frame creaking, blinked and gazed across the room. He seemed alone, which encouraged him, and all appeared as it should, though it were so infernally dark that his vision scarcely spanned half the chamber. It was a tiny place, yet he thought to see more than he did. That area by the window was drowned in blackness, as if it had been blotted out. He made to rise, intending to light his lamp and suppress all doubts, then checked himself, for at this moment a greater range of vision came to his aid, without recourse to artificial illumination.

He could see farther toward that wall than he had presumed, and it truly did appear that the opposite section of the room was not concealed by the blackness of darkness, but hidden from him because it had gone away. There was actually, so far as his senses could discern, nothing there; he was staring into a deep and unbounded distance, a vast space where nothing of the sort should exist; a space out of which he began to detect a trace of faint nebulosity. The dim radiance was at first little more than a whispering into his eyes, a hazy impression of such slight consequence that he questioned the fact, and sought to explain it in terms of the natural illusions of waking. He could not maintain this hypothesis, however, for the nebulosity grew in distinctness and intensity; seemed to approach by stealthy degrees, and to assume a more solid presence.

Finally he realized that a human form was advancing upon him out of the impossible void, and before he could properly prepare himself for the moment the mysterious personage stood before him in his remaining slice of room. She gazed down upon him impassively, as if examining him; a penetrating look, as if every aspect of his being required long and objective analysis; and then she extended an arm and lowered her hand to his, and he raised his hand to join with hers, and he rose from the bed to meet her. He gazed into her eyes, and she gazed back, and he dared not to breathe.

"Jacob Bleek," said she, in the tone of one musing over the name. Then she said, "Jacob Bleek, the wings of capricious Fate have carried you far, from one mirage of Destiny to another. Now, at last, the time of culmination has arrived. Fate has smiled upon you, and brought you to this place unbidden, to where it was ordained that you should come. It has brought you, through time and space, to me."

He dared not speak, he dared not think. He had no words or thoughts at his command, nor would any serve to capture this moment's happenstance. He knew, somewhere in the farther chasms of his mind, that something mystical was occurring to him, that he lay under a species of enchantment. Enchantment—the term rang in his brain—yes, enchantment was the word, in the truest of senses. This woman was enchanting, and her inexplicable power had enchanted him.

She was the loveliest specimen of the fair sex that he had ever beheld, a young woman of exquisite beauty, a beauty that conquered and captivated. She was tall and perfectly formed, with the natural grace and bearing of a born aristocrat. Her golden hair was piled high in curls above an intelligent forehead. The elements of her face—the strong, aquiline nose, the lush red lips, the high, sculpted cheeks—combined to suggest something beyond feminine prettiness, beyond depth of character, something more akin to what he expected of a storied goddess. Her skin was becomingly white, of the paleness of moonlight, the finest ivory made flesh. Her dress was regal, of a color matching her hair. And those eyes—how could he describe them?— warm, open, inviting, and piercing to be sure, with an intensity of vision that bored into his own. There she stood, so closely that her gentle breath bathed him. Against all seeming probability, she was real, and had touched him, spoken to him, called him by name. Once more she spoke.

"You travel the world, setting no limits to your spirit, as you seek the wisdom of the ultimate secrets. You have accepted for yourself the greatest of tasks that man can undertake. I seek the greatest of men; I desire he who stands above all other men, he who stoops to no other: the man of mind, the man of glory. Be you that man?"

Bleek replied with one word, choking out the answer that he must give, for no other answer were possible, even had he doubted its veracity. "It is good, then," said she. "You are truly he who is ordained. Never did I doubt. You shall come to me—it is so written—and with me you shall learn all, and achieve all. You see, I do know your goals, and we will speak of them, at the chosen time, but I tell you now how much I approve of you and your quest. Your long sought realization is at hand, just as you shall be my fulfillment. I leave you for the moment, but I will see you again of your own free will, at the time you condescend to designate. Fear no obstacle, for my abode will be revealed to you, and my spirit of desire shall call to you and guide your steps past all hazard." Then she was gone. Her leaving happened suddenly, literally within the blink of his eyes, yet without sensation of motion or departure. She was not there anymore. He stood alone in his little room, staring at the far wall and the vacant window. The immaculate vision of the lovely woman was gone as if she had never been.

Jacob Bleek sat heavily on the bed, rubbing his eyes and pinching his cheeks. As much as he strove to recapture it, he felt nothing of reality in his late experience. Everything was as it had been before. Had it been a dream, then? It was difficult for him to gainsay that possibility, for Bleek was a dreamer in more ways than one, and slumberous images were a regular occurrence for him, often of the most vivid expression. Normal dreams, however, he invariably knew to be such upon awakening. This experience, on the other hand, although it no longer seemed real, nevertheless struck him as a great deal more than the usual. It affected him; he sensed a disturbance in body and spirit, one which dived deep into his marrow and his heart. Bleek knew all too well when the specter of magic had fastened upon him, and he believed—he reasoned—that he felt such power now.

The remainder of a very long night passed slowly for him. He might have dozed on occasion, but he thought not; certainly he derived no rest from any further sleep that he contrived to snatch. He was fully aware of the moment when the first red tinges of dawn broke over the town, as he had for some time been residing at the window, gazing sightlessly into space. He watched as the sky brightened, and the mist rolled away and the clouds broke, revealing the horizon. In the distance he saw the hills, most of them low and round. One caught his attention, for it stood somewhat higher and apart from the others. Almost a mountain, it loomed to the east, and in the increasing light he saw, or imagined he saw, traces of structure atop its sharp peak. Yes, surely, that was a line of battlements on that far crag, perhaps towers, definite evidence of an artificial edifice built into the naked rock.

When Bleek came down in the morning Maria offered him a bowl of soup, which he accepted listlessly. Her husband was not in attendance, Radetsky being busy in back with carpentry repairs. Early customers, whose debris the wife had been clearing, had already departed for the fields. They were alone. He asked her about the distant peak visible from his window. She gave a curious answer, with much hesitation, requiring frequent prompting from Bleek. "You refer to the Kronnberg. There is nothing of interest for a traveler there, nor is there any way to get there, were it worthwhile. There is no road to speak of, and even the path is bad, so I hear. Goodness no, I've never been that way myself; I hear from others that the route is poor, and I take the word of those who know. No one goes there. Oh, who knows the path? In years past someone might have tried it, but there are none so foolish today.

"What lies on the peak?" She grimaced, obviously uncomfortable with the conversation. "You must mean the Castle Kronnberg; there is nothing else that way for three or four leagues, perhaps more. It is an old and forgotten place, best forgotten, nothing but a ruin. Well, of course no one lives there; there's no way to get to and from, that would suit normal folks, and we don't get visitors from the place. There might have been a lord of the castle in olden days—I suppose there must have—but that was before my grandfather's time, and a great deal more, I'd reckon."

Somewhat later, after he had finished his repast, Bleek (with studied artlessness) requested that a pack be prepared for him, that he might go on a walking tour of the unique and pretty countryside. Maria agreed sourly, and disappeared into her kitchen. Before long the male Radetsky appeared bearing a laden knapsack and a frown. He cautioned his guest against exploring too far on his own, pointing out that the terrain beyond the fields of the bottom land was very wild. It was quite possible for a traveler on foot to lose his way, and there were animals in the woods of the hills, wolves and such, that feared no man. Bleek assured him that he would take the requisite precautions. Radetsky averred that the finest views were to be had to the west, along the crest of the valley above the stream. Bleek indicated that the forested lands to the east had rather caught his fancy. Radetsky seemed disconcerted.

"I don't advise straying too far in that direction," said he. Bleek mused on the picturesque potential of the view from the Kronnberg. "It is too far," Radetsky said, "and there are tales— no, I don't remember them, for I never knew them—tales that were old when I was a boy. I've heard it isn't a wholesome place to visit. It has always been spoken of as such, nor have I ever had cause to inquire for myself." Here Radetsky lowered his voice and leaned closer. "I have heard, as a matter of rumor, that supplies are infrequently prepared for the castle by the farmers who live nearest the mountain, though they are still a healthy distance away, for no one chooses to reside in its shadow. I don't know if I believe that; common wisdom tells that the castle is abandoned and forsaken these many generations. If the whispers be true, however, then I believe the tenants—if any—value their privacy, and have no wish to be disturbed."

Bleek made it known that he was setting out immediately. He advised Radetsky to keep his room and belongings, tend the horse, and accept a decent advance payment to cover any costs. Maria reappeared at this juncture, to make a gift to Bleek. She said pragmatically, "We all need watching after at times," and delivered into his hand a tiny silver cross on a like chain. Bleek smiled. It was not a standard crucifix, though it could serve as such, and probably did; but rather an antique symbol of the original inhabitants of the district, whose descendants Maria and her people surely were. Rather than the figure of a Christ, or other Christian image, it bore a single eye at the intersection of the bars, representing a theological concept that these folks might dimly retain, though they never learned it in church. Bleek recognized it from his studies, and it amused him. To appease his hostess he slipped the cross around his neck, thanked the Radetskys for their solicitude, and repaired upstairs to dress for his trip, donning a broad-brimmed hat, his walking cloak and heavy boots, and taking up his staff.

He left the tavern and headed east along the main street, the only street worthy of being called such in Istrakyager. By this hour on this cloudless day people were about in town, mostly women, children, and the elderly. He was hailed politely at times, but otherwise left alone. On the outskirts of the village he crossed a bridge over a bend in the creek, then walked along a deteriorating road through fields where the youths were already active. There was considerably less farmland on this side, and he soon passed it by, to be swallowed up by the pressing forest. He spied a handful of cottages among the trees, close by the road.

At one cottage he accosted an old man leaning on his fence, who seemed more taciturn than the folks of the village. Bleek asked him about the road to the Kronnberg, only to be told, once again, that there was no road—this pitiful lane, he was assured, ran out shortly—nor any reason for one. Bleek pressed the man for information, wondering aloud how the castle dwellers acquired their necessaries. "You be friends of theirs?" the aged fellow queried. "Then you should know better than most. Someone descends the mountains once in a great while, and how he does it is more than I can guess, nor need to know. Food is purchased, and linens and the like, but not very much, and not often. That's all I know. I don't ask for more, and I've got nothing more to tell."

Bleek had further questions, but he had to keep them to himself, for the man walked away hurriedly. After that there were no more cottages on the road, nor any evidence of human presence save for the road itself, which did soon dwindle into insignificance. It was difficult to walk on, so poorly was it maintained, and he could not presume that it received any care at all. A man on horseback would have found the route a chore, and anything larger would have found it extremely problematic. There were stretches of deep mud which necessitated his walking among the pines at the edge, for the ooze sucked at his walking stick and his boots. If a conveyance ever used the road, it must pass through infrequently indeed.

The path narrowed and began to climb. This was a fearsomely wild land, overgrown with thickly growing trees that had never felt the bite of the ax, and which hung overhead, forming a dense counterfeit tunnel above his head. Little light filtered down to him; despite the brilliant sun of the lowlands, he felt here as if he were journeying under gloomy overcast or in unnatural twilight. It was primeval territory, surviving as it had from time immemorial, perhaps from the days before man first intruded into these parts. The inhabitants of the locale had, clearly, made little mark on the landscape, beyond their immediate abode, and Bleek could imagine that he had trekked to a far and primitive country, infinitely removed from the world that he knew so well.

What was he doing with himself? As he climbed the steepening slopes of the Kronnberg he asked himself this question, wondering why it had not crossed his mind before. This unusual adventure made up no part of his program, and he was at a loss to explain why this wearisome detour from his plans should matter so much to him. He had intended to be gone from the vicinity by now, yet he felt absolute certainty that he must proceed. To the Castle Kronnberg he must go; that was a given, with nothing requiring internal debate. Surely his current mood of strangeness, this odd feeling of inexplicable zeal, stemmed from his dream of the previous night. Of course it did—that had to be the answer—and yet he had not consciously formulated the thought before now. Having done so, it aggravated and disturbed him, for he was not entirely convinced that he was advancing according to his own will; and if not to himself, then to whom did he bow?

Late in the morning he came to a bend in the path, and around that he entered into a clearing below a rocky knoll. Here the sunlight reached him, and it felt good, better than it should have, for he had grown wary of the oppressive forest, which seemed too still and lifeless. In the clearing he spied an old cart, which might have taken a horse when used, but which appeared abandoned now. It could have been a fashionable vehicle once; if so, those days were long past, for now it was badly worn from usage, unpainted, in disrepair. It was parked at the edge of a formidable ravine, a narrow gash in the mountainside that plunged steeply down until hidden by treetops below. This ravine—almost a gorge—was spanned by a single long, wide plank of native wood. Bleek paid especial attention to this development, for the path ran straight to the crude bridge, continuing as a foot trail beyond. That way he must go, were he to proceed, and he had every intention, despite his qualms, of proceeding. After pondering the situation he realized there was nothing else for it but to cross, and that he did, without further deliberation, skipping quickly above the dizzying ravine, the plank shaking under him, to the other side, where he threw himself down, gasping.

He doubted not that this place attracted few visitors; the matter of access alone was sufficient to stifle idle curiosity. From this point one could, he guessed, ride down in the cart, although even that struck him as unlikely, given the conditions of the ostensible road. Above the ravine no conveyance could make its way. He saw no traces that a proper bridge had ever existed. If there had been one, it had fallen or been taken down ages ago.

Here Bleek ate and drank, and when refreshed recommenced his climb. He was negotiating a forest trail, simply that and nothing more, one scarcely designed for the comfort of pedestrians. The trees edged closer, their branches whipping at his face; the shrubs encroached, their roots and stems catching at his feet and legs. Jagged stones marred the trail, making footing precarious as the route turned ever upward. He tried to console himself by reasoning that, at this steep rate of climb, he must be making excellent progress toward the summit. That had better be true, he thought; it did not soothe his imagination to think of wandering alone in this grim forest when darkness fell.

The forest, hitherto silent and devoid of living signs, gradually began to teem with evidence of natural inhabitants. At first he heard the sounds of life: minute buzzing in the vague distance, and tiny noises of creeping, as if insects swarmed somewhere just out of reach. If that be so, he never saw them. He did spy tracks on the trail, the spoor of larger creatures that had passed this way. They were not prints of man or horse, but of other things, and he could not help but wonder if it were desirable to meet up with them. Certain tracks bore the impressions of very large claws. Bleek thought of wolves, and he hurried on his course.

After a spell he heard more sounds, as of big animals passing through the woods to his left and right. These noises were rather furtive, and he began to be plagued by the persistent notion that unseen creatures were pacing him, perhaps stalking him. That pleased him not one whit, nor was there much he could do about it at the moment. Occasionally he detected sounds below him, as it might be on the trail; and he could only trust that he would not hear them on the trail ahead of him.

There were things in the air; he noted the sounds of flitting through upper branches, and at times something like the hum of hovering farther above. He did not think of birds when he heard these noises, though he very much wanted to do so. Surely common birds would have revealed themselves. These did not. By now there was an unhappy degree of commotion about him, which caused him to long for the former silence.

Toward the last he did see things, never more than a glimpse at a time, yet enough to fill him with foreboding and make him deplore his predicament. Unknown varieties of animals were indisputably keeping company with him, paralleling his path and slowly closing with him. From the corners of his eyes (and only then, no matter how he tried to focus his sight) he caught fleeting images of heavy, ponderous beasts wending clumsily among the dense shrubbery of the forest floor. Through the massed growths creatures crept or padded, and however he analyzed these glimpses, what his brain gave back to him did not resolve itself into the forms of deer, or bear, or wolves, or anything he might have led himself to expect. He was coming around to the belief that the Kronnberg sheltered an unusual or unique array of creatures, a belief he would rather not be forced to put to the test. He was alone, and in the main defenseless; he had of necessity carried with him few resources of an esoteric nature, and thus felt himself at a rare disadvantage in regard to his environment.

And yet, despite everything, turning back was an option which did not occur to him. He had a destination, however hazily he had articulated it to himself, and he would attain it, come what may, and surely his reasons— whatever they were—would clarify themselves at the proper time. All he had to do was survive. He thought this, and it horrified him that he thought it, for what was he fated to achieve here that justified concerns of survival?

Then the masses of obscuring forest on both sides fell away without warning, and for the first time in many hours he saw the clear sky and the sun, the latter now low in the west. Most of the day had been consumed in getting this far. Bleek beheld an open, rocky plateau, on the lower reaches of which stood the scattered standing skeletons of dead trees, their bare, angular branches faintly stirring in the wind, clawing weakly like bony fingers at the air. The thin, chill breeze whistled at this high elevation, but naught else moved but the branches, for there was no longer any sight or sound of mysterious forest dwellers. From this vantage he had gained a remarkable view of the surrounding country, quite attractive in its way; he could see the rolling hills and bluish carpet of forest stretching for leagues, a wonderful vista to cheer a tired traveler, if he be the sort moved by such notions. Istrakyager, if it could have been seen at this distance, was hidden by the bulk of the mountain, and virtually the only work of civilization discernible from this awesome perch was a thin line of road slicing through the wilderness beneath the setting sun, seeming impossibly remote, like something belonging to a far off or unattainable world of dream.

All this he noted in passing, yet his attention was held by the only other evidence of unnatural feature in this realm. Before him, across the barren mountain top, there loomed above an impressively sheer basaltic escarpment the titanic edifice of the Castle Kronnberg. It looked very old, and quite abandoned, as certain reports would have had him believe. Gazing upon it now, he could understand that conclusion. In appearance it was wholly antique, with the grim, massive, rough hewn stone walls of a former epoch, a relics of the ages of darkness, bearing no trace of delicacy or artistry in its construction. The stones had never been smoothed or faced, as the fancier tastes of a later era would dictate, but rather bulged or protruded jaggedly from the vertical surfaces. The battlements were broken in spots, the short towers crumbling, scars of blackish-gray rock against a sky which was just beginning to darken. There were few windows to be seen from this side, none whatsoever in the lower walls.

The beaten path ran across the craggy plain, winding up the steep escarpment, terminating before the large outer gate. Toward this Bleek made his way. Up to the top he went, the trail here switching back and forth several times, this portion of the journey itself a difficult climb. By now he was terribly weary, and feeling the cold when he paused for breath. Presently he stood before the gate, a vast wooden door that rose high overhead, its planks rotten and held in place only by bands of rusted iron. There was no bell, no portico, only an observation slit above and to the right, currently occupied by a couple of ravens. He spotted more of these birds standing sentinel higher up on the battlements, and he marveled, for these were the only signs of life he had made out since arriving at this rarefied height. He wished they were other than ravens, however, for though he lacked superstition of the common sort, he cared not for the connotations inherent in those legendary creatures. Well, there was nothing for him to do but knock at the gate, and this he did, though it seemed one of the more foolish and useless actions of his life, for this place reeked of long desertion, and already he found himself questioning the more hopeful tales he had been told.

Despite his momentary doubts, Bleek soon received a response to his hard raps upon the rough wood. There came a noise as of metallic clanging, followed by the sound of harsh grinding, and the big gate, all of a piece, slowly creaked inward. It opened wide, then halted with a shudder. There crept forth from behind the gate a man, an immensely aged, wizened, and loathsomely ugly man, hideous to behold, yet a man dressed in the livery of a valued servant, a creature of the nobility. He stopped in the middle of the yawning entrance and, leering in an extremely nasty fashion, examined the visitor carefully from hat to boot. The man spoke no word of greeting, so Bleek, not certain how to proceed, introduced himself and claimed the hospitality of the traveler, if such be offered in this lonely abode.

To this the man replied, "You were expected, Master Bleek, and are welcome. Have you other bags?—no?—it is of slight consequence. Your needs shall be met. You may follow me now, and I will escort you into the castle." The man turned and trooped across the courtyard without another word, the puzzled wizard making haste to come up behind him. The ravens croaked at Bleek, a harsh, shrill chorus, as he passed within. Their cries unsettled him. It was a good thing to be expected at this place, with the sun fast disappearing behind the western hills, and the known world so far removed; a good thing, that is, if expectation be reasonable, which it assuredly was not in this case. Bleek observed the courtyard in passing, a deplorable, dispiriting mess like the castle exterior, with heaps of debris, trash and fallen stones, littering the dirty grounds. Rats darted under cover at his approach. Nothing he saw suggested a living place, and he wondered idly if vulgar squatters had infested this former citadel of greatness. An inner voice told him that this was not a satisfactory or convincing answer, that he should be prepared for strange surprises.

So it transpired. They came to the dry moat, partly filled with rubbish, of the castle keep, crossed over the drawbridge, which did not have the look of functionality, and passed within the door. With that last step everything changed, and Bleek began to develop a heightened appreciation for the Castle Kronnberg. Torches flared on the polished walls; embroidered rugs of vivid hues and intricate designs graced the bare stones of the floor; and a short passage led into a warm and cozy chamber, well lit by flickering lamps and a friendly fireplace. There were comfortable seats, a table, fine ornaments, hanging paintings. All was tidy, well kept, cared for as a grand residence ought to be.

"She will receive you presently," the man intoned with studied politeness, though still with that evil smirk to disgrace his already discreditable features. He took Bleek's bag and his staff. "There is cheese, bread, and wine on the table. Wait here, if you please, while I announce you." He withdrew through one of several passageways, leaving Bleek to peruse the room. Whatever hunger he may have felt gave way to his curiosity. He pored over the paintings, which seemed to illustrate historical scenes which meant little to him: local conflicts with armies in battle, or convocations of anonymous councils, all presented in the style of an antique and rather more crude artistic tradition than that which was fashionable in these times. Bleek garnered the impression that everything he saw was very old, if lovingly maintained.

He was sitting tensely before the fire, struggling to subdue or hold at abeyance the many questions jostling for preeminence in his mind, when the servant returned. "She will receive you, and is eager to do so. Even now she descends. Come this way." Once again Bleek followed him into a passage, much like the other, and they trooped past a number of closed doorways to yet another chamber, this one much larger and possessing greater ornamentation. This was clearly the receiving hall, as well as the dining room, perhaps the heart of the castle's conviviality. It was octagonal in shape, sporting an immensely high painted ceiling, beautifully paneled walls bearing historical frescoes and vibrant hangings of lovingly woven cloths inlaid with gold, silver, and precious stones, numerous full length portraits of quaint aspect depicting ancient worthies, and an array of intricately designed lamps which illuminated the space like daylight. From the cavernous fireplace at the far end warming flames roared and crackled. A tremendous oaken dining table, built to seat dozens, occupied a large portion of the floor area. Urns and bowls of gold, plates of porcelain, utensils of silver, chairs inlaid with the costliest metals, goblets of clear blown glass, a chandelier of sparkling crystal; this was the ultimate in luxury. A long sofa, strewn with cushions, took up an entire wall facing, an eighth of the room. Everything was carved, or worked, or woven with the artist's touch, with no regard for expense. It amused Bleek to think that the Graf Von Waldorff would have killed to possess a tenth as much of the trappings of nobility and power. Here it was, in unimaginable excess, hidden away in a forsaken castle atop a desolate peak in the middle of nowhere.

"Remain here," said the wretched-looking servant. "She comes quickly." Again he left Bleek to his own devices. Though his mind, in considerable turmoil, was focused upon the upcoming arrival of his hostess, he found enough spare attention to devote to the shelves which occupied much of the wall space, and which were laden with a staggering load of parchments and scrolls, as well as a number of genuine books. He extracted a scroll from its place and turned it over gingerly in his hands, feeling through his fingertips—as a result of long experience—the wonderful age of the fabric, a conclusion supported by the delicious aroma of mustiness which emanated from it. Its contents were written in an unknown script, so he replaced it and drew forth another, which was similar, and another, which was composed in a tongue he recognized. Astounding!—he held in his hands a treatise on natural philosophy written by Gordian, a learned courtier to the second Ptolemy—a priceless document, impossible to acquire, thought forever lost by scholars. Yet here it was, forgotten perhaps, or read, and if still read, then read by whom?

"Welcome, my guest. Let us know one another, and make merry." Bleek heard her voice and he turned, and he beheld her, but he need not have heard or beheld. Despite improbability, despite reason and rationalization, he had known that it would be she. This was the lovely vision of his dream in the flesh, standing before him exactly as she had appeared those eternal hours ago. "I am the Countess Kronnberg," quoth she, approaching and taking his hand as she had done before. It felt just as real, and this time he could not pretend or rationalize otherwise. Bleek bowed to her, for he knew

84

that he must, and also because he desired to do so, though he had never bowed to woman in his life. "And you are Jacob Bleek," said she, "the unique man of boundless mind and mighty dreams. I too dream, and long have you come to me as a specter. Now you are here at last, of your free will, as it was fated before ever the world was fashioned. This is a joyous night! May the joy continue without end. Yet I sense that you are tired, that the road has worn you." Bleek, driving himself to speak, allowed simply that his climb had been difficult, and that he had not slept as well as he might the previous night. She smiled—a beam of gold was that smile—and replied simply with the query, "Do you say so?" In return he said, scarce daring to whisper, that he was honored to see her again. "Do you say so?" she repeated charmingly. "Come, Master Bleek, and sit with me at table, and let us dine while we talk."

She sat, and then he did so, and she tugged lightly at the bell pull, and within the span of a few heartbeats her man appeared with a laden tray on a rolling gilt trolley. He laid out the repast and served it, a feast fit for the nuptials of royalty. Calf, pheasant, eels and other fish, sauces and a choice of ancient wines; these were made available, and much else. There was more than could be eaten by a party of visitors. "I will ring, Antonescu," said she, without taking her mesmeric eyes from her guest, and the old servant nodded and backed away as he had come, wheeling the trolley with him.

They dined, Bleek devouring the fine food in order to fill his empty belly, she picking at her selections, sampling and savoring. She spoke in due course, and when she did she spoke of him, of his self-imposed education, of his burning desire to seize knowledge from mystery, of his impossible and glorious quest. She knew everything about him, everything known to him in his mind, and some things perhaps hidden within his mind even from himself. It was hopeless, pointless, to argue with or refute what she said, nor did he think to conceal his thoughts from her. Where the value, when she knew him better than he knew himself? As she spoke of these things approval rang through her every word.

"You were ordained to me," said the Countess. "Though far away from the bustling world, isolated as I must be here in my ancestral abode, nevertheless I sensed always the presence, somewhere, of the man that is you. You are the man of inherent nobility, the Anointed One, he who lives rather than exists, who makes of the world rather than being content to let the world make of him. Your ideas are infinitely profound, nurtured by the ultimate sustenance of cosmic vision. Long ago you left behind the herd, who wallow in common, turgid fantasies of good and evil. You soar above such baseness; your wings shine in the astral fire, and your eyes glint brilliantly in that blaze, while the others dare not climb to where they are burned and blinded. I say to you that you have scaled the stairs to heaven this day, that all of your possibilities shall be realized, beyond mortal conception, and that it is meet that I should be waiting here, however long it had to be, to honor you.

"Know you, Jacob Bleek, that I am the Countess Kronnberg, born of a noble line which has reigned in this castle since before any written record will admit. My people were a great people, a wise and demanding race who once thundered across this land on foaming steeds and in hurtling chariots. We saw all, so we took all, for it was ours by right, being who and what we were. Stern, yes; harsh, yes; cruel—so fools would say—if it be necessary, for patience was never our virtue. We are scattered now, those few of us who survive, like diamonds upon a beach of black sand. Though we must hide from this world we despise, our greatness remains. Gaze upon those faces in the pictures on the walls; those are my forebears, and I honor them, as their history honors me. Born of such nobility, I have maintained it as I might, sheltering it from the lowly foulness which teems beyond these walls, and upholding this magisterial citadel until the time come that I should be joined by he who is of the same spirit.

"You are he, Jacob Bleek; you are that man. You came, and now our time begins. Here, at this juncture of the angles of fate, at this high epoch, all that can be conceived by us shall come to pass. You would know the Gods? Here, with me, shall you know them. You would know those secrets so arcane that you can not yet frame the questions you must ask? I have them at my beck, reserved for the mind that will unlock them. I will teach you the questions, and you will have the answers at your command. The culmination of your quest is at hand. With your new found power you would shake the foundations of the universe? I shall stand by your side as the willing consort to unsurpassable greatness. All this shall be ours together, for what I crave most is the vital force within you that drives your every step, and animates your soul. Give me that, and the rest is yours. Will not that suit? I say our bargain is sealed, and the deed will be done. Now indulge thyself, Jacob Bleek, for as long as thou wilt, to celebrate our victory. This is the age of merriment. Take you the wine!"

And Bleek, almost maddened by the tableau she laid before him, quaffed the contents of his goblet, and reached for more. Soon they would talk, tomorrow they would study, tomorrow they 1would explore the mysteries of life and death and the beyond, but tonight they must drink, and exalt. For him this was a new time, a new experience; the Countess had awakened something within him that he had not known to exist. Her very presence filled him with joy, warming his blood and exciting his mind as no wine ever could. What was this crazed desire that she tore from his flesh, from his marrow? What manner of conceptions now clawed at his brain? Useless to analyze; he could only feel, and accept. This was unbridled passion, a need to feed upon the qualities of mind and body inherent in another. Through her witching charms and enchantments she had brought him to this state of triumphant ecstasy. Only such a woman could have pierced his iron reserve: a woman who was not merely beautiful, but who defined beauty; who was not merely refined, but who embodied the essence of nobility; not merely cultured, but who possessed knowledge and insights equal to his own. And all this—dare he think the thought—all this was to be his!

Their party commenced and their revels raged on without bounds. They drank, they ate, they sang, they laughed. She laughed at the crucifix about his neck, laughingly pulled it away, threw it aside laughing, and he laughed with her. Through hours that seemed minutes Bleek submerged himself in desire, satisfying and sating every craving of his senses. There were no limits to his besotted hilarity and his happy lunacy. This was what life was meant to be. To think that he had denied himself so long! He would have regretted the empty years, except that he knew such regrets to be foolish. Only now, at this place, with her, was it possible. No man had ever been granted so much by woman. Was this what Josiah had known with his Ruth? Ridiculous; it was stupid to compare the two cases. Bleek had once heard the old man's prattle about love and devotion with indifference. He recalled it with distaste. There was no shred of similarity. The common emotion, even when deeply held and revered, still betrayed the baseness of its origin. For all the Jew's big talk, his pathetic justifications, his desires had yet remained nothing more than the sniffings and snufflings of an animal after its kind. Surely it was a grotesque jest to think of that in relation to the Countess, of what he had found with her. Yes, a jest—the wild laughter bubbled up from within—he unburdened himself of the thought to her, and she laughed with him. She too found it a travesty of epic proportions, for what desire of the herd could possibly compare to the cosmic majesty of their union? Love was but a word, this of theirs beyond words. They boggled at the thought, stared speechless into one another's eyes, and shrieked again with laughter.

When each moment of one's life is experienced to the fullest one may cram an eternity into a single night. This Bleek did. He lost all consciousness of time, the fruits of his pleasure ripening in their seasons with the speedy regularity of lightning flashes in a tempest. He left nothing undone, nothing untried; whatever he failed to suggest or lacked, the Countess Kronnberg was quick to offer or to provide. Whenever called Antonescu would appear to serve them, but eventually his ministrations were not required. The hours vanished, lost in revelries he could not clearly remember afterward. He became numbed to ecstasy, even as he groped for more. There came a time when he knew nothing more, and then he woke in a dark place, and alone.

In desperation he reached for the memories of that glorious interlude, for Bleek felt terrible, as with a deathly illness. He remembered the wine, and cautioned himself against its use, but that, surely, did not entirely explain his current condition. He had been fond enough of the stuff in his day, without ever feeling reduced to this weakened state. He seemed hollow, drugged, drained, more as if something vital had been taken from him. Exceedingly unpleasant, it was the utter reverse of what he had felt while the Countess had regaled him; a loss of life essence, rather than a surfeit. He turned his head and tried to focus his vision. He was in a small chamber, well appointed, sprawled naked on a downy bed, lying atop the sheets. A single candle, close to guttering, flickered on a stand near his head. He sat up, groggy and weary. His skull throbbed, the sickness mounted suddenly and almost overcame him. He noted his travel bag resting by the door. He did not recollect this room; he had not seen this place while conscious.

He strained for the bell pull which hung above his face and yanked, falling back to a prone position as he did so. His attention wavered; it may have been long seconds, it may have been a considerable span, before he heard an approach, and the door swung open, and the repellent Antonescu entered, carrying a tray bearing hot soup and a water jug. He greeted the fallen wizard in a rather undignified manner, grinning at his nakedness—quite improper behavior toward an honored guest—then brusquely urged him to eat. "For you. Restore yourself, as my Countess will soon demand your presence. Already the afternoon wanes."

Bleek, scrambling to cover himself, expressed surprise at having lost a day. "You will accommodate yourself to her ways," said Antonescu. "She loves the night, as others fear it, and chooses to entertain by the light of the moon rather than by the glare of the sun. I fancy that most living things prefer to go abroad at night, while the lesser creatures sleep. Your clothes are on the chair, sir. Be ready when you are called." The servant withdrew.

Bleek ate, feeling a little better for the sustenance, then dressed. He did not care for his current circumstances, and was for the nonce disinclined to hark back to the previous evening, which struck him as just another dream. Surely it had all happened to him, though; Antonescu was real enough, odious though he was, and if he be actual, then the rest of Bleek's remembrances must also be valid. Of course they were. Having pulled himself together, though still feeling horribly weak, he crept from the chamber in order to explore.

He was in for a bit more of a shock. The nicely prepared room had not prepared him for the dinginess of the immediate vicinity. His surroundings resembled those of the castle's exterior and its squalid courtyard. He found himself in a grimy, soot-blacked stone passage, without any light save the feeble radiance from his room. There was dirt and unswept rubbish on the floor. There might have been more—he stumbled over something hard, contained in a softer mass heaped against the wall—but he could make out little. He struggled down the filthy corridor, sniffing against the nagging odor of decay, feeling rather than seeing the wooden paneling of doors, until he discerned a patch of dim light ahead. He came to a spiraling flight of stairs. The light emanated from above. He climbed the stairs, clutching at and leaning heavily on the bannister, for with each step he feared a fall, such was his deplorable condition. Clambering to the top, he came out into a ground floor passage, one with high narrow windows like slits which allowed a modicum of illumination from outside. It was not so dirty here, although among the neglected sweepings he spied the moldering form of a dead rat. Another tiring walk led him into the maintained and artificially lighted portion of the castle, where he immediately arrived at the cozy visitor's alcove which he had first seen upon arrival.

Scarcely had he entered, longing to rest, than the uncouth Antonescu intruded, insolently tasking him for wandering about alone in an area not yet cleaned for the visitor, and demanding that Bleek make his way to the banquet hall with due speed. He did so as fast as he could, happy that the objectionable servant did not dog him further. Bleek knew the way—he remembered that clearly—and collapsed into a comfortable chair by the book shelves when he found that he had preceded his hostess. He thought to peruse the documents, that being one of his major goals while in residence, but he did not feel well enough to concentrate on them now. Also, he was chagrined by his appearance. He had brought only one suit fit for public presentation, which he had used cruelly on his scaling of the Kronnberg, and worn ever since. He considered himself a sad sight, and dreaded the fine opinions of the Countess.

Almost he dozed before she arrived. His heavy lids had sealed themselves, surely just for a moment, when she was there, all solicitude and sweetness, and the table laid. "Far be it from me to keep you waiting," said she, "not one such as yourself, who is due all my regard; duties kept me, and the sun has fully set, but the night is young, and we have much to discuss. Tonight we shall speak of great things, of import to your quest. Who in heaven or on earth knows what we shall discover?"

Her voice was as the music of tinkling bells! He had planned to apologize for his disarray, his weakness, only none of that seemed to matter now. He felt the surge of blood in his veins, the quickening of pulse, the upwelling of strength. Feebleness faded as she spoke, to be replaced by the racing passions of unquenchable life. So he had been tired by his revels— what of it?—weariness passes, and a new day begins, or night, as the case may be. "First we feast!" cried she. "Let us ever begin with joy. Food and drink await, and merriment and laughter. We live, with all things before us, so we must experience them all."

That they did. So commenced a night like the first, only of wilder abandon. It was an orgy of pure sensation and untrammeled desire, in which the mere asking brought instantaneous gratification. Nor did Bleek need always ask, for the delightful, infinitely resourceful Countess Kronnberg seemed to know his wishes before he articulated them, and offered what he craved before he found the words, or even fashioned the thought. He had wine to slake his thirst, caviar and lamb's tongue to assuage his hunger. He had entrancing conversation, for she could discourse readily on books and song, art and history. She told him of her situation there on the mountain top, laughing at the silly superstitions of the peasants below, who nevertheless surreptitiously supplied her, through her single industrious servant, with all her needs. He guffawed at those fools below, who little suspected the wonders that reigned supreme above their heads. He had her: the soft touch of her fingertips, the heaving roundness of her bosom, the warmth of her embrace, the fire of her lips. If anything she was more beautiful and vital than before; it astounded him that perfection could be surpassed and superseded, but it was so, and he could not restrain himself if he would. They retired to the inviting sofa of the octagonal room. Bleek plunged into another enduring and endearing age of bliss that must never end, but continue forever for the span of a night.

She offered him the glories of the universe, while asking so little in return. At that he marveled when he awoke in his little room, until the debilitating sickness struck again with full force. He knew this apartment now, and realized it meant the end of another crazed fest, and the beginning of everything wretched and disagreeable. He felt shattered, enfeebled unto death. The illness—the killing sickness, he feared—held him in its sway. He was barely able to rise this time, and he could go nowhere, for his door, rather to his alarm, turned out to be stoutly bolted from the outside. That was odd, yet his impaired health troubled him more.   No wine, no overindulgence, could reduce a healthy fellow such as himself to this broken state. There must be more to the explanation, yet what that might be he could not fathom. Perhaps—he shuddered at the ungrateful thought—the ways of the Countess were not altogether good for him. This business of living by night troubled him in some way, though he could not place the concern. He was no stranger to working and going about when the world was still and dark. That should not affect him here. There was more to the puzzle, if it be only his own lack of experience with the hectic life led by the Countess, a woman greedy for all the pleasure that could be wrung from mortal possibility.

And he remembered now, before the surly Antonescu returned to start the cycle afresh, that 1they had not made time to delve into those mystical secrets that had held him in their thrall throughout his life. There had been much else to occupy them, of that he was aware; he sensed that she knew much, and she dropped hints that inflamed his imagination; yet when all was done that could be done, and the revelry had concluded, he felt that his education had not advanced. He desired that, almost as much as he craved her, and the lack must be remedied. He would speak to the Countess of this matter, and she—eager to please as he knew she was—would grant him what he sought. He suspected that this night she would be prepared, unbidden, for just that occasion. Then Antonescu came and, despite Bleek's protests, lead the guest through the night-black corridor without aid of torch light. Perhaps the passage had been cleaned, yet still it stank, until they climbed out of the darkness into the lighted halls. It was strange, and annoying, that he must be led about in this disagreeable fashion, and he fain would speak of the matter with the Countess. Then she was before him, and he forgot his complaints.

Came the night, and they thundered together through the dark hours, and another night, and more, until the great sorcerer Jacob Bleek lost track of the days and weeks, or months, as if might have been, for aught he knew. His intentions, to the extent that he still possessed a will unique to himself and unshared by her, were buried beneath the avalanche of passion and earnest devotion that the Countess poured down upon his head. Truly she knew secrets of import to him, and whenever he could think to inquire of them she would laugh and draw closer still, and put her head to his, and whisper to him in her clear, low voice. "If you would know the Gods," she would say, "you must first know of Their special zones of power, where They are wont to walk on Earth when the mood takes Them." On another occasion she would say, "If you would accept the favors of the Gods, then be hard, and close your mind to doubts; for other seekers before you, men deemed worthy, have dreamed of making pact with Them, only to quail in the end." And once, when his spirit flickered brightly, and he roused himself briefly to insistence, the Countess Kronnberg told him, "If you continue with your quest you shall learn that name which must never be spoken, the name by which the brave of heart label the ultimate force, the Supreme Ruler of the Gods. When you hear it you will know it for what it is; you will know it in your mind, know it in your bones. Shall I tell you His name?" Yet then she would laugh and say no more, or promise to whisper it to him in his dreams. She demanded only his company, and in his presence she grew ever more lovely and convivial, as did he in hers, though when they were parted his circumstances were alarmingly otherwise. Though he did not care, and she thoughtfully gave no notice lest it distress him, he declined at a gradual but increasing rate until, when not with her, he became hardly capable of motion or the exercise of intellect. He had never contrived to see much of the castle—all her entertainments were held in the great hall—and as his body failed he saw less, for eventually he could only lie helplessly until the servant came to push or drag him to the nightly rendezvous. His clothes were in tatters, though she deigned not to see, and when he mentioned it at last she dismissed it as trivial, for—as she said—she wanted his essence, and thought not of his wrappings. So he did not groom or wash; it meant nothing to her, and if that lowly Antonescu insisted on offering his snide comments, at least Bleek could bask in the appreciation of the Countess. That was fair, for only she and her desires mattered to him.

Can even eternity last forever? If all things in the universe are bounded, as some philosophers have claimed, then it follows that always is but a period. There came an awakening—as so many had come before, seemingly without number—when the familiar and accepted pattern of Bleek's life at the Castle Kronnberg changed without warning. At the time he had absolutely no idea of its significance, nor that it need have any. He woke, wallowing in mounting despair in his tragic sickness, and cried aloud that Antonescu come quickly to lead him to the next orgy, to carry him if he must. This time, however, the foul servant did not come. Bleek spied cold food at his bedside, bread and water, so the man had shown, but had not forced the ailing guest to arise, as had become the custom. Bleek ate and drank listlessly, without rising, and waited for the man's return, which could not be further delayed— woe to him if he kept the Countess in suspense!—yet Antonescu never appeared. Bleek, crestfallen, fearing a monumental error, sobbed to himself throughout the night, finally falling asleep toward the morn, still whimpering piteously.

With the evening Antonescu did appear, and he hauled Bleek from his bed, and he chuckled and sneered as he said, "There is not enough left of you now to satisfy my mistress every night. Is there no more to you than this? I'm sure she is most displeased. Tonight you must prove to her that your recuperation has succeeded. If your force fails, then you are worthless to her. Think upon that, O mighty one." Then Antonescu manhandled him to the octagonal hall, where—joy sublime!—she awaited, and all was as it had been.

So he told himself. She was good, she was kind, instructing him to command her as he would, and spare nothing of his desire. Her glowing beauty had reached new heights; her vibrant physical energy overwhelmed. Once more, by her side, he felt the power building within. This night would be a triumph beyond all others... only it did not happen that way. Once he faltered, and she rushed to succor him; then dizziness blurred his vision, and she whispered sweet entreaties; and then the rich food assailed his stomach like knives, and he doubled over. The sickness had stolen upon him in the presence of the Countess. She loomed above him, saying, "This too shall pass," which comforted him, for he understood her to mean that the disease or weakness would not tarry, but release him soon, and allow him to revel with her as he had done. She led him to the sofa, the scene of former passion, and there she tended him as his nurse, ministering to his needs, imploring him to regain health. That he would—he was determined that it be so, now and forever—but it did not happen that night. He had collapsed utterly, the last dregs of energy spent. And she said at last, "There is a span to all things. We shall never dread what comes, not when we have had each other in the bliss which endures beyond mortality and memory." The festival continued, after a fashion, she engaging and considerate, he determined to please at any cost, however pathetic his efforts. Then he fell into darkness.

Next he knew pain, and rough treatment quite unlike the tender caresses of the Countess. Still Bleek lay on the sofa, yet above him stood not his lady, but the ugly figure of Antonescu, who slapped him in the face with grimy paws and kicked at his prone body. "It is finished!" the man crowed, barking his nasty laugh. "From you she can draw nothing more. In her loving kindness she regrets your misfortune, and sheds tears that your shared happiness must end. She tells me that she would keep you always, if she could. This love becomes her. Was there ever such greatness of spirit? Cling to that, Master Bleek, for you have naught else remaining to you. As it has been so many times before, so it is now. Quickly she makes other arrangements, for having grown strong through you, she would remain so, though she must seek the life essence elsewhere." Antonescu added, after a pause, "I wonder who dreams of her tonight."

What followed, for Bleek, bore of the qualities of nightmare. He was driven like an animal from the hall, shoved forward when he slacked, beaten and kicked when he fell. He was forced quickly down into the underground passage, which from his quick glimpse still looked foul. This time he was led into another chamber, a room without luxuries of any kind, a Spartan cell. There was no furniture. A soiled straw mat, crawling with vermin, served for a bed. Antonescu hurled him to the floor and closed the iron door with a resounding clang, locking it from the outside. "As soon as her new plans are in motion," the man called through the door, "you will see me again." Then the horrible creature left him, the sound of footsteps fading away and leaving Bleek in lonely silence.

How could this have happened to him? What mistake had he committed, that the creature of the Countess dare treat him in this manner? Bleek lay there in misery, his body wrecked, his spirit crushed, trying to think. A great alteration in the affairs of the castle had developed; something had changed, beyond the obvious, to lead him to this state, and make possible what had occurred. If she only knew! Could he but reach her, speak to her, might not all be as it had been?

Or might it not? Days passed, during which he was infrequently fed, and he was tended only by the vile Antonescu. Stinging pests tormented his flesh. Bleek knew neither day nor night, but only the unrelieved darkness of his prison. In that place he conceived, when his brain functioned, new thoughts, thoughts of a cast which terrified him. It was as if an evil, bemusing spell had fallen from his mind, or been allowed to lapse, and he could reason clearly for the first time in ages, perhaps since that last strange night in Istrakyager. His new views arose slowly, and he fought them with all the strength his former convictions could command, but the cold logic of the situation and his observations dictated acceptance. He had been wrong about everything—he had seen it all backwards, or through a distorting glass—where he had deduced virtue he confirmed foulness. He had imagined that the Countess Kronnberg offered much, while asking for little? That was a monstrous inversion of truth! She had taken everything of substance, that which mattered most—his mind, his spirit, his flesh—while giving nothing in return. The Countess—more than woman, more than human (and, mayhap, in some sense less as well?)—had fastened upon him through her sinister enchantments and contrived to wring from him every drop of living force that he possessed. With her smiles and her charms she had forged his chains, controlling him, so that she could eat of him at her leisure, and now, her repast finished, she had thrown him away like so much trash. In his company she had taken little normal food, only enough to be sociable. Of course that would be, for nothing served on a plate could ever sustain her morbid life. She required a different nourishment, which he had willingly provided, to the point of death.

Her spell over him had lost its power, or he could not reason thus. Had she dropped the enchantment because it troubled her to maintain it? He began to suspect the answer when he heard the music. He guessed it was after nightfall, when the castle came alive, that he detected the distant notes wafting down from far above. Somewhere up there music played, and played again, and in a fevered dream he thought to hear joyous laughter. Then, hours later, Antonescu returned, bearing a lamp, and Bleek's feared were confirmed.

"You are mine," announced the faithful servant of the Countess. "She has found another—a passing artist, a musician of renown, who fain would stop in the village for a night, save that a dream detained him—and now I may do with her refuse as I will." Antonescu hefted a spiked cudgel in his other hand and grinned with malicious glee. "I, too, seek my amusements, and ever long for the moment when I—the obsequious servant, the cringing slave—can wreak my will upon others. Know that my pleasure goes hard on my pets, Jacob Bleek; hard indeed, though not quick, for I'm a patient man, and I make the most of my rare opportunities. Such is the kindness of my mistress, to allow me to play with discarded toys. In the end you will find oblivion, but do not look for it soon; I shall jolly myself with you for a very long time." Antonescu reached with his free hand for his powerless victim.

Bleek acted. If his tormentor miscalculated, it was in considering his prey to be a common man, with common will. Jacob Bleek, the sorcerer extraordinaire, the cunning mage, was separated from his amulets and potions, and could rely only upon the profound knowledge of magical lore residing within him, but that was still something with which an enemy must reckon. Thinking fast, with the expiring effort of his awesome abilities, he pushed himself up with an elbow and gazed deep into the eyes of Antonescu. He shrieked the secret words, though his swollen tongue revolted, and through brutal mental force ordered the slavering beast to halt. Antonescu did so, for a mere moment—he froze in place, and staggered as if drunk—but it was enough. The wizard lunged, wrenched away the cudgel, and struck the man full in the face. He collapsed like a felled ox, the lamp smashing and flickering out.

Bleek fled the chamber, without pausing to check if the fiend be alive or dead, and lurched into the grim passage. He had no torch, so he plunged blindly into the darkness, his only thought that of escape. From touch and smell he concluded that the passage was as filthy and neglected as before, the natural state of the castle, he surmised, save for those few false regions where the Countess chose to entertain. If he remembered correctly, the stairs should lie ahead. He would see them, if it be day. If it be night, and she were abroad, then what horrors might lurk in wait for him? There would be no chance then. He saw the stairs dimly, and sobbed aloud with hope. He had to crawl up the steps, one agonized muscular spasm after another, but he did so willingly and gladly. The trickles of sunlight through the viewing slits encouraged him, gave strength to his endeavors. He passed beyond the gloomy, unused halls into the grandly furnished, tenanted portion of the castle. Even now, knowing what he knew, he felt a sense of welcome here, as if he had returned to a cherished home. Every second was precious to his design, yet he could not resist turning aside—how his nerves shrieked at him as he did so!—in order to view once more the banquet hall where he had lived out his splendidly corrosive months or eons with the Countess. He found it easily enough, looking much as he had seen it in his time of glory and madness. There the books and papers on the shelves, the documents he had meant always to read, and now never would; there the couch, seat of passion, scene of countless nights' rapture; there the great table, still strewn with the leavings of the most recent feast. Gazing upon this, he struggled with confusion, then reminded himself that another dwelt here now, reveling in the pleasures of the Countess. It occurred to Bleek that the other could be slumbering below at this very moment, and that he might have fled past the other's room in the dark passage. Bleek envied and pitied the fellow. If that one remained here too long he would willingly choke to death on happiness.

Bleek could give no thought to the fortunes of other victims. The poor fool must take his chances, and if he died, there was every possibility that he would do so without complaint or regret. Bleek, scarcely believing his own feelings, even envied the new arrival that, but steeled himself to tarry no longer and made his way to the door of the keep. It opened, and he passed the drawbridge and crossed the shadowed, filthy courtyard, coming to the big gate in the walls. This obstacle frightened him, for it was extremely massive, such that he could never hack his way through, and the walls were far too high to scale. Being a clever man, however, he deduced the workings of the mechanism, unhinged the gear—dreadfully difficult, in his listless, sickly condition—and released the heavy chains wrapped around the huge bolt which held the wooden slab of the gate tight in its stone frame. The grating of the metal assailed his nerves as vultures tear at a corpse. He fell against the bolt, shoving it aside, threw open the door, and passed beyond the infernal confines of the Castle Kronnberg.

The sun rode low in the east, in a clear, cloudless sky, and he recoiled from the brilliance of the natural rays which had become strangers to his eyes, yet he rejoiced, for the day was young, and he should have time to get away, unless his body failed him. So he descended from the barren plateau of the castle and flung himself into the mysterious forest that cloaked the shunned slopes of the Kronnberg. In that murky realm he lost track of himself, and could later recall nothing of the downward march. If the mysterious denizens of the mountain forest thought to molest him, he was somehow able to struggle past them. His next memory, however hazy, was one of terrible pain, and numerous concerned faces staring down at him, with the facades of cottages rising behind them. After that he knew no more until full consciousness returned, and he found himself back in his old room at the tavern, tucked under covers, at first ridiculously wondering whether he had ever left it. Then he realized, from the tureen of soup, the medicinal vapors steaming from an earthenware pot, and other items suggestive of care that were grouped nearby, that the place bore the appearance of a sick chamber. In no time at all Maria appeared to tend him, and from her and Radetsky, who soon joined his wife, he heard the tale of his return. He had been discovered half dead, delirious and injured, lying in the street at the edge of the village shortly before sundown, from whence he was conveyed to the tavern for resuscitation. Maria noted that he had been the shabbiest dressed man in all creation, his clothing dirty and torn, looking as if he had lived and slept in them since his departure. They had stripped him and burned his rags, but his other clothing was available. Radetsky pointed out that he had kept the room and Bleek's belongings as agreed, although the tavernkeeper had long ago given up on his guest, presuming him dead or gone.

Bleek told them nothing concrete of his experiences. He would not account for his lengthy absence, save to say he now agreed that the

THE COUNTESS KRONNBERG

Kronnberg was an unhealthy place, that he had wandered from the path and been reduced to a pitiable, savage condition. This he told, though he guessed it not entirely believed. Maria, in particular, seemed distressed for his sake, and once asked what had become of the crucifix she had given him. His answer was noncommittal.

His host and hostess nursed him faithfully, restoring him to vitality, for which he was grateful, as he desired to quickly leave Istrakyager. With renewed health came a reawakening of fear. When he slumbered now at night—which was often, for he slept whenever he was not eating—he was tormented by strange, vague dreams, dreams which tormented partly because they followed an unvarying pattern. Someone was calling to him, pleading with him to return, to regain that which he had forsaken. He did not quite see who was calling, but there was something familiar in the voice, its tones and manner of persuasion. There was also something oddly, horribly seductive about these visions, and Bleek had no wish to remain lest the images congeal into a semblance of reality, one which he could not withstand.

So the day came, when he was able, that he departed from Istrakyager, never to return. He realized that the evil Countess still called to him from her vile lair, and that, whatever her current monstrous amusements, it would still delight her, in some monstrous fashion, to have him crawl back up the mountain, whimpering for her deadly embrace. If he succumbed it would finish him, for she was Death personified, and from her arms he would not escape a second time. Her race, no matter the lures they used to entice, existed only to destroy, for it was their nature; it was her nature. Knowing this he left, galloping south in his carriage as fast as he could, relentlessly lashing his horses over the many leagues of rutted road.

As he rode the tears splashed down his cheeks, and he dared not look back lest his resolve crumble and he turn his steeds. For he loved her; knowing all, with sound mind and unshakable reason, he had made good his escape, yet he had left his heart in that forbidden castle on the dark summit of the Kronnberg. He loved her beyond hope or sanity and, however long he should live, there would never be anything he could do about that.

VI. Into the Catacombs

"Seek ye the Catacombs," said the blind man, "the resting place of the ancient, worthy dead since the hallowed days of the saints. With a lamp to light the path unto thy feet, thou mayest explore their grim fastness unmolested, for none venture there now, and thou may learn much of interest to a daring young man such as thyself." Jacob Bleek thought otherwise, and was like to curse himself for seeking out this man. The wizard—bent as never before on pursuing his quest for ultimate wisdom, the knowledge of all things, of all times and all places in the universe—had journeyed to the ageless city of Rome solely to meet with he whom the gypsies of Hungary and the adjoining kingdoms called the Wise One. They whispered of his insights into arcane matters; they hinted at his reputation as a seer, an esteemed personage who saw with a vision beyond sight; rumor told of his native abilities, which surpassed those of many a schooled sorcerer. Bleek, anxious to investigate all avenues, took steps to find him, tracking him down to the marketplace in the ruins of the Roman Forum, where the Wise One squatted as a common beggar, palming for alms.

Not for Bleek the glories of antiquity; he had come here only for this man, yet, having laid out in some detail his needs, he had received no more than this meaningless suggestion, that he spend his valuable time among the dry mummies of departed Christian fools in their underground vaults. He had been surprised to find the man a beggar, and blind, and now feared that the blindness was deep seated. For one who was supposed to know all, the Wise One told little. Bleek pointed out, civilly enough, that he was no peddler of religious relics, and that he had no use for such things. The blind man smiled, hunched forward, and replied, "Be not ham-strung by doubt at this juncture, my friend. I know something of thee, Master Bleek, and I learn more as we sit here on the pavement, conversing while the world sweeps around us. These busy people have no clue of what we speak, but I do know, and I tell ye truly. Thou art determined to risk all for all, so I direct thee in earnest. Seek ye the Catacombs; there are marvels within that thou hast not yet fathomed. Those centuried tunnels are the path to the answer, or shall I say, the beginning of the long road to the answers thou desirest. Those dark passages were laid down by good men long ago, but others have digged in them since, others with whom thou must reckon if thou wouldst seek thy way. Start here, burrowing into holes beneath the center of civilization, and in time thou shalt have opened to ye vistas from the ends of the earth. Say I, do ye. That is all."

Not another word would the Wise One speak. Bleek, despite his reservations, crossed the outstretched palm with silver and went on his way to ponder. He returned to his hired room at a Sabine boarding house, where he brooded long over the matter. Since venturing to Rome he had met with the most brilliant minds in the land, those of philosophers and mages, and while he had gained from the association, their scholarship had not offered anything of value to his quest. Where did the Gods reside, and what was their nature? The men of books had spun theories, the men of secrets had advised caution. Bleek was at loose ends, and he had heard remarkable things about the itinerant blind one. Might there be something in what he said?

The famous Catacombs of Rome dated from that unfortunate era after the death of Paul, when the empire of the Caesars held full sway over all the civilized lands, and had reached its apex of majesty and cruelty. The early Christians had been hounded, tortured, even killed, and their bodies denied the reverent burial which violated pagan custom. Intolerant of any public displays of the new faith, the stern Romans forbade cemeteries for its fallen elect, so the faithful chose to dig their graves deeper, where they would not be seen. At first they hacked caves out of the rock underlying the Seven Hills, and there deposited their fallen, swathed in white garments like those of their Lord, to rest until Judgment Day, as they would have it, untroubled by the attentions of malicious centurions and greedy delators. When the numbers of their departed multiplied, the Christians excavated tunnels beneath the earth, dank passages that linked the caves and created routes to still more, until finally there existed a veritable city of the dead extending for leagues below the wide, sunny lanes of the old city. The practice had become moot with the advent of the Emperor Constantine, he whom the pious styled the Great, but the Catacombs remained, the subject of legend and speculation, yet in fact a lost kingdom, virtually forgotten in their immensity by those whose boots trod the ground above the remnants of those countless corroding corpses.

Into those gloomy depths Bleek must go. He had decided; down there he would search for something—he knew not what at this stage—something that would propel him on his quest. "Vistas from the ends of the earth"; that sounded a fair beginning. He prepared for a long spell of subterranean exploration, first banking his liquid assets and leaving his goods in trustworthy charge, for he guessed that his underground adventure would take considerable time. He had heard old tales of men wandering for weeks within that benighted maze. He would not do all at once—thinking in terms of several modest expeditions—but he must be ready for contingencies. He built a traveling pack of imperishable foodstuffs and a sufficiency of water, and arranged for his extended lighting needs. He purchased a lantern, with a bag of spare candles, which should be adequate, though he supplemented these with items from his magical stores. Bleek had in his possession the handy globes of fire, curious crystalline balls of eastern make which, in conjunction with the right spells, words, and passes of the hands, could provide illumination beyond the powers of mechanical means. These he packed, safeguarding them carefully. He also prepared as much of his magical stocks and papers as he could carry, for he could not be sure what he would find below, nor how he would have to respond.

To find the nearest opening was a simple matter, for the ancient entrances to the underground world were honored as shrines. Came a morning that Bleek stood before one of these, an earthen cavity like the entrance to a mine, decorated with hung strands of flowers and religious statuettes, and flanked by the stalls of hawkers selling such ostensibly useful oddities as holy water, bits of the True Cross, and shreds of the Lord's burial linen. There were also bones of the saints for sale which, given the location, might be authentic, although the wizard shrewdly observed that several resembled the limb bones of cattle. All this amused him, but delayed him not. Surreptitiously, while pretending to admire the wares, he edged deeper into the cavity, which was strewn with trash, and when no one paid him mind he dodged further into the dark and commenced his hike into the Catacombs.

Immediately, with the sounds of holy commerce still ringing in his ears, he came to a log barrier across the tunnel, which he poked at with his stick. This feeble obstacle, perhaps meant to halt inquisitive children, he took in hand, shortly opening a hole large enough for him to squirm through. Here the endless night began in earnest, so he lighted his lantern at this point, and only then set off in search of the unknown. Moist earth gave way to damp soil mixed with stones, which in turn gave way to solid rock, the marks of the antique iron chisels still evident after the centuries. Bleek could admire the devotion which had urged men to undertake this daunting task, chopping through limestone in order to preserve their dead loved ones from the ravages of an unfriendly world. How long it must have taken them to fashion this great temple of the dead! Soon the tunnel walls fell away and he found himself in an expansive chamber, perhaps one of the original artificial caves manufactured by the pious masons. It was more or less rectangular, with the entrance crudely cut in the shape of a door frame. The door was missing, but rusted hinges bespoke its former existence. The ceiling was stained with soot. Niches had been cut to hold torches and grave offerings, and the rough, vertical walls, glistening with dew, bore dozens of openings and platforms where the bodies had been deposited. Sanctimonious inscriptions in Latin, scrawled on the rocks, praised the piety and good works of the permanent occupants.

The human remains were there still, but there was little remaining evidence of piety in this somber place. The time-yellowed or water stained bones were disordered or askew, scattered or carelessly heaped, spread about the smooth, dirty floor. Nowhere did he see an intact skeleton. All ceremonial offerings were missing, and he could only conjecture what fine items might once have graced the chamber. So, he reasoned, the Christian saints had suffered the storied fate of the pharaohs! Bleek had never been to

Egypt, though he meant to make his way there in time, but he had heard the tales. Having experimented himself, in the company of the Jew Josiah, with the properties of mummies, whole or ground to powder, he knew quite well what had become of so many of those treasured worthies. Apparently something of the kind had happened here. Meant to be concealed and protected forever by the faithful, others of equal but differing zeal had conceived other notions for these dead. Looters had been at work, perhaps scarce before the bodies were cold; but whenever they had struck, they had plundered everything of value, nor had they spared the pitiful bones. Bleek wondered, gazing upon the mortal debris, whether a single skeleton could be reconstructed complete from the bony refuse. He surmised that many a holy relic had been stripped from these remnants.

The dead could look after themselves. Bleek passed through the chamber, after indifferently studying the contents, and entered the farther tunnel. This, which also contained the occasional disturbed burial, continued in a straight line for a considerable span, then gave way to another, similar chamber. While it was all vaguely interesting, he saw nothing of particular note pertaining to his needs. In the wall to his left he saw a broken door which he assumed led back to the surface; immediately in front, another dark opening, which must continue under the earth. This course he followed, embarking upon a passage which commenced a gentle descent. He came to an intersection, one with several burials and numerous Latin inscriptions, most of them illiterate. On the other hand, there was less disorder here. There were articulated skeletons, and a few bodies still possessing their tissues, tough and brown or blackened. They were not much to look at, but they stood a chance of surviving intact until their promised resurrection. In addition, a great quantity of grave offerings—little figurines, woven messages, even desiccated food and empty jars of drink—remained to litter the floor. He had already passed beyond the area frequented by the ghouls of greed.

One tunnel inclined upward at this point, the other continued to descend. Choosing the latter, he shortly found himself in a mystifying maze of criss-crossing passages, heading down into what he now knew to be various levels of the Catacombs. It was like an immense building of many stories, only all underground. In the lower depths the accommodations were crude in comparison to the upper levels. Here there were no major chambers, just the tunnels lined with the hacked out tombs. Where the native rock proved inadequate, rough masonry provided support for the straining walls. Black earth spilled into the passages where the bricks had crumbled or the mortar given way. In spots grimy water dripped from the low ceilings. The tomb niches, mere holes in the wall into which the dead had been inserted lengthwise, mostly contained well preserved corpses, properly shrouded. Bleek pulled out a couple for close examination. The ancient shroud cloth, cheap fabric in any case, tore at the touch. The flesh of the old, forgotten bodies felt leathery. The fabled morticians of Egypt might not have approved, but it occurred to Bleek that the typical peasant was unlikely to expect more, or receive better. This far down, surely, the dead were safer from predation than any honored denizen of a pyramid. The Catacombs, therefore, had served their purpose.

He passed through an especially wet region, where he sloshed through mud, where all the mortal remains had long ago rotted, then came back onto a dry surface and made good progress as he journeyed ever lower. He estimated his depth at ten rods or more, and thought to ask himself how far toward Hell the antique Christians had chosen to dig. There were still plenty of wall tombs, crude wall writings, simple offerings, and mummies. The dead in their countless thousands beneath Rome, Bleek mused, constituted a vast tenancy indeed, and he absently pondered the question of relative population figures. Which was greater: the thriving, boisterous city above his head, or this incredible, quiescent necropolis below?

Such a line of study, however, could not claim his attention, and he had begun to consider himself again on a fool's errand when, quite suddenly, he noted a change in the appearance of the Catacombs. He had been striding purposefully and quickly, his shadow leaping ahead, paying little heed to the burials about him, when he realized that, having descended yet another level, he had entered a region of renewed disturbance. It had not caught his eye before because the grave offerings were untouched, and he had assumed that the human remains were similarly undisturbed. Then he spotted a wrecked mess of dusty, broken bones and dry, shredded viscera on the floor before him. This corpse had been fearfully and unkindly mutilated, rather like those of the upper chambers and tunnels. He backtracked, examining the contents of niches. Some were empty, all the others trifled with in an unpleasant fashion. He proceeded, uncovering further evidence of post-burial action visited upon the bodies. It was like, yet unlike, what he had seen before. He paused to refill his lantern.

The light restored, he surveyed the scene afresh, giving the minutiae of the curious evidence heightened scrutiny. Undisturbed goods, disturbed bodies; how, exactly, were they disturbed? Yes, that was what troubled him. Certain bones cracked just so—others scraped, with marks of scratches plainly visible—masses of wilted flesh ripped away in chunks; these data lent themselves to only one solution. Bleek could scarcely credit his eyes, or his formulations, but there was no mistaking the facts. He beheld the leavings of a ghoulish feast! Someone, at some point in history, had passed down into these depths and fed upon the remains of the dead.

So he concluded, and having done so, several entertaining scenarios flitted through his mind, which he logically juggled as he sought a rationale for what he had learned. As it turned out, there were elements of truth in his ideas, yet soon he found it necessary to adjust them. Going on, he spied fresh changes in the aspect of the Catacombs. He descended again down a long, steeply inclined passage, then noted that the wall burials had ceased, the offerings had left off, and the inscriptions vanished abruptly. Indeed, these walls were of an entirely different nature from those above. They were sheer, smooth as if sanded, composed of primordial granite. The excavators had accepted needless difficulty in delving this far down, where the rock would soon blunt any iron tool, and in being so fastidious as to erase the marks of their chisels. Why down here, and not above, where it would have been much easier? The tunnel was smaller, too; Bleek had to stoop now as he strode, and contrived to bump his scalp twice in a most painful and annoying fashion. He sensed that he was entering a radically different realm, and wondered whether he might find something here pertinent to his goals.

The passage continued on a mathematically straight, plunging course, growing so steep that he must needs watch his footing. He descended rapidly into unforeseen depths. No deviations, no variations, the path shot ahead without the relief of any other signs of workmanship or occupation other than its own existence. He could not grasp the purpose for this tunnel, knowing only that he wanted to know. Presently the walls fell away, and the ceiling receded from his head, while the floor immediately leveled out. He thought himself entering a new chamber, and he eagerly anticipated hallowed secrets of some sort. When he ventured forth, however, he could not discern the size of the room, for his light dwindled into the distance, falling short of obstruction. This benighted chamber must be of great and unusual volume, and therefore—he hoped—possess untold riches of the esoteric knowledge he craved. This place would hold, if any did, the justification for his underground expedition.

Yet, as he walked across the plain of the widening floor, he found nothing. To his surprise and dismay he progressed for several minutes without reaching a far wall. A room as big as the interior of a cathedral—at least that large—and that room devoted to no purpose! There was something strange about this business. It would have taken an army of laborers years to excavate it. Try as he might, he could not pretend that it was a natural cavern. How, then, to explain its reality? Then the floor dropped out from in front of him, plummeting into inky blackness. He stood on the verge of a seemingly bottomless underground cliff. He walked to his left along the edge for a fair distance, eventually coming to the smooth cave wall, without learning more of the unexpected obstruction. He retraced his steps, which left faint marks in the dust, and having reached his former position proceeded along the dangerous drop the other way. Advancing a similar distance to the right—as much as a hundred rods—he attained the next wall, and here found something in addition. By the wall, at his feet, he spied a notch in the stone, which closer examination revealed to be the top of a worn foot path, an entrance to a narrow downward trail. So this weird, unexplainable chamber was not the end of the line.

Bleek paused to eat, rummaging through his stores, and while he did so he considered. Confronted by mystery, it was his custom to investigate. "Seek ye the Catacombs," the Wise One had said; he had done that, and sure enough, awesome possibilities were opening to him, though their meaning remained elusive. He sprang up presently and perused the dusty floor. He noted traces left by others than himself, the prints of unshod feet. That was most odd. More odd still was the shape of those prints. They were passably human but, unless his wavering light tricked him, those feet had borne only three fat toes, with large nails. This was yet another development for which he had not prepared. A wild, improbable idea occurred to him. He shut his lantern for a brief period, which ought to have rendered him as sightless as his blind mentor. For a spell he saw nothing, but as his vision adjusted to the Stygian darkness he began to discern faint suggestions of luminosity at the limits of sight. There was a dim, misty red radiance emanating from the gulf below.

Reopening the lantern, he stepped onto the trail which led into the vast depths and plunged down into the unknown, thrusting aside the questions that plagued him. They persisted in nagging him as he descended. He was no longer in the kingdom of the dead which the pious called the Catacombs. How could that be? Others had digged upward to meet those who had dug down. Why had they done so? Obviously, he reckoned, not to honor the dead. The cherished remains of the departed served another purpose for them. Who were they? That was the big question. Another race of beings, their presence hitherto unguessed, dwelt below. What was their nature? What he could deduce filled him with apprehension, but he knew too little to judge properly. Might they be of value to him? That, too, left a blank spot in his mind instead of an answer, but there was only one road to knowledge in this case. Wherever the trail would lead him, he must go down in order to seek unsuspected truths.

This path was narrow and steep, designed for beings as sure-footed as goats. Bleek nerved himself to set one boot before another, bracing himself with his staff, hugging the wall on his right, averting his eyes from the frightful chasm at his left. Fortunately the excavated path was perfectly smooth, so that he need not fear stumbling. Despite that modest advantage, he nearly did stumble when he happened across a small object in his way. It was a fragment of human skull that caught his toe, a single eye socket staring a grim warning. Someone had dropped this piece while descending before him, whether a day or a millennium before he could not say. He consoled himself by reasoning that little remained within the Catacombs to attract ghouls in this age, however famished.

Down, down; a league he marched, ever downward, into the pit of ultimate night! A furlong in elevation he descended. The terrestrial world, even the murky realm of the Catacombs, lay far behind and above. The glow of his lantern illuminated his steps, but provided no information beyond its circumscribed radius. This being so, he reached the floor of the gulf without warning. Suddenly he was there; the wall to his right fell away, and the path disappeared into a broadening floor. He strained to see, but could make out nothing. The burning lantern, paradoxically, constituted a hindrance to observation, for it blinded him to all features at a remove. The radiance he had spotted from the upper shelf was so weak as to be masked by the rays of the flame. It was a difficult situation. His lamp oil was almost consumed in any case, and he had his candles and magic fire globes for emergencies. Thinking this, he dowsed his lantern, and waited for his eyes to adjust.

The soft reddish luminescence was there, and as the minutes passed he grew accustomed to the gentle, velvety shining. He saw that he had reached the bottom of a titanic natural cavern, one so vast that he could merely speculate as to its dimensions. The ceiling he could not decry, its zenith being lost in the overhead gloom. He conceived a general sense of a wide plain, with occasional hills, its geography broken by scattered hints of structure. There were large, regular, geometrical shapes out there. There were isolated forms and, he thought, a suggestion of congregation at the limits of visibility. That far jumble in the dark must represent a dwelling place, even a city. A city of men, or something like men, existing beneath the world. There would be wonders to explore! He made as if to rush forward, then checked himself, recalling the nasty disturbance of the burials in the lower Catacombs. Thinking of that, he left his empty lamp oil tin as a positional marker and proceeded with care.

A low ridge loomed on his left, a flat-topped mound bearing a single squat structure in the shape of a cube. He made for that, scaling the crumbly slope, and along the way discovered the source of the cavern's natural light. He happened across a patch of sprawling fungus, of the texture of toadstools, only growing in profusion like a blanket on the ground, faintly luminous. This was a phosphorescent form, emitting a mild red glow, analogous to minor varieties on the surface, which here must grow rampant throughout the cavern in order to provide the light it did, little as that was. This freak of flora, perhaps, was all that made life possible in the abyss. He was thankful for the favor, though he wished for a more appealing color. Now he approached the building. It was small, composed of granite, with a circular opening in each wall. It might, he thought, have been a guard post, where a watch was set on the trail leading to the higher levels, but if so, it was no longer staffed, for it was empty of occupants and furnishings. He could not see into the tiny interior, yet he felt his way easily enough, meeting with nothing. This finding was unremarkable, for there was little need to protect this inner world from intruders. These people, whatever their level of civilization, were best shielded by the inaccessibility of their frightful location. Bleek doubted whether any dwellers in the sunlight had ever penetrated this far or, if having made it to the bottom, lived to report their findings to the upper world. Certainly he was aware of no such tales.

Immediately upon exiting the structure he detected a sound, a definite hint of movement close by, and such was his situation—the unnatural ruddy gloom, the weird surroundings, the vague forebodings in his mind—that, though he cursed himself for his weakness, he was nevertheless seized with stark panic. He cringed in terror against the wall of the cube, staring wildly into the murk, straining without success for signs of movement. He heard the sound again, a distressing stumbling, shuffling noise, only nearer now, as if making for him, and quite loud. A shape bobbed up on the faintly glowing slope—he bit his tongue—and the dark form resolved itself, as it waddled by, into the shape of a four-footed beast.

Jacob Bleek breathed easier. It was no such animal as he had ever cast eyes upon before, yet it resembled a pig—of sufficient similarity to call it such—and it seemed absolutely harmless. It was heavy and round, with a broad snout and atrophied eyes. The wizard doubted that it possessed sight to any great degree. It snuffled among the gleaming fungus, then appeared to note his presence, suddenly starting. He called softly to it, and it forthwith bolted downhill, quickly disappearing from view. Bleek chuckled nervously, choosing to accept the encounter as an object lesson, reminded himself to be aware of his situation at all times, and set off down the slope himself.

As he progressed into the cavern he came upon other examples of living things, though in no great numbers or variety. The weird, red-litten abyss contained a modest array of growing plants, aside from the ubiquitous luminescent fungus. There were mushrooms and other fungi sprouting in low, damp places, mosses and lichens blighting the rocks and the surfaces of carved stone. He discovered thickets of rubbery shrubs, from the branches of which depended hard, tiny fruits or berries. Then, too, there was animal life. He crossed the paths of more cave swine, creatures always skittish in his presence, sometimes browsing blindly in small groups. There were little things like rats without tails, that dashed away or dived into holes at his approach. Creeping insects resembling beetles infested many of the plants, though they avoided the glowing fungus. Once something swooped down from the darkness above and flapped close by his head, brushing his broad hat as it flew. He did not see it, so he could not tell whether it be bird or bat; he suspected the latter, that being more in order with his knowledge of conventional caves; though he could not be positive, for he could not convince himself that conventions applied in this strange case. This world well might have rules of its own.

He found water, small pools arising from springs or condensation, and then running water, in the form of a creek, brackish to the taste, trickling through a narrow cleft. Beyond that he approached the limits of the city. So he termed it, though he saw little of detail, for the overall impression was of considerable size and complexity. As he made his way into the place his progress became painfully slow, for he harbored misgivings concerning its inhabitants, yet before long his worries seemed unfounded, for he chanced upon no one, nor did any sight or sound suggest occupation. He had entered, it appeared, a dead city, whose giant blocks of primordial stone and wide avenues spoke of former greatness, while its dilapidated condition and uncleanliness indicated a fall from glory in ages past. Bleek did not recognize the architecture; it looked purely functional, without style, even rather dreary. On the other hand, the buildings he observed required a fulsome knowledge of advanced geometry in their construction. Perfect cubes and square slabs of stone dominated the scene, the cubes often being stacked into towers of imperishable solidity. The angles of the conjoined slabs came together, in every case, with praiseworthy precision. Windows there were none, but every ground floor structure contained at least one circular entrance. Often the round metal doors remained intact and shut. The buildings increased in height and volume as he neared the center, with granite walls of incredible massiveness and durability, attaining a size comparable to what he had seen in his travels over the face of the earth. The creators of the nameless city, whatever their other merits, had been educated and clever men.

At the center several avenues came together, like the spokes of a wheel, meeting at one structure greater than all the rest, a low, broad mass of almost solid stone, bearing only a single entrance in the long, rectangular facing he could see. That opening was dwarfed by the monumental size of the edifice, which must rival the pyramid of Cheops at its base. Bleek guessed that this hub of the city might be especially worthy of investigation, so he re-lighted the dregs of his lantern and ventured within. The door pushed aside with a metallic shriek, which distressed him exceedingly, he not being accustomed to loud noises in these parts. He found the enormous building to be virtually hollow, for as soon as he passed beyond the thick walls he entered a vast emptiness which, so far as he could tell from his pale illumination, occupied the majority of the interior. It might once have been a communal space, where throngs gathered for religious or social ends. As he strode across the space he detected bits of debris, in such broken condition that he could merely speculate that the remnants had formed chairs or some such useful devices. Against the far wall he spied an alcove at the top of a wide flight of stone steps, and these he climbed. Flanking the alcove were two metal, perhaps bronze, images on pedestals, sculpted or cast presentations of winged deities, as he judged them to be; for the images were harsh and blocky, suggestive of geometrical interests rather than fair design. They bore frightfully stern, grimacing faces with large round eyes. Within the alcove he found—yes, this was what he sought—he found books, or what must have served as books for these people. Stacked on ledges were thin, square metallic plates heavily inscribed with an unknown script. The words, indeed the letters, were like nothing he had seen before, consisting of a myriad harsh, angular shapes interspersed by jagged lines. He hefted one in his hand; it was remarkably light, grimy to the touch, but not visibly corroded. He could read it easily enough, once he cracked the code of the language. These records, obviously of supreme importance to the ancient inhabitants, surely contained priceless information vital to his career. He scooped up as many of the plates as he could handle, sequestering them in his bag. He collected a mere fraction of the whole, trusting that one day he could return for the rest. He then departed the small chamber, and after probing the limits of the great hall left the building.

Bleek thought there must be other wonders to explore in the mysterious underground city, but that would wait for another occasion. He had been beneath the earth for a very long time; his lantern was now truly exhausted, and his activities within the great structure had also consumed a number of candles; his food supplies were limited, and he grew weary. He needed sleep before he commenced the long climb back to the world. Across a plaza from the city center he chose a cube with one entrance and sealable door which he could barricade, to an extent, with his possessions. There he rested, experiencing during deep slumber a troublesome dream in which the Wise One, along with a gathering of learned, three-toed philosophers, sought to explain to him a subtle matter of supreme importance to his quest. For the duration of the dream he felt himself on the brink of ultimate revelations, but of course he lost this certainty so soon as he opened his waking eyes onto darkness.

Some undetermined period later he rose, made himself a meal, and then set out from the cube to make his way back through the city and then up the cliff path to the Catacombs, from where a few hours walk would return him to the welcoming, sunny splendor of Rome. He discarded the empty lantern at the door, dropping it on the granite flagstones. Echoes answered the clink of metal on stone, the sounds continuing and multiplying until he was not so sure that only echoes answered. Some of the sounds seemed to assume unique aural forms quite unlike the original noise he had thoughtlessly generated. That disturbed him woefully. He paced down the avenue, carefully taking his bearings from the main building. The slap of boot soles on stone offended his ears, sounding unnecessarily loud, as did the dreadful pattering responses from without the reddish gloom. Though he had been preoccupied when he entered the city, he could not but think it a noisier place now, full of echoes lacking sufficient cause. The sounds died down when he paused, which pleased him, yet they were hesitant about doing so, which pleased him not. Need they possess qualities of furtiveness, and must they sound so unlike their presumed source? Bleek found this unpardonable.

THE JOURNEY OF JACOB BLEEK

His brooding thoughts took another turn askew scarcely before he had traveled a block when, assailed by the erstwhile echoes, he halted abruptly, holding his breath. This time the noises continued far too long to suit him. He could not further fool himself: something was out there, at no great distance, treading as he trod, but with feet unshod. He thought of the cave swine, considered what he knew of their habits, and most unwillingly dismissed that explanation. The curious pigs did not creep as did these unseen things. He went on, approaching a relatively open space between a cluster of low buildings. As he reached the center of the space the sounds attained a new and frantic pitch, and his eye caught a suggestion of movement in the murky pseudo-twilight. Some thing—no, more than one—had passed between the narrow gap separating two cubes. This was too much for him. Jacob Bleek cried out a warning shout, containing all the threat and bluster that he could muster.

And the things advanced upon him! Suddenly he saw them, rushing forward in a furious throng, a mass of pale, lithe, loathsome figures. They were human, after a fashion—at least they walked or ran upright like men— but mere mockeries of humanity were they. Unclothed, they raced at him on feet bearing three large toes and heavy, horny nails. Their skinny, extended arms ended in gnarled hands with three big, dangerously curved claws. Their heads bobbled atop scrawny long necks, and those faces! The faces, grotesque caricatures of the human norm, were beyond belief; Bleek felt himself confronted by living nightmare. They had no nose save slits for nostrils, nor external ears, nor hair; they had thin mouths from which glistening, dripping fangs protruded, mouths that twitched and worked and drooled as they emitted thin, nasty squeaks; and eyes that dominated the ugly features. Their eyes were like saucers, fishy ovals spread across half the face, never blinking, staring damply at him as the things closed in. Bleek saw all this in one horrific instant, then turned tail and fled with a scream back the way he had come, dashing off of the avenue and behind a cubic structure in a feverish attempt to lose the creatures. The hideous monsters were hot on his trail, however, and more charged forth from other angles. He ran on, heedless of direction, twisting and turning between blank-walled buildings in an all-consuming effort to escape.

He ran forever, as he imagined it, pursued by a horde, of which the slightest glimpse induced lasting disgust and mortal terror. He knew not where he fled, nor did he think or care of such matters; his only thought was to get away from those freaks of life and nature, to put distance between them and himself. He hurtled down roads, dodged around walls, pausing never, turning in flight but seldom, and then only in order to judge his success at escape. Inevitably they came on, pattering and squeaking, moving as fast or faster than he could at his utmost. They were so near to him now—more were issuing from the lane ahead, a lane which bounded one long wall of the central edifice—he had fled in a circle! He had gained nothing, and they were all about. He clutched at the wall for support as he turned a corner of the tremendous building... and here came still more, their vile claws tearing at the air. One opening remained; he staggered down a narrow lane, wove between cubes for an eternity of anguish, and there, in an unknown location buried deep within that ghastly city of madness, he found himself facing a high wall of granite, with no egress before him, and the horrors close behind.

Stricken, at the last extremity, Bleek thought to ward them off with charms, and he shrieked out words of power that sway the minds of men, and struggled to formulate a spell that would check them. All for naught; they were not men, only travesties of such, and would not be swayed or checked. As they reached out for him he fumbled in his bag for a fire globe, hoping to frighten them momentarily and use surprise to get himself through the unspeakable crowd. He produced one, a scintillating glass ball the size of an egg. As their claws groped at his cloak he whispered the words and held aloft the globe, which sparked and flashed into brilliance. It lighted— bright white light bathed the scene—he released the globe, which hovered of its own accord in the air, and he fell to his knees.

With the explosion of fierce illumination he heard a sibilant hiss from countless throats, and when he looked up Bleek saw the creatures staggering back as if in agony. Their claws clutched at their faces, their large, inky pupils contracted to points, and wet, filmy lids slid down over their eyes. They could not tolerate the flare of the globe! The sudden brightness, which caused his eyes, grown accustomed to the murk, to smart, critically wounded their own. So long as the globe burned, they were helpless. Once again, through his esoteric resources, the clever mage had turned a leaf in the book of fate. He rose, the globe rising with him, remaining just above his head, and made his way through the wretched, cowering crew, the beneficent ball of blazing radiance moving with him. The beasts moaned and squeaked as he passed them, but made no attempt to interfere with his progress. As he crept by he noted their coloration of unhealthy looking bluish-white, which had been masked by the pervasive redness, and shuddered uncontrollably. It nauseated him to think of such vermin crawling about under the feet of the civilized world.

Having escaped the immediate peril, Bleek sought a way out of the dreaded city—which now seemed infested with the things—into open terrain where he could see farther, take his bearings, and return to the surface. Eventually he attained the outskirts without incident, although by then he was feeling a sensation of extreme weariness, which slowed his steps and fogged his mind. He was well aware of the problem, an inevitable effect of the sustained reliance upon magic. The fire globe, amazing as it might seem to the uninitiated, was not a perpetual motion machine of the sort favored by ill-educated tinkerers. It did not burn endlessly, nor did it provide something for nothing. The mystical process which animated it fed off of his own life energies, steadily converting small quantities of his material substance into radiation, and he could not employ it with abandon. He must maintain it until he was clear of the present danger, when it would be necessary to rely on the red fungoid light for a period.

He fled, at a greatly slackened pace, behind a hill, and from there put considerable distance between himself and the dead city. When he could go no further he betook himself into a thicket of rubbery bushes, drew down by hand the globe, and willed it to extinguish. Then he collapsed into exhausted sleep. Awakening to the hateful, dull red world , he ate something to restore himself, surveyed the vicinity for lurking enemies, and pushed on. He marched up and down ridges through increasingly rugged country, and as the time passed he grew fearful once more. He could not see the city, nor had he come upon the cliff with the path that led to the surface. In every direction he saw the same unpleasant, undulating landscape. There were no cardinal points in this terrible region, no well defined landmarks. He had lost himself in these wastes, and knew not where to go.

Onward he trekked, through what he estimated as days of wearisome journeying. He began to realize something of the extent of this place; it was truly another world, a vast underground kingdom stretching for scores of leagues through the semi-darkness. His food and water gave out, but sustenance was at hand, if he was willing to drink from the streams— sometimes fresh, often brackish, always untasty—and chase down cave swine for slaughter. Such necessities injured his sensibilities, yet sustained him throughout the ordeal. One day—as he called it, though day and night were meaningless terms now, memories of fading dreams from what seemed a former life—he approached a broad mound which bore a city similar to the first, though considerably smaller. Here the ghoulish cave dwellers again assailed him, and again his employment of the fire globe saw him through unscathed. That one reached the end of its utility, flickering and dying like a dampened flame. He had four more, all of equal potency, but he knew they must be conserved were he to survive.

He speculated, as he journeyed aimlessly into the unknown, on the natural history of the troglodytes. What manner of beings were they? The embarrassing likeness unto man suggested an undesirable linkage, but it was not such as to be altogether convincing. That the ancient builders of the underground domain had been men he doubted not; the creatures that plagued him so could never have fashioned those impressive, if uninspired, structures. What became of the builders? Perhaps the troglodytes had made away with them. They seemed little more than animals. He was sure in his mind that they were responsible for the ghoulish feasting in the Catacombs, nor had he questioned for an instant their intentions for himself. They might, he mused, have been the original denizens of the cavern, into which a tribe of men had long ago intruded. They had fought, and the men had perished, but not before the men had erected cities. Surely those wise fellows could have repelled the primitive threat of the pale monsters! His reasonings did not satisfy, but he lacked the information necessary to even hypothesize a solution to the mystery..

Beyond the second city Bleek entered a dreary region of perpetual dampness, a land rife with sluggish streams, turgid pools, and stinking marshes. In time he found himself skirting the shores of a vast sunless lake, an extensive sea hidden within the bowels of the earth. Its waters lapped quietly, without rising or falling, appearing a dark veinish red in the gloom, and they tasted poisonous to him, so that he dared not drink of them, but must rely on the problematic streams which emptied there, having flowed from unknown sources. He wandered shores of the lake for a dismal age. During this period hope began to fade in his breast. Whichever way he journeyed, he seemed farther than ever from the world he knew and desired. He had left much wealth and vital records in Rome, yet now he was reduced to this crude state, with less and less chance of recovering his goods, salvaging his fortune, or of saving himself. He remembered, with soul-shaking dread, the terrible curse laid upon him by the misery-crazed hermit of Cracow, and brooded through the grim hours and leagues on its significance and possible ramifications. Had the broken old man's curse taken hold of its victim? Must his current tragic state constitute its fulfillment? It was almost more than Bleek could bear, to think such things and yet keep going forward.

While it proved difficult to keep track of his course about the lake, the woebegone wizard thought he had followed the arc of a roughly circular sea, and when he happened upon still another small, abandoned city, he guessed that he had walked around to the far shore. In this shadowy metropolis he faced his supreme test, for despite all precautions the troglodytes got at him. He had seen none about, daring to believe that they might not inhabit these parts, but in this assumption he was wrong, and the error nearly killed him. He awoke in the darkness of a cubic interior, to find the door shoved aside and the grisly things pawing at his outstretched legs. In another moment they would have been at his throat, with all his unfulfilled potential going to fill their abhorrent bellies. He screamed and fought and clutched at a fire globe, managing to ignite it before the weight of their filthy bodies crushed out his efforts. The foul creatures lurched back against the walls as if struck a blow, and Bleek fled past their hissing, writhing forms. After that he forbore relaxing his guard, and even sleep came seldom in the unhappy days ahead.

Traveling across the murky red country, treading in fungi and crunching insects, eating pig and drinking muck, he one day approached a very large city which stirred feelings of remembrance within him. It was so like his first glimpse of the great city by the cliffs. Could this be the place? Had he come round again to a realm he knew? He entered with infinite caution, seeking the massive edifice in the center which he should recognize. The troglodytes came on again, and while their attacks always shook him, he feared them not so long as he was aware and armed with white light. He chased them away and pushed on for the tell-tale building. He found it—the outlines were unmistakable—and then his hopes were dashed, for it was not the same, but a similar edifice, this one sporting an uncharacteristic stone tower rising like a needle from the middle of the flat roof. This city must be a near twin of the first, yet need not be anywhere close by.

He entered the building, which afforded no surprises nor anything new save for a zigzagging flight of granite steps leading up into the tower. These stairs he scaled, and the termination of his climb took him to a round chamber at the top, a platform of observation with many vacant windows. From this vantage he could discern, dimly, the layout of the entire city, and despite his desperate situation he found sufficient wonder within his breast to enthuse over its painstaking geometrical precision, a consideration which must have passed for art with the ancient builders. He saw something more, which at first he could not credit. He spied, far above him in the absolute darkness which reigned up there, a remote speck of faint yellow light.

This was no place he knew, to be sure, yet he could not mistake the import of that distant glow. He beheld an opening into the outer world! What he could see with his eyes, perhaps he could reach with his feet. He had found a way down elsewhere, and he might have discovered another way up. This was an opportunity that did not brook delay. Down the tower steps he ran, across the empty hall, through—with the hesitancy of experience— the ominous city, and away across the ridges and valleys toward the remote, beckoning speck. Down on firm ground he lost to sight the lovely vision, which aggravated his fears and made him question his senses, but it must have been a fold of rock which blocked the view, for he came to observe it again, and now he trekked unerringly. The terrain rose gradually—it rose steeply—he stumbled into a paved avenue which he had missed before, a road of polished stone which pointed upward like an arrow at the light. Upon this he strode, ever uphill, the broad path curving back and forth as he climbed. It was not an easy journey; the road was long, the light far, and he was forced to pause once when the craved illumination faded wholly away. So accustomed was he to the laws of the unchanging underworld that he had to puzzle out an explanation. Up there night had followed day, as it was ever wont to do on the surface. He waited to be certain, and when, after many fretful hours, the light returned to bathe him in its soft glow, he set off once more with furious determination.

Nothing lived in the upper reaches of the ancient road, so he journeyed without nourishment, while his water supply dwindled and failed. Still he pushed onward, stopping for nothing, until time and consciousness seemed to blur and shimmer. He lost all awareness, save that of constant motion, for an indeterminate period. He knew a pain in his eyes, a fire in his throat, an emptiness in his stomach, and an ache in his legs, and no more. Then he was bathed in warm light, a dry, ferocious heat beaming down on his exposed flesh, his boots shuffling slowly through deep, soft sand. There was nothing around from one horizon to the next but hills of wind blown sand. He had emerged into the sunlight, blindly marching on until he had lost any sign of the cave from which he had escaped.

Wandering tribesmen found him there, still trudging like an automaton on will power alone, and marveled that this strange man should be alive, in the midst of the great desert, without provisions of any kind. These were tough, independent folk, well adapted to the cruel environment, riding and transporting their commercial wares upon oddly humped beasts as if they were horses, though they were not. They carried with them only a small store of pity, yet his unlikely presence fascinated them, so they stopped and offered him succor, in hopes of hearing his tale. The famished and dehydrated Bleek eagerly accepted a modicum of food and a tortured stomach-full of drink, and as he sated his starved and parched body he asked of them their knowledge of the shortest route to Rome. At this request they looked to one another, shaking their turbaned heads and covertly winking, and let it be known that they were aware of no such place, nor could they guess in which direction it might lie. They wondered aloud at this, for their knowledge of the world extended all the way to the jungles of the remote south, and to the mountains by the great sea to the far north. They had seen with their own eyes many wonderful cities, such as Tarissa, Alican, and magical Apharia, the city of mages; yet never had they so much as heard mention of a Rome on any of their travels.

Then he bowed to their demands, explaining how he came to be in their country, and upon hearing his story they laughed, and pushed at one another in a good-natured fashion, and made waggling motions with their fingers about their ears. Much amused, they begged him not to regale them with the stories of children which, while entertaining, had nothing to do with the world of reality. Of course the tribesmen had all heard, at an early stage of youth, the marvelous tales of the Ancient Ones, that mighty race of men who, facing catastrophe in the almost forgotten days of yore, had descended underground into mysterious caverns where, over the span of long ages, they had been transmuted into awful demons in the service of the Evil One. They had all heard that one before, so there was no point in trying out the jest on them. Bleek, fearful that these rude men would flash to anger and abandon him, admitted his confusion, apologized for the scattering of his wits, and fain would recall something of having been accidentally parted from his caravan.

THE JOURNEY OF JACOB BLEEK

They agreed to let him journey with them, on the understanding that he moderate his craving for precious water, and he thought to make his way to Apharia, where he might learn something of geographical parts he knew, and which, anyway, sounded like a worthwhile place to visit. So off they went, the wizard of the known world with the wandering traders of the unknown, and during the course of his lengthy travels with the nomads Bleek had ample opportunity to take stock of his rather undesirable situation. He was cut off from Rome and the bulk of his possessions and money, with little chance of recovering them before discreditable types made off with them, which was likely enough since, not having planned a long expedition, he had made no arrangements to especially safeguard his belongings. He had with him a handful of coinage and the goods he carried in his bag. For the time being, at least, he would have to shift for himself as he had done when first he set out on his esoteric odyssey.

Bleek chided himself, however, for the unnecessarily gloomy cast of his thoughts. Against all the odds, he lived; there were possibilities before him. His quest for the Gods and Their ultimate knowledge went on. The Wise One had advised him to set out on "the path to the answer", and by doing so he had, in a wholly unexpected fashion, reached this strange realm, where otherwise he might not ever have gone. There would be occasions for gaining wisdom ahead of him across the burning sands, of that he was certain. Furthermore, he had with him in his bags the sacred plates rescued from the mysterious underground city, which might—must, if there be merit to his sufferings—contain lore of benefit to him.

Jacob Bleek commanded himself to find contentment in these musings. He had triumphed over all perils, and was prepared to face those, perhaps even more terrible, still to come. His great journey would continue, whither it would lead him, and let no foolish man, or no foul thing, stand in his way.

VII. The Conclave of the Telkonians

In the course of time the wizard Jacob Bleek came unto the sunny and warm city of Apharia, which rose by the shores of the placid, muddy River Nelas on the eastern marches of a tremendous, uninhabited desert. Through this desert he had made his way and, though Apharia was small and ancient, being composed more of mud brick from the river than stone blocks from the hills, he nevertheless felt grateful for any of the appurtenances of civilization that it could afford him. The people were bearded, swarthy folk, modest tradesmen and subsistence farmers, who spoke a language with which he must learn to struggle, but Bleek was adept at such things, and he was willing to take on the task as a necessary chore rather than an insufferable burden. Of greater concern to him was his immediate position in the grand scheme of the world, which did not look good, and which must be bettered were he to carry on as he saw fit. Recent experiences had reduced him to beggary, which caused him to spend his first few days in the town sleeping in doorways and by the roadsides, and cadging alms from sneering, heartless pedestrians. Such a life did not suit him; it gnawed at his gut, filling his heart with blackness, smiting his mind with calculating rage.

He thought to earn his living by peddling common incidentals of his magical skills, a humiliating need, but one which he had indulged before to his profit. This time, unfortunately, he found major obstacles standing in the way of his plan. He had lost, by one means or another, practically all of his magical commodities, and books or other sources of ready information, so what might be termed his commercial stock was woefully low. In addition, here he found no such ready market as had sustained him elsewhere. These people had little use for the wares and ministrations of an itinerant sorcerer; indeed, as he came to realize as he gradually mastered their tongue, they felt themselves overburdened by the enormity of the magic which already plagued their simple lives.

"Another magician!" shouted a sturdy peasant, whom Bleek thought to tantalize with a charm. "Aye, I'll buy your magic, and more mud for the river, too!" Shrieked at him a miserable crone, "I'll mop my floors with your potions, if you provide the soap as well!" A frowning, turbaned merchant whispered, "I'll pay you a bauble to leave me alone, and something more, if you'll not tell your fellows of the rejection." At every turn he was confronted with refusal, and occasionally a suggestion of fear. Facing this, and the prospect of not eating, he had no choice but to accept the traumatic fact of helpless indignity, and join a work gang in order to survive.

This he did, saving copper coins and living in a hovel while ignoring all but the most impertinent demands of hunger, which allowed him to accrue a tiny sum while he learned the essentials of his new milieu. Eventually he might, even at this rate, establish himself, but he had no intention of tarrying long in these circumstances. He had journeyed to Apharia solely because he had heard dark and amazing claims concerning its wizards, who were accounted a mighty force in the land. Apparently this was true, and although that had so far hindered rather than helped his career, he hoped to make contact once back on his feet, and thereby enrich himself materially or mentally.

He had gathered nothing by way of concrete knowledge concerning the local mages, and not much more save rumors that they comprised a secret society, a shadowy kingdom of esoteric scholars rampant within the city, who passed unseen among the folk, yet whose power and influence unsettled even the sheik who pretended to rule these parts. What he heard proved overly obscure and inconclusive, so that he knew not how to seek out this august body, nor how to make his presence known to them. It was a sad period for Jacob Bleek but, being who he was, not an entirely unproductive one. He had borne out of the frightful inner chasms of earth the mysterious metal plates which contained the writings of the fabled lost race. Those leaves of aged metal, by the light of day, shone with a dulled silvery sheen, and he suspected that they were of an unknown alloy containing that lovely metal, smelted for durability, as would serve for the preservation of important or sacred documents. These he diligently, during his pitiful spare hours, set out to decipher.

The unlocking of an antique script is a difficult matter even for a learned warlock who possesses secret sources of information. The task is made possible, barring a mystical revelation, only when the unknown script can be made to connect to one which is known. In this Bleek experienced a major stroke of luck. Though the writings of the underworld men had initially mystified him, resembling nothing familiar in his wide knowledge, he had discovered that the modern people of the region in which he now resided employed a script rather similar to that used by the olden dwellers in the gloomy depths. Both scripts were generally angular, sharp, and harsh to the eye, and several figures were identical. From this Bleek deduced a kinship between the old and the new; the living folk were, perhaps, in some fashion descended from or otherwise related to the great ones of the distant past. Knowing what had become of the ancients who hid themselves away in the morbid caverns, Bleek blanched at the thought of such linkage. The lost ones had been men, like any others, before their terrible fate befell them. Nevertheless, the connection should serve well.

It would not prove that easy, however. He gathered unto himself fragments of current literature that fell into his hands, and compared them to what he read from the plates. When Bleek took the symbols of the script written in contemporary Apharia, and applied those to the plates, and when he matched the sounds and word meanings of the new to the old, he derived gibberish. He had discovered that, while the scripts had retained similarities, the actual languages themselves had lost most of whatever affinities they had ever possessed. At this stage he was able to read the ancient numerals and tease out a few corrupted place names, but nothing more of value.

Bleek insinuated himself into the idle chatter of his neighbors and strove to hear more of the legends concerning the underground race. Few took such tales seriously anymore, although not all were as skeptical or amused as the pragmatic nomads who had first introduced him to the stories. From the common folk whom he, quite unwillingly, rubbed shoulders with, he derived a word which connoted a city of the red gulfs. This word, "Klexel," he took for a place name, and searched for it in the plates. Sure enough, he located a term—transcribed into the symbols of a triangle, a bent and jagged line, and a rhombus—which could be phonetically read as "Klexel." Within the plates he found this term routinely associated with others, as in a list of important places: Klexel, Angorak, Phrax. These were apparently cities of the inner world, maybe the very cities he had explored at such peril, and where now dwelt only subhuman horrors. So, by minute steps, he progressed.

He sought patterns within the writings of the plates. He identified the simple connecting words, the "ifs", "ands", or "buts". From these and other basic structural forms he put together the framework of the language which still challenged him. He could now tell at a glance the logical sense of a sentence, without exactly knowing what the sentence was about. Infuriating this was, yet encouraging. He made strides, and Jacob Bleek had the raptured patience of a born scholar to see him through. Also, he possessed the trained, extraordinary mind of a fully developed sorcerer, one who could observe where others only saw, and perceive where others only wondered. His keen abilities to wrench out secrets from the darkness of ignorance were not to be underestimated.

One plate, replete with long arrangements of numbers, appeared to contain population counts for all the cities, broken down by men, women, and children, and various social classes. He gleaned more words from these. Bit by bit he established the system of the language, uncovering a golden nugget of phraseology here, excavating a crucial item of terminology there. As his knowledge acquired breadth and depth he spotted a handful of further parallels to the modern tongue, mostly horrible corruptions of names, but these he added to the mix, and with his keen insight and honed bookish skills the dead, dry bones of the forgotten language slowly grew flesh and sinew, until such time as he had restored it to a passable semblance of life.

Thus came the evening that Jacob Bleek, breaker of stone by day in the ditches outside the ramparts of Apharia, read with some ease the recovered records of the ancient race calling themselves the Rhexellites, whose name and very existence had been dismissed to oblivion by history. The documents dated to a period in the heyday of the underground kingdom, before the loathsome transformations began, yet long after they had abandoned the outer world as a result of what they ambiguously termed "The Time of Sorrow". The chronology was difficult to extract, but Bleek learned enough to deduce that he was reading material dating from a time thousands of years before his people had granted the development of writing, and many years before some would admit the creation of the earth. Most of the plates dealt with commonplace day to day matters of interest only to the historian, though they must have been deemed important by the ancient scribes. Several plates, however, dealt with arcane matters of special interest to the translator. So he read of great empires of prehistory in which magic had been exalted to a profound degree, where wise men strove to pierce the veils that shrouded the human mind and bring forth rare fruit from their expanded mental and mystical energies. He read of vast walled cities erected by magic, and glorious mages who ruled benevolently in the selfless devotion to wisdom. He found references to amazing discoveries in the natural world which painted a—to Bleek—daring and unusual picture of the universe and the place therein of its inhabitants. He found still more references to cosmic delvings into the realm of the supernatural, and he grew aware that his miserable world had not yet relearned much that had been forgotten from that former epoch. And (here he felt jolts of excitement) he read of the Gods, as those people had understood Them, and what they had professed to have learned about Them.

It seemed that the Rhexellites, whom Bleek came to think of as his intellectual forbears, had thought hard upon the question of the Gods of the Universe, the Creators and Shapers of all things, and had sought to investigate the real and tangible evidences of Their existence and natures. There were, to be sure, elements of mythology in the accounts, including the old, standard, self-serving claim that the Rhexellites had descended from the Gods, but the records tended to present the presumed facts within a construct of logical philosophy rather than devout faith. What particularly intrigued Bleek—nay, what inflamed his passion—was the statement, presented as accepted knowledge, that the great minds of the elder race had deduced and confirmed the verity of the Gods, for there were known geographical locations upon the face of the earth where They had been seen to walk among men, and those locations could ever be discerned by the traces They had left behind Them. Reading of this, Bleek recalled what the evil and beautiful Countess Kronnberg had told him: "If you would know the Gods, you must first know of Their special zones of power, where They are wont to walk on Earth when the mood takes Them"; and, having thought of this, he read on eagerly.

These locations were mighty foci or vortices of cosmic energy, where all the powers of creation and destruction were funneled through the planes of time and space, and through which the Gods could step as readily as a man may step across a city street. A vortex was, in effect, a hole in the universe, through which the unbearably majestic radiance of the Gods would flow. These were awesome and terrible places, where men ventured at their peril, yet they were also sources of unimaginable possibility which drew the wise who were desirous of ultimate truths. From the savage beginnings of mankind these vortices had been seats of pilgrimage and strange worship, and in later eons often the centers of kingdoms constituted by men who managed, however precariously, to tap the endless streams of power gushing from the supernatural fountains. Kingdoms rise and fall, and believers fear or forget, but the vortices had always existed and always would exist, awaiting the clever seeker willing to bend heaven and earth to find them and to meet They who reigned forever supreme on the other side of reality.

Of this Bleek read with mounting astonishment and joy, and thought to dash out immediately, with such coppers as he had in hand, in search of the vortices and the Gods who would favor him with Their powers. With further consideration, he realized the magnitude of the odyssey before him, for he had still very much to learn, and the plates were frustratingly reticent when it came to particulars of location. In addition, as he was shortly to discover, trouble was being brewed for him, and it was no longer a question of when he would recommence his journey, but whether he would be allowed to do so at all.

One evening, after a dreary afternoon of mindless drudgery on his part (a local nobleman desired a new wing for his villa, along with a statue of himself to grace his garden, and the materials had been urgently ordered from the fawning suppliers), Bleek received unexpected visitors. A young, slight man, with a wispy beard, dressed in dark brown, accompanied by two large, beefy men, heavily bearded, dressed in gray, entered unannounced into his shack, driving out his fellow occupants after a few harsh words. The young man faced Bleek and began, without ceremony, thus: "I speak on behalf of the Telkon League. We noted your arrival, yet gave it no thought other than to maintain watchfulness. Our agents reported periodically on your case, and we have come to realize that you pretend to dabble in magic. This is not agreeable to the Telkonians, who hold a monopoly in these parts on all knowledge esoteric and arcane. We are aware of the secret plates, and it has been discerned where you must have acquired them. Even now, I admit, the *how* of your acquiring them eludes us, but that is of little consequence; in time all will be known by us, and we can best attend to such matters ourselves. I have been sent to formally take possession of the plates, and to warn you against further delvings into ancient wisdom. Do not attempt to molest me in any way; such action will do me no harm, while it will prove fatal to yourself. I am an adept myself, and these men are authorized to kill you with physical force if you interfere with the removal." At that the speaker collected the plates, which were in full view at that moment atop a makeshift bench, and deposited them into a leather bag. "Pray, Bleek, that you do not meet me again," he added, and then he departed, followed by his henchmen, who kept dull, hard eyes on the wizard until they passed his door.

This was not the crushing disaster it might have been—Bleek had already transcribed the plates in their entirety, both the original writings and his translations, and those documents had neither been seized nor sought— but the event, once he recovered from his surprise, left him seething in frustrated fury. At last the sorcerers, of whom he had heard so much fearfully whispered, had shown themselves to him, and this had been their manner of dealing with him! It seemed they considered him a lucky buffoon, a fool with pretensions in their line, someone who could be threatened into acquiescent impotence. They were wrong, of course, dreadfully wrong; they, in their arrogance, had woefully misjudged him. He began devising subtle means to prove to them how wrong they were.

The next day Bleek found another filthy hovel in which to live, one which he need not share with others who, for all he knew, might be spying on him on the League's behalf. It was a wretched place, and the expense strained his budget, yet he valued the enhanced sense of privacy and security. Also—and this took every miserable coin he had saved—he began surreptitiously purchasing such items of magic as he could find in Apharia, in order to replace a portion of the stocks he had left behind in Rome. He could not put his hands on a great deal here, most likely due to the organized wizards of the League laying claim to them; but, being the sort of city it was, a place where strange wisdom was taken seriously and nurtured, he acquired enough to put him back on a sound footing, along with the little he had retained, and his vast experience as a practicing mage. He wished to be prepared as he could for whatever was coming.

With the paper documents, the writings in his own hand, he continued his studies, and learned more of benefit in the days ahead. His translations continued apace, with fresh facets of ancient Rhexellite history being uncovered within the records. He did occasionally hit stumbling blocks, and one in particular, for no reason that he could consciously state, especially mortified him. There was a word, a meaningless word, which appeared once, in a phrase which might have been the title of a priestly volume, and nowhere else. The title was *The Book of Xenophor*. It was a strange enough work, but it was that curious term in the title which puzzled and aggravated Bleek. There was no context from which he could derive a definition, and the text was incomplete due to missing plates, but the very pronunciation of the word "Xenophor", as it rolled off of his tongue, excited and perturbed. He felt it important to know about it, as if he had made a vital find, yet the word also displeased him somehow, as if he were better off knowing nothing about it. In fact, the sound of the word made his skin crawl. It was a mystery, one destined, as it turned out, to haunt him for a long while; but for Bleek there was always joy in confronting and grappling with mystery.

All was not well with him, however, for a grave portent arose which heightened his anxiety. One night he returned from his embarrassing labors to find his room ransacked. Someone had searched for something, and he guessed that it was magical items and lore which were the objects of the hunt. After a moment's distress he examined the concealed pit beneath the rags of bedding on the dirt floor; there, under a cover of boards, were his essential belongings. This fresh attempt at theft had failed. Why had they done it? Either they had become aware of his special purchases, or they had sought what he knew of the plates. Either way, it obviously mattered to them, and he surmised that they would return. In the early morning before dawn he dug several small pits outside the flimsy structure and secreted his magical assortment in such a manner that the League, in the future, could not finish him at one go. This plan apparently succeeded, yet it merely led to the next, and rather more dire, confrontation.

The same young fellow returned, of an evening, with two different brutes. The man pointed an accusing finger and cried, "You have been warned! The Telkonians know all. We will not be ignored. Surrender what you have, and leave Apharia now. Do this at once, for otherwise I have been delegated the task of settling our dispute permanently." He may have expected Bleek to cower and crumble at the threat, or at least beg for terms; if so, he and his masters of the League had seriously underestimated their man, who had made ready a sinister scheme of his own. Bleek roared the words of power and threw down his last remaining globe of fire (all the others having been expended in the chasm of the Rhexellites), which burst at the feet of the three, shedding its full energy in one dazzling moment. Flaming gas, blinding and choking, overwhelmed them. Then Bleek bellowed more words, the horrific Chant of Death, formulated in antique times by the morose and morbid magicians of fallen Babylon. This was not such a spell as to catch unawares a prepared wizard of good standing, but this man was unready and, as his cool and wary opponent surmised, no great intellectual light in the land, but merely a factor of those who sent him. Indeed, he went down and stayed down, never moving again, for he was stone dead on the instant. That was the end of him, of his snide warnings and bluster. His goons lasted a little longer, having fallen gasping into the dirt, where Bleek made short work of them before they recovered their wits. He chose not to waste precious magic on them, instead slitting their helpless throats with his dagger. Then he dragged them away into the night, one at a time, and buried them in concealed and unmarked graves.

Having thrown back the gauntlet that had been flung in his face, he could only bide his time until the next move. How would the League react? The answer came two days later in the early morning when, just before Bleek was setting out for his inane labors, a single visitor appeared at his door. This, a white-haired old fellow dressed in black robes, announced himself by name as Zarbitah, and courteously bade speak with the occupant of the hut. Bleek, with equal formality and pleasantry, bade his guest enter and be seated, to enjoy the rude offerings of his host. Zarbitah agreed with a slight smile, and after refusing refreshment got down to his business.

"Good wizard Jacob Bleek," said he, "I come to you as a sitting member of the lower council of the Telkon League. We, the masters of sorcery throughout the southern kingdoms, have noted your presence among us, and seek to acquaint ourselves with you, and you with us. We feel that we may have much to share, of great benefit to all. It is not often that a stranger of the esoteric orders enters the realm where we hold sway. Pray tell, to which order do you belong?" Bleek, with a certain unconscious haughtiness, retorted that he held membership in no body, but rather stood upon his own education and experience. Zarbitah seemed nonplused by this, yet recovered easily and continued, "So you represent only yourself, and serve no one? That is most interesting. Here we organize affairs very differently. All true power resides in the League, as those fools of the uninitiated learn to their cost when they dare transgress against our whims. Peasant or prince, it is all the same to us. Ours is a secretive sect, but our reach extends far, and we maintain order and peace here as it suits our needs and our desires. It is, I assure you, a happy system, one which we cherish, and would not willingly relinquish." Bleek allowed that it must be so, a good way indeed, yet wondered—for the record—why his concerns should be theirs, when he had no designs on them, and intended only a short sojourn, until he had accrued sufficient funds to leave their land.

"There is much to discuss," replied Zarbitah, with sharpness underlying his gentle tones. "We can seek glad accommodation with one another. Surely you are capable of learning from the massed minds of the finest mages of our era? And we would know more, if you will, of the nature of your researches. It is a trade, a swapping of ideas, of which I speak. Now, as it so happens—quite by chance, entirely so—there is convening, at this very moment, a conclave of the Telkonians, called to discuss sundry matters of everyday import. That, perhaps, would be of no interest to you, yet—it occurs to us, by the by—it just might be an excellent moment for the assembled mystical colleagues to make your acquaintance. Therefore, with all due respect, the invitation is made, and you are asked to attend, as an honored guest, our combined councils, the upper and the lower, which meet this evening at a secret place."

Bleek accepted with every outward appearance of joy at the proposal, though he suspected that the convening of the conclave, if that be truly happening, had more to do with him than any "sundry matters." He accepted because he was wise enough to realize that refusal would avail him not; that it would at best continue the present unsatisfactory situation, and perhaps lead to immediate reprisals, which he could not ward off indefinitely. Verily he would go, for to accept and then abscond—an alternative which crossed his mind—might also prove unfortunate to him, for these shadowy agents of the League observed too much and too closely to make escape a reasonable risk and, furthermore, he was simply not prepared to bolt at this stage. So he agreed, and asked for the time and place of the meeting. "I will come for you at dusk," replied Zarbitah. "The place you need not know, for I know it." Then the Telkonian would take leave, but before he departed he asked, in an offhanded manner, whether Bleek had recently received visitors. "One of our members proposed speaking with you, and he may have come with friends. I do not know what came of the notion. Can you shed light on the matter?" Bleek feigned befuddlement, looking blank and questioning in return. "It is of no consequence," said Zarbitah, who then left forthwith after additional professions of mutual respect.

Bleek did not go to work that day; one way or the other, he guessed that his days as a digger of ditches and stones were over. Instead he went back to sleep, and despite a certain uneasiness concerning things to come he rested well. That was good, for he wished to be fit and clear of mind come the evening. In the afternoon he gathered all vital possessions into his bag, and spent the remainder of his time mulling over formulae and the magical wonders available to him. Thus he was ready, as ready as he could make himself, when with the failing light Zarbitah returned, again alone although now driving a closed horse carriage, to escort him to the conclave.

The Apharian wizard insisted on a blindfold for his charge. Bleek balked at that, but Zarbitah assured him that it was a necessary factor of secrecy; the location must not be known beforehand. Bleek did not like it, for he dreaded the thought of a knife in the back while helpless, but consoled himself with the thought that they could kill him any number of ways, if his death was all they sought. So he agreed to temporary blindness, and when the deed was done his escort led him into the carriage, which he sensed was vacant of others, and then the man mounted the carriage and whipped the horses into a canter.

The route to their mysterious destination seemed long, but it was not a continuous drive, rather one with many stops and turns and doublings, so that Bleek knew not how far they traveled as the crow flies, nor whether they had left the city entirely or merely circled back to a point just down the road. Of course he removed the blindfold once they were in motion, and chuckled to himself as he did so, but it did him no good. The carriage lacked windows, and the doors were securely fastened. He chose not to break a door, an act which might initiate trouble too soon. That being the case, he rode along as peacefully as he could be with his thoughts, and retied the blindfold when he felt his conveyance come to a lengthy halt.

THE JOURNEY OF JACOB BLEEK

The door creaked, the voice of Zarbitah spoke, and the guest was gently propelled across a gravel walk. They entered a chamber, and they proceeded for another span, and then Bleek felt the fabric unfastened from his face and he beheld Zarbitah once more, this time in a small, unfurnished room. The man said, "The conclave awaits beyond that door. Truly this is a grand occasion." Having said, he opened and passed through the door, and Bleek followed him.

He found himself within a broad hall of stone, dimly lit by a few flickering yellow torches on the walls. He stood behind a kind of podium, from which the flagged floor rose gradually. Upon this floor rested five semi-circles of stone benches, of like material to the walls, and upon these benches sat about a score of black-robed men, currently much engaged in mumbled conversation among themselves. Above the main hall Bleek discerned a high, black-draped balcony, unlighted, yet in which he spied hints of furtive movement. He was led to the podium across what he likened to a small stage, a dais which gave him such view as was possible of the entire large room. When he reached the podium all discussion stopped.

"Brother Telkonians," cried Zarbitah, "I have brought you the man!" At that there were sounds like muted cheering, and even some clapping of hands. When this died down, as it quickly did, Zarbitah exclaimed, "Weighty matters await us this night. There is much to consider, and something to be gained, I expect, so I take this moment to--"

A harsh, screeching voice from above cut him off. "To business, I say! There is only one item on the agenda." A torch flared on the balcony, and Bleek beheld there another gathering of black-robed men, half a dozen of them, much like those below, only somewhat older and bearing scarlet sashes about their waists. It was one of these who spoke, an immensely aged man who glowered upon the invited stranger, his countenance radiating raw hatred. "I proclaim this conclave of the Telkon League in session, with due authority to pass judgment upon this Jacob Bleek. There need be no further delay. Let us kill him and be done with him."

There came murmurs, some in approbation. Bleek turned to Zarbitah and meant to chastise him, but saw that it was useless. The man had stepped away, and gone was the veneer of geniality, to be replaced by deep-seated coldness. Zarbitah's eyes shown like orbs of ice as he said, in a steely voice, "Do not deny us or oppose us, Bleek, for we will have our way." Then he called aloft, "Grand Master Philates, of the upper council, speaks wisdom as is his wont. This Bleek can be destroyed as we please, and he shall be, when we please. I add only that first, solely for our purposes, we must extract every bit of information that we can derive from him. He knows something, and through him we will know that, and more. Let us make haste to glean the truth, so that we may rid ourselves of him at our leisure."

This seemed to satisfy the majority of those present, including the

126

ominously quiet members of the upper council, who looked to one another and then nodded. Zarbitah smiled grimly and said, "It is like this, Bleek. We of the League have no use for amateur interlopers intruding unthinkingly into our territory. Once you understood the situation of our organization you should have been gone, but you dared to stay. That must have been immediately fatal to you, save that we learned of the ancient plates. We acquired them—yes, they came into our possession—and their secrets are being unlocked. Our best minds have been busy with them, and we have learned much. We have yet to decipher all—although surely far more than you could ever manage—but we have made a start. We know of the vortices, what they represent, and we have deduced your motives, which offend us."

Bleek was intrigued to learn that their collective scholarship had so far failed to entirely decipher the plates, a feat he had accomplished alone. That tickled his vanity; unfortunately, they knew or guessed enough, as Zarbitah's next words proved, to desire his condemnation. "So you crave power, do you, Bleek? Power over the kingdoms of the earth, power over the primal forces of the universe, would be yours, you believe, if you could master the energy of the vortex. That may be so; therefore, we would reserve this power to the League, for no one can be allowed to supersede us. As for this matter of the Gods, whom you fain would greet; I know not what to think of that, but if there be anything to it, then it must be the League who deals with Them, and no other body or individual.

"We are aware of the stories concerning the Rhexellites, who it is said crept into the bowels of the planet long ago, taking their secrets with them. Until now we thought that a tale of nonsense, but we increase in wisdom, thanks to your fumbling efforts. We grant you the privilege of enlightening us once more. This is what we would know from you: where is the underground realm; what remains of its people; are more plates to be had; and have you gleaned the whereabouts of the vortices? This knowledge we demand, and we will hear it from you now, of your own volition, or at the cost of that excruciating torment which reaches even beyond death."

Thus spake the cruel mouthpiece of the League. To the peremptory demand Jacob Bleek issued a blunt refusal. He might, he declared, have been willing to share information as an equal (though in truth he never would have done so), but he would not as a servant or a captive. They had made their position clear, and he laughed, and was like to spit, at their awesome pretensions. Let them terrorize peons and fools; he cared nothing for their threats. Now he would take his leave—with all due respect to the gentlemen—and he defied them to hinder his departure. Bleek responded brutally, for he knew that they meant to murder him, and therefore nothing was to be gained by bowing to them.

Uproar erupted in the lower chamber. Zarbitah descended the dais to the main floor and cried, "So be it!" Philates shouted from the upper chamber, "Finish it! We will wrench the secrets from his dead brain!" A storm of approval rocked the hall. Bleek gripped the podium and waited tensely, in readiness. A fellow of the lower council rose and stepped forward, a supercilious grin on his rat-like face. He glanced around at his colleagues, then haughtily cried, "Leave him to me, my friends. I shall annihilate this pest on my own. Come forward, thou babe of a wizard, and meet thy doom!" Bleek stepped forward and threw open his cloak. "Be easy with him, Micra," called someone from the back row. "Kill him quickly!" Micra snorted with amusement, raised a hand in the air, and began making strange and artful motions with his fingers. He commenced a singsong mumbling.

And at that moment Bleek struck. He thrust two fingers at the man and hissed his own magic formula. The effect was immediate and devastating. Micra halted his incantation, his mouth frozen in mid-syllable. He shuddered, a curious rolling shudder that started at his sandaled feet and raced to his head. His eyes bulged; they glazed over; the pupils vanished, leaving ugly orbs of red-streaked white; and then bright blue flame burst from the sockets! Micra screamed as the fire rapidly spread and consumed his entire frame. Before his body hit the floor he had been reduced to charred, smoking meat.

The wizards of the lower council sprang into action. The room resounded to the chanting of murderous spells and the invocation of vicious demons. Clouds of stinking vapor from magical preparations gushed into the air. All this happened at once... and Jacob Bleek fought back! Less well armed, but with consummate experience and esoteric wisdom at his beck, he took on them all, and the battle raged. A poisonous winged thing, angrily conjured, flew at him; Bleek hurled back a flying viper that strangled it in its mystical coils. A fireball landed on the dais and bounced at his face; with a wave of his hands Bleek sent it spinning back into the shrieking crowd. His quick ears detected the initiation of the chant of living mummification; with a second to spare Bleek shouted the symbolic word—a hideously pagan word, born out of the dark madness of prehistory—that shriveled the unwary speaker to dust. One of the conclave—yes, it was Zarbitah himself, he of the false tidings—attempted to leap onto the dais, bearing in his hand a weirdly figured amulet; what it might have accomplished Bleek never knew, for he sent the fragments of its possessor, sodden and steaming, raining down upon the throng. On and on the struggle continued, with Bleek standing his ground and dealing out death to his opponents. He took what they sent his way—and he would ever bear the scars to prove it—but when the shouting had died, and the conjurations had disappeared, and the noxious haze had cleared, it was Bleek who still stood, his clothing in rags, his face begrimed, his body aching from minor wounds. Not so fortunate were his enemies. Indeed, it says much for their courage that they thought not of quarter, or flight, or surrender. They fought to the last, until they were no more. Bleek had erased from existence the lower council of the Telkon League. Every member of that group had perished.

Throughout the conflict the upper council had held mysteriously aloof. Having mastered the immediate situation, Bleek braced to face their wrath. To his surprise, they were nowhere in sight; the balcony was empty. The grandest minds among the Telkonians had withdrawn without a fight! It was inconceivable, but it seemed the case, and Bleek did not hesitate to employ the sudden calm to his benefit. Having made his point, in a manner of speaking, he now longed for nothing but a peaceful escape from the unknown building, and a chance to depart the precinct without further difficulty. He darted through the door from which he had come and dashed down the murky passage. He had hoped that it would lead straight to an exit, but it was not so; he found himself in a distressing maze with many blank, unmarked branches. The corridors curved and split into several new passages, so that he must trust to luck in order to find the right path. Either the structure was very large, or else he made the mistake of crossing his trail and doubling upon himself, for he wandered a considerable time. When he spied a large room at the end of one torch-lit tunnel, he suspected that he was approaching once more the chamber of the conclave, which irked him, for it meant that he had failed to progress, and he harbored no desire to tread upon those magic-blasted remains. His supposition, however, proved incorrect, for he was approaching a fresh chamber; one, as it happened, well occupied by the living.

They sat there, as if waiting for him, in their black robes with the scarlet sashes, Philates and the other gentlemen of the upper council. Serene and somber they looked, and unimaginably dangerous. "Enter, Bleek," said Philates quietly. "We called, though you knew it not, and you came here to us. Come to us, and to your fate." The wizard entered the room and stopped before them. They eyed him now, dispassionately, as if he were an interesting specimen that had gone astray, or an experiment that must be put right. There was some curiosity in their gaze, and some amusement, perhaps, but no kindness, nor pity, nor mercy.

"You have had your fun," said Philates. "We trust that you enjoyed yourself. It entertained us to watch you in action. It also served our purposes to allow you to test our lesser members. They have been found wanting, and are dead. It is a trivial matter, for we will recruit more, and recruit better. We have learned from the experience, and will seek a superior class of underlings in the future. That will be of no interest to you, of course. Sadly not, for this, Jacob Bleek, is the end of the road for you." Then they launched their attack.

They did so without movement, without histrionics, a quiet onslaught out of stillness. Without warning a great wave of psychic force crashed down onto the brain of Jacob Bleek. The concentrated minds of the League's most powerful sorcerers focused upon him and willed him to die. They willed his arteries to rupture, his veins to burst. They commanded his heart to stop, his lungs to hemorrhage. They ordered his guts to writhe, and knot, and rot within his belly. They sought to beat down his mental control of his living system, and to replace it with their own control, for his destruction. At the first blow Bleek felt his body giving way, every aspect of his mortal frame unraveling. He could neither see, nor hear; he felt exquisite, fiery agony. Stunned, for one split second he sensed himself slipping away from life.

Yet he could still think, and standing there, the merest trembling betraying the intensity of the struggle, he marshaled his defenses and fought back. He gripped his mind with firm ethereal hands and steadied his consciousness. He located the points of extreme danger and endeavored to ward off the damage his enemies would bestow. His liver began to give way under a storm of burning pain; he erected barriers to shield it. His heart pounded slowly, like a mighty mallet crashing down onto a titanic anvil, each beat slower and more labored; he regularized the beats and kept the blood flowing to his brain. It seemed as if his skin were peeling from bleeding flesh; he cloaked his skin in clothing of mental force which scattered the corrosive rays of murderous power.

The tension eased, although it did not wholly recede. The august gentlemen of the League still sat there, unmoving, unblinking, as if nothing had happened, as if no death struggle were underway. Bleek still stood, shaken but unbowed. He had weathered the first blast. "Most interesting," spoke Philates; "This one holds to his life as if it were a rare gem. My friends, I propose--" He said no more aloud, for it was unnecessary. His colleagues knew, and acted on the thought. They renewed the attack.

The first surge of black power had been directed at many points simultaneously. For the second round the upper council of the Telkon League went solely after his mind, the engine of the body. If it were crushed, victory would be theirs. Another merciless hammer of force, of far greater intensity, bludgeoned the brain of Bleek. Their minds crowded into his own, seeking to destroy, seeking to dominate the seat of his intelligence, to replace his vital being with theirs. He staggered under the blow. They chewed his brain, they stirred it into slush. Darkness clouded his mind, the desperate thoughts trickling rather than pouring through their channels. If his thoughts winked out—if his defenses lapsed for an instant—it would be the finish.

Bleek did not quail, nor falter. His brains bulged within his skull—they were like to explode and boil over—he felt the bones cracking in his head. "Lie down and die, Bleek," chanted unemotional voices, voices which whispered directly into his ears though the speakers were across the room, though their mouths never moved. "Peace, Bleek, rest, and die, Bleek." He did not, he would not. They drove him into a corner of his brain and there he fought from behind his last rampart. Their psychic legions scaled the walls of his citadel, they fought bitterly on the battlements, the outcome of the magical struggle hovering in the balance... and he hurled them from those walls! The fiercest surge repelled, Bleek counterattacked, fighting to clear his mind of the invaders. The minds of the League recoiled, and his brain was free.

The anvil had not shattered the mallet, however. The Telkonians were strong and clever, and would rush his defenses again, and again, and perhaps again, until they ground out his spirit and destroyed him. Now was the moment, while they were briefly in disarray, to launch his own decisive assault. Bleek blasted them with his psychic powers, a cunning, clinical use of his inherent and well trained energies. Methodically he pounded their minds, utilizing every scrap of ability and wisdom inculcated by study and experience. Through the years Bleek had learned much, far more than his enemies had reckoned upon. He had read and absorbed knowledge that few students of the arcane ever conceived, much less mastered, and he had perfected his esoteric skills, under the tutelage of expert mages, to a degree that might have surprised his teachers. Huysman, his old mentor from the days of his youth, had taught him much; kindly Matthias of Heidelberg had revealed still more to him, even while trying to restrain him, as had the doomed Helvetius, albeit unwillingly; and good Josiah the Jew, the grand magician of Cracow, had opened to Bleek every secret door he knew as part of their unfortunate bargain. All this power was at Bleek's command, and he brought it craftily to bear for the ultimate annihilation of the League.

They fought back hard. As the full force of the mental barrage hit them they rose to their feet and frantically struggled to maintain their own enormous mental integrity. They had miscalculated; they had underestimated him; it may be they had grown soft, operating unchecked for so long, trampling upon foes unworthy of their ethereal steel. Regardless, the one man against six proved an even match. The outcome of the battle could have gone other than it did; it was that close, and all bets were off almost until the end. Bleek had acquired the high ground, but if he had flinched ever so slightly they would have pushed him off of it. He did not flinch. He bored away, swinging and punching with his extraordinary brain, gaining the upper hand and maintaining it, increasing his lead. One of the upper council collapsed back into his chair, clutched his head and moaned, then went limp. The remaining five redoubled their efforts, but it was too late. Bleek shocked their minds with another furious blast; he envisioned their deaths, and another man crumpled and fell, sprawling on the stone floor. A third dropped his defenses and staggered forward, crying for mercy; Bleek conceived an ugly thought, and the man's head literally blew up. What was left of him went down, a ghastly mess. The last three, whether from courage or despair, gave no thought to surrender, choosing to defend their honor if naught else. In the end lone Philates, their ringleader, abandoned by the deaths of his fellows, saw the uselessness of continued struggle and chose gesture for his final act, pulling himself up and shaking his fist at his tormentor. Then he bellowed in rage and mortification, stumbling backward as Bleek's total power of sorcery burned into him, and he tumbled and crashed to the floor, scattering chairs as he impacted the stone. Philates was no more—he had joined his colleagues in darkness or in Hell—the weird, wholly mental battle was over! Jacob Bleek, worn, weary, and wan, had conquered all.

The last conclave of the Telkonians had met in formal session, with the result that their League had ceased to exist. Possibly the local folk would cheer the event, although that counted for nothing with Bleek. He had not sought nor required such an outcome, yet, as he recovered himself and considered the matter, he thought it for the best. It was dangerous to have such a great organization loose in the world, one which knew of his grand designs for himself, one which would act out of self-interest to hinder and oppose him. Better that they were gone, and better still that he was in the choice position of picking up the pieces, for he must be on his way. The unknown road of his journey beckoned; the quest must continue, and there was no time like the present, when he left a clear field behind him, and he could help himself to the full resources of the late League. So Bleek ransacked the building, searching within every nook and exploring its most secret fastnesses, and took for himself all the accumulated writings of magical lore and instruments of sorceric power that he could bring away with him. The Rhexellite plates he found, and he melted them down to slag, for he had his notes, which would travel better than masses of metal, and he had no desire to leave the plates behind for others. Having performed this action, he made his way from the building.

Morning was breaking as he beheld, for the first and last time, the exterior of the secret conclave chambers of the Telkonians. He appropriated from the courtyard a wagon and beasts of burden, and he filled the wagon with his plunder: food, other necessaries, and his priceless magical booty, the fortunes of war. Then he drove away and out of Apharia, never looking back, already dreaming of the glories that lay ahead.

VIII. The City of Dyrezan

He first heard the story in Egypt, that ancient land of marvels and strange tales, into which he had ventured from the desert kingdoms to the south, journeying down the great river Nile. Jacob Bleek had traveled well, once again a man of wealth and substance, for the coffers and storage chambers of the Telkonians had supplied him with all his wants, both as a man and as a wizard. He made for Egypt, so soon as he had pieced together the route, for there he expected to find much scholarly information and antique lore, carefully preserved through the ages, of value to his quest. All things were possible in Egypt, he felt, and perhaps they were, yet he did not gain his initial knowledge of the story from any of the expected avenues. He did everything required of a determined, cold-blooded delver into the unknown: by day he visited the pyramids and temples as a nonchalant tourist, properly impressed by the outward grandeur of the past, while by night he stole into the ruins, accompanied by hired ruffians, in search of secrets that would intellectually enrich himself. He read the exotic inscriptions on the walls, studied the writings on jeweled scarabs torn from a mummy's breast, explored forgotten passageways beneath mountains of devoutly carved stone. He did everything he should, and rather more that he should not, yet he did not gain the first gleanings of useful wisdom from these sources. The feeble flickers of enlightenment came to him, recited casually in a marketplace, by way of a merchant's tale.

That gentleman, a well-to-do trader hailing from another ancient land, told him the story of a kingdom far to the east, long remembered in poetry and song, which was like unto an earthly paradise. It was a veritable garden land, a realm where magic ruled and made all things possible to men, who need not work for a living nor slave for others, but have all blessings for the asking. It was a special place, governed by a great city wherein dwelt the wisest and most learned minds of the human race. It was so far away that its particular attributes had fallen into rumor and legend, though the merchant had still heard whispers of it at the limits of his eastern travels, and he had dreamed of one day leading a caravan there and partaking of its bounty. Bleek was familiar with popular stories of this kind, and tended to dismiss them as nonsense, but for once he was disinclined to do so. This account, wispy as it might sound, jibed in its broad outlines with conceptions of import to him.

Armed with the evidence derived from the Rhexellite records, Bleek was now obsessed with locating the fantastic sources of magical power which, in certain geographical regions of the earth, flows or had flowed from the cosmic vortices, those gates into other universal dimensions which had been thought, in olden times, to marks the doorways of the Gods, the fabulous

Old Ones, creators of all things, who alone could grant him what he sought. The Gods must exist, were he to succeed, and therefore the vortices must exist, as the wise men of the underground world had written. They had stated, as fact, that incredible cities of magic had been erected at one or more of these points, and furthermore—as he had gathered from continuing diligent perusal of the transcripts—that a major center of power, a most pervasive vortex, had existed somewhere in mysterious lands to the east. Bleek considered these tantalizing hints, juggled them with the odd story told by the merchant, and wondered if there might be a connection.

There was nothing for it but to head for the east, making for the distant lands where the merchant had picked up his rumors, and continue the search from there. This Bleek did, leaving Egypt by the caravan trail curling along the southern shore of the Mediterranean Sea (which, remarkably, he had never seen before, having passed under it, as he eventually deduced, during his freakish odyssey within the vast, red-litten caverns), then plunging straight across the deserts of Arabia, the shortest, if most difficult, route to the east. He accomplished this trek and, when he regained contact with the lazy civilization in this part of the world, found himself within sight of the wonderful and morbid ruins of Babylon, by the green, fertile banks of the muddy and sluggish Euphrates.

Here, he trusted, there were secrets to be learned, if not from the crumbling bricks of the fallen city, then from the living descendants of that ancient greatness, for it was a thickly populated, if rude, land, a quiet, pleasant kingdom of river farmers. Poor they were, almost to a man, yet loquacious as well, and from them Bleek did pick up further indicators which might aid him. Some of them knew the story as the merchant had known it, and some fewer were willing to volunteer extra details which served to heighten the eager sorcerer's fascination for the topic. Indeed, there was such a place, they assured him, a mighty city—the greatest city that the world had ever seen—only it was to be found far, far toward the rising sun, at the edge of the known world or, as it may be, just a little bit beyond that. Bleek was rather chagrined by the continued vagueness of location, for he had already journeyed far to the east, and had wished that he were close to his destination. The stories he heard now, however, while differing in minor aspects, were very like what he had heard before, and he did not feel himself much the wiser for his efforts. A great city lay out there somewhere (to the east, apparently), a city where magic pervaded every thread of the living web, a city of gold and riches incomparable. There even the peasants were wise and noble, and skilled in arts that would frighten the vulgar of other lands. It sounded like the kind of place that Bleek sought, but how to get there?

1Whither he might go, he could not leave without plumbing the depths of the broad earthen mound that concealed the remains of ancient Babylon. The natives had brought to his attention the brick seals and tablets of baked mud or clay which bore the peculiar script of those hoary days, priceless objects to the scholar, often used as building materials by the locals. There were still a few men of parts who could read them, to a tolerable degree, so Bleek hired men to dig through the countless levels of the mound to find more documents. He spent days in a dusty mud hovel examining his finds. One batch of tablets, to his delight, referenced the wonderful city to the east. He acquired little in the way of further detail, but the unusual, blocky writings, consisting largely of slanted wedges impressed into the clay (it thrilled him to note that the script somewhat resembled that of the Rhexellites, although, alas, the language itself proved radically different), contained one more clue that could aid him in his quest, this being the name of the legendary city. From the odd literary forms he extracted the following three syllables: DY-RE-ZAN. So he sought the city of Dyrezan.

To the east, to the east he must go, in hopes of further evidence, tales and signs, that would lead him to his destination. Away to the east he traveled, riding with caravans that annually journeyed to the known edge of the world. They rode for profit, and so did he, a kind of wealth that would make the holdings of kingdoms seem like ashes. His traveling companions had never heard of Dyrezan, although some of them recalled stories of a marvelous city of the sunrise. Always the indications pointed to the east, yet this seemed to be the case no matter how far east he ventured. He amused himself, grimly amused, thinking that eventually east must become west; if he lost the true path, whatever that might be, and chose not to turn back, then one day he would circle around on himself, having spanned the globe, and ride east into Europe, a mighty achievement and a grotesque failure. What an awful joke that would be!

At the borders of India he reached the limits of the world as known to him from scholarship. Beyond were realms known to him only by traveler's reports and gossip, lands left blank on maps or peopled with half-imaginary races. At this point the caravan turned back, its master satisfied with the fruits of his commerce, not caring to tempt fate by adventuring farther from his already distant home. Bleek went on, naturally, pushing east alone into a languid but civilized land where he thought to learn more of the magical city, and perhaps to find it. He found cities galore, though not the one he sought, and as a rare stranger in those many principalities, a stranger who quickly identified himself as a man of the mind, he was honored by the grandees and rulers of those cities. Through their benevolence, inspired by indolent curiosity, he became acquainted with the wise men of the land, respected priests who lived like the lowliest of peasants or beggars, yet were well versed in the lore and history of their people. One such was the sage Murrhatta, to whom Bleek gained introduction at the court of Delhi. This man told him many things, for he knew the name of Dyrezan and somewhat that it signified, which was good, for this marked the first time that a living man had admitted knowing the mysterious word. What he had to say was not altogether pleasing to Bleek, but it was spoken with sincerity and the force of acumen, and musts needs be vital to him.

"Indeed yes, my earnest friend," sayeth Murrhatta, "I have ever heard the tales of Dyrezan the marvelous, that great city where all things are known to men. In my youth, in the days of my vigor and strength, I dreamed of visiting it, and would have done so, had ever I learned a passable way to reach it. I regret to tell you that it is not to be approached by any road known to my people. Dyrezan lies a long journey to the east, on the far side of the great snowy mountains which form the borders of our domain. Those mountains, locked in snow and ice since the beginning of the world, form an insurmountable wall, as travelers will tell it, across which no man can pass. Teach yourself to fly, if your arts permit, and you may see the city with your natural eyes."

Yet Murrhatta had more to relate. "It is strange to speak of it, but there are tales that have passed the heaven-kissed peaks. How they come to us I know not, save that they wing their way to us atop the dreams of the seers of old. I read once a description, in a sacred book now lost to me, which contained an account of the mystic metropolis, which it called the City of Burning Gold. The scribe wrote that the city blocked the rays of the new born sun, so vast was the place, and that, when the light of the declining sun fell upon it, it flamed into golden brilliance, as if its magical substance had become as fire. I have tried to view this city, in the light of the sunset, through my dreams, as must have others before me, but I have not, for I am not worthy."

To the east, ever to the east journeyed Jacob Bleek. He crossed plains, forded rivers swarming with monstrous reptiles bearing huge jaws and great teeth, hacked his way through jungles in which enormous, striped cats prowled and giant snakes slithered. He flattered and questioned holy men, he charmed and terrorized chiefs of primitive tribes. When he derived any information from them, it was always the advice to seek the mountains and scale them, if that could be done, which all his informants doubted. Came the day that he spied a jagged line of shimmering white on the eastern horizon, and he knew that he neared the mountains. Not entirely was his assumption correct, for he traveled many leagues and days before the distant peaks grew larger to his sight, and he realized that they were great mountains indeed, unlike any he had seen before. Approach them in time he did, the ground rising about him, the trek becoming more wearisome as the last roads failed and he must negotiate the mounting slopes and swelling crevasses. Then he stood before the mountains, at their very feet, in a rude land where the peaks were worshipped as gods, each with its name and function, and there he was told that he could not and must not go farther, for it was impossible and impious.

THE CITY OF DYREZAN

So Bleek went onward and upward, for nothing and no one could stop him. Since his victory over the Telkonians he feared no man, and nature existed solely to be tamed. He paid staggering sums for supplies and guides, and he marched forth into the everlasting ice and snow. The supplies ran low and the guides ran away, but nothing could deter him. He climbed—oh, how he climbed!—trudging up narrow paths, pushing aside the nimble wild, hairy goats, up slippery ledges where one misstep meant a fall from a sheer precipice; he climbed, dangling from stout cords on the faces of slick, ice-coated granite cliffs, trusting his life to twists of fiber; he climbed, higher and higher, until every physical effort was an agony, and his life's breath rasped hollowly in his straining lungs. No common mortal could have done it as he did it. There came moments when he must call upon his esoteric resources, and he would make magic to warm his freezing flesh, or call upon friendly spirits to guide his feet, or bargain with grudging demons to ward off an immediate peril. Thus he won through, and he scaled the mighty mountains, and stood so briefly on a summit, alone above all the world, and then without hesitation he descended the other side, facing the same difficulties and terrors as before, until such time as he attained firm earth on the high plateau beyond.

He entered into a new land, drear and cold and wind-swept, yet one surprisingly well populated by a folk new to him, curiously yellow, slant-eyed folk who marveled to meet him. He found them quite as civilized as the people to the west of the mountains, more so in some respects, and deeply religious as well, for their lives seemed to center on the ubiquitous stone temples which marked the center of every habitation, be it city or town. Whenever he asked questions of the peasants they unfailingly directed him to the nearest temple, where they assured him that all answers were to be found. Therefore Bleek, once he had gathered something of the ways of this land, repaired to the largest temple he could find, in the city of Comdrec, seeking there wise men to instruct him.

There he met Ubalassa, the eldest of the priests, who sat on a satin cushion before an urn of spicy, smoking incense; rocking gently to the tinkling rhythms of unusual stringed instruments, and the melodious whining of flutes, played by unseen hands; flanked by two large statues of their chief god, a nodding, benevolent-faced fellow with folded hands. At first he offered no answers, but quizzed Bleek much, asking who he was, whither he had come, and—unusual question—the purpose of his being. Bleek replied as he would, providing considerable truths on certain points, combined with a pragmatic reticence on others. When he had satisfied the elder (a lengthy process) that worthy deigned to speak of the subject most dear to the suppliant.

Ubalassa had heard of Dyrezan, proving a font of wisdom on the great city. It was, he warned, a tremendous distance to the east and north, a discovery which was like to dishearten Bleek, who had developed a distaste for one particular cardinal point. On the other hand, the priest alluded to the north, which was an alteration of the usual advice, and seemed to suggest better knowledge of the city's whereabouts. To the east and north it lay, then, and there the traveler must go. First, however, Ubalassa had incredible things to relate, an account that merely whetted Bleek's appetite, yet convinced him that he followed the true road to wisdom, that Dyrezan was indeed the goal which would successfully cap his quest.

"O seeker," said the learned priest, "Dyrezan is the jewel of cities, the source of every legend, from every land, that speaks of a paradise on earth. Dyrezan the Eternal we call it, for it is verily so, a city erected by brilliant sorcerers shortly after the Creation, enduring to this day, and ever after. Our oldest sacred writings, yellowed and crumbling with age, refer to the city as already ancient beyond the imagination and memory of living men. Yet it can not die, as do men and the common works of men, for Dyrezan was builded from dreams and ideas rather than sweat and brawn. Strange, unearthly magic is the secret of Dyrezan; conceived by magic, created by magic sustained by magic, it is the ultimate, lasting symbol and the center of all things great, wise, and noble.

"Know you that the fabulous city was the material child of keen minds who, at the dawn of terrestrial life, unlocked the mysteries of existence that most still consider unfathomable, who delved into the underlying fabric of the universe and, in search of wisdom and beauty, laid bare the foundations of reality. In the elder times chosen men—mighty heroes of the mind, rather than the sword—spoke with the Gods, and They benevolently revealed all to Their most devout worshippers. The Gods led them to the focus of cosmic power, or vortex, the bridge to the domain of the Gods, and there those men tapped the endless energy of the cosmos for their own majestic ends. There they built their city as a tribute to the Gods, a city which would outshine all others so long as They should condescend to believe in the universe and its inhabitants; for it is Their belief, you must know, that is the First Cause; our belief in Them, or in any aspect of reality, counts for little in the grand scheme of nature and supernature. And I tell you that the city they built, those wise mages, is a feast for the eyes, though I have seen it only with the eyes of the mind. There are sky-flung towers, massive temples, vast palaces of exotic stone, and broad avenues which spiral through the city from the central monument, a gigantic statue to he who first dreamed of the city. I fail to remember his name—perhaps I knew it once, but have forgotten, for I am an old man—but this king of priests and wizards, the founder of Dyrezan, must be the greatest mortal who ever lived, a man at whose feet I would gladly sit. Then again, all who dwell within the holy confines of Dyrezan are unlike other mortals, for they are saturated from birth with the bright, revealing rays which ever flow from the fountain of the vortex. They are all wizards, keen and magically clever, and they are all near to the Gods, who may be considered, in some sense, their immediate sires. The people of Dyrezan are the offspring of the Gods, as you would know if you ever beheld their faces."

Still more could Ubalassa tell him. "I have not yet mentioned the most wonderful tale about the heavenly city, one which I would refrain from crediting, were it not reported, from various worthy sources, in the sacred texts. We are informed that the great men of Dyrezan, desiring to honor the Gods in a fashion unlike, as well as superior, to other tributes, did not rest when they had completed their marvelous city. Vast, beautiful, ornate, awe inspiring; all these things it was, but those would not fully serve the purpose of their devotion. The highest tower kissed the faces of the Gods and scraped Their gates, but this was not sufficient for them. So—hear this, Jacob Bleek, and do not forget, for I relate now the final wonder of the ages—they employed their magical skills to devise one more supreme achievement for which they must be forever renowned. Utilizing the surging, relentless forces of the vortex, that fire of the Gods, they assuredly lifted their grandiose city away from the restraining confines of the earth. Up from the ground they willed it to rise—think of the incredible power that required, power that only demi-gods could harness—and through the intense determination of sheer mental energy, focused by godly magic, they hurled their city into the blue skies, to hover over the land as a beacon for all to see. Wonderful it was, if they had done but that, only this was no mere gesture, but the way they had chosen for their people, the way of always. They lifted Dyrezan to its celestial perch, floating among the clouds in the realm of the eagle, and there—mark you!—there they have maintained it to this day. Dyrezan, the city of wizards, known in antique song as the Sky City, still rides the waves of the air, like a fairy vision, a vision vouchsafed only to the most devout and eager of travelers. You may see it, if you persevere, for much is possible in this world, but I have never heard accounts of travelers who have actually entered that famed citadel of age and power. That it is eternally denied to the common herd I know from faith, and it wearies me to wrack my brain if I ask, as you must, how may any man of the earth, who walks on legs, ever stride those magic streets in the sky? Dreamers and seekers have faltered at the end of the road, for the city lies not there, but above, toward heaven. I believe that only the most holy of men could attempt it—to raise themselves to that rarefied height—much less succeed. If that describes you, then perhaps there is a chance for you."

Having gathered unto himself all available lore—from Ubalassa, from lesser priests, from the old and cherished texts of the temple of Comdrec— Bleek pushed onward, in a purchased wagon with two strong horses, descending from the chilly plateau by way of an unfrequented mountain pass, moving north by east into ever more unfamiliar territory. He entered a lower, still rugged, land of scattered tribes, rude people not unlike those of the plateau, only less learned and, therefore, less helpful to his quest. They worshipped many gods, but these were casual deities, spirits of the trees and the rocks, not the sort to interest or intrigue the wizard. The people recognized, from his elaborated descriptions, something of this Dyrezan that he sought, yet offered in return only vague tales that contributed nothing to his stock of information. Irked by this (for he had hoped himself once more close to the goal), he wended his way tediously through their lands and ventured, after considerable pains, into still lower lands, an extremely populous domain of many villages clustered along numerous big rivers and surrounded by endless watery, wind-rustled fields of unfamiliar grain. These folk—short, slant-eyed, yellow of skin, black of hair—resembled those he had been lately meeting in his journey, but they counted themselves a different race, and lived according to differing codes, and worshipped in very different ways. As far as Bleek could tell they looked to no god or gods, but rather reserved their devotion for the dead, the departed of old being honored and prayed to in thousands of tiny temples erected in each home or hut. The folk marveled at him, for they had never seen nor heard of his like before; his white skin—pale even by the standards of his race—drew stares and gasps from them, and they were civil enough, too, and they made his wanderings among them easy if they could, yet they expressed little interest in his quest or its object. Of the Gods they knew nothing and cared less; they laughed at such superstitious and barbaric conceptions. "There are no Gods," they assured him. "We have our ancestors, who watch over us, and therefore have no need for Gods, who in story and song are always capricious and cruel. We do not need Them, therefore They do not exist. It is so." As for Dyrezan, while they were familiar with the story, and were amused by his additions to their own version of the tale, they thought such notions more fit for children than wise men.

Their language was impossibly complex, and during the initial period of Bleek's passage through their land he learned only its rudiments, and therefore often doubted the worth of his translations and his understanding of their views. Their outlook, if he grasped it correctly, struck him—the wanderer, the scholar, the seeker—as infuriatingly provincial. They did not dream of magic cities, they had no need, for they themselves were the fairest and most civilized people of the earth, in this time or any other. They were all citizens, so they informed him, of a tremendously powerful and widespread empire, which they called China, stretching from the savage tribes of the west all the way to the big sea far to the east, the sea which marked the edge of the world. Everything of value in the world they already possessed; beyond the limits of their empire there was naught but stupid barbarians and worthless wilderness. These opinions nettled Bleek, but nothing he could say would shift them. Their elders—incredibly polite, soft-

140

spoken fellows all—gleefully showed him maps of the earth, which illustrated terrain entirely unknown to him. So far as he could discern, these were mainly generalized maps of their empire, which apparently consisted of one vast mass of farm land, with a few large cities many hundreds of leagues away, while all the rest of the earth's lands were squeezed unrecognizably into the scanty surrounding margins, which also bore intricately sketched depictions of fearsome, glaring monsters. Bleek could make little of it.

Here he gained nothing of intellectual value, and yet he did not leave these people empty-handed. Quite to his surprise, as the matter developed, Bleek took to himself a traveling companion.. Of all those who heard of Bleek's quest and his amazing adventures, there was one whose imagination was fired by the accounts.. A mere youth, scarcely beyond adolescence, a native of a nondescript village where Bleek stayed for a few days, he had made it his habit to stand back of his elders as they courteously disdained their guest, and he, unlike them, gaped and sighed at what he heard. In no time it became his custom to follow around after the odd foreigner, in order to hear what wonders he would next impart. Then the wizard publicly let it be known that he must leave and get on with his curious business, and that evening the boy came to him at the cottage where he had been staying.

The boy's name was a lengthy, unpronounceable mouthful of gibberish, and Bleek always styled the young man Ting-po for short. The boy announced that he wished to join the stranger in his journey, and to see wonderful things, and to visit wonderful places. Bleek sought to dismiss him with scorn, for he had no use for others, but sharp tones and brusque words failed to stymie youthful desire. Said the boy, "Honored master, I do not laugh behind your back, nor hide contemptuous smiles behind my hands. I delight at your words, and would learn more of wisdom at your feet. My people are happy and contented with their lot, finding joy in splashing through our fields and harvesting our grain; but I am not happy, nor contented, and I would fain turn my back on the farm, the very sight of which tires my eyes and wearies my heart. Let me see the world with you; take me as your humble servant and, when you surely succeed in your quest, show me the enchanted city that floats on the clouds." While the earnest entreaty irritated Bleek, for it took his mind from better things, he nevertheless gave it thought, as he would think about anything to his profit, and it occurred to him after a moment's ponder that it would do him no harm to have at his beck a willing beast of burden, one eager to aid him, and who asked for no pay, as well as a useful translator for the difficult local language, which was apparently spoken, with minor variations, throughout an enormous territory. So the sorcerer diffidently agreed, on the conditions that the boy obey his every command without question or hesitation, and that he expect little by way of reward for his services, however extensive those might be. Ting-po bowed at each demand, enthusing aloud that his new master should be so warm and generous to one so unworthy as he. Then Bleek commanded him to make ready, for they should depart on the morn.

Ting-po joined him before the dawn, took upon himself the packing of the wagon, and situated himself by Bleek's side as his master seized the reins and lashed his steeds onward. In this manner began their shared odyssey throughout the eastern empire, a course which led them over endless, densely peopled plains, down rivers which made the Rhine and the Danube seem creeks by comparison, and so eventually to the sea, which appeared to be an ocean hitherto unknown to Bleek and the mariners whose haunts he had frequented in youth. In this region they visited great cities, unlike any he had seen before, and were he a different sort of man he would have made much of these opportunities. All he wanted from these Chinese, however, be they high born or low, was information, for these villages, towns, and cities were not what he sought. The pursuit of the elusive Dyrezan continued unabated.

There was much of learning on things old and new hidden away in the palaces or the temples, those places where hoary men of knowledge congregated, and though the course was long and twisting Bleek picked up hints and indications that his goal lay somewhere within the confines of this colossal kingdom. The best minds of the better classes, the philosophers and the magicians, were familiar with the story, and some were prone to waxing ecstatic on the theme, claiming to know further secrets of the marvelous Sky City. Ting-po proved invaluable when it came to discoursing with these eminent gentlemen. Indeed it existed, they said, had since the beginning of things, for the empire itself derived the blessings of heaven from those people who long ago raised their city upon the Fountain of the Ancestors, a curious term of which Bleek made much. That was, he decided, how they styled the vortex in their dialect. They did not speak of the Gods, that conception not being in accord with their more recent views on such matters, yet they praised their ancestors—especially those they called the "Celestial Ancestors"—so extravagantly that he felt them one and the same. In this manner he reasoned, and thus he progressed, from one tidbit of promising lore to another.

The empire possessed records galore, compiled by legions of scholars since time immemorial. Ting-po could not read at first, which humiliated him before his master. "I have no books," said he; "I was told they are not useful for those who live only to sow and to hoe. Reading and writing are magic to me." Bleek chafed him for that and ordered him to study, while the mage did likewise and thus gained insights from the weird local script. Within months he learned to read as the natives did, to the point that he felt comfortable with their peculiar letters and could think their thoughts as he read them from the page. References to Dyrezan were ubiquitous, and every reference served to enhance the glory, the charm, and the might of that fabled place

Ting-po commonly spoke for the elders of his people. "They say," he reported with delight, "that Dyrezan is the origin of all knowledge, where learning began in the days when the Celestial Ancestors walked the earth. Everything is known there, nor is anything hidden from the mind of man. When we get there, honorable master, you will learn what you will, and you will be the greatest sage of them all." For Ting-po had come to understand the mind of his master, who was like a hero to him, and he knew that Bleek sought the profoundest secrets of the universe, and that he expected to acquire all that without effort from the people of Dyrezan. In this Ting-po was right, for Bleek, having concluded that those magical folk had learned all before him, thought that he need only present himself among them in order to have what they had, and then do with the knowledge as he pleased. In this fashion the culmination of his quest for the Gods would be made easy.

The legends as related by the easterners placed the wondrous city within the empire; very good, but China was a big place, and since entering their domain knowledge of directions, however hazy, seemed to slip away. Dyrezan was somewhere—it was this way or that—seek ye the city, he was told, beyond that hill, or over that river, or at the end of that imperial road, or somewhere hard by the astounding wall of antique masonry which bounded the entire kingdom to the north, separating it from the savages beyond. On they went, Bleek ever more obstinate in his determination, giving ever more years to his quest, while Ting-po tagged along happily, accepting such crumbs of lore as Bleek would cast his way, meanwhile seeing the world and chortling with joy at each fresh experience.

Jacob Bleek, being a great sorcerer—perhaps already the greatest—naturally chose to employ his esoteric arts in the furtherance of his quest, in addition to the legends, traveler's accounts, and documents that typical scholars would use. He had done this from the first, far back in Egypt and Arabia, now thousands of leagues and so many years away, and had continued his attempts at magical delving to the present. He possessed arcane skills which ought to grant him knowledge of far places, skills which he had used to advantage under proper conditions in the past, and he had hoped that they would serve him in this extraordinary case. They did not do so, at least to any spectacular degree; in the beginning he gained nothing from his efforts, which might have been due to the effects of extreme distance, but he had expected more as he trekked ever eastward. After passing the great mountains beyond India he derived certain faint hints, results which intensified slightly once he passed into the eastern empire, but never did he learn enough to guide his feet. He stirred his potions by the midnight moon, and he inhaled the acrid vapors, and he let his mind wander into a soothing, dream-like state, and he peered through the fog of reality toward his destination. Evidence of location came not to him; that was always troublesome at best, to be sure, but in this circumstance the method did not avail at all. It distressed him that a real place, with real geographical roots, should so shift about and drift in his mind. On the other hand, the technique did require a certain clear-cut, personal grasp of the tangible essence of the goal, and this too was in short supply. Within the realm of his dreamy magical state he endeavored mightily to garner a visual impression of Dyrezan, which should aid in establishing its place in the world. Here as well difficulties plagued him. During the earlier portion of his quest he saw nothing but otherworldly murk; much later he began to receive images from the mental mist, but they were never more than suggestions of form, outlines of shapes. He came to see, very late in the day, a shadowed skyline in gloom of a peculiar cast, embodying architectural designs of types never before seen or imagined by him. There were towers like minarets that speared the sky, and others that curved and looped upon themselves. There were intricate geometrical forms like sculptures, some so delicate that they seemed to defy the pull of the earth, only they were buildings the size of cathedrals. He sensed a massive bulk in the void, and an emptiness below, and far beneath that a vague landscape, a vast bowl-shaped hollow encircled by sheer cliffs and stately mountains. This he saw, but this was all; never more did he see of the city or its surroundings, and of the inhabitants and their ways nothing came to him whatsoever. The impressions remained the same from one session to the next, so he knew that the visions possessed something of validity, despite their illusory appearance. He rationalized this mystery by supposing that the masterminds of Dyrezan had thrown a magical shield about their city, so that strangers could not peer within and snatch from them their secrets. He could believe that, for it was what he would have done in their place.

Over the course of their wanderings their path led them back to the west, and far north of Bleek's original route into China. They entered into a less settled land, where the thinly scattered folk made their scanty livings from the products of their goat herds, for there was little otherwise in that unproductive region but grass and rocks. These people moved about with the seasons, dwelling in camps rather than villages. They were less accommodating of strangers, perhaps because they had little to lose, and were therefore jealous of what they had, or perhaps because their experiences with strangers in the past had made them unfriendly. Bleek and Ting-po happened upon a herders' encampment one evening, in the bed of a dry river at the bottom of a grim, arid valley above which rose steep, boulder strewn ridges, and they settled for the night within sight of the natives. Ting-po went forth to ask for succor, which was hard to come by in these parts, but the request was denied. The wizard sent him out once again with coin in hand, and this time he returned with a few morsels of jerked goat's flesh. When they finished their fairly palatable repast Bleek ordered his servant forth again, to quiz the folk about Dyrezan. Since arriving within this harsh territory he had heard no news of the mysterious city.

Ting-po returned with his brown eyes flashing, sputtering in hot indignation, but he had something to relate. "These men," said he, "are as stupid and dirty and smelly as their goats. I go to them, in the name of my master, the one and only Jacob Bleek, and I ask of them big things, concerning that which you know. To me they owe nothing, for I am only a servant, but I am the honored servant of Bleek, which I would rather be than a king, and I expect those fools to realize that. I ask questions, and they laugh and spit and throw me another scrap of their foul meat, and tell me to be gone. That I don't do; I stay, by your command, and ask again. Out of contempt they hurl stones—see this bruise?—they are but animals. I persevere; I explain to them that what my master wants, my master gets, and if they displease him, he will turn them all into goats, and we will eat them fresh as man should eat. That makes them think. They have seen you, and are puzzled by your fair skin, and they wonder who you are and what you may do to them. This time I laugh. Only then do they pay attention to me, and heed my questions.

"They tell me this. Dyrezan they don't know, nor any cities anywhere, but they know of a very strange thing. They speak of a valley, many days journey from here, far over those mountains on the horizon. The valley is a big circle, surrounded by mountains, with just a single pass leading inside. It is a shunned place; no one goes there, for legend warns them to stay away. It has been so since their people began wandering this wilderness, many years ago. None of them will admit to visiting the valley—they stay away—but they know stories.

"They say that in the old days, in the time of the Ancestors, brave men crept close to the round valley, and they saw this: the rocks of the ground and the mountains shine as if they had fire in them. They're lit up as by the light of the moon, only they do this when there is no moon. The old men say the valley is a place where magic comes from the rocks. The earth underfoot is magic! Even in story they don't go closer, so they say nothing of cities, but everything there must be magic. Is that good for you?"

Jacob Bleek felt a thrill of exhilaration at this report. He had only the foggiest of notions as to what might be expected at the site of a vortex, but to untutored barbarians, certainly, and perhaps to their betters, such a place could be described in the simple terms he was hearing. There would be incredible energy latent in the location, and in the nearby territories such energy might manifest itself visibly. The earth would be saturated with the substance of the Gods. That night Bleek made his magic again and sought, armed with this new information, to receive a clearer glimpse of his goal. Before he had focused on the city, which continued to elude him save as insubstantial impressions, but now he saw, as if with his physical eyes, the sacred valley of the vortex. Yes, it was round, curiously so, as if sculpted by design out of the ringing mountains. There were peaks above, recognizable shapes he would know when he saw them in life. He observed the pass, almost a tunnel carved through the primordial granite, cutting straight as a road through the rock. He could not see the glow of which he had been informed, which he guessed was dimmed by the same cunning magic which obscured the city from his sight, but he strongly suspected that it was there, waiting to be seen with eyes of flesh.

It was enough; through Ting-po he pumped these folk for whatever more they could tell, trading a handful of worthless baubles for their knowledge of directions and terrain conditions, and late the next morning he set out to the north with his companion. The land grew increasingly dreary and sinister, harsher still than the range of the herdsmen. Bleek and Ting-po crossed a barren, rocky plain swept by miserable winds, then began to climb as the land rose gradually around them. Through the trackless wilds they rode, the rocks about them looming in weird forms, sanded into odd shapes over the eons by the ever present wind. They approached a line of forbidding peaks. When they rested (Bleek drove hard now, insisting on progressing through the night, so they had little sleep) the wizard employed his magical eye to discern the location of the pass through the barrier. It seemed that he had found it, for he gained a definite sense of its whereabouts, and with first light he pointed out a distant ridge and they made for that. The going was terrible, and at times Ting-po feared that they must be forced to turn back, only Bleek would not countenance the thought, even for a minute. Willing to hazard all, there was nothing that could stop him now.

So, as the shadows lengthened and the afternoon drew on, they found the entrance to the pass. It was not easy, for it was partially choked with boulders which had tumbled from the cliffs above, and they were like to miss it, but Bleek had seen the place in his mind, and knew what to look for. Apparently the pass had not been traveled in countless years, a considerable surprise to him, until he remembered the extraordinary attainments of those who dwelt on the other side, and realized that they had no need of commonplace conveyance, or for that matter of contact with the outer world. The inhabitants of Dyrezan must be sufficient unto themselves, living lives of wonder and plenty. By this time it was also obvious to Bleek that they had no desire, in this age, to advertise their presence, otherwise all the peoples of the earth, through admiration or envy, would be singing their praises and bowing before them..

The pass was narrow and dark, and Bleek, despite his eagerness, could not see his way to advancing further until morning, so he spent the night tingling with anticipation, imagining to himself that a citizen of the great city might emerge to invite him within; for with their legendary knowledge and abilities they must know he was there, and he believed that they would welcome a man of his type. No one came, however. He must be patient, then, until he brought himself to them, at which time he would learn their secrets, the very secrets of the ultimate Gods, and gain for himself all the wisdom of the earth and the universe. He could barely contain himself. Ting-po did not fret, on the other hand, for he reveled in each aspect of his new experiences, and would gladly wander forever in search of the fabled city. To him it would be a new place to visit, and one that would please his master, and that was enough.

Come the dawn they made ready. Bleek's sturdy wagon could not be driven through the piled boulders in the small gap—it constituted a near miracle that they had gotten it this far—so Ting-po unharnessed the horses, packed them with supplies, and led them as he followed behind his master on foot. The sheer walls of the passage rose up above them; the gloom of false night descended, for no sunlight penetrated here; the straggly scrub of the outside world died out at the stony blockage, and naught else grew within. The pass, as Bleek had seen by his magic, cut right through the mountains in an unwavering course. Many rocks had fallen within throughout the ages, and been suffered to remain, which made their final trek more arduous than predicted. They tramped for a league or more along the shadowed path, with Bleek expecting developments at every moment. His eyes strained for a marvelous vista ahead, his ears attuned to catch the sounds of wholesome life. Presently a grayish sort of half-light seemed to filter from regions before him, and he quickened his pace. Then he ran forward, panting in a frenzy of fierce desire, leaving Ting-po to catch up as he might. A final lunge carried the wizard over a heap of boulders, and he saw the sunlight once more.

Ting-po had lagged well behind with the horses; the passage did not suit them, and they seemed inclined to skittishness, ready to bolt, so he must work with them as he marched, and proceed with unsteady, halting gait. Shortly, however, he too emerged into the region where the sun beamed down, and he saw the valley with his own eyes, the curiously round valley of which the goat herders had spoken and his master had seen by his mysterious arts, and the stark mountains that enclosed it. Ting-po noted this, yet for the moment his attention was captured by a sight that he had least expected: that of his master, the cunning sorcerer Jacob Bleek, groveling on the ground, his face in the dust, screeching unintelligibly as if possessed by devils of madness. Ting-po, stricken by panic, dropped the horses' reins and rushed to Bleek, endeavoring to raise him from the dirt, but the man clawed wildly at him and sobbed uncontrollably. The young fellow squatted and waited for his master to recover his wits, and while he did so he cast his gaze upon the valley which lay before him. He did this, and he began to wonder, and he tried to think, and he rose slowly to his feet, and he spoke with furrowed brow. "Honored master," said he, "there is much I do not understand. This is the valley as foretold; it is round, as if dug for a great well, and there are the mountains, even the one you saw with the twin peaks, as you described to me. This is surely the place, isn't it? But master, you must explain to me. Tell me we have come to the wrong place What is all this lying on the ground before us, and where—O, where, master—is the beautiful city that floats in the sky?"

And Jacob Bleek shrieked, not at Ting-po but at the fate that had led him here, and he half rose in undirected passion, sustained by a paroxysm of rage, before he collapsed weakly against a big stone, unable to move. For this was the place, indeed; he had found the magical valley, only there was no magic here, and no home of the children of the Gods; the great Sky City, the incomparable city of Dyrezan, was no more! Its ruins, the pitiful remnants of that once heaven-flung fortress of cosmic secrets, lay smashed and scattered, as it had fallen, across the floor of the valley. The wreckage was there sure enough: the crushed and splintered blocks of many colors, even through their thick coating of dust exhibiting the rainbow hues of the finest stone, bearing worn and cracked carvings of what appeared to be lidless, staring eyes; twisted fragments of intricately worked metal, corroded now beyond even imagination to reconstruct, and glinting shards of glass; and a chaos of formless, rotted debris, heaped and splashed across the titanic stones, the essence of a dream reduced to trash. As far as he could see, to the limits of the far wall of the valley, he beheld only time-weathered and time-worn devastation, the enduring evidence of a dreadful catastrophe which must have occurred countless ages ago.

The destruction was complete. From the pitting and cratering of the ground he could tell that the now broken masses had crashed down from their former dizzy heights. Everything he had learned over the years, from his painstaking accumulation of evidence, was accurate; there had been a Dyrezan, and it may well have been as glorious as legend told. That was true, then, but it was old information, sadly out of date. The city, its people, its knowledge, were a chimera, lost forever to the world, beyond hope of recovery. Furthermore—he sensed this, and knew the sensation to be real—there was no magic here, had not been for a long time. The rocks did not shine, if they ever did; they were substances of the common clay, nothing more. The vortex itself was defunct, deceased, dead, and with it, perhaps, had died Dyrezan.

What terrible doom had befallen the city of marvels? He might never know, though he could hazard guesses, and speculate as he chose. Maybe the denizens of Dyrezan had grown greedy through the eons, and squandered the strange power available to them. The energies of the vortex might not, after all, be limitless, and once used up, there was nothing to maintain the city at its lofty aerial perch. It could have happened that way. Maybe the noble folk of Dyrezan had grown prideful, and the Great Old Ones, the Gods, had stepped in to punish them, and withdrawn this vortex from the earth, thereby depriving the city of its support. He knew many an old myth which recounted such events; the fate of Dyrezan might constitute the grandfather of all such stories. Then again, if it be the actions of the Gods which were responsible, it might have been no more than capriciousness on Their parts, as the Chinese would have it; They may have chosen to pass elsewhere through the spheres, thus leaving this location dry of magical potency. There may have been no good reason for it at all, but it was done, not to be undone, however much he reasoned or theorized.

He remembered the obscurely recorded fate of the Rhexellites, and an unpleasant thought struck him. They, too, had known of the Gods and the vortices; perhaps they had made use of the latter, or built their cities near, and the use or the proximity had destroyed them in the end as Dyrezan had been destroyed. It was so terribly difficult to be certain, given the lack of firm evidence, but he began to fear that the vortices were inherently dangerous places, and the Gods, perhaps, dangerous masters.

Bleek felt his quest to be in shambles. In order to acquire the wisdom of the Gods, he had sought the storied city, the city of supreme mages and the ethereal vortex, and he had found neither city nor vortex. Both had been stolen from him, cruelly ripped from his grasp. He had spent years of his valuable life on what proved to be a worthless detour, and now he must pick up the pieces as he might. For a moment, in his despair and sorrow, he thought verily that it would be more rational and sane of him to try picking up the pieces of Dyrezan. In his mind's eye the baleful face of Josiah, the Cabalistic Jew, suddenly swam before him, and he remembered the old man's curse—that he should never achieve his grand goal—and he asked himself bitterly (as he was prone to do at times of crisis) if this were the fulfillment of that evil prophecy. Crushed by the magnitude of his loss, when victory had seemed so near, he felt a mounting hopelessness.

Then he recognized again the existence of Ting-po, whom he now realized was tugging at his cloak and shouting into his ear. "Master, master," cried his servant, "what do we do now? We must leave this place; it is not a good place. There is nothing for you here. Let us go and seek wonders. Take me to them, show them to me and explain them to me. Somewhere in the world we will find what you want. It is there, for you are wise beyond all men, and you can't be wrong. Take me there. Now is not the time to lie down and die."

Hearing this, Jacob Bleek growled an inaudible reply and hauled himself to his feet. No, he would not die, nor would he surrender to abysmal fate or vile curses. That was not part of his plan. While he lived he, the power of his brain, not mere event or misfortune, controlled his fate. He had reached a dead end, but there were other ends, other roads, and one of them would lead him to his destiny. He would explore the valley and sift the wreckage of once majestic Dyrezan for whatever items of value could be retrieved, and then, whatever the result of that investigation, he would go on. The quest would go on, and in the end—tomorrow, or at the finish of the world, if it must be—he would triumph.

IX. The Vault of Azamodias

The world turned; the seasons marched forth, spring giving way to summer, summer to autumn, and the cycle came round again, renewing itself, ever onward; and the wizard Jacob Bleek, with his faithful companion Ting-po, marched ever onward across the face of the earth, in pursuit of the great quest for the Gods and Their wisdom, which Bleek would fain make his own. The years came and went as they journeyed from one strange land to another, ever seeking the clues which would lead Bleek to the mastery of the natural and the supernatural worlds that he craved, power that would raise him above all mortal men, make him the undisputed king of the sorcerers and of the cosmos. With the passage of the years the boy Ting-po matured into a fine, stout young man, and always he devoted himself, without reservation or question, to the service of his master. Still time swept by, sweeping away maturity and vigor as it had youth and wide-eyed wonder, and it came to pass that Ting-po grew to a contented middle age, white of hair and lined of face. He had lived a long life, according to the standards of his eastern farmer folk, and he looked forward to many more years, so long as his health would sustain him, of traveling the world, and seeing and experiencing its thrills, by Bleek's side.

Now the strangest thing of all was that Jacob Bleek did not truly age. He matured, to be sure; his cold, angular features grew hard from care, from worry, from the ravages of the elements, from devotion to grim and morbid thoughts; and since his cataclysmic expedition to the ancient rubble of fallen Dyrezan his jet-black hair had been shot with the gray of iron. He had paid the price of his unusual life, but otherwise he did not materially change. In this time he could be seen riding hurriedly down the lanes of cities with his dark hat low over his eyes, or striding purposely across the lands and through the dwelling places of men; a tall gentleman, lean and strong, with staff firmly in hand, his black cloak flapping in the breeze. A short, cultured beard adorned his prominent chin; his hawk-like nose suggested strength and will to command; his eyes, dark and keen as ever, were known to frighten those who gazed too long into their unfathomable depths.

Such he was, and had been for a very long time, and such he had begun to assume with reasoned joy that he always would be. It was not natural, this, the combination of the mind and attitudes of a hoary, learned graybeard with the body of an ostensibly young man; this amazing effect was no product of respectable nature, nor of any arts that he had visited upon himself; this pleasing result, which promised indefinite life and health, could only be the logical outcome of the weird bargain he had sealed with the tragic mage Josiah those many years gone. Bleek had long felt dubious about his relations with that man, who had ended his bitter enemy, yet they had made a deal, and Bleek—after his fashion—had lived up to the compact, and had often wondered throughout his life whether the day would come when he knew that his old partner in esoteric delvings had lived up to his side of the agreement. Now Bleek did know, and the knowing was good, for he had spent a lengthy span on his quest, and at the present moment there was no apparent end in sight.

Of course Ting-po noticed this curious development (or lack of same) in his master, but such was his high, even worshipful, opinion of Bleek that nothing could surprise him. He had seen the wizard do things incredible, heard him speak of possibilities more so; Bleek, to him, was the greatest man in the world, and if he did not age as did other, lesser, men, what of that? In so far as Ting-po dwelt upon the matter at all—and he never indicated, by look or deed, that he did—it seemed entirely fitting and proper to him. Bleek was Bleek, better than all other men, greater than they in all ways, and everything about him was a surprise and a marvel, so in time Ting-po was surprised by nothing, and it came to take much to cause him to marvel.

Through the years they trekked into the seemingly endless voids of unknown lands, Bleek ever alert for evidence of value to him, fresh avenues of knowledge by which to guide his quest. The secret of his success, he realized, lay in finding an active vortex, that awesome bridge to the realm of the Gods, by which he could meet Them and parley with Them. This he must find, in whatever distant or difficult part of the earth it lay. He and Ting-po called no land home, but passed through all, stopping to inquire and investigate, then moving on, ephemeral presences that came and went. During the course of their wanderings they sojourned for extended periods within every old city of China, and visited strange nations upon its borders, and when those vast realms were exhausted—a long process indeed—they turned north into a harsh wilderness of unguessable extent. Bleek possessed no maps of value, nor at this stage any reckoning of the route he must travel, so he set horses and carriage toward the north, where he had not been, in hopes that he would learn, out of the unknown, what he had not from that which he knew.

The region north of Ting-po's great people was a desolate, unproductive, and frigid land of raging rivers, somnolent pine forests and stormy tundra, the least inhabited area Bleek had ever seen. The folk were woefully primitive, desperately poverty-stricken tribes, without fixed villages, who chased large deer during the brief summers, and languished within caves and rough-built ice houses throughout the long and brutal winters. They had not books, nor any of the accouterments of civilization which ameliorate the lot of man. Though they were hospitable enough in their poor way, honestly and earnestly striving to please odd visitors—which was ironic, for they had so little—one could reasonably assume that they would have nothing to offer Bleek.

THE VAULT OF AZAMODIAS

Yet they knew stories, and were keen that others should know them. Bleek discovered a world in which the telling of tales about the past was a respected occupation, and often he and his servant fell in with traveling singers and poets who made livings according to the caliber of the ancient stories they sang or recited for the amusement and edification of their brethren. These men, the handful of elders and their many younger acolytes, ventured from one unsettled band to another, presenting their lays, speaking of secrets from antique days. There were occasions when they sang of matters that much intrigued Jacob Bleek: legends concerning lost Dyrezan, and the ways of the Gods, and the gushing mystical fountains of the vortices through which walked the Old Ones when it pleased Them. Bleek heard these things (and other statements, certainly, somewhat less to the point), and thought to himself that his journey into the wild, unexplored north might not have been in vain after all

They knew magic as well, which surprised him exceedingly, even more so than their rich stock of accumulated lore. Their wise men had developed an esoteric school, as he called it, .devoted to a form of magic which did not manifest itself, in any plain manner, via material aspects. This was a strange, narrowly focused form, at first incomprehensible and unnoticed by the wizard of the west, which served to enhance the innate powers of the mind to an extraordinary degree. These sorcerers, few and old and wizened, spent the long nights of their land gathered within sacred caves, rocky chambers adorned with frightful images of wood and peculiar carvings of bark, and there they inhaled aromatic vapors of boiling potions derived from jealously guarded herbs which they collected themselves, trusting none of their uninitiated fellows with these vital substances. The outpourings of these potions served—as Bleek analyzed the situation—to create linkages within their brains, opening doorways of the mind which were closed to others. Natural skills of thought were greatly increased; marvelous insights containing genuine knowledge sprang forth; and they could see, to a seemingly infinite degree, that which other men could not see.

Bleek's chief informant, the man who set him upon a new path, was the sorcerer Ingmakok, a perfectly dreadful old fellow who appeared ever possessed of some mysterious glee untinged by kindness, and who clearly knew more about his visitors and their schemes than was wholesome or tolerable. "Did you enjoy your stay in fair Dyrezan?" he asked out of the blue, much discomfiting his guest; "Where will you seek your vortices?" he queried, to which his visitor was too stunned to offer reply. Bleek hastily reasoned that the generalities of his local inquiries had been transmitted by the natives to the clever seer, but when the old man pressed him for particulars—"Shall the Gods dance for you, O traveler, and grant to you a share of Their power over all men?"—Bleek knew that he could keep no secrets from this one, for he had never let on the nature of his quest. He also surmised that the mocking sorcerer could tell him much, and indeed, Ingmakok had a tale of interest to relate. This was no story retained in holy writings, nor even passed down through the generations from hearth to hearth, yet Ingmakok knew of it. He saw it, after a fashion, as it had happened, for he could see old events as in life, could plumb the murky depths of history better than any of his fellows, who rightly revered him for his mystical ability.

Long ago, he said, in the days of the ancient fathers, another white man, himself a learned wizard, had come out of the west on a mission to find the legendary city of Dyrezan. He was a great man, of such importance that he counseled his people and, in time, ruled over them. His motives were obscure—even the seer could not read the minds of the ghosts who passed before his inner vision—but he was brilliant, and demanded much from his world, and perhaps sought greatness and renown, in his own way, as did the modern traveler. "As I say, long ago he came to the east, yet even then Dyrezan was naught but a forgotten ruin. In those times, however, the cruel world had not effaced all the glory of those toppled towers; much, rather, remained of value to the wise, and this man gathered unto himself all the lore and the emblems of magic that he could carry. The fading wisdom of Dyrezan he took away with him, back to his own kingdom, where he achieved much or little with it, as the case may be. As with all men his span closed, and he died, and his kingdom too, in due course, passed away, but mark this, Jacob Bleek—mark this, young stranger who is somehow older than I can understand—his secrets did not die with him. The records he kept still exist, hidden near him, to this very day, and the bold man may retrieve them and do with them as he pleases."

Bleek searched his brain, but first thought himself aware of no such tale even from vulgar legend, much less scholarly documentation; and yet it seemed to ring a bell. Wait; long ago the wise and worthy Josiah, he of the pathetic life, had told him a bare story about a man, "a wonderful scholar of the far north in olden times", who had written concerning the Old Ones. Bleek insisted upon more: what was the name of the ancient mage?—when had he reigned?—from whither had he come? The irksome fact was that Ingmakok did not know, or would not tell. Bleek would have tortured the information out of him—imagine possessing priceless lore descended from Dyrezan itself!—but he could not incite hostility among these crude people in this wild and treacherous place, and likely the seer spoke the truth, for as he said, "That which is too far away I see as through a dark mist. He came from the west in a former age, and then he returned. Find what survives, then, far to the west."

Far to the west Bleek must go! Yet it was a dispiriting thought, to think that, after all of his efforts had directed him to the east, he much now turn about and seek his fortune at the other end of the earth. Far to the west lay his own land, Europe. He laughed harshly at himself, regaling himself with the foolish notion that the anonymous wizard of yore was buried beneath the very boarding house of Bruges where Bleek had grown to manhood. Would not that be a fine joke on him? Furthermore, the clue was so slight, so vague; should he gamble on it? Bleek knew sorcery, and he knew sorcerers, both subjects at which he excelled. He believed the hazy tale of Ingmakok, and must needs act upon it.

"We go to see your own people," cried Ting-po happily. "Be it so? There we'll see many men like you, and none like me? There must be such a land, I know, but I can't picture it." Bleek admonished him to silence and ordered his servant to prepare the horses. They were heading west, he admitted, so far as the trail of evidence and signs would take them. They had never traveled for amusement, the wizard pointed out, nor did they do so now. On a journey of such import only cold, steely determination would suffice. This Bleek said, as he had decreed oft before, at which Ting-po bowed gravely, but though he had never argued and never would, he also had never agreed, for try as he might to imbibe the ways and views of his master, his journey with Jacob Bleek had been nothing but an extended joyride for him, and the whys and wherefores counted for nothing at all.

There is much that could be told of their great westward trek, for it took a long time—considerably longer than Bleek's solitary procession to the east—and led them through many wild and fascinating countries. They struggled against the elements, fording rampaging rivers in flood, losing their way in trackless forests, careening over mountains and riding horses to death on the cold plains. They encountered a myriad savage tribes, many of whom welcomed strangers to a degree, others of whom did not, and trouble was known to flare. Once Ting-po saved his master from a poison-tipped spear wielded by a hostile warrior, receiving an agonizing wound for his pains, and another time Bleek faced down a cabal of native wizards who frowned upon his pointed inquiries, and sought to stir up their people against him. Where remonstration could not rescue the situation, Bleek's magic did; the news, scarcely capable of embellishment, concerning the doom he visited upon his foes spread far and wide, and for many leagues they traveled in security, no one daring to molest them. By slight gradations, day by day, they continued west, until there came a time when they entered the kingdom of Russia, a land of which Bleek knew by former report.

It seemed to him almost a homecoming, to come to a place actually marked on familiar maps. It was rather more primitive, on the whole, than most of the old Europe he had known, this land—named for the powerful Norse tribe of the Rus during the epoch of darkness— but the folk were mainly white, and they spoke a language recognizable to a well educated scholar. In short order Bleek could converse with the people and seek contacts among the gentry and nobility. Ting-po was amazed by this land, so much of which was new to him. He could still meet a sprinkling of easterners rather like himself, but the rest of his fresh acquaintances, their manners and customs, entertained and awed him. To him all of these types looked exactly like his master, and he lived for days in expectation of Bleek hailing an old friend or relative. This did not happen, of course, for Bleek had neither friends nor relations, yet the sorcerer got along well enough, and soon learned that which was of interest to him.

Throughout the wild lands he had occasionally gleaned hints concerning the wandering wizard of yesteryear, who had apparently left his mark wherever he had passed, but only now did Bleek acquire worthwhile particulars. He learned them from a colorful source, a man who called himself Prince Alyesky, though he was really chief of a formidable and ancient Cossack tribe. The self-styled prince, who lived in a mud and thatch manor surrounded by his faithful villagers on the endless, empty steppes, spoke poor Russian, but read it better, and as a man of letters in an illiterate land had gathered unto himself all the lore and wisdom of his people. He knew things, and had heard things, and he had for the telling a very old story, partly derived from a monkish book, partly from legend; the tale of the wonderful olden mage Azamodias.

In a time not long after the Flood (so ran the Orthodox written account by the monk Gregorias) clever Azamodias, the fabled Lost Patriarch, came down from the north, from his kingdom in the ice and snow, as he traveled about the reborn world, seeking all the knowledge of the earth for the great testament which he planned to write as a record for all the generations which would come after. He was a warlock of profound cunning and ability (so said the vulgar legends), who astounded and frightened all who came before him. Eventually he departed for the east, where he sought the now hidden land of Eden, that happy realm which had been torn away from mankind after the inglorious Fall. A lifetime later, according to both sources, he passed through Russia again on his way home, having learned all there was to know from man, and perhaps from angels and demons as well. Thence he returned to his kingdom, where he resided in the ice-bound citadel of Krothag, and there he died as even a patriarch must, full of the wisdom and contentment which long life and (so wrote the monk, legend demurring on this point) godly goodness bestow.

"Make of it what you will," summed up Prince Alyesky; "I read that Azamodias returned joyously with a light heart, having achieved his mission in life, yet I hear that he came back bitter and black of heart, having failed to find what he coveted, suffering from cruel disappointment. Know you this man? Does my story, in any version, correspond to your own?" Bleek allowed that it did; he granted now that all this time he had been on the track of Azamodias, and had but needed to attach a name to the tales that chance had thrown his way. "Then let me help more," said the prince. "You say you seek wisdom, which is sweet to mine ears. All the stories speak of the Eternal Knowledge of Azamodias. The lore which he made his own is indestructible, and may be possessed by the man who walks in purity with God. If thou art the man, his wisdom is yours for the taking. That would be a pretty end to your quest."

So it would, Bleek averred, and it only remained to him to find the last resting place of the Lost Patriarch—a term which the wizard interpreted as referring to a great man of his own kind—and seize for his own use the ancient knowledge diligently recorded by his predecessor. That still left the dubious problem of the location of Krothag, the reputed home of Azamodias, a place name which meant nothing to Bleek. He knew the geography of Europe, yet Krothag seemed as fabulous as Dyrezan once had. The prince could not aid him there, save to advocate a journey north, as far as human conveyance would carry him.

"There is more to see!" cried Ting-po, delirious with joy, when told that they must resume the march. "It is a wonder to me that I have not visited it all. Is Europe so big as a province of the empire?" By this he meant his own land of China, which he had once thought all the world. Bleek gruffly informed his companion that the civilized west was quite as large as the whole empire, and a good deal more satisfying to him. They would see of it that which was necessary, and then go where fate dictated. The body of Azamodias reposed to the north; thus they took leave of Prince Alyesky, who with his priests blessed their trip—though Bleek laughed grimly at that—and ventured north, across the face of Russia; over the steppes, through cooling forests and swamps, to the old Viking town of Novgorod, now a boisterous city of proud nobles, raucous serfs, and demanding churchmen.

From the latter Bleek learned, for a hefty stipend, a fact which filled him with wary hope. In the weather-worn wooden palace that they called their cathedral the priests of Novgorod maintained their records, and among these were items of information, collected over time by traders and military adventurers, pertaining to the far north. In these documents Bleek found numerous references to an old military outpost, on the shores of the northern sea, in a wild country through which the occasional conqueror had passed, but never long resided; a forgotten town or village, yet in former times a habitation of some note, which the records styled Crothakkias. Knowing how names are wont to change over time, slurred by disuse or altered by variations in the conventions of language, he thought to himself that Krothag and Crothakkias might be one and the same.

From Novgorod Bleek passed out of the traditional domain of the Rus and pushed on into the frigid realm of the fierce, hardy Finns. These were not a schooled people by any means, but they were long natives of their land, and they had tales to tell. From them he learned, around their bonfires by night, that they knew of Crothakkias, the forgotten fortress of another age found at the edge of the earth, where land meets the impassable sea which freezes solid in the winter; they sang lively songs of Crothakkias, wherein was found the castle of Azamodias, the dead sage of yore whose mighty deeds and wisdom ever lives. Difficulties remained to confront Jacob Bleek and his servant Ting-po, but with this information the way was clear, and in the fullness of time they indeed came to Crothakkias, the ancient town once known as Krothag.

Modern Crothakkias was a small place, an impoverished village of fur-wrapped coastal dwellers, lying on a barren peninsula sticking out into the cold sea which still, at this warmest time of year, was barely liquid, with only a dirty, icy slush slopping up onto the rocky shores instead of clean, lively waves. The inhabited area was nestled at the foot of a steep crag which rose hundreds of feet above the surrounding flat, ocean-washed landscape. The folk dredged a bare subsistence from the sea, fishing from leather boats in season, hacking through the ice elsewhen, but as Bleek soon learned they remembered better days when antique Krothag had constituted a wonder of the world. Tangible evidence of former glory remained. It had once been a considerably larger town, as testified to by the earthen mounds and heaps of worked 1stones that littered the peninsula right to its narrow neck, where the icy waves crashed and frothed at both sides of the road. There was much in these ruins to interest a scholar, but Bleek, from the moment he approached, had eyes only for the spectacular remnants of colossal architecture which adorned the oddly level summit of the fearsome crag.

The people of Crothakkias were a mixed race, part Finn, part Scandinavian, mild descendants of the warlike Goths. History had long passed them by, but they remembered much, and it pleased them to recount what they remembered of their heyday. The village possessed nothing like an inn, so Bleek and his companion were forced to accept the graciously offered back rooms of a private house, a building superior to most, which were often little more than huts or wind shelters. From their host they heard something, from others still more, for the legends of Azamodias were well known here. At every opportunity Bleek asked of the austere ruins perched atop the crag, and in short order his suspicions were confirmed.

They were no less, he was confidently informed, than the surviving walls and battlements of the ancient castle of the mysterious wizard Azamodias, who had raised his fortress through the employment of dark arts in the youth of the world, in a time even before the Vikings embarked upon their fateful rampages. A legion of demons, so went the story, had torn off with their stony teeth the mountain peak in one stormy, thunderous night, and had graded the top of the remaining crag with their red-hot iron claws. Then Azamodias had conjured anew, and he bade the pitch basalt of the ground to rise up at his pleasure; and the rocks did this to please him, and they spun in the darkness of the screaming night until they assumed the forms he desired; and then they came together, like well-drilled soldiers in formation, and they fashioned themselves assiduously into the contours of a grim and foreboding fortress of nightmare, so dark that its outlines could only ever be perceived by light of day; and then, the tellers of tales proudly asserted, Azamodias had commanded the mystically shaped stones to fuse, and so they made up, on the outer walls of the castle, one titanic block of sheer, unseamed black stone, and the similarly wonderful and impossible palace within. Thus with the dawn the erection of Azamodias' home was complete.

What did they know of the man himself? As Bleek heard it, there was no marvel that could not be imputed to the memory of Azamodias. He was the sorcerer to whom others of his brotherhood bowed in respect and dread. Wise and clever, knowing all that scrolls could teach, and limitlessly powerful, he was everything noble and evil, kindly and cruel, sagacious and demanding. When absolute mastery over his blood-chilling dominion lost its savor and failed to satisfy, he set forth alone on his fabled wanderings in search of new knowledge which would increase the scope of his already unrivaled majesty. After a lifetime of magical adventures he had returned to his gloomy abode, a wiser man still—never has there been a man to compare with Azamodias!— yet sadder as well, for whatever he had sought, that, apparently, he had not found. And so he remained, absorbed in his studies or sorrowing over lost possibilities, until the day he died, and was interred under the castle keep. His people honored him as he would have it (though there were those glad to see him gone), and buried him with all his treasures and his mystic scrolls, in a stone vault deep beneath the keep, within the permanent ice which underlay the crag.

Since then no man, no matter how courageous, had scaled the crag in order to visit the ice-bound tomb where Azamodias rested. History or legend alluded to brave fools who tried, but there was no recorded case of success, or even of a return in health. The mere climbing of the crag was held to be a tricky business. What perils might lie in wait within the wreckage of the castle, or inside the tunnels of ice leading down below the level of eternal frost, or within the treasure vault and burial chamber itself, no man living could guess, for there was no one now who would dare the attempt. The lair of Azamodias was a holy and a shunned place, sanctified and cursed, forbidden to all by wisdom, by prudence, by terror.

All this Jacob Bleek heard, and forthwith began the laying of plans. Folk who thought themselves worldly asked him if he intended claiming the legendary treasure for himself, and he could reply with unfeigned honesty that he had gold enough for his wants, and a bit for his pleasures, so that the treasure of Azamodias was safe from his greed. The response, perhaps, satisfied them, yet Bleek continued with his arrangements. In fact the treasure could rot *in situ* for ought it mattered to him, but he craved those scrolls, which he knew must contain magical lore of awesome power, including, as it might be, the age-hallowed secrets of the Old Ones as revealed to the extinct mages of Dyrezan. For those records there were no limits to the risks he was willing to face.

Come an evening, when all was ready, that he explained to Ting-po what they must do. His servant had sensed something big in the works, but when he learned what it was he blanched and quailed at the thought of the deed. "Tonight we violate the tomb of the great dead ancestor?" he tremulously queried. "We break open the vault, we take from him that which he took to the grave with him? Good master, I know that you are wise and strong, and that none living can stand before you, but the dead are jealous of their sleep, this fellow maybe more than most. I hear so many stories, for these people wonder at me, since I'm not like them, and they crowd around to see me and talk all the time. I ask of your old friend Azamodias"—for faithful Ting-po could not shake the charming delusion that Bleek knew all of his people, those alive now and those of the unspecified past, especially other wizards— "I ask them, and they tell me of one young man who laughed at the dead, and climbed to the castle in search of riches, and next morning they find only his head at the foot of the big rock. Then there was another, who would make himself king with all the gold and jewels up there, who climbed up laughing, for he was not afraid, and later climbed down still laughing, and he kept laughing until he died. Then there were the others, a band of brave men who went up together, each man to protect the back of the other, and they thought themselves safe, but these people say differently, because the band never returned, only awful screams were heard that night by those who waited for them in the village below. These stories they tell me, and more too, for every man has his own story to tell, and they all make me unhappy. Your friend Azamodias is dead, you say, and you would know, knowing all as you do, but maybe something still lives up there, something without manners or respect, that is not nice to visitors." Bleek, worked to a rage by these unhelpful doubts and worries, bade his companion to shut his mouth, and do as he was told. Ting-po agreed without a moment's hesitation, though his wrinkled face was still more creased with concern, and so they stole into the night and up the shunned crag.

They lighted their torches when they reached the base, after assuring themselves that none of the superstitious villagers were about, and then they climbed. There was a path of sorts—not often used, certainly, and never maintained—a sad sort of rocky, bumpy trail which wound up an exposed, crumbling ledge. Bleek had scouted it by day, and thought himself ready for it, yet found the going more problematic by the light of sputtering torches. An icy wind tore at the men as they gained elevation, clawing at them with a cold scarcely held at bay by the fur jackets they had purchased. Along the northern face of the crag the wind was so fierce that it threatened to extinguish their light; they shielded the fires with their bodies or cupped their hands uncomfortably close to the flames. They progressed, however, for the vertical ascent was not so very high, and as hard as the climb proved, Bleek realized that it was the mystique of the place that warded off visitors, not the magnitude of the crag. Round about midnight, or a little later, they gained the summit, and strode wearily onto its remarkably flat surface. Truly, Bleek thought, Azamodias must have been an amazing fellow, to build his fortress of secrets in such a locale. There was the morbid basalt castle, barely visible under the twinkling swarms of stars; woefully dilapidated, its mighty walls broken asunder, collapsed wreckage within. Once it had been a weird marvel of the earth, and now... well, time was the unconquerable enemy to all things and to all men, except, perhaps, to Jacob Bleek.

He commanded his man to establish a camp and prepare their belongings for the duration of their stay, which would be of unknown length, depending upon the quickness of Bleek's investigations. Ting-po performed this task with his habitual skill, saying to himself all the while, "There is nothing to fear here. We dared the slope of death, yet we live, untouched. Nothing came out of the cliff to trouble us, and now that we are here, nothing walks from the castle to threaten or kill." Yet he was leery of that vast dark pile, and ever dreaded signs of furtive movement from within its awesome ruins. His master, on the other hand, was all eagerness, and scarcely were they established, with a big campfire blazing by the tents under the lee of the crumbling walls, than Bleek had entered the confines of the citadel in search of egress into its depths. Worthwhile labor, however, was impossible under such conditions, so he gave up the effort and took to his furs in order to catch some sleep before daybreak. Ting-po strenuously insisted upon standing guard until his beloved master should wake. The tired sorcerer said nothing to dissuade him.

Come the bright, cold, breezy morning, Bleek left his servant to rest for a period while he resumed his efforts under more promising circumstances. Now he could better discern the plan of the castle interior, and was able to make his way into the lower chambers of the keep. There he found only the empty rooms of black stone, their fragile furnishings having long been destroyed by the corrosive action of time and rain and snow. Knives of ice hung from the low, oppressive ceilings, with curious-looking frozen mud pools mounded below them on the dirty floors. A staircase ran upward at sharp angles, blocked by fallen stones. Another circled into the depths, also plugged by debris not far below the level of the floor, which must surely lead to the subterranean vault of Azamodias. In this case the stones would have to be moved, for Bleek wanted what he had been told was down there.

Before he had clambered back to the surface Ting-po joined him. Rising to find himself alone, the faithful easterner had come running. Bleek sent him back for tools, and when Ting-po returned they tackled the obstructions which hindered their descent into the murky realm beneath. It was tough going, but large stones can be broken into pieces, and the pieces can be removed and hauled out of the way, and where will and determination exist, there will always be progress. They chipped and shattered the rocks, manhandled them up the steps and dumped them in the chamber above. During the course of hours an impressive pile of shifted rubble grew in the room. Down below, the pair continued to inch farther downward. They passed under the masonry of the castle into bedrock, where they found their advance easier, for not so much debris had tumbled into the lower depths. Still deeper they labored, until they encountered another, more surprising difficulty: the walls of limestone fell away, to be replaced by enclosing surfaces of ice, through which the stepped path descended for a short span before terminating in a solid barrier of pure ice. Azamodias, it seemed, had built his fortress atop a cave—or he had hollowed out the crag via his demoniac arts—an ice cave, now entirely filled, or at least massively plugged. Bleek could not estimate the magnitude of the blockage, but he feared the worst, and after a period of ineffectual gouging with axes he gave up on the attempt, for the moment, and ordered a return to the camp for the day, there to refresh and reconsider.

While Ting-po cooked their meal Bleek sat by the fire, turning over the situation in his mind. If the ice barrier be too thick, he said aloud, or if the underground cavity be naught but ice, then the sharpest steel would not do the trick. Fire might serve, however, or extreme heat, generated by natural or other means. The latter course appealed to the sorcerer, and while he ate he devoted himself to study, seeking the right combination of materiel and incantation which would open the way to the subterranean vault of his eons-dead predecessor. The more he analyzed the possibilities the more he grew confident of success on the morrow, and he took to his warm bedding in excellent spirits. Not so his stout servant, who sat up glumly into the dark night pondering, as best he could, what was to come. After the wizard retired, exhausted, at dusk, his companion had wandered to the edge of the summit, there to rest and to think, staring out at the splendid view of little Crothakkias on the wide flat land this side of the isthmus, gazing upon the primeval landscape and the rolling sea. A bitter wind nipped at his wizened yellow cheeks, but he thought of more serious matters. Ting-po too feared the worst, in a very different sense than his master had done. Of course that great man would open the vault; Ting-po never doubted it—what was possible the wise Bleek would perform with alacrity, while the impossible would merely tax his cunning somewhat longer—but what then? What perils would his master gleefully embrace once they penetrated into the death chamber beneath their feet? Ting-po felt that the dangers which lay before them were more frightful than any they had previously faced. There were those absolutely dreadful stories told by the locals, and the mysterious and horrid tales of wonder told in many lands about this Azamodias. That this was a place of spirits Ting-po solemnly believed, and hostile spirits at that, though they had so far refrained from showing themselves. He disliked the thought of his adored Bleek charging heedlessly into the unknown. It occurred to him that he could yet again be of service.

"The night is young," he muttered to himself, "and I am strong. Maybe there is only a little way to go before the ice gives way. I shall take my torch and my ax and work through the quiet hours, and maybe the job will be finished when he wakes. If I find within anything unfriendly or bad, I will deal with it, or, if it's something that only my master can counter, then I will be able to offer him fair warning, and he may chant and boil and mix as he sees fit, knowing—thanks to me—what waits for him. That would be a good thing. I will do this, for him, and he will be pleased." So Ting-po returned to the camp, verified that Bleek was slumbering soundly inside his tent, and then slipped away, with a light and a tool, to carry on or complete the unhallowed task they had undertaken.

Bleek did sleep, though it was an eventful rest. His quiescent mind was disturbed by visions of Azamodias' stronghold in the days of its glory, when Krothag was a fair city of peaked houses, with polished pine walls and oiled, shingled roofs, and trading ships of distant ports docked at the base of the peninsula during the short summers. He saw that lovely black citadel brooding in the moonlight, a symbol of power and permanence, a fitting seat for a king of mages, and he thought to enter into it. This in dream he did, and immediately he was strolling, disembodied, through warm, lighted halls decorated and furnished in austere splendor. He seemed to drift into a great room containing a large, handsomely carved desk, and on that desk lay a book with a heavy leather cover, bearing no title on its front, but inscribed with the gilded outline of a circle, and within that circle the stylized representation of a multitude of staring eyes. Bleek approached, eager to examine the contents of the tome, which he knew consisted of the assembled wisdom and learning of the unseen proprietor. Then the book opened of itself, and a breeze from nowhere rustled the parchment pages, and they began to turn stiffly, faster and faster, as he tried to read them. It was no use; scarcely did he focus on one page than it turned, and the next leaf flashed into brief view, illuminated by flickering light, a tantalizing glimpse which was itself gone in an instant. Bleek woke convulsively, recognizing the drab interior of his tent, thinking that the magic he had made earlier might have granted him an image of the castle in its heyday, and then his preternatural senses detected a presence at short remove, which he assumed must be Ting-po. He crawled from beneath the canvas shelter, gazed across the dying fire, observed a dim form at the limit of observation. It was Ting-po; undoubtedly that was he, and yet Bleek's nerves tingled, snapping him to full awareness and placing him on alert. Something was wrong—his man's carriage and attitude were unlike him—and why did the gray-haired fellow stand there wan of face and regarding him gravely, silently? Bleek called gruffly to his servant, and Ting-po responded, in a listless monotone.

"Wise and benevolent master," said he, without stepping forward or moving any part of his body save his lips. His eyes, those odd eastern eyes, never blinked. "Master, know that I have always served you with all my heart, and it is my final joy to do so once more. I went inside and below while you slept, and I return to tell you these things. Do not go down to the vault. It is there, as you were told, but there is nothing for you there. What lies in the vault is not good, not kind, not helpful, nor can it truly lead to what you desire. There is great evil and danger down there, and if you go to that it will surely kill you. Please, master, do not go there. Remain where you are until the morning, and then descend the crag, and flee far away from this spot, and never think of it again. Do this, live long and happily, and think no more of Azamodias or his secrets. They are death. Think of me, if you will, and light a candle and burn incense to my memory, as is the custom of my people who would honor their ancestors. This I would have you do for me." Then a fierce wind blew, the howling of a sudden gale, and Jacob Bleek beheld an astonishing sight. His loyal companion Ting-po began to come apart and blow away like chaff in the wind, tiny fragments of him streaming away into the darkness. Within moments he was unrecognizable; within a minute he had lost identifiable human form; in another two he had completely disappeared, the last particles of dust vanishing into the close night. The wind died down to normal levels, the mystifying drama concluded, and Ting-po was gone! Bleek realized that it had not been a corporeal entity which confronted him, but the lingering shade of something that had passed beyond life, and he guessed—what proved to be the case—that he would never again see Ting-po in this world.

While Bleek had idly dreamed great matters had been afoot this night. He realized that his servant, a useful enough fellow in his own way, had taken upon himself the task of meddling where he should not, and had thus paid a grim price which was, perhaps, merely personal destruction. How the ghostly visitation had come about Bleek could not say, but the spectral occurrence thrilled him with what it suggested. There were indeed powers at work here, queer vestiges of the magic that once saturated the locale, and Bleek imagined that he was sufficiently astute to harness those waning powers for his own disposal. Anticipation devoured him; he could not wait for the dawn, but must strike while the fire blazed within his breast. Down to the cave of ice he must return, not to emerge until he had won his way through the barrier and seized that which was his by right.

With his torch, and his satchel of tools and magic, he picked his way through the ruins to the stairwell and plunged into the dark passage. Past the masonry walls, past the bedrock he went, to arrive where the dense ice had formerly brought him to a halt. Now he discovered that an evil miracle had been worked. Ting-po, certainly, had not achieved this with his puny efforts, however earnest they may have been, though that lost unfortunate's ax lay on the steps at the wizard's feet. No, someone or something else had intervened, for now the path through the ice lay open, the worn and fractured stone steps descending clear of obstruction into the inky dark. What Bleek had determined to do had been done for him.

Slowly he trod the cleared steps of basalt, downward into the interior of the curious ice cave. Presently the walls of smooth ice receded from him, opening into an expansive ice chamber, a pocket of emptiness which extended beyond the range of his torch. This room, for such it could be called—with an appearance of having been carved like stone or sculpted like clay, rather than melted or scraped—bore unfamiliar bas-relief designs cut into the glassy walls, and smudged with black, sooty matter to make them stand out. On the slippery floor he spied a collection of locked, iron-bound chests of antique make. Bleek assumed, for want of a better idea, that these chests contained the legendary treasure of Azamodias. It could be; another man would have been fascinated at the prospect, but Bleek hunted bigger game, and for the nonce broke open the ponderous lock of one chest with a steel spike solely in order to verify that the box contained nothing of greater interest to him. When he heaved up the lid a sprinkling of antique gold coins fell out and rolled away, and when he threw it back he indeed beheld a generous portion of the precious metals and gemstones which the ancient sorcerer had hoarded. Very pretty they were, and Bleek did not doubt that many men had sacrificed their lives for them, but they were not his present priority.

At the back of the ice chamber, which proved oblong in shape, he cast his gaze upon a bas-relief which he did recognize, though the knowledge derived from the weirdest of sources. It was the circular image of many eyes he had seen in his dream. This must be a portentous symbol, fraught with meaning; and it reminded him a little of the strange carvings he had beheld upon the smashed granite wreckage of Dyrezan. He immediately noticed a dark, square cavity beneath it in the floor. He approached, peered into gloom, found that the basalt stairs resumed here their course. So there was yet another level to the cave. He descended warily, for he was at this time overcome by a sense of dread, tense expectation, as though something were about to happen whether he willed it or no. Down he gingerly stepped into the narrow passage framed by ice, and then cracked black masonry swallowed him up again. He had, he knew, discovered the shunned vault of Azamodias.

What was this? A pale, sickly light spread before him, an ambient glow that irritated his eyes and even the flesh of his exposed face, and one having nothing to do with the wholesome illumination he carried. He trod upon black pavement, saw clearly stretching before him a rectangular chamber of basalt, and away toward the far wall a further scattering of heavy chests, grouped loosely about a long box of darkly glistening metal which looked very much like, and he supposed actually was, a coffin. It was a massive affair, its thick lid chased with what seemed to be geometrical or other abstract designs. He would have investigated this without delay, only he stood transfixed by the hurtful radiance which flickered and beamed from beyond the gruesome object, and by the shadowy form which stood within the feeble gleaming.

And a hollow, reverberating, icily cold voice called out to him, saying, "So you have come, Jacob Bleek. I allowed you to get this far, for I had no real desire to see your end, and I hoped that you would turn back when the difficulties of terrain and excavation defeated you. That would have been the optimal outcome. I do not gladly suffer the approach of fools, and am prone to dealing harshly with interlopers. When your man came on alone, I dealt with him after my chosen fashion, as I would with any common mortal, yet even then I returned him to you as a fair warning, and hoped you would be gone. A vain hope, as I should have known, but you are truly a kindred spirit, Bleek, and out of my mercy I offered you that last chance."

The form advanced, showing itself in the thin, nervous light which emanated from its body. There was nothing about it of wispy spirit or earth-clinging shade, but the form of a real and potent man. He loomed large, tall and heavy set, wreathed in black robes, with a high, domed forehead, his bald pate fringed with white hair. The mouth was cruel, encompassed by a mass of white beard, the nose fleshy, the hard eyes bright as ice. There might have been traces of amusement in those eyes and even, so one might fancy, a twisted tenderness, but no pity. "There is no need for introductions, Jacob Bleek. I know you, know what you are, and you know Azamodias. Do not be surprised to meet me. I perished in my time, as the greatest of men must, and was buried in this secret vault, the storehouse of my secrets which serves also as my mausoleum; yet such was my magical might of mind, the tenacity of my trained and lore-enhanced intellect, that my consciousness has not entirely departed from the vicinity of my remains. The coffin harbors my carcass, frozen by the eternal ice which preserves rather than disintegrates, and while the shell exists, protected by the frigid conditions from the gnawing of the worm, it may be that the effluvia of my brain shall haunt these precincts. Think not of me as a ghost; though my organic remnants lie stony within their case of bronze, this is the genuine flesh of willpower standing before you, and it is the true essence of Azamodias which shall destroy you."

Bleek, without further hesitation, commenced a spell of death, such as would lay low any normal man. Azamodias chuckled to himself throughout the recitation, and when it was finished, and nothing of note had transpired, he laughed, a ghastly sound like the throbbing peal of a funereal bell. "Would you say me down?" he asked. "You can not kill me, Jacob Bleek; I am already dead, in a curious state of decease, having left but not gone. I would discuss

166

it with you, as we could discuss many things, but we must postpone that talk, for it is your time to die, perhaps to dwell with me in the vault, more likely to cross over as you should. I bring doom upon you but, my friend, do not confuse yourself with wild imaginings of my hostility. There is none. You are myself of another age, and the one service I can perform for you is to take your life, and put an end to your journey.

"I know why you have come, Jacob Bleek; I know what you seek, and what you would do with it if you could. Think hard, O wizard, giant of your kind, and feel my sincerity. I conceal nothing from you, as you can hide nothing from me. So you would behold the Gods, the Old Ones who are the Lords of All Things, and wrest from Them Their secrets? And you believe that my wisdom can lead you to Them? In that you are correct. These sealed chests contain treasure, but not the base baubles you found above. Rather, they hold the massed records of my wisdom, the knowledge acquired from all the olden seats of magical power, including—hark to this!—including what I was able to derive from the rotting annals of fallen Dyrezan. I saw it in an age when its rubble retained somewhat of its glory, and its mysteries had not wholly faded away. These chests hold that and more. Therein you could find precise descriptions of the vortices and how they function, how the Gods employ them to stride about our world and to far stars, and to the unimaginable beyond. Nor is that all I can offer you. It is crucial to your quest that you find a living vortex. I tell you that, within the metal casket, beneath my frozen corpse, lies a book, my book of ultimate secrets. Among its revealed wonders you would find a map which marks the geographical location of every existing vortex, including the most powerful of all, that most favored of the Gods. It is all there, Jacob Bleek, for you as it was for me; and yet, as I chose, at the last, not to employ that foul knowledge, so shall I prevent you from doing so!"

Azamodias struck at Bleek, without movement, without fanfare. Suddenly Bleek buckled and dropped, gasping, to one knee. "It is no use," intoned the dead-in-life warlock to his victim, "it was never any use. Your quest, like mine before, is founded upon false premises. I learned the truth, as I was being drawn in by vain beliefs, and I recoiled, just in time, from the monstrous reality. Others before me were not so fortunate. You know the legend of Dyrezan and its masters: the great and noble men of that city, giants of wisdom who walked and talked with the Gods. I learned enough from their wreckage to marvel at their achievements, and to discern the nature of their fate. Do not console yourself with puerile romances of natural disasters, cosmic vengeance, or misbegotten hubris which annihilated them. They did not deviate from the path; they held to it surely, as I meant to do— as you would if able—and it lead them to oblivion. Their final folly was to learn what you would learn, and it finished them! The knowledge of ultimate reality broke them, overthrew their plans, throttled their dreams. They could not go on, knowing what they knew, so their civilization, and their glorious city of the sky, died. So too they perished. I uncovered the bare beginnings of what they learned in its totality, and my slender wisdom was almost too much for me. I halted my research; I refrained from further exploration, though I had the requisite information in hand; I gladly returned home to die! I stopped for the good of my soul. I would not accept the destiny of the fallen heroes of Dyrezan. You, too, must be stopped, for your own sake, brother, though I see that your will is too strong to succumb to argument."

Bleek hurled at him a spell which should have banished any spirit. It was a chance that availed him not. Azamodias did not flinch, but hammered again at Bleek's mind, and the living sorcerer collapsed, writhing on the floor. "Know you," queried Azamodias, "of the mighty name Xenophor?" Bleek weakly acknowledged that he did—indeed he knew the word, for it was the disquieting, indecipherable term from the Rhexellite plates—a riddle which had continued to fascinate, though he admitted now that it meant nothing to him. "It is a name beyond horror, beyond foulness, beyond sanity!" shrieked his tormentor. "Xenophor, Master of Creation and Destruction— Xenophor, King of the Gods—Xenophor, Lord of All Things, who rules supreme in heaven and on earth; Xenophor, the most cunning of Serpents. He exists. He is the fundamental reality underlying all. He can offer you what you desire. Will you bow down and serve Him, as you must if you proceed on your road to self-damnation? Would you do that, Jacob Bleek? I could not, though I strove to placate him by cherishing his everlasting symbol: He of the Million Eyes that never sleep, but see all and know all. And yet you would accept Him into your heart and mind; that you would, with ignorant joy. Not if I save you from yourself, however. Before you cease to be, let me tell you the particulars of the vile fate that awaits those who are impressed into or volunteer for His service."

Bleek heard no more. With a despairing effort he struck at his enemy, which was not the man Azamodias nor his eidolon, but rather the magic which the fearsome mage of centuries past wielded as a weapon, and which still maintained his quasi-existence in this world. Bleek croaked the vile, the despised—the professionally abhorrent—Spell of Obliteration, that which attacked the essence of magic itself. Wizards dreaded the spell, rightly shunning it, for it bit as savagely at those who delivered as at those who received. He spoke the olden words—chanted them in a bare whisper, yet they resounded throughout the vault—Azamodias opened his mouth to shout, yet no words issued—he gesticulated wildly—he ceased to be! On the instant the dead one vanished from sight, and the ugly, hurtful light faded away, and Bleek was left to himself, almost in a swoon, weak as a babe, feeling as if death had come for him at last.

It was not, however, his appointed time. Overdue though it might be, the end of his life and career were once more postponed. Bleek had guessed well. Magic was the major part of his being, to be sure, but he still possessed a natural heart that beat, and lungs that billowed, and brain that thought. His human, or his animal, functions, those fundamental systems of corporeal processes that form the framework of feeble life, were sufficient to sustain him, by some slender margin. The great, the invincible Azamodias, his spirit held together solely by utter magic, on the other hand had possessed no remedial support at all for his being, so the oblique attack succeeded. He was gone.

Bleek ailed, but he lived. The power of magic was as much a matter of knowledge as it was an essence, and that power would return to him, so long as his body remained intact. At first he could do nothing but moan unhappily and miserably. Then he crawled to his torch and fed anew the sputtering light with fresh flame. When a modicum of strength had returned, and he could feel the red blood pulsing through his veins, he staggered to his feet and immediately, if slowly, made his way to the grim container that formed the centerpiece of the vault. That coffin he would open, and he did, after much exhausting effort, and there he beheld the mortal remains of his storied predecessor. Azamodias looked much as he had in life, though livid and leathery. In these frigid precincts the worm had not gnawed, nor time considerably defaced, the nobility and brilliance which once dwelt there. A strange and curious moment, one suitable, perhaps, for reflection upon the odd ways of fate and time. Bleek struggled with the heavy corpse, pulled it up from its eternal resting place, and dumped it unceremoniously upon the floor. In the coffin, within a small recess below the dead sorcerer's former resting place, he found the book of Azamodias, the very book of his dream in every particular, including the evil, multi-eyed symbol of unspeakable Xenophor on the ragged cover. This book he extracted and made his own.

There was much else that he planned to take with him before he put the vault, the castle, and the forlorn site of the ancient city of Krothag behind him. Before he left this place he would ransack the chests for all the wisdom of the ages that he could carry with him; and there was base treasure in plenty, as well, which he need not entirely disdain, for it would pay his way and that of his cargo. For now, though, he had thoughts only for the book, which in time he would read, translate, and decipher. Before he gave attention to food, or drink, or other bodily cares, he perused that book, examining every fragile page, until he came upon the one he eagerly sought. There it was, the priceless map of Azamodias, his amazing map of all the world, and the locations of the celestial vortices. Never had Bleek seen its like. Was this truly the earth on which he resided? He recognized portions, could puzzle out others based on his travels, while vast regions were lands of total mystery to him. The vortices were clearly marked and labeled in old Latin, the geographical points denoted by tiny spirals of rainbow coloration. There were quite a few of them, though widely scattered. The dead vortex of

Dyrezan, he now saw, had been ever the most readily accessible, so there had always been logic in making for that place, however great his initial disappointment. One vortex—in a far, far land—was marked differently from the rest, symbolized by a minute circle with many smaller circles or ovals within. That, he knew without further research, was the Great Vortex, toward which he must guide his feet.

He would learn more presently, but he knew much now. To the Great Vortex he must go, heedless of peril or cost. No man should stand in his way, no spirit dare hinder him. The Gods Themselves he would defy, though They threaten and bluster. In time he would come to Them, and he would deal with Them, and of this They could be sure: such was his determination to win for himself the sources of all power and knowledge—such was his might—that when he did finally meet with Them, it would be on his terms, at his dictation.

X. The Mountain of the Old Ones

In the course of his great quest the marvelous wizard Jacob Bleek, that man of guile and wiles and mystery, did come home again, as other men might be accustomed to think of such matters; for he came again to the Europe that he had known in former days, and during his travels across the continent he passed through or by the scenes of his earlier adventures and triumphs. These storied locales were of no consequence to him, nor was it a matter of personal satisfaction to him that he shortly made his way to the seaport town of Bruges, the scene of his youth and early, remarkable education, where he had grown to manhood and made of himself, at a tender age, a force to be reckoned with in the august ranks of the esoteric scholars. He did not return to Bruges with the achievements of life behind him, prepared to bask in glory and contentment; no, it was, rather, yet another destination, one more stop, on the long road which stretched behind and before. The journey was not yet over; another fantastic expedition lay ahead, and in order to accomplish that Bleek required a port with ships and men, and Bruges had those things, and he knew the city and its ways, or had once done, so that place would serve him as well as any. He drove into Bruges through neighborhoods which were familiar to him, with their narrow lanes were he had walked and their markets where he had purchased books and talismans, and he passed near the house where he had dwelt as a student, but he thought nothing of these. He arrived with money, and possessions, and the fruits of his magical collecting and delving, and made straight away for the wharves and the docks of the waterfront, for what he presently sought was to be found there.

Among his effects Bleek carried the complete lore and wisdom as transcribed by the ancient sorcerer Azamodias, especially that prized possession, which he now held as his personal property, the fabulous map of Azamodias. This was a curious document, one as yet unlike any produced by mariners or cartographers. It revealed to him the existence, far across the sea to the west, of a vast land, a whole new world on the other side of the earth, and there, in a remote region of that land, the exact location of the Great Vortex of the Old Ones, the main portal through which, Bleek was given to understand, the ultimate Gods of the universe come and go, and through which They can most readily be approached. Such a place actually existed—or had in the dim past and might still—and it was definitively marked on the map. Bleek, that old and experienced traveler, could follow any map, so, knowing the geographical coordinates of his goal, it was simply a question of how to get there. First he must cross the ocean, and for that he needed a ship.

Ship and crew were to be had by any man with the requisite funds. Bleek carried the treasure of kings in his chests—of kings, some would say, though it truly came from the ruined citadel of a dead wizard—so price was no obstacle. To a seafaring merchant of Bruges he presented a straightforward offer: an ox-load of gold and jewels, in return for a sturdy ship. The offer was swiftly accepted. To the merchant's best captain, he made another offer: a princely sum, on which the master seaman could retire if he chose, in return for one voyage of indefinite duration, to an uncharted location, and a subsequent march on land of some length. This offer, too, was accepted, with certain questions being asked and brusquely ignored. Then, to the handpicked crew of stout sailors, still another offer: top wages, with a magnificent bonus at the end of the voyage, if they would agree to convey Bleek whither he would go, without murmur or complaint or quarrelsome restlessness. Not every man approached would accept this deal—none of them were fools, while all of them were superstitious where matters of the sea were concerned—but enough of them eventually did accept to complete the ship's complement, and all of these swore on numerous profane sailor's oaths to obey Bleek at all times, and to follow without hesitation whatever course their salaried captain should set for them.

Deals struck, bargains made, the ship's hold loaded as if for an impossibly long voyage, and one fine morning, when the winds and the tide were right, Jacob Bleek and his crew of the good brig *Gloriosa* set sail. As a trading vessel the ship and her master, a worthy old salt named Piter Hoch, were wont to make stops at many ports, but the new master had taken her in charge, and he directed his captain and crew through the channel and charted a course, south by west, into the unknown. The men chafed at their instructions, for they knew little of the world beyond the confines of their old and familiar trading routes, but their wages were to be envied, so they congratulated themselves on their good fortune and held their tongues.

Ever west and south they sailed across the wide, empty, placid sea. In the evenings Bleek would perform his calculations by the stars, ordering the course to be held or adjusted as he found fitting. With the captain he conversed little, with the crew not at all, preferring to remain in his cabin mostly, poring over his manuscripts and scratching reams of notes with his quill. Piter Hoch was complacent, for he stood to acquire riches to set him for life, but the hired hands grew querulous as the voyage continued, days giving way to weeks, without landfall. They did not especially care for Bleek and his solitary, furtive, and mysterious ways, and the farther their homes and families receded to the east, the less grateful they were for their promised wages, and the more they doubted the safety, and even the piety, of the cruise. The potential hazards loomed larger in their minds, and they began to question—among themselves at first, then to Captain Hoch—the point of the expedition. They carried nothing to sell, and they knew not whither they were going. It began to seem a bad business to them, and imagination conspired to conceive all manner of perils known or unknown. Finally, after the first big blow swept down upon them, and the storm had tossed about the *Gloria* for two strenuous days atop mountainous waves, the crew grew alarmingly restive.

Hoch notified Bleek of brewing trouble. The latter dismissed the subject by alluding to the terms of their contract, and went on with his studies. He was entranced by documents, in Azamodias' hand, relating to the great God Xenophor, whose name still gave Bleek qualms whenever he dared whisper it to himself. He would not be distracted by trivial difficulties, when horrifying and splendid secrets beckoned to and tantalized him. Meanwhile the crew grew surly by degrees. They still obeyed orders, but their servile snap was gone, and they came to begrudge the simplest commands. Behind Bleek's back they hissed and catcalled, a common enough practice among sailors, but though they vented steam, the pressure continued to build. Another week passed, while the stars rotated in the heavens, and no land appeared, and the supplies of food and water dwindled, and a delegation, led by a common seaman, approached Hoch with formal requests for information. The request was passed on to Bleek, who casually responded with allusions to uncharted lands requiring exploration. This answer did not suit, and shortly the delegation demanded a timetable for the voyage, a firm date by which they must turn back. Annoyed, Bleek broke his routine long enough to address the men, curtly insisting that they cease their muttering and do as they were told. He made it clear that he would brook no interference with his plans, threatening dire punishment to the complainants.

The leader of the delegation called his own private assembly of interested parties on the stern deck, urging action. He advised seizing the ship, before they were hopelessly lost to the world they knew, and steering a course for home. Hoch intruded, for he feared such unauthorized gatherings, and demanded that the men disperse. To his dismay, a hard core of malcontents refrained from immediate obedience. Harsh words passed back and forth, and the chief delegate, accepting at his followers' behest an exalted position of power, leveled his own demands. At this point Jacob Bleek appeared on the scene.

Bleek intoned, in a sibilant whisper, the frightful Spell of Dissolution, and thereupon something terribly evil happened to the mutinous leader. The men recoiled in horror from the sickening mess, and even Captain Hoch could summon only enough courage to request proper burial. But no; Bleek ordered the vile remains cast unceremoniously overboard, and threatened a similar fate for all who tried to disrupt the voyage in the future. He assumed that would settle the matter, for terror is a potent weapon, yet he judged wrongly, for fearful, desperate men are capable of extraordinary actions. Though the crew dared not confront him to his face, their hatred of Bleek drove them to new conspiracies. One evening, not long thereafter, they cunningly insinuated a dreadful poison into his food, one bite of which was like to end him. Unfortunately for them their intended victim detected the ploy, and later that night two sailors, seemingly chosen at random, died in a noisy and lingering manner which defied conventional description. On the following morning a lone, very courageous, sailor attempted to approach Bleek from behind in a narrow, darkened passage below decks, the man carrying something long and sharp and metallic in his hand. Above decks the men waited silently, expectantly, for the result. Imagine their distress when the would-be assassin appeared before them with seaman's knife in hand, crying out loudly for mercy and salvation, and staggered awkwardly, as if compelled, to the railing, and climbed up, balancing precariously, and there slowly but surely raised the knife and drew it across his own throat, at which he screamed and plunged from the side of the ship into the sea. Then Bleek emerged from the lower darkness, and the men scattered to their posts.

How it might have ended none could say, for after this series of grotesque events even Hoch walked in dread of his employer, and was driven to make common cause with his crew, but on the very next day the lookout sighted land, and for the moment different concerns loomed large. The *Gloriosa* sailed along the unfamiliar coast until her captain spied a safe natural harbor, and there he put in. Then Bleek took charge, dictating that camp be made on shore, and his belongings unloaded. This was carried out as ordered. He also told off, for the morrow, the sailors who should serve as his porters for the overland journey to come, and delivered explicit instructions to the captain for the disposition of the ship while all members of the party, save only a small watch, should continue the journey on foot. All this Bleek required, and captain and crew agreed to everything, even when warned that much travel remained before them; but, given the sad state of affairs as it had developed, the shunned warlock had little doubts as to what would follow so soon as he turned his back. His greatest fears proved correct: while he slept that night, far apart from the others for security, in a hidden place among a dense stand of trees, his opportunistic hirelings, forsaking the wealth he had promised them, re-boarded the *Gloriosa* and sailed away, being already out of sight when he woke on the morn and rushed down to the water's edge. They had taken no chances on his intervening, for in their haste they had thought only to save themselves and place distance between themselves and he whom they feared, and most of the offloaded supplies remained on the beach untouched, despite the fact that the ship had contained little to sustain life. Bleek could only wish that the traitors, as he deemed them, would meet a deservedly miserable fate on the high seas.

So Jacob Bleek found himself alone, stranded, on an unknown shore, cut off from his world with no obvious means of return, friendless and defenseless save for his formidable esoteric skills and knowledge. His situation was most unpleasant, for he was nowhere near his destination. He knew, from the wonderful map of Azamodias, that he stood on the verge of a vast, unexplored continent, and that the Great Vortex which he sought lay somewhere within the remote interior, hundreds of leagues from his present position. With no men to serve him he would have to complete the journey on his own, carrying what few necessaries he could on his back, along with the most vital documents of import to his quest. He would have to live off the land, and to seek such aid as he could from the inhabitants along his route, if there be any such, and if they be disposed to help him.

A hundred monks could fill a hundred volumes in recounting the tale of Bleek's journey across the unknown western lands, and still not tell the whole story. There are adventures that could be described: marches, staff in hand, through endless dank forests and steaming swamps and burning deserts, the scaling of awesome mountain ranges, the crossing of majestic rivers. One might multiply accounts of strange animals and unusual plants not found elsewhere on earth. One could read of the incredible privations that he faced, the accidents on the march, the incidents of hunger and exposure to inclement elements which rivaled or surpassed his former experiences in wild or exotic realms. There are the myriad meetings with the unusual inhabitants of those lands, the tribes of coppery-colored men belonging to a new race hitherto unknown to him, who lived in primitive fashion, dwelling in small villages and skulking after game in the woods or farming little plots by the streams. With these people Bleek necessarily had much to do, for intercourse with them was critical to his survival during the long months and years that he trudged ever onward toward his goal. By turns they were friendly, hostile, or wary of the newcomer, but regardless of their stance he must needs deal with them, making common cause when possible, terrorizing them with his magic when circumstances dictated, or fleeing from them when he failed to overawe their strength and instead kindled their anger. In the better times (and Bleek was a wise and cunning fellow, so he always attempted, according to his reasoning, to smooth his path among the natives) he lived with them in a manner resembling comfort, learning from them what stuffs in nature were edible and which were not, gaining information on the best and safest routes westward, and ever plaguing his hosts with demands for lore pertaining to his quest. In the bad times—and there were many, for Bleek was not always the most congenial of guests—he crept through the wilderness like an animal, living a pathetic hand to mouth existence, subsisting on berries and roots and what small creatures he could catch in his desperation. Through good times and bad he consulted the stars, consulted his map, through sheer cleverness and willpower forcing himself onward, step by weary step, toward the anticipated glory that awaited him at the terminus of the long trail. He consulted his dreams, on occasion, for as he delved deeper into the forbidding and barren lands of the farther west weird dreams came to him, visions stimulated by his dark arts, which seemed to hint at otherworldly marvels lurking ahead.

All this could be described in ponderous detail, yet that epic march was for Bleek but the means to an end, another hurdle requiring surmounting, and from his standpoint it suffices to say that he accomplished the trek, and there came a time when he sensed that his long journey, which had consumed the span of a human lifetime since he first set out upon the road in the last blush of youth, approached its conclusion. One warm afternoon, following many hours of scrambling through a parched region of limestone ridges and scrubby, needled trees, he strode forth through a windswept pass and beheld stretching before him a spacious valley ringed by mountains, an oddly circular valley extending to the far horizon which bore, to his imagination, the appearance of having been carved or stamped out of the surrounding terrain by forces other than natural. If he had read surely the map of Azamodias, if the dreams which increasingly festered by night hinted rightly, then this was the place marked with the ugly little symbol of the many eyes; somewhere out there in the broad expanse below he should find the exact location of the gateway of the Gods. Along the rim of that curiously regular stony bowl he sought the local inhabitants, who were easy enough to find, for in this area the red men dwelt in large, crude houses or even castles of plastered mud and rock. Shortly he discovered such a village on a high point, a single big structure with many rooms where lived a tribe of a hundred extensive families, and he parleyed with them in such of their language as he had previously learned from related peoples, and they accepted him with the customary reservations, for as always they knew not at first what to make of the pale stranger. Bleek spooked them with his tale of a long lifetime of travel, for he did not look so old as he claimed, but something in his manner convinced them that he spoke with veracity, so they treated him as a favored one and gladly responded to his peculiar, even impertinent questions. He pressed them for their knowledge of the strange valley, and they proved to have much of interest to tell him.

His primary informant, the chief or priest—perhaps both—of the tribe, was a venerable gentleman named Tonipah, who wore the skins of wolves, and feathers in his hair, and dabbed red and blue ocher on his face; steeped in the lore of his people, he told of the valley as best he could, eking out his tale with signs when speech failed him. The notions which he merely volunteered, without prompting, thrilled Bleek with their implications. The valley, said the old man, was known to hoary legend as the abode of the Gods, where They dwelt in ancient times when the world was young, and where They were still prone to pass when the moon and the stars were right, and the black clouds gathered over the hills, and the lightning flashed down onto the highest peaks of the land. Tonipah, as he made clear, spoke not of the trivial gods who bless the tribes as they choose, but the Old Ones, the primordial Gods, the masters and makers of all things. He actually mentioned—in a shuddering whisper—the dread name of great Xenophor, that ominous grouping of syllables which represented, wherever it was spoken on earth, the supreme power underlying the universe, the King of the Gods, a being so all-encompassing that the other original Gods, however They were differentiated, might truly be no more than cosmic facets of His grimly immense totality. The Valley of the Old Ones was Their kingdom, and though it was a fertile land, with flowing water, lush grain, and many delectable game animals, it was not a good place for man. Many eager tribes had wandered into the valley, seeking to live there amongst plenty and be happy, but misery had come to them instead of happiness. There was something about the valley, in the air or in the rocks, not healthful to those who sought long residence. This was true for all things that lived: plants grew strangely there, assuming frightening forms, and beasts developed unusual sizes and peculiar shapes, while men sickened and even died there in disproportionate numbers and without understandable cause, just as their children tended to be born lame, or feeble, or misshapen. Throughout the ages the story had been the same, with many men coming, only a few leaving, the rest lost, struck down by the remorseless emanations of the Gods. Their castles and villages lay empty now, in ruins, prowled at night by the wolves and the native lions. The valley was a holy place, sacred to and cherished by the worshippers who lived about the rim where normal habitation was possible, but it was not a good place. Such was the wisdom of the Old Ones, the wisdom of eternal Xenophor, who knows all, sees all, and acts as He will.

Bleek averred that he would meet the Gods, and gaze into the thousand eyes of Xenophor Himself, at which Tonipah drew back affrighted, declaring that it was sacrilege to speak of such things. There was a shrine, he admitted, a natural temple of blood-colored rock which rose like a tower from the floor of the valley, to which daring pilgrims were wont to go, for from the top of that high red spire one could gaze, from a safe distance, upon the Mountain of the Old Ones, where it was said that Xenophor held court. Tonipah himself had visited as a priest the wonderful temple that the Gods had fashioned for believers in the elder times, and he gazed upon the mountain, and dreamed strange dreams in its presence. The generous old man offered to lead Bleek to the crimson crags of that summit which served as the cathedral of his people (an offer which the wizard accepted at once), for the devout ought to travel that far, but no farther. Tonipah cautioned that no man should attempt to scale the rightly shunned Mountain of the Old Ones, and furthermore that no man could, as the white stranger could soon learn for himself, if he were crazed enough to attempt the forbidden feat.

Bleek urged his host to make ready with haste, for—as he told it—he desired to pray within the red rock cathedral. Tonipah agreed that they would set out for the sacred shrine in the morning, and reach it by nightfall. That suited Bleek's plan's perfectly. He knew quite well, from all that he had heard and deduced, that the great Vortex was to be found atop this Mountain of the Old Ones, and if the reverent Tonipah would lead him to within sight of the prize, then Bleek could somehow, no matter what it took, complete the rest of the journey on his own. That evening he slept well in a small chamber set aside for him, after a welcome meal of dried venison and pounded grain stew provided by the folk of the tribe, who were impressed by his apparent piety. He slept well indeed, but in the morning it seemed to him that his rest had been filled with visions of lights and sounds and motions that he could neither identify nor decipher upon awakening.

Tonipah and Bleek descended into the valley, the women honoring their departure with song, the men with the bellowing of talking drums; but no one chose to accompany them. The elderly red man allowed that very few wished to make the pilgrimage these days, relying rather on the infrequent reports of their wise men. The pair entered the valley, finding the going easy, advancing rapidly across the rolling plain and along the fecund streams. During the course of their progression Bleek noted some of the floral and faunal peculiarities of which he had heard, and wise Tonipah pointed out still others to him. Once they spied a spectacular ruin on a ridge overshadowing the river they were fording, an impressive site which resembled a secure fortress, now overgrown by large spiny plants the size of trees. Bleek wondered that such a choice dwelling should be vacant, but his guide assured him that it was so, nothing stirring there under the hot sun but fat, multi-colored lizards and swollen black spiders, both extremely poisonous.

They entered a region where all the rocks were red, of a hue that did suggest fresh blood, and before them there rose gradually into view a high hill, and atop that there loomed a chaotic, massy jumble of red stone that assumed varying morbid forms dependent upon minute gradations in the angle of viewpoint. From one angle it appeared as a crumbling tower lost to time, with strewn rubble at its base, while from another it looked much like a solid structure, a sort of building chiseled by giants, with one steeply raised end in the manner of a platform. This stony pile, with its peculiar aspects of unusually shifting geometry, was the so-called shrine or temple, provided by a surprisingly architecturally minded nature. By the lowering sun of the late afternoon they hiked the rocky trail which wound up its slopes, and before the light began to fade they had attained the summit and stood in the lee of the incredible walls and spires of bloody stone. A path more suitable for a goat than a man led upward into that rocky wilderness, a path which Tonipah negotiated with practiced ease while his guest struggled. They reached the level of the rugged platform which capped the highest peak of stone, and Bleek gazed out upon the landscape before him on the far side, and he gasped in astonishment.

He looked out upon a rough plain backed by sheer cliffs of red, cliffs pierced by the entrances into mysterious canyons that wound into the bluffs and vanished in the mystery of distance. In the center of this plain, rising up to heights incalculable, rose a vast cubical mass of night-black stone, a titanic mountain the likes of which no other land could boast. Nor would any other land be eager to do so, for there was something not right, not wholesome, not pleasing to the eye in that weird vista. The ugly black rock of which the mountain was composed resembled nothing found in the area; it was unique, stark, eerie, hinting at a graceless state of counter-naturalism. The base of the mountain appeared distressingly regular, as if shaped by hands that could sweep away cities with a swipe. From the base the objectionably angular walls (for one could not speak of slopes) rose vertically in a solid mass, up, up into the scanty clouds, to where the top (for one could not speak of a peak) terminated in a perfectly flat plain of enormous extent, a world of its own raised above the common world. From what Bleek could tell the amazing edifice constituted a solid cube, perfectly formed save where the weathering of eons beyond number had dented its unholy symmetry. It frightened him to look at it, indeed it did, for he sensed that this was something that did not belong, something that had not risen from the earth through the known or guessable operations of time and nature, but rather been placed or dropped here by forces beyond the imagination, powers for whom the world and the universe were but trivial playthings. It was something not of this world or of sanity as men know it, but something wholly, inescapably *other*.

"Behold," cried Tonipah, "the Mountain of the Old Ones!" Bleek did not require this announcement, for there could be no doubt on that score; nor did he relish the advice that his companion now proffered. "This far we may go, and here we may remain in safety, if we tarry not long, but no farther must we go. The great Gods who frown down upon Their creation are jealous and cruel; They hear our supplications with amusement, reject our advances with contempt, and are wont to break those toys which do not perform as They would have it. The Mountain of the Old Ones is forbidden to all men; to approach it is sure death. Here in Their temple we will pray, here we will sleep, and in the morning we will return to the abode of men."

The coming of dawn found Jacob Bleek far away. That wizard had waited until Tonipah snored and then slipped away with his bag of provisions and magic, heading down the far side of the steep hill, where no trail existed to ease his progress. Morning light found him on the plain, a tall, gaunt figure cloaked in black, his broad-brimmed hat shielding him from the warming sun, his long staff pawing the ground as he marched. Behind him rose the red rocks, from this angle appearing as a large, bloody hand grasping at the sky, while before him stood the strange dark mountain. By the time the sun hovered overhead he stood at the base of the mountain, where he paused briefly, considering what he must do. That colossal, cubic tower of stone was, truly, never intended for climbing. It seemed to be formed from nothing more than a series of impossible cliff faces. There were, however, slim fissures cracked and scoured by the scrabbling fingers of time which offered possibilities. He set out on a walk around the base, his eyes peeled for useful indicators. Presently he came to a thin gap in the intimidating wall of harshly black rock, a kind of ravine choked by stunted, spiky shrubs, with something slightly resembling steps smoothed by the action of running water. The narrow gorge, which apparently wound up and into the cliff face for some distance, was bone dry now, and Bleek thought he could manage it at least so far as he could see. He entered this fissure, and the bulk of the mountain swallowed him.

For a hot, tiring spell he clambered through this passage, rough walls and sere, snaky vegetation enclosing him. Then he emerged under a rock shelter gouged from the cliff, and from this vantage he could gaze out upon the plain and surrounding ridges, and glimpse the far red temple, which was already beneath him. He saw that the sky had changed, becoming dark and menacing, with the fierce sun nowhere in evidence. The gloomy clouds clustered about the high top of the mountain, with daggers of lightning darting down to blast the grim stone. The sounds of thunder rolled and reverberated among the rocks, and Bleek imagined that he detected other sounds, barely concealed by the low rumbling, sounds almost like words, words in a language he could not classify, a dim shouting which echoed interminably from every plane and surface of the unearthly black pile from which he dangled precariously like a fly.

Acutely examining the position, he thought he spied a narrow ledge creeping off to the right. This way he went, and did find a continued foothold, a deliriously dangerous path on which he would not have trod for all the money in the world, and which only the greatest of cosmic boons could lure him to attempt. One misstep, the slightest false scraping of loose gravel with his frayed boot, would have sent him plunging hopelessly to his death. The ledge proved lengthy, then steep, tipping sharply upward, while the sky darkened perceptibly, and he dreaded the real and grotesque chance of being pinned to that ledge when night fell. Already he received more illumination from lightning than from the shrouded sun. He would have lighted a torch if his hands were free, or conjured a spell of radiance had he maneuvering room by which to reach the magical items in the pack on his back. As he was growing frantic with worry the ledge widened into a modest platform, and there he collapsed, exhausted and sore, lying there breathlessly and long before he could drive himself to make a camp.

There were sticks and bits of dry scrub with which to kindle a fire, which he needed less for warmth than for light, and to ward off hostile animals. No creatures of this world appeared to menace him, however, nor, for that matter, had he seen any beasts since commencing his climb of the mystic mountain. Even the birds seemed to shun the place, so he was able to sleep free of molestation or company, assailed only by the awesome boom of thunder and the dreams, which returned to disrupt his quiescence in full force. Again he remembered mainly a chaotic, random series of sight and sound impressions, a blurred, kaleidoscopic jumble of obscurely horrible sensations which twice jolted him awake. Both times he returned to consciousness aware of a sense that something vast and formless had been peering down at him as from a great distance, awakening each time when it seemed to rush violently toward him. After the second, weirdly distressing experience, he slept no more, but crouched by the dying fire, fashioning a meager meal, until the dismal, fog-smothered sun rose amorphously, sufficient to allow his ascent to continue.

He resumed the climb under deplorable conditions, a warm, damp mist cutting off all view of the world beyond the gigantic black cube to which he clung, closing in and concealing all beyond a few rods. Now he could not plan nor calculate his march, being reduced to struggling forward a handful of steps before previously hidden terrain appeared to confound and perplex him. Progress, of course, was pitifully slow. Thunder rumbled at all times, occasionally preceded by a muted flash which did little to alleviate the dank, impenetrable gray gloom. He could not keep track of the time when he could not judge the direction of the sun, nor measure the rate of his advancement in the absence of landmarks. He knew it was daytime, and that somewhere on the earth far below him the skies were bright and clear and cheerful, but none of that meant anything to him now. He walked, he squeezed through briar-choked clefts in the rocks, he scrambled over piles of weathered stone, for an endless age he did these things and naught else until, without any prior warning, as a still denser gloom closed in around him, he found himself treading easily upon a broad and curiously level surface. A few minutes more confirmed his hopes: Jacob Bleek had reached the top.

Visibility was even worse up here, so after gingerly walking along the edge of the frightful precipice for a period he took the bull by the horns and plunged into the unknown, unseen interior of the upper plain, lighting a torch to guide his way as the inky night fell. The black rock of the surface was worn, cracked, and pitted, but otherwise offered no obstacle to sound footing. As he went aimlessly on across that huge horizontal face he noticed that the unpleasantly dry and spiky bushes had disappeared. Nothing known to man lived or grew at this rarefied height. He made out, far away to his front, a flickering sequence of flashes resembling lightning, and he waited expectantly for the dull throbbing of thunder, but it did not come. Pausing, he considered for a long, ghastly moment what he was seeing. That was not lightning; something else lay ahead of him that flickered, twinkled, and winked in an array of rapidly shifting colors, white, red, yellow, blue, now indigo and green, all emanating from a narrowly circumscribed location. With quickening steps he made for the source of the strange lights. As Bleek approached he felt an invisible barrier rise up before him, tangible though unseen, a wall of fear that strove to check his journey on the verge of its culmination. This was not his imagination; something real barred the way, gripping his boots to slow his pace, gripping his heart and filling him with sickly dread. No common mortal could have withstood that force, but there was nothing common left inside Jacob Bleek; he had expended the long span of an unnaturally enhanced lifetime to reach this place, a span in which he had grown incredibly wise and incredibly hard. Fear was an enemy, like all others to be pulverized and skewered, so he mastered this enemy as he had all of his enemies, striding onward with his head high, and so he came in time to the cave.

A heap of large, angular boulders marred the alarming smoothness of the plain, a startling mass which rose incongruously from the flatness, a strange jumble which he imagined had been grouped by cunning rather than by nature. From a wide cleft in this black pile there radiated the lights, now harshly flashing and flickering. Weathered markings about the opening, scratched into the rock face, might have been intended to represent a myriad of baleful eyes. If so, he wondered who had carved them, and whether the artist had suffered for his daring. As he entered the cleft the variously colored lights winked painfully like exploding stars, then subsided into a homogenous carmine glow emanating from somewhere before him. He discarded the torch, then marched down a narrowing stone passageway deep into the interior. He found himself, presently, squeezing through at last upon the verge of a cave, a wide, high rock room of jagged, irregular shape, with walls of multifaceted stones, oddly angled stones with edges sharp as razors. He stepped, cautiously, further into the chamber, the walls receding from him, obscured by the glow which spread about him like mist, so that he could hardly make out the spatial confines of the cave. A curious sound now drew his attention, a sound which thrilled yet which annoyed, for he thought it like a sort of mocking tittering, as if something laughed at him. It seemed to come from above.

Bleek turned up his head, lifting his gaze to the dimly perceived ceiling, and as he did so the tittering swelled and burst into a cacophony of harsh, discordant mirth. This might have irked him still more, only he was too astonished to feel a petty slight, due to the grotesque sight which he now beheld. Things hung from that craggy ceiling; very strange, very terrible things like the disquieting leavings of a ghastly nightmare. They crouched as they hung, hunched and huddled like giant bats, with broad, leathery, membranous wings that fluttered and flapped nervously as the creatures jostled among themselves for a firm perch. He thought of bats, because of the wings, and the claws of the hind feet which scrabbled on stone, and the clumsy claws of the ugly hands, the big, pointed ears and the wide fanged mouths; yet the initial thought was error, for they were not bats. There was something manlike in their overall form, a kind of distorted humanity in those repulsive, naked bodies, and there was that in their faces which bespoke a cruel and heartless intelligence unlike that of any beast. Those eyes, especially—keen, knowing, bright and evilly eager—entranced him. Bleek wondered, however, what such monstrosities were doing here. That they were demons he did not doubt, demons of a certain power or ability, with nothing normal about them, nothing natural; their presence in this place could not be due to chance; they must serve a purpose, or have a purpose of their own, and it remained for him to find out what that was. Uneasily he addressed them, and in so many words demanded of them that they state their business.

Came again that loathsome tittering, followed by a chorus of rasping, sibilant voices in horrid unison, a weird imitation or parody of human speech which stunned his ears and engendered within his breast a longing for flight. Bleek did not flee, for such was not his way, nor would it have helped to gain him what he sought. He listened instead, paying heed to their words, and learned what they would make known to him.

"You stand, Jacob Bleek," hissed the voices, "within the Great Gateway, the entrance to the Ultimate Vortex. Behind you lies the meager, feeble world that men know and imagine to be all; beyond lies the mysterious realms of the Gods Themselves. You are but one step away from Their abode, though it resides in impossible regions an infinite distance in time and space, in far planes and spheres of existence. You can not walk there, nor sail, nor fly, yet you can be there, if you choose, for you have come to this place.

"Would you speak with the Gods, Jacob Bleek? They are not prone to speaking with men, nor with any of Their playthings, but perhaps They will show tolerance in your case. We may know, if we speak with you, and learn the reason of your coming, for we deem ourselves the Messengers of the Gods, the go-betweens standing betwixt Their domain and yours. Talk to us, Jacob Bleek; reveal to us your mind and your heart; open to us that which is important within you, and we will—if it pleases us—open a door unto you."

Succinctly the wizard explained his situation, and nervously as well, for he knew not of these Messengers, nor of their powers. He did not care for their presence, nor understand it. He had moved heaven and earth to reach this far place, thinking that the attainment of the Vortex would be the end of his journey, and yet he had met with what seemed a fresh hurdle or barrier. The idea infuriated him, and he contemplated wielding his magic to sweep the creatures aside. He believed that he could conquer—he no longer recognized limits of any kind—but he never, except as a last resort, sought trouble when such was avoidable. So he restrained his mounting anger, eulogized patience within himself, and treated with the Messengers.

"Your soul is strong," they rasped, "and we hunger. There is much meat in your spirit. Give us that, and you may pass." Now Bleek knew what he could only have suspected before: the nature and desires of these beings. Demons indeed they were, of a sort referenced through the ages in old stories and forbidden tomes. Given his long experience, he imagined that every serious quest, in the end, came down to moments such as this. It seemed a little price, yet he adamantly refused. He pointed out that his soul had been a cheerful companion to him through many strange years and countless strange events, and he felt no need, at this time, to break asunder that beneficial partnership. He would pass, one way or another, with body, mind, and spirit intact.

"Your position is not reasonable," they said. "You ask for all, Jacob Bleek, while we ask for nothing of consequence. We see in your brain that you have offered much to less than we; placate us—just that—and you may go on your way in peace. We, too, are able and willing to stand firm." The clever sorcerer thought about this, and he remembered ways and means of his former life, in the olden times long ago when he had scraped for a bare living among the markets and tradesmen of the home of his youth. He denied them that which was essential to his being, and granted that he bore with him no prizes, that he carried no surplus souls to hand; the mundane world, however, possessed these in plenty, and when he chose to return to that world he could gather up such morsels as he pleased. He made them the offer, then, of a future boon—of a soul on account, as it were—that he would gladly provide to them at the earliest practical date. He suggested the soul of Tonipah, which would surely make a mouthful for them. The Messengers buzzed and fluttered with glee. "Can you do this?" they asked him. "Will you do this? That one we would relish." Bleek agreed to provide them, at the next available opportunity, with that particular soul, and he made to them a solemn oath, and rapped his staff three times on the stone floor, and he drew forth a dagger and sealed the bargain in his own blood. "It is enough," they cried. "We agree, Jacob Bleek. Do not disappoint us; if you renege, there is no place in the worlds you know, or will know, where you can hide from us. So be it. You may pass." The Messengers screeched and flapped their wings, then dropped from their stony perches and descended to smother him with their vile, noisome bodies. Their vicious faces pressed into his own, and though he shuddered and shrank away, their repellent flesh pressed closer, soiling his own. Bleek, despite himself, made as if to scream.

Then darkness enfolded him, an absence or banishing of light. Sight, sound, sensation, in a blink were gone from him, a shroud of nothingness spun from the great wings and fetid breath of the Messengers. It was as if the last remnants of the world he knew had died, leaving only him, a presence in limbo. He could no longer see the floor beneath him, although he seemed still to be standing on a surface; at least, he still possessed the sense of upright balance, and facing forward. He was definitely aware of himself; somehow he lived, breathed, and thought, in nothingness. He also sensed, without any objective impressions derived from eyes, ears, or brain, that he was not alone. The Messengers remained with him—somehow he knew this—and he felt, without the true and normal feeling of man, that they had taken hold of him, and were conveying him thither.

He felt that he rushed forward. Then a hole opened in the darkness, a circle which swelled and expanded rapidly, sweeping around him, and he hurtled into another place. He seemed to be racing headlong through space, with an incredible vista spread before and around him. He could see it all, though he saw not himself nor his grim companions. He had left the world of men, plunged through that transition of nothing, and come out elsewhere, into a very different realm of force and matter.

There was much darkness remaining, but there was light as well, the light of objects within this new universe; for he admitted that, as the Messengers had warned, this was no place that man or magician could reach by walking, or sailing, or soaring, or by any known or unknown natural means. He had entered another cosmos, one which operated according to rules of its own. There were suns, and there were worlds, or so he supposed, for everything he saw was so strange to him. Bleek wondered if his eyes were meant for such visions.

Those bright, glaring objects that flamed and smoked were the stars of this universe—he guessed this, or a sibilant hiss of words quietly informed him—and there were many, countless numbers of them, far and near, but those that he could see well were formed into crazy, intricate shapes. There ahead of him he saw a string of crimson diamonds flaring in the night, while to his right burned a scintillating blue circle strung with bright, pulsing beads, a celestial necklace, and to his left, very close, steamed a vast yellow latticework of harshly radiating brilliance. His magical course took him across this and down, so that he passed close to one furiously blazing network of fiery bars. The light source dazzled but did not harm him, although he knew that, in his conventional body, such a monstrous object would have destroyed him instantaneously. Then he was beyond it, and he could see more clearly the other wonders of this mysterious realm.

As there were suns, so there were worlds, though at first Bleek failed to recognize what he saw. He now focused upon these other images, gigantic planar shapes that stretched in every direction unto infinity, softly illuminated in broad areas by the fierce burning of the weird suns. These impossible surfaces extended endlessly, slowly rotating or shifting in space, cutting through one another and through stars without catastrophe, or incident of any kind. There was something ethereal about them: at a distance they seemed to shimmer as with an aura of unreality, and when, in the course of its revolution, one plane passed in front of a particularly bright, kaleidoscopic congeries of multi-colored lights, he could still make out the sparkling lights beyond the plane. He could see through the vast, wide surface, as if it possessed no depth at all, but were a mere film of semi-transparency overlaid upon the universe. The plane continued to turn toward him, and when it faced him directly he realized that he was diving straight into it.

At his extreme, though unfelt, velocity, the surface appeared to zoom dangerously at him. He approached a portion lighted by the shining latticework, and only now did he grasp that he was gazing upon the face of another world (though a quiet, nasty, muttering voice seemed to be trying to impart this information to him). Across that thin plane were etched the mighty crags of jagged mountains, expansive seas of oily liquid, winding rivers, and other features of terrain which would have been considered natural and normal had they appeared in a less uncanny milieu. There were still more features which he noticed as he rushed at the surface, then sensed an inward wrenching as his trajectory suddenly altered. Now he coasted rapidly above the land, where he spied immensely long, straight lines chiseled into the luridly litten landscape, and major conglomerations of softly glowing lights. The former he deduced to be artificial avenues, the latter great cities. At one point he soared quickly over a city, and in the blink of an eye he glimpsed strangely twisted pinnacles of gleaming metal, and wild, ropy towers that turned and curved and circled upon and through themselves. The denizens he had no time to see, but he imagined that they might be as curious to behold as their city and their world.

Then Bleek was being pulled away from the surface, back into space, and he knew, somehow, that the Messengers were still with him, guiding him, and an inner voice—he thought it to be an ugly, inhuman, rasping voice— told him that a clearly defined destination lay out there before him in the mysterious cosmos. He flew very high, then began to veer toward another planar world, moving speedily in the direction of a surface bathed in the painfully flashing light of an indigo sun that hung in the dark sky like a titanic figure "X." During this fast journey the plane tipped far up over his head, revealing one side to him, through which he could dimly make out the indigo flashing, then rotated upon its infinite axis, actually sliding through him, to expose the other face. It continued to rotate until he reached a point at which he was, as with the previous world, plunging into it.

This time he did not pull away. The surface swelled; there opened before him a huge dark crater, the mouth of an incredibly large, perfectly circular volcano—the black walls rose up about him—and he plummeted breathlessly into the heart of that gaping maw! At first he expected to perish, then thought better and waited to emerge out the lower side of the plane, yet that, also, did not occur. Utter darkness encompassed him, and he found himself within another formless void for a period, and when he eventually emerged from this, he found himself in yet another place entirely.

There was much darkness, some light; he might still be within the esoteric universe, but if so he was now leaving it at a dizzying rate. He looked down upon an outrageously colored massing, extremely dense to the appearance, of distant stars, an enormous swarm of lights hovering in a void of emptiness, and as he watched the vast aggregation it perceptibly receded from him, dwindling in size and brightness, gradually fading from sight. Before long he could detect nothing but a minute patch of glimmering dimness in the everlasting dark. Then he had to strain to see even the fuzzy, feeble glow of that far universe, and shortly it was altogether gone. Total night reigned supreme all about him; not the blinding darkness of the transitions, but only an absolute emptiness of content; no matter, no force, no thing of any kind. For the moment Bleek felt as if he were forever lost, divorced from every other aspect of creation in all the universes and dimensions of being. He felt, too, a despairing and uncharacteristic loneliness, for he knew of a certainty that the Messengers had departed, abandoning him to face on his own whatever lay in store. Either they had betrayed him, leaving without even pause for a last laugh, or their mission was done.

He hung suspended, so it seemed, in darkness, with no sense of motion to hint at progress, no awareness of eventuality, nothing to indicate that anything was happening or could happen. This dreadful period lasted for seconds, or for an endless age. Bleek could not judge; even his thoughts seemed frozen. Then he observed something at the extreme limits of vision, a minute speck of light, the merest pinpoint. He watched it with rabid intensity. Yes, it grew—now it was a somewhat larger dot, suggestive of a far round body in space—grew, and as he saw it more clearly he detected a hint of greenish radiance. He surely approached the thing, although he knew that the Messengers were no longer guiding him. Perhaps it possessed a kind of attractive property which drew him toward it. If so, the force must be extremely powerful, for it was very far away, the only object that he could detect in all the universe of darkness. He wondered: an entire universe, maybe, containing only a single body. What did that signify? He wondered, and waited, as he neared the thing.

It grew, and neared, and swelled into an inconceivably vast and majestic globe of seething greenish mist, a roiling, bubbling, erupting mass of dull, featureless green. There was no question that he was diving right into it. As the wizard approached he thought that his velocity increased; certainly the incredible object appeared to expand at a mounting rate. Bleek told himself that it was a solitary sun, lost like him in the empty cosmos, but he did not believe this. The thing belonged here, and it drew him.

He plunged down into the green mist, and he saw nothing but formless dull green, but he sensed and, thus, knew more. This was no natural feature of this unnatural realm, but a focus, a concentration, of strange power. There was intelligence here, vast intelligence; limitless intelligence, a mystery of utter mind, and having conceived this, then Bleek knew in a flash where he was, where he had come. Not intelligence, but Intelligence—not mind, not anything merely rational nor understandable, but Mind Absolute—the totality of cosmic knowledge and power, dwelt here. This, he now realized, was the place for which he had striven, the center of all creation. Having thought this, it seemed to him as that his invisible, unfelt motion ceased. He beheld naught but mist, but he sensed that he stood again upon solid ground, where there was no ground. Nothing tangible confronted him, but he had stopped in space and time, saturated by the overwhelming force of Mind. The long journey was over.

Jacob Bleek had arrived—he knew beyond question, beyond life—at the ultimate source of the Great Vortex, the celestial portal of the Old Ones, the Gods of all things and all times. The journey was complete, and now the goal of the quest must be honored. And he cried out to the unseen Old Ones, announcing that he was Jacob Bleek, the sorcerer beyond compare, the wizard who knoweth all the ways and secrets of man, the mage who would know the ways and secrets of the Gods. Bleek demanded of Them that They grant him the boon of Their unlimited knowledge, for he would make of himself and the world what he would. Bleek wanted to drink from the goblet of power which was Theirs, to know all, to see all, so that with this power he might control all that he could grasp or conceive. Bleek demanded this as a right, the right of one who had come far, struggling against perils and ignorance, overcoming all obstacles, mastering all men. Now he chose to master fate, and he would defy even the Gods to stand in his path. Bleek issued this challenge to Great Xenophor Himself, King of the Gods, He of the Thousand Eyes, the Creator and the Destroyer: obliterate him, Jacob Bleek, now from time and space, if the Great One darest—nay, abolish even the memory that Bleek once was, if He so wilt—or grant now unto the claimant that which he sought and craved.

This Jacob Bleek said, and with the saying Something gazed upon him out of the dull green glow of the mist, and he knew It looked upon him, though he could not see It, nor could he discern from what direction It gazed, for It seemed to peer thoughtfully from all directions at once, from the left and the right, from before and behind, from above and below. And a voice whispered, ands then rose to a low roar, a voice or voices reaching him not through his ears, but passing around and through him; voices speaking and vibrating from within his own flesh, so that he shook and shuddered at each solemn intonation. It (or they) spoke not in his or any language—there were no words as such in that thunderous travesty of speech—yet he heard and understood what was being said. The voices that were not voices varied in intensity, such that he could not be sure if a conversation were underway, or whether a single entity were musing to Itself.

"He has come at the appointed time, to the appointed place. As We devised and

foretold, he is here, and the demand has been laid before Us. All has been arranged and determined according to Our plan, and We find it meet that the demand be honored, as was always Our intention. This is the time, this is the place, the act has occurred, and now the next action inevitably follows. He would possess the pure, perfect knowledge of the eternities; he would see and know as We do; he would accept this as a boon. So it has been written, here and now it comes to pass. This is the will of the Gods, the will of Xenophor. Jacob Bleek, the power you desire above all else is yours."

On that instant Jacob Bleek felt the power fill his mind. He questioned, and answers flooded into him; suddenly he knew, for the asking, the age-old, primal secrets which underlie all reality. The truth came to him as if he were reading a book, absorbing the knowledge as swiftly as he could turn the pages. The critical fundamentals of natural philosophy, toward which all great thinkers had striven, came to him in a flash. He attained the limits of magical understanding as quickly as he could formulate the wish. Now everything he had previously known, the fruits of devoted decades of study which had made him a giant among his peers, seemed paltry by comparison with what he gained now without effort.

That was only the beginning. He gazed into the distance, and the glowing haze fell away, and he saw with a new and indescribable species of sight. He saw the earth under his feet and all around him as if he were there, he saw everything happening upon it as if he were there, standing near to scrutinize, and he saw beyond the earth, into the heavens. The mysteries of the cosmos which he had sought to probe lay revealed. As if he were there, he cast his mind into the heavens, and he saw worlds without number, and flaming suns, and dense gases drifting among the stars. He knew it all; the entire universe of men was his palace, through which he strode as a king, all of that universe which so many before him had hoped to fathom, and the many planes of existence, the other dimensional realities which exist side by side with his own; all these he knew. He looked to the edge of the universe, and infinitely beyond. He beheld the weird universes through which he had passed, and more, more and stranger, universes or spheres of existence without number. All this he saw, and knew.

And as he mastered the secrets of space, so did he conquer the mysteries of time. He blinked dazzled eyes, and he saw the past, not merely knowing it as from moldy records, but seeing it unfold before him. Events long wiped from the slate of history, and those never known to history, came to him readily, effortlessly. He experienced the grand sweep of history as if he had lived it himself. He saw empires rise and fall, and thunderous battles, noble victories and grave defeats, the erection of glorious cities and their tragic decay. Prior to the feeble span of man he observed earlier races of strange beings and beasts, the shifting of lands and seas, traveling back in his mind to the steaming, fulminating creation of the world. He saw everything that had ever occurred on the earth, and everything that had ever occurred elsewhere. He knew the magnificent, weird, and terrifying entities that had populated other worlds, and knew all of their histories as well.

And still more: as the past appeared to him in the here and now, as real and present to him as his own breath, so did Jacob Bleek see the future develop and come to pass as if he lived every moment of it. He saw the titanic events that would shake the cosmos throughout all the eras of its existence, he watched the continuing triumphs and dooms of alien beings throughout the worlds, he read the story of the earth to be as it transpired. He learned of great men and small men, good men and evil, wise men and fools, who would dream or struggle or stumble forward, and thereby fashion the future as it would be in every age from tomorrow until that distant time in the shadow of eternity. He saw it all, laid out for him like a theatrical pageant staged solely for his amusement. No pathetic prophet of old had ever dared pray for such a view.

It seemed incredible to Bleek that one fleshy mind, even his own, could contain this stunningly boundless accumulation of total knowledge. He feared that his brain was like to burst under the strain, but it did not, for there was no strain. He knew everything as easily as the Gods did Themselves. It was a heady, exhilarating experience like none he could have believed. He grew giddy as he quaffed this strange wine; he laughed and shouted with abandon, he screamed ecstatically for joy with his initial thoughts, those first intimations, of what he could accomplish with this monstrous gift. There were no limits to his power; absolute knowledge meant absolute possibilities, and he had only to conceive in order to achieve.

He had seen the past and future in strokes of the broad brush, yet the particulars of cosmic totality were available to him as well. He could as quickly delve down to the level of the individual, and no one person mattered more to himself than he. He thought upon the tale of Jacob Bleek, and there it was before him, to be lived again. He beheld, from a strangely fresh vantage which illuminated moments previously obscure, the days of his youth, the time of study in his cramped quarters in Bruges. Again he learned the basics of magic, again he dared grasp at greater marvels, again he conceived his mighty quest. He saw himself set out on the great journey, experienced anew the triumphs, disappointments, and horrors of his travels. His few forgotten friends aided him once more; legions of dead enemies appeared again to plague him and to succumb to his wrath. Now he bested Helvetius, and humbled the Graf; now he bargained with the wise hermit of Cracow, and left behind him a sinister, raving madman; now he fled in love and terror from the delightful and deadly Countess Kronnberg; now he plumbed the voids of inner earth and trod the benighted streets of the damned Rhexellites, annihilated the wizards of the Telkon League, stood before shattered Dyrezan, wrestled with the fearsome spirit of Azamodias. He watched—living it as he watched—his approach to the present victorious point, and then—and then!—he saw laid out for him his own, his entire future. It began, of course, with the selling of Tonipah's soul, as he had agreed to with the Messengers; a bit of unfinished business, and then more and more, and on and on, ever into his private futurity. There were the 1accomplishments, there the failures, the wins and the losses of his life to be, a staggeringly long life; and he saw with stark clarity what would eventually become of him.

He could not help thinking that there was much about his future career that he did not like. There were those failures, those checks and overlooked opportunities, which displeased him, and from his godlike perspective he was less prone than ever to accept displeasure. As the tale of his life opened to his eyes he concluded that it was not unrolling down the proper channels. There was much to suit him, to be sure, but a distressing quantity of his futurity mortified and angered him. That should not be—that he would not tolerate—so he pondered the matter, and Jacob Bleek willed his future to change into a course of his bidding.

Still the parade of his personal events ran on as he had seen them do. That was not correct; with all knowledge should come all power, and there should be no difficulty in diverting his own life into other, happier, more satisfying avenues. He had but to envision the life he would lead, and he would in time perform the requisite acts, and that future would be so. This he thought, this he demanded... yet nothing changed. What he saw was what he had seen, forever rolling down the same road. Why was this? What trick of his newfound abilities had he not yet mastered? What more did he need to know before he could prepare to rearrange his story to his satisfaction? As he brooded over this conundrum he became uncomfortably aware of that Presence or those Presences which had not left him, the definite sense of many eyes upon him. He thought that he heard, muted and far away, the cackle of laughter, and a deeper, steady growling that might have been amused or contemptuous chuckling. He looked away from the worldly images that concerned him, gazing into a black void, and out of that void there stared back at him eyes beyond number. A thousand, a million, a trillion eyes glared at him, still more; and he imagined that they were yellow and cold, never turning from him, baleful, watery yet never blinking, inhuman and implacable.

He cried out, invoking the awesome name of Xenophor, insisting that he be told what was wrong, and what he must do to right it. And the voice (Bleek thought now that it was one voice only) spoke to him again, feigning words that he knew, quivering throughout the fabric of space and time as it said: *"Thought he to see as the Gods do, and thereby become one of Us? This one, this Jacob Bleek, hast gained all knowledge, as he desired, and so it shall always be. The gift is his now—solely his, for none other who has ever dared ask has fully received, and it amuses Us that none other ever will—but he must not imagine that he has become one with Us. To know all lies within his power forevermore; he may revel in his power as it pleases him, yet he must think not that he canst change that which has been written since the beginning of time.*

'For in a place outside of all space and time We conceived existence and eternity, and We fashioned them according to Our will, and made them be; from the first to the last We dreamed these things, and they are so; this and every other cosmos is an instrument of Our devising. To Us everything is known, for everything is as We have chosen for Our own ends. These ends this Bleek, this meaningless speck of dust, can not understand and shall not judge. The grand sweep of what he deems time, as it is, pleases and amuses Us, and what We have created, from the first to the last, can not be uncreated by him. Past, present, and future, which he believes or pretends to be separate states, are merely aspects of the totality of creation which We formulated as a whole—as Bleek is merely an aspect—and they have been carved into his universe by Us forevermore. All is written, all endures, until the abysmal end of eternity itself."

With these words Bleek began to grasp the magnitude of his error, and the discovery was like to kill him. Mighty Xenophor and His minions had created the universe in its entirety, every material object from stone to man to star; had invented them from scratch and then designed a story for them, into which each object had been inserted at what the Old Ones considered the fitting place and time; had thought upon these things and composed them, as a scribe writes a book; and this great, this grotesque, Book of the Ages had already been written, from beginning to end, the final chapter prepared with the first. The wizard Jacob Bleek, with all of his cunning and his wisdom, constituted no more than a footnote of that eldritch tome. He had been granted—as a morbid jest, perhaps?—the amazing ability to read the book, yet he was truly still only a character within it. He could read to his heart's content, but he could not rewrite a single line, a single word. The long sought gift of Godly sight had rendered all power, all schemes, all goals, meaningless.

Whatever he might desire to accomplish for himself, now he would always know beforehand, beyond question, exactly what the results would be, no matter how much effort or thought he expended. What Xenophor had written must come to pass, and no kicking against the pricks could alter that; nay, it already had come to pass, and there remained only the dreary task of living a story already known. All of the boundless possibilities of his life had, at a stroke—by his own demand—dwindled to one fated certainty, which could not be avoided through any action of his own. Indeed, all of his future actions, whatever they might be, must inevitably lead to just the outcome he dreaded, no matter how he twisted and squirmed against it. The act of avoidance, along with its failure, were already givens of the cruel and heartless patterns of the universe as they must develop. At every turn his escape from this maddening doom was blocked. The more he thought of it, the more he realized the implications for himself, the more that fate disgusted and horrified him.

Jacob Bleek shrieked in dismay, and out of his righteous anger he demanded an accounting from the Gods, and ordered Them to save him. They rumbled with mirth. Bleek screamed in terror, begged for mercy, pleaded with Them to release him from his chosen destiny, even to destroy him if that was the only escape. The Old Ones laughed, and the universe trembled as They laughed, and Bleek knew They had rejected his supplication—had always rejected it, as They had always gratified his first demand—and he felt reality crumbling beneath him. In a panic he turned and fled—his spirit fled, dragging his unseen body—through the misty abyss, desperately attempting to hide himself from the eyes that pressed upon his soul, from the lurid, scintillating lights and grotesque, disembodied motions that now crowded about him, images which he recognized as stray motes of thought, leakage from the minds of Them, fragments of the true universal reality he had long sought to know. He fled, and the green mist faded, and darkness swallowed him alive, and then he was on real, honest ground again, running across a stone floor, with mocking laughter echoing from a familiar stone ceiling above his head, and he scrambled through the fissure as the rocks quaked and fell about him. As he emerged from the cave—that cave atop the evil mountain, the cave he had entered those ages before—the black, stony mound sagged, and toppled in upon itself, burying the cave under rubble and sealing or filling it. A cloud of thick dust blinded and choked him. When the dust had settled, and he could see and breathe, all was gone— even the stones of the mound had dropped away into an ethereal void—and he was left standing alone under a clear, starry night, on the smooth dark surface of the mountain top.

All of this he had known would be. It was written, as he was written, the comical, oafish, insolent, stupid plaything of the Gods who styled himself—as They allowed it—Jacob Bleek. He knew everything, and he had nothing but a long, agonizingly long, life of predestiny before him. That life he would live, as he must, because the Gods willed it; he had nothing, for the drama and the passion of a life unknown and unknowable was forever denied him.

Epilogue

Bleek contrived to descend the loathsome Mountain of the Old Ones, putting behind him the scene of his disaster; he crossed once more the plain and climbed to the mysterious cathedral in red stone, and gazed miserably upon the far summit to which, as he now thought, the Masters of All Things had called him; he made his way through and passed beyond the unholy Valley of the Gods, and collapsed at the feet of the native priest Tonipah, who took him in and succored him; he sojourned with the noble old man until health was restored, and then went on his way, after first casting the poor fellow into the darkness, as had been promised to the hungry demons. All this Bleek did, yet he cared not, for he need not care. He knew that he would do these things, though he chose otherwise; for it was ordained.

He trekked again across the great continent of the west, and many an adventure he experienced along the way. There were fierce scrapes with warlike or murderous primitives, hair-raising flights and defiant stands, tense moments when his skills of persuasion or his magical abilities came into play and saved him. Every conceivable obstacle he confronted, faced, and defeated, each one a story worth telling, and yet Bleek thought little, or not at all, of these things, for he knew what would happen in each case, and what would be the outcome; for it was ordained.

He arrived at the far coast, and there lies one of the most incredible tales concerning the wonderful homeward journey of Jacob Bleek; for he arrived upon a desolate wilderness shore, among barbarians who were incapable of aiding him in his progress; without a ship, without any legitimate chance of hailing one, since no mariners of his world ever passed this way; completely cut off from any reasonable regress from that unknown land. It was an absolutely hopeless situation, so it would seem, even for one so clever as he, and yet the learned wizard deduced a way out of his difficulties, and in due course he did commence his return passage across the seas. How this came about is one of the marvels of the ages, and yet Bleek thought nothing of it, and would not have thought the deed worthy of recording, since he knew already exactly how it would come about; for it was ordained.

He returned to the world of civilized men, and here the new pattern of his existence continued as he feared it would, as it must. With his limitless knowledge, his Godly power to peer into and behind all creation, he could imagine the boundless vistas that must open before him, and yet, whatever his schemes and means, he found himself always traveling down a particular path which was growing wearily oppressive to him. With his great quest over he found that, within a relatively short period, his days on the road were over. He had nothing left to learn, and there was nowhere left that he would go— as he knew—so eventually he surrendered to his fate and took up an abode for himself in an old and obscure village, where he built himself a house. There is much wonder in this as well, for he raised his house out of nothing in a single night (a trick he had learned from his forebear Azamodias), and come the morn the villagers gazed up at the high, barren hill overlooking their town and beheld the strange house there, where there had been nothing the previous evening; a house surrounded by a dark, cloaking belt of dense forest, which also had not been there, full of ravening beasts; and the villagers gasped in surprise and dread. It is remarkable that Bleek could do this, but he could, and he knew he would, so it was done. How he did it, that he did it, mattered little to him; for it was ordained.

He thought often, throughout the years, of the hate-driven curse of Josiah, which had once so disconcerted him when he pondered its possible effects on his future. He no longer feared it, for he had gazed beyond such terrors. If the curse had been potent, and had wrought evil upon him, it was of an evil laid down at the instant of creation, long before Josiah was fashioned by the Gods in order that, one day, he might utter his curse. Bleek detested the thought of the future to come, but he could not summon the energy to fear it. Whatever he thought of the matter, that future would be.

In his house Jacob Bleek dwelt, in black, brooding solitude, all the days of his weirdly long, yet—to him—precisely known life span. He had his books, his implements of magic, his inescapable knowledge, as his only company, and that was, peculiarly enough, as he desired it, for the world of men, any world of which he might be a part, appalled him. Shunning all, he imprisoned himself within his house, where he ought to be lord and master, save that he was master of nothing, a mere puppet dangling on strings from the fingers of the Gods who had casually made him. There he stayed, avoiding the world, though there would be incidents to come at known times, when daring or foolish men would seek him out, having heard rumors of his learning and powers, and brave his frowns in an attempt to tap his secrets. These he would drive away or destroy as he would, as it must be; for always, always, the consequences were known to him, the result ordained.

There be those who claim that Jacob Bleek still lives in that old house on the lonely hill above that ancient village. Who now can say for sure except Bleek himself, and if he can say still, then he cares not to say, for it has been long that anything really mattered to him. In gaining the gift of the Gods, which he had craved above all other prizes, he had lost that which is most important to man: the ability to hope, and to dream.

THE FURTHER ADVENTURES OF JACOB BLEEK

Beyond the Crossroads

In olden times the wizard Jacob Bleek, seeker after strange mysteries and stranger wisdom, undertook a journey through the Black Forest that he might come quickly to Frankfurt, where would shortly convene a conclave of learned men. Amongst those assembled sages he wished to find precious knowledge for which he would bargain hardly, hoping to gain much while revealing few of his own secrets. That was his way. The accumulation of such exchanges had made him respected and feared among his peers, and this was still early in his legendary career. As matters transpired, Bleek was fated to miss that meeting. Nevertheless, adventure befell him.

At a homely village deep in the woods, where the main road curved unpromisingly to the north, he inquired of the way, putting his question to the considerate innkeeper who sheltered him the previous night. That stout fellow said, "If you would reach Frankfurt from here, good sir, you must travel east and south through the hills and forest. Take the east road, which is a fair path-- though few pass upon it except at market time-- until you come to the crossroads. There you must take the turn to Yost, which is a decent village like my own, full of goodly people who will see you on your way down the river and to the city. Do not, at the crossroads, take the road to Crost. That would be an unfortunate mistake. Long ago that was an evil place, Crost; folk say the devil danced there of nights, at the desires of the people, until they and their abode came to a bad end, one well deserved. There are no folk there now. Crost is no more, affording no hospitality to the weary traveler. Be sure you take the road to Yost."

This vagary of a tale intrigued Bleek, and he thought idly to look into the story one day, but now he was in a hurry, so he heeded the innkeeper's words and went forth from the village early that morning, in his little wagon with his few belongings piled in back, that he might come to Yost and thus depart the dark forest. His tireless pony trotted merrily between the farms girdling the eastern road, until the trees closed in again and hid the quaint cottages from view. Thereafter the beast worked harder, for the hills mounded up and steepened. Afternoon came before Bleek descended into a narrow valley with meadows in the bottom land, and there before him the road forked.

Bleek would go to Yost where, he had been assured, good folk would attend to his needs, yet the taking of this simple choice placed him in a conundrum. There intruded a galling element of ambiguity in his decision. He dismounted from his wagon to study the case. The road he traveled had deteriorated from disuse, was gullied and overgrown with increeping weeds. The paths beyond the crossroads looked similar. There was a sign, of course, a wooden post with twin boards pointing the way; one indicating Yost, the other Crost. The sign had turned, however; whether due to tempest or hooligans, it shunned philosophical certitude. The information it conveyed should have been obvious. It was not. At a guess, Bleek felt that Yost lay this way, and Crost that; so, after irritated pondering, he chose this, resumed his position in the driver's seat, reined over the pony with diffidence, proceeded.

The dank forest pressed close once more. Indeed, this road was very bad, and scarcely had he advanced a mile before misgivings assailed him. He was like to turn back and try the other fork when a shadowy glade came into view on his left, a mossy clearing by the banks of a thin brook. Three figures at the far end beneath a spreading oak caught his eye: a tall, elderly man dressed in a long black cloak, upholding in one hand an ornate silver implement, facing a young man and woman, also garbed in black, who bowed and repeated in unison a chant as directed by the old one. They took no notice of Bleek, not so much as acknowledging his presence. He rode on at last, mystified by the ritual, which he deduced might constitute a local wedding rite. He did not recognize their dialect, but then, their words had been indistinct at that distance. The appearance of human beings, though, cheered him, for it proved that he moved toward habitation.

The first glimpse of roofs past scattered trees caused him to falter, for they seemed awfully dilapidated, but when he rounded the bend in the wretched road and saw the place squarely he thought himself mistaken, for it was a fair village, well kept, spread throughout a hollow under a wooded bluff, with smoke trickling from several chimneys. The scene was oddly dark, as if the sun had fled behind cloud, but it was picturesque and warmly inviting at this stage of the afternoon with its lengthening shadows. This had to be Yost.

Jacob Bleek drew up at the inn, one like so many others that formed his itinerant homes. No one was in sight. Yost was a quiet town. With the thought he discerned a face staring at him from a cottage window up the street, then others, and he detected from various points muted whispering hitherto unheard. He must be tired not to have noticed. He dismounted with his travel bag, entered the inn.

The main hall was large, absolutely dark, apparently untenanted, the fireplace vacant. Bleek knew himself to be alone, then realized himself mistaken, for the landlord stood at his station behind the oaken counter, and there was light after all, dim but serviceable, from sputtering twin lamps on the bar. The man hailed him cheerfully. Bleek requested lodging for the night. The man said, "We don't entertain many guests here... this time of year."

He came round the bar, a short, stout man in apron, with a furry moustache and scanty hair. "Allow me, sir, to introduce myself," he said with a smile. "I'm Tobias, your eager host, at your command. My lady will serve you. You do require food?" Bleek granted this, requested shelter and board for himself and his pony. "All will be done," cried Tobias. "I'll see to your animal now. Matilda! We have a guest!"

His shout brought out from the kitchen a painfully thin woman with long, lanky black hair threaded with gray. Her sharp features were bent into a bright grin. "My wife," said Tobias. Bleek introduced himself to both. The woman replied, "This is an unusual honor." Tobias added, "We must make the most of it. Good sir, eat and be merry, while I care for the beast."

Bleek took table, waited no time at all before his meal arrived. Matilda laid before him a platter of beef and dumplings, set beside it a mug and a jug. The food gratified his palate, the wine teased his tongue. The piteous neighing of his pony, on the other hand, distressed.

Tobias returned presently. "Your beast," he explained, "takes none too kindly to strangers. Fear not; his accommodations will suit. Yours will be even more satisfactory, I trust."

He urged on his guest a second helping, directed his wife to quick action. Bleek, seeking to derive from the man information as to the journey ahead, allowed that he was fortunate, given the poor state of the roads, to arrive at Yost.

This much amused Tobias. "Do you hear that, my lady?" he called. "Our guest counts himself lucky that he has come to Yost. So you think this Yost a grand place, sir? I dare say there are better. Aye, the roads are bad. One can't be too careful. A wrong turn may lead to an ill day."

Matilda cackled a laugh as she heaped Bleek's plate afresh. "Some days more than others," she said. "I recollect an old story-- the tales folk tell!-- I don't know how I came to hear it, but it was about that other place. What was it called, husband?" Tobias only stood and chuckled, so after an awkward moment Bleek took a stab and suggested Crost. "Aye, that was it," cried the woman. "A dreadful town it was, that Crost, to hear about it."

"Never did I hear a good word," Tobias admitted.

"Surely not from the folk hereabout." Matilda went on, "Bad people, bad doings all around, they say. Crost is gone now, eaten by evil, only some do say that kind of evil doesn't die, but lingers in spots, festering like a biting disease. And there are those special days, the peculiar ones. Those naughty folk in Crost had one in particular."

"I know the one you mean," interjected her man. "That was the high festival in honor of Azamodeus. Isn't that a weird name? Who might he be? I reckon the fell folk of Crost knew."

Rejoined his wife with a snicker, "I reckon they did."

"Oh, they knew, all right. They kept that day holy. It meant more to them than life. Every year they celebrated that one. It was about this time of year, I fancy... if old stories tell true."

"They as told them are long dead now," Matilda observed.

"And a body would expect them to keep quiet," Tobias added. "Don't you agree, sir?" Jacob Bleek, puzzled by this unusual outlay of untoward information, conceded the point. Had he been so inclined, he might have discussed with them the reference to Azamodeus, an ancient term which he recognized from his occult delvings in the most hideous of contexts. He refrained. In rare humor his host and hostess left him then to finish his repast.

Night advanced apace. Before long Bleek craved the comfort of his room. Tobias appeared at the appropriate moment to direct him to the upper floor, last room on the left, the door open. Bleek trudged with his bag up the creaky stairs, down the hall to his obvious destination. The room was small, with few furnishings, a little musty, but sufficient for a night. A small closet behind a sticky door contained only unswept dirt. A drab, dusty curtain concealed a small unpaned window. Bleek peeked outside. Lights moved out there in the dark village, the scattered flare of torches. The yeoman of Yost, he noted, were more active by evening than by daylight.

His bed was a ratty affair, a straw-stuffed mattress atop a decrepit wooden framework, with a single blanket and misshapen pillow. Fortunately the nights were warm in this season. In short order Bleek disrobed and made the most of that resting place. Sleep took him quickly.

It did not let him lie, however. He awoke from a dimly remembered dream of unpleasant nature into stark blackness. His scalp crawled with nervous tension, his heart raced. Possibly the dream had jarred him awake. He recalled discordant images, a throng gathered in hectic merriment, loathsome feasting, praise shouted from many maddened throats to the "Lord Azamodeus". It was an ugly vision, yet more than the spurs of slumber galled him. Fear assailed from an unknown quarter. His well honed instincts screamed at him of imminent danger.

He heard nothing to justify sudden consciousness. Possibly the smell of the room had intensified. A subtlely rank stench offended his nostrils. He fumbled for the oil lamp on the rickety bed stand, lighted it with the matches he had placed there on retiring. The faint glow revealed the room vaguely. All was as it was. No wind ruffled the curtain. The closet door stood slightly ajar as he had left it.

Bleek stared at that closet. The mounting odor emanated from it. Something had changed there. Yes, he saw it now. The untidiness of that enclave had crept out beyond the door. There was a dirtiness about the door which had somehow extended itself to the adjacent wall. He likened it to oily grime-- nay, more-- to a damp encrustation of greenish-gray fungus. It looked unhealthy. Askant looking told him still more. As he watched the foetid stain insidiously spread, threw out tendrils upon the boarding, a thin coating of filth heralded by yellowish spurts of powdery spores. With a snap of attention Bleek unfocused from that spot, realized with disgust that much of the wall facing him, and very close to his face, was vanishing under a silent tide of noxious growth. Just then a puff of spores landed on his pillow, a mere two inches from his nose.

Jacob Bleek sprang from the bed. Hastily donning his clothes, he grabbed his bag and made for the hall door. A miasma in the close air choked him. He coughed out a breath of yellow dust. He threw open the door, which sagged on broken hinges. He dashed over the warped floor-boarding of the dark hall to the stairs, made to race down them, then proceeded gingerly, for with each step he took his life into his hands. Somehow he reached bottom intact, to confront a barely perceived scene of abandoned decay and rotting debris. He fled through it. The outer door toppled at his touch.

Menacing silence greeted him, the silence of a frightfully dead town bathed in the sickly glow of moonlight. He dared the unknown region behind the inn to locate the stables, found merely a weedy lot where his wagon and pony stood, tied up and unattended, amidst ruinous foundations. The poor beast practically cowered in terror, and its equine cries were terrible to hear. Bleek mounted hurriedly, lashed the animal into motion. It obeyed with alacrity.

When he turned into the empty street he heard the sound. The hissing and buzzing and scraping came at him, swelled monstrously, and then a wave of detestable vermin poured down upon man and conveyance. Flies, gnats, hard winged beetles flew into his face, crawling things sprang up from the dust, chitinous things with a myriad of scuttling legs. Bleek's pony reared, tried to dash itself to death against a crumbling stone wall, but its master, heedless of the assault on himself, sagely mastered the animal on which his life depended and drove it by main force back into the lane. As they galloped on their way past flashing images of unspeakable decay and aged neglect Bleek muttered to himself an antique charm, the sole defense he could conceive at the moment, a whispered protection against the mysterious outer powers that lurk at the rim of mind and matter.

The moldy wreck of a village fell away. The vile pests dropped off. The bumpy road, leading back the way he had come, darkened under the encroaching trees of the great forest. His pony assumed its accustomed demeanor. Bleek supposed he was safe now. The baleful influence of the ghastly town did not extend into the unspoiled realm of primordial nature. He had escaped the unquiet force that lurked in that place, though not by much, he reasoned. Maybe his unorthodox studies had prepared him, awakened him to perils beyond the ken of the typical traveler. He shuddered to think what would have happened if he had slept on in that chamber this night.

The bright after-dawn found him at the fateful crossroads once again. Jacob Bleek paused to examine that two-faced sign post with grim mirth. He suspected, naturally, that it mockingly lied, had directed him surreptitiously to Crost, a properly dead village of old evil where, quite possibly, said evil lived on dormant, perhaps to raise itself unbidden to the unwary at certain times; and he made a note to himself to look into the specific date of the festival of Azamodeus, wondering if remarkably bad luck had played a part in the night's adventure. Otherwise, the choice before him dismayed Bleek exceedingly. For if he had, after all, come rightly to Yost, and Yost was reckoned in these parts a goodly town, then what must ill-regarded Crost be like?

Morstenburg

Jacob Bleek, the dark scholar of long ago, student of things uncanny and alchemical, practitioner of black arts, once experienced a peculiar adventure hard by the waters of the gently flowing Main, while he sought Frankfurt, where a gathering of enlightened professors—meaning men of magic, wizards all—promised fruitful knowledge and, perhaps, brisk business in learned trade. Bleek was fated not to attend, for he lost his way amidst the seldom frequented forest tracks of that bleak region, lost a day endeavoring to find the river again, and when he did so came out not on anything resembling a thoroughfare, but on a difficult path hugging the steep banks which strained his pony and almost overset his wagon piled high with his only belongings. The rutted trail wound along the stream to its terminus, which a sullen, solitary farmer identified for him as the village of Morstenburg.

Bleek rode into town as shadows lengthened into evening gloom and a chill wind begin to rustle his black cloak and wide-brimmed hat. There was a castle there, of sorts, but the burg, on its low mound, looked ancient and abandoned, a mere keep of olden Gothic fashion now crumbling away. Around it lay clustered the many rude dwellings of the cottagers, and not far from the decrepit pile a brooding inn, two stories of raw lumber and rough-hewn logs. Bleek looked askance, but the day was done, he required shelter for his animal and himself, and this seemed the only accommodation. The inn promised a stout roof, if nothing else, and faint yellow lights burned within. He tied the pony and entered the dining hall.

The fat, stubble-faced proprietor behind the counter greeted him in jolly fashion, after a disturbing, staring pause. "Pleased to be of service," cried the man warmly, "though surprised I be to see you. Few folk from outside pass this way. Most of my clientele be local. Call me Branden. I manage the place and do the dirty work, while my wife handles the cooking. Yes, I have rooms, not ready now, but one will be, so soon as I get my lady onto it." The innkeeper bawled for the woman, a rather slovenly type who appeared from an inner chamber. "A guest waits, Mistress. Give him stew and bread and ale, and prepare a bed while I see to his beast."

Dinner was served, a fare which suited the weary traveler. Branden returned. "A fine animal you have there, which I fitted up cozy," said he. His wife descended from above, announced Bleek's room ready. She said to her husband, "'Tis a marvel that he come now, right before Festival. There's a meaning to it." "Hush your jabber, woman. The fellow's tired, and he craves a decent bed rather than a ditch by the road." He sent her back to the kitchen for another bowl of stew. He chuckled. "I have to watch her, sir, or she'll talk your ears off. A regular chatterbox, she is. Now me, I keep my own counsel. You don't require my foolishness this night. Funny, however, the timing of it all; you coming at Festival, that is. It's tomorrow day, our annual celebration, by which I mean we hold it once every year, on the Eve of St. Viteglius. But you're an educated chap, by the look of you, and you don't need such explanations. There's naught special in it, as a rule, our gathering, save a tradition that guests are to be honored. That's what the wife meant."

Bleek nodded pleasantly during this harangue, inclined to accept what he heard, whilst laughing inwardly. His studies had told him a thing or two of the archaic underpinnings of the Viteglius tale, one which had been handed down from fearsome pagan times. It amused him that these common peasants should embrace the later Christian veneer, forgetting utterly the dark legends lying beneath.

Hunger sated, Bleek ascended the creaking stairs and ensconced himself in the prepared room, a tiny chamber with low bed, a stand with water jug, and a single shuttered, paneless window. He threw open the latter for air, as it was quite close and musty inside. He exited once for his toilet, then settled in for a sound sleep.

In the morning Bleek woke early to considerable racket emanating from below, and the sounds of activity at his door. Flinging it open he beheld the mistress of the inn and two serving wenches clattering buckets and pans as they cleaned the floors. "Go on down, sir," said she. "Your hosts await." He came down presently, intending to seek directions and be on his way, to find a goodly gathering of locals, male and female of all ages, in the hall. "Here he is now," cried Branden, "the man of the hour. Rest ye merry, Master Bleek. Join us, that we may fete you and offer boon." The visitor accepted a heavy breakfast, during which the innkeeper stood before him and expounded. "As I told you last night, today we hold our Festival of St. Viteglius. There will be feasting, song, and amusements. Today we rejoice, tonight we feast. We feel it our solemn bound duty to invite you. Stay for this day—if no business presses—and allow us to honor you as chosen guest. You will please us, while we devote ourselves to entertaining you. Your beck is our command. One day, sir; little to ask, much to give. Find you that agreeable?" Jacob Bleek agreed. Surely a day he could spare, and the harsh life of the road was not so happy that he rebelled at breaking his journey. Then, too, this matter of the Festival intrigued him. He might learn something from the experience, knowledge of value to his studies.

Bleek knew the standard, popularized tale of St. Viteglius, the determined True Believer of ancient times, he who proved instrumental in driving out or destroying paganism in the land. It was said that he dared confront a coven of witches who sought to lure him to his doom, evil ones who offered him bounty as a trick in order to seize him for their sinister sacrifice. As their guest St. Viteglius joined them, but at the moment of truth he called down another guest, one unbidden by his hosts; an angel of the

Lord, an avenger who slew all the heathen with righteous fire. So ran the story Bleek knew from childhood.

There was a peculiar variant, however, to which he had been exposed by arcane research. If yellowed, crumbling scrolls and antique illuminated manuscripts were to be believed, there was an earlier, perhaps more accurate version of the tale. In this account there was no St. Viteglius—the man had never lived, never existed—but only the grim truth of the cult of Vitegeras, the unspeakable demon God of Torment, a monstrous thing which demanded worship and craved offerings alive and screaming. This cult had terrorized that part of the world, so much so that many a hoary legend spoke of the dangers that befell unwary travelers. Bleek thought it likely that the old stories had grown corrupted with time, so that the distant horrors of Vitegeras had been masked or overlaid by the somewhat more hopeful tale of Viteglius the Saint. If Bleek stayed and paid attention to the minutiae of the Festival, then he might glean the logical elements of the story-telling transformation, which would be something rewarding to add to his book of strange matters.

At Bleek's acceptance of his role as honored guest the crowd roared with joy. The beaming Branden ushered forth a comely young lass, blonde-haired and blue-eyed, announcing, "Master Bleek, meet Gretchen, designated our Rose of the Festival. If this fair one pleases you then she shall be your escort for the day, from this moment until the evening feast. Ask of her anything, and don't be bashful about it." The throng laughed and snickered at this. Gretchen blushed but looked invitingly upon Bleek. Continued Branden, "The great day begins! We all have tasks and pleasures before us, save our guest who expects only the best of the latter. Let's get to it."

The group broke up, leaving Bleek and his charming hostess alone. She asked him, in a rather forward manner which seemed to suggest much, how she could best serve him. Bleek allowed that he harbored great desire to see the town and the developing celebration, to which the girl nonchalantly agreed. They went forth, she clinging devotedly to his arm, into the bright morning of Morstenburg.

The hours after breakfast, while the townsfolk made ready, the couple spent touring the place. They enjoyed a pleasant stroll by the river, the sole area void of activity. Of the village itself there was little to note save the bustle of peasantry, all gaily dressed in what passed for their finest. At the low end of town Bleek observed the church, a typical structure of its kind, here much run down and appearing desolate by its little unkempt cemetery. Bleek opined at this, finding it remarkable that the house of God should look thus.

"'Tis very sad," replied Gretchen, she of the lovely face and, as it happened, musical voice. "'Twas many years ago—before my birth, so I'm told—that our good and wise minister met with his unfortunate accident, a disaster which, tragically, encompassed his whole family. You can be sure there was much mourning that day. Indeed, all such kindly men and their kin tend to be sons of misfortune and unhappy happenstance in these parts, have been for many a generation. It is most pitiful. The far away Church Fathers that last time deigned not to send a replacement to us. So small and lost is Morstenburg, maybe, that they forgot us. Whatever the cause, we have lived without official holy guidance ever since. An unhappy state, sir, I grant you, but we've made do. Our hearts are sound, and we know who rules here eternally, and we make proper obeisance to Him."

To the castle Bleek would go. Dilapidated though it was, the ancient pile bore picturesque allure to a student of the bizarre, and he spied signs of frenetic activity in its vicinity, but when he gave voice to his whim Bleek discovered that his unbounded privileges possessed limits after all. "There we can not go," said Gretchen, with an air of heartfelt remorse. "It is considered unlucky for the noble guest to enter its confines until the hour of the Feast, which is held beneath its ruins. Sate yourself on all else, sir, until the time come, when we will enter there together."

This irked Bleek, as did other curious instances during the course of that day; irked and sobered him to unpleasant possibilities. The signs and portents which led to his mounting unease were few and subtle, yet his mind was subtle, and he detected them, weighed their meaning, pondered their significance. The minute steps of his reasoning fell into place as the merriment of Morstenburg developed. By noon booths had sprouted in the outlying meadows, where light repasts were hawked and trinkets bartered. The former were free to him, and his many self-proclaimed servitors would foist their meat pasties and fruit pastries on him, begging him to eat well during the course of the day, despite his reservations; for should not he save himself for the Feast? His statement to that effect drew cackles of laughter, not all graceful to his ear. One eminent worthy—the burgomeister, it turned out—boomed with a silly grin, "Aye, sir, we will save you for the Feast. Then we will serve you well." Leers and winks among those present, and a giggle from sweet Gretchen, and a muttered rejoinder from a wiseacre, "Too be sure, served on a platter of gold." The latter items for display and sale were more, Bleek realized, that cheap gewgaws, rather nice artworks of gold and silver, bracelets and necklaces of decent craftsmanship and dubious aspect. There was nothing saintly about them. Several bore symbols familiar to Bleek through necromantic delvings, and he shuddered slightly that such seemingly simple folk should possess or fashion imagery the import of which must cause a learned man to quail. The good people of Morstenburg implored him to decorate himself with their finery, offering as much as he wanted as a gift. This troubled him the more because it was impossible that the little town could generate sufficient wealth to give away, in such manner, on an annual basis as they would have it.

MORSTENBURG

Come the afternoon and the singing and dancing began. The booths were abandoned, all the people great and small poured forth to revel. Bleek was sullenly enclosed within the web of their masses, Gretchen earnestly tugging at his arm whenever he made to slip away. The folk seemed to be working themselves into a frantic state, the mob surging and swaying with apparent mindlessness, while ever closing upon the relic of the castle. Branden rushed past on one occasion, pausing in stride to cry wildly, "The hour approaches, sir. Shortly we feast. For you is reserved a special place, Master Bleek. Truly it will be the glory of your life."

Bleek pieced together the slender evidences and came up with a theory that both amused and horrified him. The sequestered village with its holy day founded upon obscure and evil pagan rites; the absence of official church influence, the hint of morbidity underlying that absence; the odd insinuations and increasingly strange behavior of these folk, culminating in their granting him their relative treasures, which as a matter of logic he could not be allowed to retain; these pieces Bleek fashioned into a possible whole, deriving from them a picture which gratified him not. Deduced he that they were survivors of the dreadful cult of Vitegeras, retaining furtively their olden ways, enticing him with honeyed words and baubles that he might be lured to the time and place of sacrifice, one which must bear—if he guessed rightly from their chortling hints—cannibalistic overtones. So Bleek reasoned, so he foresaw, and as night dropped upon the torch lit throng and he was propelled toward the castle door, so he wove his plans.

Once alert, now wary, Bleek did not fear the people of Morstenburg. He possessed sorceric arts, tricky methods and difficult yet powerful, by which he could shield himself from sudden hostility and repel murderous attack. He laughed to himself when he imagined how he might deal with these fools should they lay hands on him. Thinking thus, he climbed the mound and stepped lightly within the wrecked castle, into a shattered chamber of broken stones and rotten hangings, pressed from all sides and urged onward by his hosts. They did not ascend the tottering remnants of the spiral staircase to the forlorn tower, but surged across the room and plunged steeply down a narrow stepped passage, down through dank and dirty gloom onto a lower, subterranean floor, where by the flickering light of standing torches Bleek spied a double circle of limestone benches enclosing an octagonal dais littered with choice foodstuffs, calves and swine roasted whole, and scattered elements of gold and silver jewelry.

"Behold the throne, Master Bleek," bawled the burgomeister. "Take your place, man of honor." Bleek was rudely shoved into the circle toward the dais, Gretchen joining in with sardonic laughter. The townsfolk—there seemed an incredible number of them in that confined space—swarmed onto the benches. The Morstenburg fathers, a group which included the ever buoyant Branden, donned the white robes which hung from pegs at the entrance. Said the innkeeper, "I trust ye shall relish the Feast so much as we." Bleek prepared to make a magic that would blast the fellow, and any other who came near.

Intoned the burgomeister, "Aye, we will dine presently, but first we look upon the true Feast. Our lord Vitegeras grows impatient. He will be appeased. Unto you all I say, Begin!" And the crowd started to chant, an eerie keening and wailing in an ancient and largely forgotten language, words chanted here since the dark times of lost eons. They recited in echoing unison, and as they did something weird happened.

Jacob Bleek had erred. Having readied himself for a physical attack, common enough regardless of motive, he discovered now that greater peril assailed him. Hard it was to face this resurgence of survival of the Vitegeras cult, more distressing still to confront the focus of the cult in His flesh. The folk of Morstenburg might be evil and sly, but they were no fools; the basis in fact of their hateful religion appeared before them on the dais, tangible and monstrously real.

This foul thing they worshipped, this lumpen, slimy, glistening mass of foulness was their master. It quivered, jelly-like, turning to face Bleek, a face of many spidery eyes and gaping maw. Jagged teeth protruded from the drooling mouth. Bleek stood as if stricken, unable at the moment to comprehend the enormity of the danger, the magnitude of his miscalculation. Vitegeras slopped toward him, whilst from that filthy heap of disgust incarnate radiated a strong, insidious influence, a silent calling that sought to draw the chosen victim into it. Bleek could not calculate, could not puzzle; he must act by quick instinct and sound training in the possibilities of necromancy. He flung himself to the hard floor, eyes closed, face to the cold paving stone, fumbled in a pocket of his cloak for an amulet and a vial of powder that he knew should be there. He whispered arcane words, words of eternal power, as hot, stinking breath panted down his neck. He rapidly mumbled the mystical words of ancient Artocris the Mage, the words of Final Protection...

And Vitegeras drew away from him! The unspeakable creature growled angrily, yet the baleful calling continued, intensified, reached out. Then Bleek heard sounds of restiveness and smothered exclamations from the audience, muffled pleas and oaths, followed by the shuffling of halting footsteps. He heard the steps approach and pass, then choked cries and a nasty slobbering sound. More such sounds, more still, interspersed with a sickening crunching noise. Forever it seemed that cacophony lasted, while Bleek remained immobile, whispering his chant over and over. Finally the sounds died away, came a little pop and a trace of rancid stench, and only then, in the reverberating silence, did Bleek raise his head to survey the scene. He was alone. He rose to his feet, hugging tightly his cloak, looking in every direction. The chamber was empty save for himself. Vitegeras had gone back into his plane of existence, whether that be an astral realm or pit of Hell, and the pious folk of Morstenburg had gone with him. The animal offerings too had vanished, perhaps as a casual afterthought, a reasonable supposition given the choice of delicacies at this feast. Only the items of jewelry remained, splashed with daubs of gore.

Jacob Bleek vacated the chamber and departed from the drear emptiness of Morstenburg soon thereafter. Before he left the underground room he helped himself to all the gold and silver he could carry. The stuff had been promised to him, after all, and an itinerant wizard was ever in need of goods convertible into ready coin. A harrowing experience this visit to Morstenburg, he thought, but one in all profitable, and not without elements of interest. He felt that he had relived the tale of St. Viteglius, while uncovering its bitter reality. Bleek was satisfied. Men of his type were famed for acquiring informative lore via strange means.

The Crags of the Schwartzenburg

Jacob Bleek, wanderer of a benighted age, was a scholar of strange and forgotten lore, and his unusual studies had trained him to sniff out the furtive signs of the uncanny and the arcane. As he rode now on the tiring mare along the rough trail across the steep, densely forested slope, an inner sense told him—not in words, but it was like a voice in that it informed him clearly and unmistakably—that a dark presence lurked nearby, a force beyond that suggested by the gloom and chiaroscuro of the wild landscape. Somewhere south of him, perhaps this side of an evening's ride, lay the wide Danube, and Bavarian towns with civilized folk and lights and comfortable inns, but here, at this moment, he beheld the rude world as it had been since time's dawn, and felt the breath of undefined, mystical menace.

Yet the first sight of interest did not so indicate. Coming round the slope, a gap parted in the pines before, revealing the stark outlines of a very high hill or low mountain across a little valley, cloaked in trees save where ragged crags of black basalt protruded, and atop the pointed peak of dark bare rock stood a simple white cross, a wholesome image scarcely evocative of threat. To be sure, Bleek's inclinations toward esoteric knowledge were such as to alarm or offend the religious authorities of many lands through which he had traveled, and as he advanced southward he learned that toleration for his intellectual oddities markedly declined. Still, he knew that this distant, unadorned symbol was not the instigator of his developing unease.

The horse, too, sensed something. She balked at continuing along this course, so he had recourse to the lash, and she proceeded then, eager to display unwillingness at any opportunity. So by fits and starts Jacob Bleek descended the trail, encouraging and cajoling his beast as need be, until he reached bottom where a placid, shadowed creek forlornly trickled.

He followed the gentle flow until the forest drew aside to make way for tilled fields and pasture, which in turn stood aside for a narrow lake which curved closely around the wooded cliffs at the base of the notable mountain. The trail became a cart path. At the end of the lake he observed the earthen dam which provided sure evidence of human construction, with confirming glimpses of solid habitations shortly downstream. In another minute he entered the village.

The furtive hints of evil remained, though there was nothing in this fresh scene to justify disturbance. It was a tiny, backward, slovenly place, hardly promising for a night's rest, yet of a type familiar. There the church, the only building that stood out above a huddle of thatched cottages and anonymous wooden structures, and there—over there, to the right—maybe an inn. He would investigate that.

The citizens of the village came to Bleek in the street, to hail this stranger, with his pale face and dark robes, formal bearing and educated manners, and to inquire of his business. Little information he offered, save that he was a scholar of antique rarities, but he asked after their hospitality, and they proved good-natured enough, perhaps because a reading and writing man demanded their respect. It was Herr Tollmann, a portly fellow with an easy smile, who said to him, "Welcome to Ganich, good sir, and well met I say, for the shadows grow long, and the clouds gather over the Schwartzenburg. If you seek to stop here, I beg that you confer with me. An inn for the gentleman traveler we have not in these parts, nor will you find one this side of the big river, and ere the moon rises the ferry will cease to run; but I own the public place, the only one in Ganich, and I can arrange accommodations which shall not distress. Say the word, sir, and I and mine are at your command."

Bleek grinned to himself, answered appropriately, was beckoned down the lane to the building previously noted. Herr Tollmann spoke truly when he refrained from describing it as an inn. A tavern, yes, with a cramped dining hall and bar drawing several patrons, some sort of kitchen, and store rooms and closets in back. One of these, as it transpired, would be cleared for Bleek's benefit.

The traveler, with weary geniality, expressed satisfaction with the arrangements. The landlord's beefy son Dieter saw to the mare; Tollmann's stout wife Olivia concocted a filling stew; his daughter Merta, not yet in her prime, eagerly served Bleek at table, bearing steaming bowl, a wooden spoon, an earthenware cup and a tankard of amber beer. Bleek gave thanks for small favors, relinquished a couple of coins, thought himself decently disposed.

With his belly replenished, he thought to stoke his mind. Something in or about Ganich nagged at his brain. Bleek commenced artfully jovial conversation with his host, asking of conditions thereabouts. That man gave commonplace, unconsidered replies until Bleek, in praising the local scenery, opined that fine views might be had from the heights that loomed over the village. At this Herr Tollmann paused uncomfortably, stared intently at nothing for a spell, answered after inordinate hesitation, "One does not climb the Schwartzenburg."

Bleek casually contested this, alluding to the cross mounted on the far peak. Someone, he suggested with a fey shrug, had planted it up there. The topic seemed to make Tollmann nervous. He said shortly, "You will find a pretty walk along the stream and by the lake. The lake path is a popular favorite with the young. I can recommend a stroll so far as the Vendras Gate; thus far, no farther. Beyond that, on the black mountain, lies unrewarding country."

Herr Tollmann announced himself called away at this juncture. Bleek was left alone to finish his repast and muse over these tidbits of information. Though he did not show it—not so much as by the flicker of an eyelash—

the reference to "Vendras" confounded him, for he somewhat knew the term from his scholastic delvings into the darker arts. The Vendras Circle, as he understood it, was a cult of degenerate priests who, in a former century, had practiced abominable rites devoted to objectionable gods. Tales of their bizarre enormities formed the stuff of nasty legend, and served to justify historical anecdotes of their vicious suppression. Until this moment Bleek had heard of them solely in a past context.

By degrees he managed to quiz the rest of the Tollmann family. Little Merta, while clearing the table, admitted that she dared not approach the gate, for fear that ghosts would clasp her there or come to her by night, but that her parents went there on days of the saints to lay charms on the steps to ward off those who dwelt beyond. The mother Olivia intruded, chased away her daughter, apologized for her fanciful stories. The laying of charms, she averred, was a harmless local conceit authorized by the church. She closed the subject with a certain asperity. Dieter, leading Bleek to his room, had more to say when asked about the route to the top of the Schwartzenburg. He said, "The black mountain is forbidden to men. Our priest tells us that evil lives there, old evil which is wont to invade our homes when disturbed. We do what we can to ward it off. I have helped lay charms at the Vendras Gate with my father. Always I carry one with me. Here it is." Dieter drew from his pocket a purplish oval stone cut in the fashion of an eye with a minute cross etched in the pupil.

Slumber tarried in coming to Bleek in his rude lodgings that night, and when it finally did it brought a peculiar dream. He found himself in darkness, with the impression of dank walls enclosing him. Out of the oppressive black miasma he spied a glittering yellow orb, then another, then many, countless pale ovals tightly grouped, suspended in nothingness. He realized they were eyes, eyes without face or face unseen, but surely a presence of bulk and substance occupied the indeterminate space with him, watching, observing, calculating. He sensed a baleful, pitiless intelligence that scrutinized, seeking his sum as it prepared to act. Then the eyes rushed forward, wrapped him in greedy, hungry vision. He awoke. He fingered the ornate gold talisman hanging at his throat. Fashioned in the shape of a rhombus, it enclosed the image of a grinning skull with green eyes of jade. Herr Tollmann had looked askant upon this item, been fobbed with a lie pertaining to a collegiate club. Bleek bethought to himself that his studies had granted him knowledge of magical charms surer than those of the villagers. Dream it may have been, but Bleek suspected that he had experienced a close call.

Come the morning Jacob Bleek would not go. He allowed that he would spend the day partaking of sylvan pleasures, tasked his host with making up a pack of food and drink. This modest request apparently troubled Herr Tollmann, who urged his guest, "for God's sake," not to wander too far afield. Bleek left him to his simple task, and concealing his necklace within his cloak sought the priest in his church, the only stone building in town. That worthy served alone, as was customary in such a small village, eking out a bare but earnest living from sporadic donations. He crossed himself when asked about the Schwartzenburg, did so again at pointed mention of the Vendras Gate. That term meant nothing specific to him, though in his statements the priest clearly treated that location across the lake as the edge of decent and healthy territory.

But what of that obvious cross on the peak? Here Bleek heard a remarkable story. The priest told it this way: "The cross dates from the time of my father's grandfather. In former years there were bad men who lived up there, worshippers of the devil I fear, who plagued damnably the honest folk of the valley. Their fell cravings instigated frightful murders and inexplicable disappearances. Finally the king's men marched against them, slew them or drove them away. So it should have been, only there remained influences, presences barely seen, if commonly heard at night. Still there occurred occasional atrocities, committed now by no men known to be living. My ancestor was also priest. One sunny day he scaled the heights with two companions, bearing with them materials for a standing cross, previously bathed in Holy Water. They gained the top, planted the cross, made their way down. During the descent something happened. One man did not return. The two survivors refused to explain. They said he was dead—as the tale came to me, they hoped he was dead—but they would not describe his end. Sad to relate, their godly quest was for naught. The cross stands, but the black mountain reeks still of evil. Just last year a boy vanished from our midst. There were screams from the high forest that night; screams, and laughter. I tell you, sir, that was never human laughter."

This was, for Bleek, an entertaining and wholly absorbing tale. He returned to the tavern to collect his pack, fending off Herr Tollmann's questions and smiling at his heartfelt advice, and with staff in hand set out through the village to the lake. He crossed over the foot path atop the dam, made his way onto the lonely east side where the rocky roots of the black mountain extended dark fingers among the reeds. In time a cliff barrier rose up at the shore, and the trail ascended a flight of rough-hewn carved steps up the face of the stony mass to a narrow gap barred by a heavy oaken, iron-bound door. This was none other than the ill-spoken Vendras Gate. On the ledge fronting the weathered door lay a scattering of crudely made amulets of purple, semi-precious minerals carved into simple shapes. There were crucifixes, but not in plenty; the eye images predominated, many with superimposed crosses situated so as, he reasoned, to blind the eyes. Bleek remembered his dream, wondered which was cart, which horse.

The high door creaked open at the touch of his staff. There was no lock. Having passed the gate Jacob Bleek immediately experienced an intensifying of the gloomy sensation that had assailed him since entering the valley. Truly, he thought, ominous powers dwelt here. A rock path scaled the basalt barrier, led him into shadowed forest which knew not the kiss of the ax. A furtive breeze rustled the needles of the pines. His boots squeaked as he trod earth and stone. Otherwise, silence reigned. The mountain seemed devoid of life.

In lieu of better, Bleek directed his feet toward the distant cross way above him on the highest crag. He marched without formal direction, but the vague trail led ever upward, which took him the way he wanted to go. He climbed swiftly, pausing at times for a gulp of water. Once, between a thinning of branches, he spied Ganich below, already appearing small and forlorn. Then the forest swallowed him.

The path (trodden by whom?) practically gave out as he stumbled amidst the loftier crags, where the wind commenced to howl. Unfazed he continued, however, for now he had a sure shot of the white cross directly ahead, framed by the trees, centered squarely on the utmost pinnacle of a blocky mound of pitch basalt. A deal of huffing and puffing got him beyond the tree line and to the top, and there he momentarily enjoyed the sweeping view of the slender valley, the sullen loop of lake, the toy village and its patchwork fields.

Bleek examined the cross with care. Taller than a man it stood, of lovingly planed, white-washed lumber. An inscription in clumsy Latin evoked the mercy of God, pled for release from undefined peril. So much he expected. Deduced he had, too, the worn, dilapidated aspect of the wooden fabrication when viewed at near remove. What intrigued him was the apparently subsequent, corollary inscription, in better Latin, partly scratched over the original. A thin, claw-like instrument had written, "As the world endures, so reigns Xenophor, He of the Thousand Eyes."

This was meat indeed to a scholar who hungered for knowledge of the mystic and the arcane. In a cloistered monastery the student Bleek once perused an incomplete illuminated manuscript which dared relate, in halting, fragmentary paragraphs, the abysmal legend of Great Xenophor, Lord of All things, Creator and Destroyer, the focus of a primordial religion sinister and secretive, old when the Egyptian sorcerer Imhotep planned the first pyramid. This marked a curious intrusion of theme. Bleek connected his discovery to the Vendras Circle, the details of whose worship had been a mystery to him. More he understood now. But who had scrawled the words?

He garnered no sense of protection from the cross. He thought that another power ruled the black mountain. At present it seemed that his explorations were at an end, that nothing remained but to descend the steep trail and return to the village bearing augmented mystery. In this he was mistaken. Picking his way carefully down the crags and between black fingers of standing stone, with the lively wind frantic to pluck him into deadly space, Jacob Bleek noticed regularities among the dark rocks to his left. He veered to investigate. Those rectangular openings in the basalt truly resembled windows. He circled a difficult tongue of rock, faced a larger, cone-shaped opening through which a man could readily enter. This Bleek did.

From supplies he brought with him he made a torch, which he lit and carried before him into the interior. Bleek entered a series of spacious chambers chiseled out of the living rock, a sequence of rooms connected by short corridors and radiating from a central hall. Bare of furnishings they were—save for infrequent heaps of smashed or burned debris—yet expansive enough that he likened them to the chambers of a small castle gouged from the stone, rather than built on it. The dusty stone floors were perfectly level, the ceilings high and sooty. The walls were adorned with paint, red and yellow ocher on stone that still kept their vibrant colors despite the uncounted years of neglect. Several images were defaced. Bleek hazarded the obvious guess, based on the priest's account, that the king's men of long ago had sacked the place when they raided the mountain retreat of the evil ones. They had overborne that which was material, that which would fall before sword and pike.

The paintings interested him exceedingly. They consisted mainly of clustered yellow eyes enclosed in nebulous red forms, no one quite the same as the other. The insidious glare of those eyes, so artfully rendered, held him aghast. Bleek really felt as if he were being watched from all sides. There were inscriptions here, too, in Latin and the common script, praising or imploring Great Xenophor. Still more inscriptions were entirely indecipherable, but he supposed the meaning of a certain recurring group of letters or runes writ large.

The big room at the heart of the complex contained a kind of altar, a massive slab on which stood a heavy basalt basin. Around this were flat-topped stones arranged like seats. The basin was encrusted with gritty, odorous black powder. Within and around it were a surprising number of disarticulated human bones. They were hacked and scorched. They were also much too recent to constitute evidence of ancient ritual or conflict. The smaller remains, those of a youth, were appallingly fresh.

At the realization Bleek staggered under a wave of dread, an induced fear funneled against him by enemies unseen. He gasped at the psychic weight of the cruel torrent. So the powers that haunted the Schwartzenburg were aware of him, knew his location; knew, possibly, the contents of his mind? Ethereal tendrils plucked at his consciousness. He felt them, through their sudden emanation sensed the invisible embodiment of that which had not died nor been extirpated, but lingered on, less active in this wilderness waste but scarcely dormant. The spirits of the Vendras Circle lived, clinging to their gathering place of old, craving as ever the sacrifices by which they adored and propitiated their awesome master!

With a smooth mental effort he turned aside the ghostly emotional weapon. He was not to be mastered that way. Not for nothing had Jacob Bleek dedicated his years to uncovering the secrets of the weird and macabre forces that swirl around the blandly materialistic shell of life. He muttered certain words, motioned with his fingertips, via these simple means surmounting the moment. This revelation of ability did not pass unnoticed by the invisible enemies infesting the place. They redoubled their efforts. This time they presented him with images. Of a sudden a gory tableau was enacted before him, in which he was granted audience to a scene of supernatural sacrifice, possibly the most recent carried out in that chamber. Bleek beheld misty forms pushing and dragging a cringing, screaming lad in rustic, contemporary attire to the altar; pressing him down onto the stone; the startling gleam of a big, hazy blade; a gurgling shriek, gouts of blood.

This was more information than Bleek desired. He intoned a stronger charm that wiped away the brutal vision, leaving him alone in the empty stone room, but he wondered now if his quest for forbidden knowledge had led him astray on this occasion. These doubts were reinforced when the attack against him assumed a more solid, less psychic character.

This time the fear he felt was not entirely due to an exterior funneling. He heard a hoarse, guttural chanting, punctuated by fiendish laughter. A pale yellow light permeated the chamber. It coalesced into a foggy mass, which then splintered into a hundred or a thousand twinkling sparks. These faux stars subsided into a dire suggestion of many disembodied, unwinking eyes. Then they zoomed toward him, dashing at his face like a swarm of angry bees. He heard the raucous cry of "Xenophor!" and at that instant the hateful eyes disappeared. The priests of the Vendras Circle stood before him, seven of them, clad in robes of black and crimson, knives in hand, their faces covered with scarlet masks through which glared their implacably hostile eyes. They stepped forward.

Jacob Bleek ran, ran madly, but not away from his foes; no, he dashed at them, head bowed, clutching at the odd golden talisman that dangled from his neck and swiping wildly with his staff. He heard the terrible sound of blades ripping through air, felt the bite of razored metal at his shoulder. He hit the floor, rolled, came up at the altar. He tore the talisman from its chain, planted it on the altar, thundered the monstrous word *Astrodemus*. The chamber rocked with the frightful echoes. Astrodemus—an olden designation for a power that haunted the spheres outside of stale reality—an aggressive, blighting force that ate into and nullified other, competing powers; Astrodemus, to whom Bleek had called during a particularly dangerous experiment that he might further his studies into the darkest principalities of ancient lore; Astrodemus, whose essence dwelt in the magical talisman! This he carried with him always against special peril. This he now employed in desperation to negate the concentrated evil surrounding him, by planting it squarely in the heart of the menace.

THE JOURNEY OF JACOB BLEEK

His cry or prayer was answered. The fruits of his arcane scholarship held good. He felt the opposing force diminish. It indisputably weakened, but only by degrees. The dead priests of Vendras, servants of Xenophor, hesitated, gargled screams of rage, but then they came on again. Bleek swung with both hands his stout staff like a club, bashed through to the door which led to the outer chambers. He fled frantically through these to the outside air. The priests and their knives did not follow. Did the talisman constrain them? It might be so, but the wind howled a gale, and black clouds scudded across the sapped sun, and the very crags shuddered as with strange fever. Bleek noticed the cross above swaying on its stony perch. He practically hurled himself off the ledge and into the trees.

He found the path, a thankful blessing, but he was, so to speak, not yet out of the woods. The obviously faltering force threatening him was scarcely obliterated. Its fangs, blunted, were still long and sharp enough to inflict damage, perhaps lethal. The journey down the mountain seemed endless, impossibly longer than the weary trudge up. The trees bent toward him, clawed his flesh and clothing with spiky branches. Stones thrust themselves at his ankles. Thick shadows—not robed priests, mercifully, but something more tangible than wisps of darkness—stepped out from the corners of his vision to grope at him. Twice an influence swelled in his mind, demanding that he return and retrace his steps to the heights of the mountain, where he should acquiesce in the justice of unhallowed vengeance. This he did not do. The strength of the talisman defended him at a distance.

Once he passed the Vendras Gate the persistent low level onslaught ended. Bleek realized he was trembling, bathed in oily perspiration. He could feel still the unpleasant emanations from the upper crags of the Schwartzenburg, but they were latent now, relatively harmless. Either the force of the talisman was conquering, or the contest of powers up there was muting the evil radiation. Whichever the case, the festering mood of darkness which he had sensed since approaching the black mountain had definitely lessened, to the point that he felt no longer a perilous presence waiting to pounce.

Of this development he informed his hosts in Ganich, and grateful they were, as well as astounded. Said Herr Tollmann, "Never thought I to behold you again, Master Bleek, this side of death. I suspected your destination, deplored what I deemed your recklessness. I should have reckoned that a man of books and letters would know more of these matters than we." His wife said, "Miracles are cause for celebration. This day we shall feast you, at no expense to your purse. Would there were more we could do in your honor." The priest sought him out, came to him and said, "It is necessary that I understand. Before you leave us, tell me all. This knowledge I will inscribe, against the growth of fresh terrors."

All this was nothing to Jacob Bleek, who treated with them all on their

220

terms, made the most of bounty bestowed. When he left them the following morn to continue his journey he did so replete with satisfaction at the wisdom accrued, which he vowed should soon direct his studies into profitable channels. The acolytes of the Vendras Circle, whether living or dead, were capable of instructing him in a great deal of peculiar insights. He regretted, though, the loss of the talisman of Astrodemus, a potent tool sacrificed in order to save his life and soul. That gold emblem had been his most costly possession, and one acquired through extraordinary difficulty, for he had paid much for a devious and greedy agent to purloin the thing from the rotted neck of a long dead wizard buried in a guarded tomb. It would not be easy to replace. In his quest for unearthly lore he would surely stumble into dire circumstances yet again. Before that happened, he swore to himself that he must be well armed.

The Companion of Jacob Bleek

In the olden times the great sorcerer Jacob Bleek journeyed to Egypt in quest of secrets. There, in that already ancient land of weird mysteries and ominous marvels, he thought to uncover strange knowledge which would serve to increase his magical wisdom and enhance his wizardly powers. He had heard much, naturally, of that kingdom, and had read many an account by former seekers of earlier ages, travelers who had sought the wildest wonders that the earth could bestow, and who had found—or failed to find, or perished trying to find—those kernels of esoteric lore which ought to make a keen-minded man mighty and fearfully respected by his peers. So there Bleek went, to Egypt, arriving in caravan out of the merciless desert, and having arrived, he sought the city of Cairo, the gateway to Egypt's lost past.

Those who plague the casual tourist (for there were such, even in those days), the Arab guides and peddlers and so forth, swarmed about him in the Cairo bazaar when he came, but they did not harass him long, for there was that in his tall, lean, pale-faced presence which disturbed them and suggested that here was a man with whom they dare not trifle. Bleek wrapped his black cloak about him, shook his oaken staff and declared that he had no use for trinkets and tale spinners. He hungered, he said, for the genuine secrets of the pharaohs, those mysteries that reside in forgotten chambers within the pyramids and in papyrus documents eternally entombed with the hallowed dead. Hearing this, most of the smiling, congenial parasites fell away, leaving only one, a man of courage and greed named Atabarsis, of Greek extraction, who claimed to know something others did not, an avenue to real knowledge that might impress a true mage. Bleek listened warily.

Forget, said Atabarsis, the popular monuments which once awed the legendary Greeks and Romans. They were but pretty hills of rock, long plundered of their princely treasures and their marketable wares. Whatever mysteries had been buried in those places had been mined in former ages, and were surely common coin to a practicing magician of note. Bleek allowed that it was likely, and urged the man to say on. Atabarsis told him then of a scarce known pyramid, a small and badly weathered edifice which had never known the thrust of the spade, yet which was one of the very oldest in the land, and about which antique tales were still whispered. It was not easy to find, unless one knew where to look, but it was not far away from the greater pyramids, and he, Atabarsis, could direct the visiting gentleman there. What, asked Bleek, was the significance of this pyramid? It was, said his informant in a low voice, the last resting place of the revered Egyptian sorcerer Imhotep.

They hammered out a deal on the spot, the wizard offering gold, the native supplying information. For Jacob Bleek knew well the hoary reputation of Imhotep, that fabled mage of the world's youth who had explored the arcana of existence in the misty past, when the heyday of ancient Egypt was still but a dream. Eons ago that man, more than any other, had laid the foundations of civilization in the shadowy precursor kingdom of Khem. Counselor to the pharaohs, man of mind, medicine, and magic, he had stamped his genius upon the earth by the Nile and out of it sprang perpetual glory and a new age of the world. The first architect, he raised the original pyramids, monuments to others which, in Bleek's estimation, served only to honor Imhotep and his amazing mind. In his day he had known all that man could know, and among the fraternity of wizards it had been ever held as verity that many titanic discoveries, quietly hinted at through the centuries, had died with him, and perhaps—a tantalizing possibility!—the records of those accomplishments interred with him.

Why, demanded Bleek, had no one raided the site and stolen the intellectual treasures of that incredible repository? Because, he now heard, the location was nondescript and uninviting to craven looters, and because, to those who knew a little more, the place was said to be accursed. There were stories—not such as to hinder a clever mage—of dangerous, lurking forces that watched over the honorably dead worthy, and tales of obscure but horrific tragedies which had come upon the inquisitive. Atabarsis acknowledged his own concern, and his own desperation; he would not go there himself, but he would show the way, and the noble sir could do with the information as he pleased.

They went their separate ways until nightfall, while Bleek busied himself with preparations, gathering about himself a gang of tough and bitter men who would risk anything for a gold coin apiece. When the Egyptian sun fell into the endless desert Atabarsis reappeared and led his master and his men with their tools onto the dusty plains of Gizeh, where they made for the brooding Sphinx which crouched ever before the mightiest of the pyramids. Atabarsis pointed to the time-blighted face of the curious monument, and drew a line directly from the stone beast's right eye, the one which, at that time, still bore its original golden orb worked tightly into its limestone socket. He drew a line from the eye to splendid white Sirius just descending to the horizon, marking the angle with pebbles. Look there, he said, to the edge of the plateau, where the bright star grazed the earth, and there one might dimly spy a bump in the landscape, a subtle discontinuity. That low mound, far removed, was in fact the jumbled remains of the pyramid of Imhotep, old already when the artificial mountain of Cheops was young. Dig there, he said, where no one had thought or dared to dig, and Bleek would find whatever lingered there, untouched until that day. The wizard acknowledged this but paused, contemplating the speculative nature of the information. Already out of pocket for the laborers' pay, he would spend no more of his own capital, but—by way of honoring his deal—muttered in a quiet chant certain odd words of power, at which moment the wind whipped up and, to the amazement of all present, the golden right eye of the Sphinx popped out of its socket and fell to the ground between the giant's paws. Take that, said Bleek, if thou wilt, and go. Atabarsis hesitated, locked in superstitious terror, but the lust for gold overcame him, and he leapt forward, seized the priceless old object and ran, vanishing into the cloak of night. It is to be hoped that he gained from his boon, and that misfortune never came his way due to his brief acquaintance with Jacob Bleek.

With the simple course charted for him, Bleek led his men across the plain in darkness, allowing no torches, to the distant ridge marked by the wildly twinkling star. Sirius soon dipped below the rim of the earth, yet the path was true and constant, and before an hour was out they attained their goal. The wreckage of Imhotep's monument was surely nothing to impress, and it did not surprise the foreign mage that it had been largely overlooked. Little of the structure's original shape remained intact, the pyramid now resembling one more pile of rock and dirt, grand in size, yet unappealing and uninspiring. There were no carvings or paintings in evidence, no indications or clues whatsoever. Testily Bleek commanded to his foreman, Ali Bey, that the men dig, so the Arab shouted harshly to the others, who produced their spades and haphazardly dug. A hole here, a pit there, now the beginnings of a tunnel; until well after the warm midnight they strenuously worked, turning over the soil, sifting the debris, shifting with stout levers the limestone blocks, many of which weighed a ton or more. Eventually they discovered, on the flat underside of a square stone, traces of what Bleek recognized as a funereal painting, and further excavation at that spot turned up a chiseled band of hieroglyphics, fragmentary and crude—its very crudeness a delight, for it suggested staggering antiquity, a period when the written script had not coalesced into the polished form well known to the most devoted of esoteric scholars—containing, within a faded red cartouche, the welcome stylized pictorial syllables of the crow, eye, and stalk of wheat which translated as Im-Ho-Tep. Doubt ended then; the Greek had spoken truly to that extent, and the great Imhotep lay buried beneath those ruins.

Minutes later they found the top of the burial tunnel. Bleek ordered his men to dig down there, and they did, gradually descending a man's height and more until they ran into a stone slab, a plug of faced granite which, unlike most of the upper blocks, was still in situ. The workers produced hammers and chisels, attacking the barrier, smashing and chipping their way through. The stone cracked; the fissure widened; the barrier splintered and broke into pieces. Bleek pushed to the forefront, thrusting his torch into the black hole. The flame flickered as a noxious vapor gushed forth. He peered within. Then he dismissed the men, giving to each payment for services, and an extra coin apiece to hold their tongues. Having been paid they departed, leaving quickly, with obvious relief.

THE JOURNEY OF JACOB BLEEK

As soon as they were out of sight Bleek entered the crypt, which no living man had beheld for thousands of years. The adornments of the death chamber were simple, for Egypt had not yet garnered great wealth in those days, and the deceased, for all his merits, had not been a pharaoh, but there were silver statuettes of the gods, some gold inlay on ceremonial plaques, vivid colors on painted mahogany, and images of freakish dog-headed priests adorning the walls. Then there was the sarcophagus, a massy oblong box of sanded greenish granite, the lid firmly in place, as was intended for all time. Here the mortal shell of the honored one would rest through eternity, as commanded by Thoth and Osiris, if those who laid him there had their way. An inscription on top warned of the dreadful fate sure to befall any who tampered with the casket. Bleek planted his torch securely and employed an iron bar, discarded by his hirelings, to raise and topple the lid. It fell with a crash, exposing the grim contents. The wizard stared briefly at those desiccated remnants of humanity, the dry, crisp wrappings, the patches of tough, leathery, time darkened flesh, all that physically remained of the magnificent and wise Imhotep. After that pause he tumbled the corpse from its stone box and probed the interior of the container for items of worth. Finding nothing, he search the small room for hidden materials, damaging the priceless furnishings in the process. Still finding nothing, he then (and only then, for which he gave himself credit) ripped into the mummy.

He tore off the head and felt with his fingers into every cavity, pulling out the false eyes of garnet and tugging loose the real teeth. He broke off the fingers as he unfurled the clenched fists. He ruptured the papery abdomen and reached into that broader space of emptiness, and there his search bore fruit. He extracted from the opening a wad of flattened scrolls, tied with frayed cord, onto which a long dead priest of the ancient ones had pasted a waxen seal, now worn and distorted, which Bleek could barely read. The implied threat referred to the extreme danger of those sacred writings, should they fall into the wrong hands. He flicked away the seal with a fingernail and gingerly separated the tightly coiled papyrus sheets, seven of them, hastily examining their contents. Yes, there was much here of value to him. He wrapped the scrolls in heavy canvas, placed them within his travel bag, retrieved his torch and prepared to exit the forsaken chamber. He stepped over the mummy as he made for the upward tunnel.

And a hollow voice spoke to him from out of the gloomy room, saying, "Jacob Bleek, I know thee, as I know much that is beyond the ken of mortal men. We are kin, you and I, brothers in mind and spirit, so I desire not to strike thee down, as is my choice. My greatest and holiest of secrets reside within those documents. Use them well, if thou wisheth, if thou canst, but I give you in fairness this warning. Beware He who followeth in the night and in the shadows, He who approacheth stealthily with foul intent. During my life I learned much, and had cause to suffer much. Thou hast learned, and would learn more, as I did. If thou keepeth the scrolls, then gain great wisdom, and despair of life and sanity. If this does not suit, then replace the scrolls and depart in peace. Again I sleep." Bleek, shaken, thought the breathless voice spoke to him from the shattered head on the floor, but he could not be certain, and it spoke no more. He fled from the benighted chamber, taking with him the scrolls.

He gave thought, in the days to come, to the strange and menacing discourse from beyond the grave, but only those scrolls could fascinate him. He, Jacob Bleek, possessed the lost writings of Imhotep! As soon as time and leisure permitted he spread the seven priceless documents upon the table in his primitive lodgings by the banks of the Nile, and there he studied. He translated the archaic pictographs and he read. As he read, marvelous vistas of hitherto concealed knowledge sprang out at him and seized upon his fevered mind. Imhotep wrote of the Gods; not the conventional, popular deities of the common herd, but the true Entities of boundless power which reside behind all life and existence, the creators and governors of the universe. The Egyptian described complex magical formulae by which the Great Ones could be contacted, and he broadly hinted at secret places on earth where such spells would prove especially effective. He alluded, in expansive terms, to the grandiose personal benefits to be derived from such contact, and made quite clear, in a roundabout fashion, that he had indulged in such traffic, and had gained thereby. This was exactly the sort of information that Bleek craved, for he had, as he saw it, acquired all that knowledge which the material world could bestow, and must needs reach outside for more. Imhotep provided him a blueprint for sorcerial action.

Jacob Bleek was a man without nerves, a lifetime of morbid delving and frightful research into monstrous realms of thought having burned from his soul the petty cares and concerns which tax what he considered lesser brains. Nevertheless there were moments, late at night, or during the uncanny hours before dawn, while he perused the manuscript by the feeble rays of a guttering candle, that a sensation of icy unpleasantness would creep upon him, and he would suddenly turn, and glance behind into the darkness of the room, and imagine that someone had quietly joined him from out the shadows. Never was this the case, but the feeling troubled him, and troubled him more as he read on from Imhotep's words bearing on dire corollary matters.

This line of investigation, wrote the Egyptian mage, encompassed furtive dangers. The Gods were not eager for congress with men, and they had fashioned servitors to guard them against unwanted meddling. These horrific beings dwelt within a sphere outside of time and space, below that of the Gods, beyond that of man, and normally were prone to leave mortals alone, but any instance of magical tampering at the celestial gates could conceivably draw their attention. The magnitude of the attempt largely determined the force of their response, which could be considerable, and was always malevolent.

Quoth Imhotep: "In their sphere they dwell unformed, shapeless, without mind or purpose, like poison clouds or wisps of deadly mist; yet should arcane supplication pass through them, their potential doth concentrate and focus upon the supplicant. They are drawn to the seeker like the many-toothed crocodile of the Delta is drawn to the hapless goat, and perhaps for the same purpose. They are enabled by the offending beam of magic to enter into our world, and to cloak themselves in vile bodies or foul semblances of same, and if they desire they will send one of their number through the mystic portals to fasten upon the mind and soul of the unwary wizard who disturbs them. Their intentions are utterly evil, their power immeasurably vast, for it descends from the will of the Gods; and one must be alert at all times for their baleful intrusion."

Imhotep added, "I write from cruel and miserable experience. I sought the Gods, utilizing the formulae I have here cunningly outlined, and gained results to astound and amaze; yet I gained somewhat other, which transformed my happy life into nightmare. That was long ago, but it presses me still, darkening my days and sapping my joy among men. My tormentor is too cruel to kill me, reveling as it does in my suffering. Never have I uncovered the secret of banishment, though I would gladly trade all my fame and wealth for an instant of peace. At times I pray for death, which I hope will grant me balm or oblivion. I say to he who comes after me—should any other read this—ponder long the first step, lest the road be an interminable and weary one."

Troubling business indeed, but Bleek could not restrain himself. He held such valuable lore in his very hands, and come what may he would study, he would learn, he would implement. He felt himself close to monumental discoveries and decisive results. Greatness always demanded a price, and perhaps he could afford the cost in return for benefits received. Then, too, it seemed that virtually every supernatural gift came wrapped in threats and warnings, or so it was ever claimed. This had proved a falsehood in the past, and might well in the current instance. Why should Imhotep's fate of thousands of years gone necessarily apply to the present? Bleek assured himself that it need not, and plunged forward.

He had been warned; retribution followed swiftly. It began with what he thought, at first, a disorder of the eye. His peripheral vision teased him with a suggestion that someone was barely within sight of his field of view, at a considerable remove. He would be out and about, by day or night, in the streets and markets of the city, and something would minutely intrude upon his consciousness, the merest hint of a form or shadow, and he would glance in that direction, only to see nothing there whatsoever. Puzzled, he would further turn, thinking that a fellow pedestrian had passed that way, but never did he spy anyone whose appearance adequately corresponded to his fleeting glimpse. While he concentrated on matters immediately before him he was largely immune to the effect, but when attention strayed the annoyance was sure to arise. On occasion he would note the subtle form after he had turned to face it, though it would once more reveal itself only at the boundaries of vision. The ailment, as he tried to call it, irked him exceedingly, and did rather more than that as it gradually intensified.

Bleek continued to devote himself to absorbing the spells of power vouchsafed him by his deceased mentor. He analyzed formulae, computed equations, practiced inscribing certain hieroglyphs of latent magical potency. All this he did, dreaming of the approaching moment when his studies must culminate in world-shaking revelations; and he fretted and grimaced, cursing his fortune, for he knew now that all was not well with him. The supposed optical disorder began to impress him in a new and evil light. There definitely was something quietly lurking in his vicinity, allowing itself to be seen just enough to induce dread. He knew this because, with the passage of days, it grew apparent that the thing was, by infinite degrees, approaching him. Each fresh glimpse, not quite out of sight, showed him the unwelcome presence stealthily advancing. It never spoke, nor did it generate any sound at all, but it was there. He could not escape it; it was always there now, inflicting painful wounds upon his concentration. It seemed to Bleek that, when the insidious visitation first occurred, that it had hovered about thirty feet to his left or right. By the time he managed to discern details it had inched forward to within six feet.

Jacob Bleek did not care for his new companion; in fact, he loathed its presence and its features, such as he could make out. As he feared, it was not a man, though there was something vaguely manlike it its general outlines, which he thought unclothed. It was a dark thing, and tall, with a hint of soft corpulence about its frame, for it seemed big in the body, yet insubstantial, as if inadequately molded. The shape did not remain precisely the same from one view to the next, but there were sufficient similarities to convince him that he dealt with the same entity at all times. There were stout, thick legs which he never observed moving, although he imagined that he caught them on the verge of movement, a beginning of motion in his direction; and there were arms, of a number he could not establish to his satisfaction, if they were proper arms, for he could not detect any hands. These upper extensions appeared grotesquely long, and thin, and whip-like, and they did, so far as he could tell, appear to be in constant, gentle motion. He sensed that they were waving at or reaching towards him, most probably the latter.

Of the head and face of the thing Jacob Bleek preferred not to dwell, yet he did so frequently. Minutiae of that black visage were hard to pin down, but he saw sufficient to induce quaking disgust. The skull was a sagging, lopsided mass with a shiny black covering of stringy, chitinous hair, beneath which stared two large, dull yellow eyes. There was a strangely protruding beaked nose and a broad muzzle of a mouth, black jaws which appeared to encompass many spiky teeth and a fat, elongated black tongue. This much he could make out, after a course of observation painful to the eye, and he suspected that there was more to be seen should he ever have the unpleasant opportunity to focus on the thing. The creature was absolutely horrible, completely unearthly, and Bleek could not doubt that the curse which had befallen Imhotep had similarly fastened upon himself.

He would not despair, however; his great work must continue, and he had faith in himself and his abilities. No man or monster could best Jacob Bleek. Most unwillingly—for it cost him time from his favored research— he turned to the thorny matter of banishing the repellent being. He knew that the methods of antiquity were ineffective, else the Egyptian mage would have relieved himself of the burden, but Bleek had pried into the practical secrets of magic farther, he felt (perhaps with justice), than had any other scholar, and he demanded of his mind and fate that there be a way.

He read in his copious notes of possible solutions; he gathered potentially useful materials, rare herbs and specially blended mineral compounds and fuming acids; he mixed and boiled and simmered his potions; he uttered queer words possessing weird meanings in both this world and that beyond. All this he did, while still endeavoring to carry on in what passed for his as a state of normality, yet all this time his horrid companion edged nearer, and never did Bleek's formulations rid him of the agonizing intrusion. The hideously waving black feelers or tentacles of the creature—rather more than two, he now saw awkwardly but plainly—groped through the air by the side of his face, were soon like to touch him, a notion he found unbearable.

It must be understood that Bleek could not call upon any conventional aid from his fellow men. He had realized early on that only he could see the beastly thing, a truth impressed upon him after he initially made a fool of himself in public by loudly and violently reacting to its presence. Other people ignored the creature regardless of its proximity to themselves, and once he thought he saw a native gentleman actually pass through the form without awareness. The entity was, of course, an apparition, existing within this plane solely for the dubious benefit of its chosen victim. The foreign sorcerer had actually stooped to paying a call on a local wizard (there were some in those parts), contriving a flimsy excuse, in fact wondering if another mind trained in magic to a reasonable degree could detect the horror. The native mage did not; Bleek was hopelessly alone in his misery.

The situation deteriorated. The thing, spirit or demon or whatever it might technically be called, had now approached so closely as to stand, partly seen, at his side at all times. Even within Bleek's tiny rented cloister, which had served as a refuge for a time, he could no longer avoid it. The monstrosity would appear at his left, the black feelers lapping around behind him to his right, or vice versa. Probably it was always there, but enormous willpower could blank it from consciousness for short periods. Those intervals decreased at a steady rate. He concluded that the moment was coming when half-sight of the horror would become permanent and oppressive to his sanity.

He knew when that moment came. For many days he had felt himself going to pieces under the silent onslaught. He could hardly think an unbroken or rational thought, while his defensive measures faltered, and even his vital studies suffered. He had hoped to be communicating with the Gods by now; instead, he cowered in his room, contemplating a tragic future. He could not fully relax, and sleep came only with utter exhaustion. One night, after a day's pathetic labors, he did throw himself into bed and drop into slumber, only to awake at some point with a start, an abruptness induced by a nagging dream, the tail end of which he remembered. It had seemed as if a repulsive, growling voice, accompanied by a rapid hot breath, was muttering incomprehensible words directly into his ears. A moment's thought identified the language as a crude variant of Old Egyptian, and once Bleek realized this he immediately knew what had been said to him, and he was aghast at the concepts conveyed. Awakening, though, did not rescue him from distress, for on the instant he felt the presence of something sharing the bed with him, something snuggled closely along the length of his naked body. It was clammy and cold, soft and pulpy, and at several points sensations as of soggy fingers twitched and writhed across his exposed skin. He sprang up with a cry; it had touched him, a genuine physical interaction! There was nothing in the bed, but he had felt it, and when he lighted a candle and the flame burned steadily he saw that his demonic companion still lurked silently at his side, crowding him now as if to permanently press against him. There was no longer a hair's breadth of gap between them; they must necessarily become as one.

It was the end. Jacob Bleek could not go on. The curse of Imhotep had defeated him at last. He knew fairly well from the ancient account that the monstrous illusion—a misleading term under the circumstances, for this was no figment of a diseased brain, but a legitimate aspect of his reality—would not kill, but torment him slowly unto death. Bleek craved long life, and he could not bear to pass his days in such conditions, with such company.

One ray of hope remained. In that supposed dream, that invasion of his subconscious, the creature had spoken to him in the antique dialect of Imhotep. That should not be required of a visitor from the dark realms of the other dimensions. It had so spoken, deduced the wizard, because the curse was a derivation of that which had been wrought upon Imhotep himself when he risked all with his spells and incantations in the bygone centuries. The clinging menace had been chiefly intended for the original transgressor, and must linger now via some medium, a tangible source easy to guess. It was the scrolls, the wonderful documents inscribed by the hand of Imhotep, founts of wisdom, yet impregnated with inherent evil. The curse existed in this world only through them.

With the realization came decision, and with the decision, action, though it were a sort akin to cutting out his own heart. Bleek seized the first scroll and thrust it into the candle flame. The papyrus charred, flickered, blazed and crisped. A glutinous black smoke streamed from the flaring document, filling the chamber. A filthy stench assailed the nostrils of its destroyer. Neither were normal consequences of the combustion of parchment, but that he expected. He lit the second scroll with the first, then the third, continuing relentlessly until all seven were destroyed. He could take no chances, so he gathered up his own notes, upon which he had transcribed critical elements of the scrolls, and annihilated them as well by fire. When everything of inestimable merit was gone he staggered, choking, from the room, and only then, away from the opaque vapors, was he in a position to subsequently verify that his hateful companion had indeed vanished.

Thus ended the remnant curse of Imhotep, and so ended Jacob Bleek's immediate dreams for grandiose wisdom and power. All had been lost—a loss, the magnitude of which struck him as physical pain, for he had been close, so close—but the redoubtable sorcerer had never been one to surrender to ill fortune. He had suffered a setback, no more, monstrous though it was. His mind and soul were intact, and there were other pyramids beneath which he could delve, and other strange parts of the world to which he could journey and investigate. The gateways to the cosmic secrets existed, and he would find them. It was time for Bleek to move on.

The Love of Jacob Bleek

Long ago Jacob Bleek came to the little village, and built for himself the tall, towering house on the heavily forested, sunless peak of the brooding hill which loomed close over the town. In those days he was still young, and an unknown quantity, which his cold demeanor and craving for solitude did not quickly dispel. Much time passed before the fine village folk realized that they had in their midst a great sorcerer, a formidable man of antique and odd learning, who read strange books, wrote stranger ones, practiced dubious arts and indulged in mysterious experiments utilizing materials brought to his chosen abode by taciturn foreigners in the dead of night. The worthy fathers of the community did not know what to think of him, but they suspected the worst. They observed the curiously colored lights which gleamed from the windows of the far off house, and noted the strange rays which shot up from there in the hours before dawn. They feared what they guessed was black magic, and some of the more daring among them suggested that something ought to be done about the intruder who quietly labored on menacing projects right above their heads.

They did attempt to take action—nothing serious, perhaps no more hostile than warning him to be gone—but it was the last time they ever made that mistake. They entered unbidden into the grim house of Jacob Bleek, remained for a period, and then left it. Not all of them did, so it seems; it appears that the deputation had shrunk in numbers since entering, and those who returned had certainly lost their eagerness for their stated mission. After that the village folk concluded that it was best to leave the reclusive wizard alone. The stories they told concerning the fates of the missing men were wild and marvelous, and perhaps need not be taken at face value; yet those men were never seen nor heard of again. One man who did return, a stolid, sober blacksmith, had suffered a crisis of the brain, which forever afterward reduced him to the level of cringing, gibbering idiocy. He died some years later, still unable to speak coherently of what he had seen in the Bleek house, or of what Bleek had done to him. Some of the other survivors considered him a fortunate man.

As the years rolled by the people of the village learned to leave Jacob Bleek alone. They found that he was, in the main, willing to return the favor. He did not come down from his dark hill to stalk their lanes by night and terrorize them; he did not issue cruel edicts or crazed demands from the fastness of his shunned citadel. He did not go out of his way to do anything to them, or to have congress with them in any fashion. Sad to relate, however, that his ill-repute lingered. There were troubling incidents, ongoing hints that all was not well in the formerly complacent burg. Those who met up with the legendary sorcerer by chance told scurrilous tales of the cloud of evil which seemed to envelope him. Others spoke of his penchant for lurking near the ancient cemetery near the base of the big hill, and of the occasional signs of disturbance which marred some of the graves. Then, too, there were the infrequent shipments of alien supplies which came for him, packages and crates of which pious folk suspected the worst. One inhabitant from those days—a cleric, possibly a fanciful one—recorded in his diary a peculiar event. One evening a heavy oblong box arrived in town, intended for delivery to Bleek. The careless wagoneer lost control of his horse, and his insidious freight tumbled to the ground and broke open, whereupon he promptly fled. There was much excitement over what was found within. The villagers were not sure what to do about it. There was talk of interring the contents in the burial yard, but they were not convinced that such a dreadful thing ought to lie alongside decent Christian remains. To make matters worse, they were not entirely of one mind that the thing was wholly ready for burial; it actually occurred to some of them that it might object. What, then, were they to do? They had no interest themselves in retaining the material. They might have sent it back from whence it came, but they lacked an address. Therefore, they made the best of a bad situation and sent it on to Bleek, who may have been grateful to them, although his response was not written down for posterity.

There is recalled from those days the extraordinary fear and hatred that the village folk felt for their unwelcome neighbor. They had nothing good to say about him—if they remembered him in their prayers, it was to curse him—they wished him far away, and all determined to keep their distance from his ominous stronghold. No, wait; there was an exception to this rule. The innkeeper's daughter, a young and lovely lass, well raised and gentle of mind, did not share the common approbation. She had been taught by her widowed father to practice all of the feminine and godly virtues, to take them to heart and to live them, and this she did. A more kindly and warm-hearted soul never walked the earth. She, it is written, did not walk in furtive horror, as did her peers, at the man of mystery in their midst.

The history of the times has not retained her name. There are documents which allude to her story, and one batch of papers which purports to tell all that befell her, but even the latter avoids precise identification. At strategic points in that manuscript there are carefully placed blots of ink which appear to conceal her name. It is hard, at this distance, to grasp the meaning of those convenient accidents of penmanship; into them may be read the calculating superstition of the author. Regardless, she is remembered as the innkeeper's daughter, and so she must be referred to here.

She deplored the attitudes of her contemporaries. Their ignorant rejection of Bleek, their unwillingness to grant him the respect due a newcomer, earned her righteous contempt. She denounced the lurid stories told about him. No man on God's earth could be so evil. They had misunderstood him; in their narrow provincialism they had failed to offer to a stranger the benefit of the doubt; they read the blackness of their hearts into his own. It was their duty to show Christian charity to the man. If they would not fulfill their social obligations, then somebody else must do so.

She conceived the alarming plan all on her own. One morning she made up a bag of delectable viands, which she had prepared herself—she was known as the finest cook in the village—and, slipping unnoticed from her home, the innkeeper's daughter set out toward the huge hill which friendly counsel would have had her avoid. She marched, with some trepidation, past the graveyard, the sight of which brought to mind the recent baleful connotations connected with it, and then proceeded up the densely forested slope along the weedy dirt track which few ever traveled, and none of them townsmen. It took her an hour to reach the top, and that journey was frightening enough to halt many a stout heart. The gloomy woods pressed close upon her, and shadowed her every step forward. Things moved in that unhealthy murk, things which behaved not quite like birds and deer, the familiar animals known to her. She did not see them clearly. Dimly glimpsed shapes rustled in the tangled undergrowth, and something large and clumsy kept pace with her during her climb. She had been told that the hill had not been such an awful place before the coming of the wizard Bleek—that he had introduced a factor of wickedness into the very landscape—but this she dismissed as a childish fantasy, shrugged, and tried to think of it no more.

At last the forest with its secretive denizens fell away, and she attained the crown of the hill, and found herself on the edge of a wide clearing, a sere, barren meadow, and in the center of the clearing, at the very peak, she spied the house of Jacob Bleek. New it was, compared to the humble cottages of the village, and yet it looked old. She had never seen a house like it before. A vast wooden structure, square, it boasted three stories, with tiny windows configured into curious geometrical shapes. From the center of the peaked roof rose a high, narrow tower, like a minaret, which terminated in a chamber entirely sealed save at the top, where an angled glass ceiling caught the oddly muted sunlight. It was an imposing, impressive edifice, and she may well have wondered how it came to be built, how Bleek had managed it without local aid. Many of her fellow villagers wondered.

At first she had thought that a light shone from within the tower chamber. That might not have been true, for a second glance revealed nothing. She warily approached the great paneled doors, stopping at the foot of the flight of granite-flagged steps which led up to them. The world around her seemed eerily silent, and she was tired, what with lugging her burden up that hill, and just for a moment she was not sure how to proceed. There was something about the place, an aura of mystery, not altogether welcoming.

Then the innkeeper's daughter saw the face in the second story window above and to the left of the doors. A hard, cold face stared down impassively at her. That must be the man. Then it vanished. She took heart, somehow, and mounted the steps to the porch. She found that the doors were ornamented with unusual carven images, pictures of animals or entities unlike anything she had ever seen or heard of before, creatures which appeared to swim and undulate on the broad oak surfaces. She raised the star-shaped silver knocker and lowered it with a reverberating clang. She did so twice more.

Presently the doors creaked open, folding inward to reveal the host of the manor. The great and terrible Jacob Bleek confronted her in the flesh. What did she see? By collating various reports, a guess may be hazarded. There stood before her a tall, gaunt figure, cloaked in Stygian black and wrapped in an air of unearthly menace. Cruel dark eyes, a hawk nose, thin pursed lips, and a strong chin accentuated by the short pointed beard, made up the face which assailed her with its inhuman hostility and superior cynicism. Not a trace of warmth glinted from those fierce eyes, nor a breath of humanity in his forbidding manner.

What was said at that meeting was never taken down, nor is it recalled that Bleek spoke a word to his uninvited guest. The innkeeper's daughter managed—haltingly, one must imagine—to make the purpose of her errand known. She offered him the comestibles as a token of good will. Given the type of stories told about Bleek, it would not surprise if this tale ended here, with him devising some extraordinary means for removing her permanently from his presence. It did not happen that way. He stood aside, and allowed her to enter the dreaded Bleek House.

In due course she returned from her mission, reappearing at her home in the village later that day. Her story, although it contained no trace of weird nastiness, shocked her neighbors and horrified her father. She made clear that she had been treated with respect, that Bleek's behavior had been thoroughly correct, if formal or even rather frigid, and that nothing unpleasant had occurred or caught her attention for the duration of her visit. This account did not satisfy her father. The innkeeper punished her severely and forbade her to ever approach the spooky hill again, much less the evil house at its summit. His methods of persuasion, though extreme, failed to have the desired effect. His daughter, although she did not openly defy him, developed a penchant for day long jaunts, the purposes for which she could not adequately justify. People claimed to have seen her near the old cemetery, or wandering in the vicinity of the base of Bleek's hill. One man claimed to have seen her, from a distance, conversing with someone by the woodland road which ran to the sorcerer's house. She had little to say by way of excuse, but there can be no doubt that she did undertake the climb again, and soon, and this time, as it transpired, she went to stay.

Shortly thereafter Jacob Bleek caused a decree to be published, through which he proclaimed a most marvelous announcement. Henceforth he and the innkeeper's daughter were to be considered as man and wife. He made clear to the townsfolk that the union was official, according to ancient custom and law. This puzzled and perplexed the villagers, for the local priest and the town recorder knew nothing of the ceremony, nor would they have taken part in it had they known. Assurances that the marriage had been properly authorized and witnessed pleased and satisfied no one, for they all loudly wondered among themselves as to the monstrous nature of the authority, and the character of the witnesses. That Satan and his imps had presided over the affair seemed the most likely explanation. Bleek might have clarified the matter further in order to soothe uneasy minds but, as was his wont, he chose not to do so.

For all of the scandalous talk and hard feelings, the villagers chose to do exactly nothing about the situation. If it actually had been a real wedding, as they tried to convince themselves, then interference on that score would prove fruitless. Then, too, there was the character of the groom to consider. They might not like him—they might have good reasons to dislike him—and he might not like them—as they possessed abundant grounds for suspecting—but they dreaded the notion of converting him into an enemy. It was not wise to seek trouble with such a man. As for the poor, lost little girl: well, that was very much too bad, and her father certainly felt his loss most keenly, but that was very often the way of the world, and there was little they could do about it anyway, without risking extreme disasters (imagination supplied all sorts of tragic scenarios), so why not just let the matter lie, and try very hard to make the best of admittedly disagreeable circumstances? Call it cowardice, if that suits, but it had been their way for some time now, and so far had served them well.

In the course of time the new wife of Jacob Bleek presented herself in public. She handled all of his business in town—no one ever figured out how he had gotten by before—and her appearances became frequent. She seemed contented, as cheerful as ever, though she provided few details of her married life. Certainly she exhibited no ill effects from the union. The village folk treated her with amazing courtesy, which was apparently the right thing to do, because no difficulties of any sort arose. She did not involve herself in local society to any great degree, and her husband not to any extent, and there were several who continued to deplore her choice, but life went on as before, and without hardship or pain the years rolled by.

Then the woman of Jacob Bleek, who had once been the innkeeper's daughter, died. This happened much later, long after the shadowy wedding, and there may have been nothing untoward about the sad event. All who are born must die, and according to one prevalent account, her time had simply come, as it eventually comes to all. There is a competing tradition which must be noted. According to one popular story, which descends through the ages without clear references or solid backing, she had remained the good and faithful wife all that time only because the evil, black-hearted Bleek had cunningly contrived to shield her from his conjured horrors. Then, late in life, she had accidentally stumbled upon one of his morbid obscenities, some vicious rite or criminal activity which had shocked her and shaken her to her soul. She had remonstrated with him, argued, recoiled from him in fright, perhaps, toward the last, even tried to kill him for the safety and sanity of the world. Bleek, not accustomed to defiance, prone to reacting hotly to any opposition or rebellion, had, in that unguarded moment, blazed furiously at her with the boundless power of his loathsomely astronomical mind, and through the sheer will of his titanic rage had struck her dead.

Which version be true? At this great remove, it may be only a matter of taste. History, such as it is, records that she died. Legend offers alternative options as to the cause. Regardless, she was gone, and Jacob Bleek was alone. He laid her body in a sealed stone chamber beneath his house—no public burial for her, and no mourners allowed—and with her remains deposited in the private tomb, he pondered.

A regular folk tale, at this point, would expound upon the ephemeral nature of the things of this world, and serve to instruct in the methods by which man deals with the subtraction from his life of fleeting joy, or expose the vanity and hubris of those who embark upon a futile campaign to deny fate. One might derive fine lessons from such a tale, but that is not the sort of story told about Bleek, in this case or ever. It is told that he refused to bow to the dictates of destiny. Unlike the innkeeper father, Bleek had no intention of accepting his loss, for the wizard had truly loved his woman, after his fashion, and it did not please him to acquiesce in her passing as any other man must do. He was a strong man boasting incredible resources and an inventive mind, and he determined to retrieve her from the eternal darkness into which she had forever gone.

As local lore relates, he first attempted to call up her shade from the realm of the dead. Whatever old books of spells were required, he possessed them; whatever incantations must be recited by the midnight light of the moon, he knew them by heart; whatever pacts must be made with infernal powers at whatever cost, he was willing to pay the price. He knew what he had to do, he did that, and it worked. He raised up before him her spirit, the ethereal, flickering ghost of what had been his wife, and he spoke with her at length. Two versions exist of that conversation. In the one, derived from the claim that he cruelly destroyed her, he pleads for her forgiveness and demands her return, yet she still recoils from him, and begs to be left in peace. In the other, which acknowledges her natural death, she reaffirms her vows of love for him, and begs that he employ his mystical arts to rescue her from cold oblivion.

The differing threads of the stories intertwine beyond this point, for they agree that while the brilliant mage had resurrected her spirit, she was only a phantom, insubstantial and untouchable. This was not what he craved. She was no good to him in this formless state. So it is written, and more often told orally, that Jacob Bleek went back to his books. He studied every scrap of mystic lore at hand and pried from them astonishing secrets that no one had ever imagined to exist. That did not turn the trick, so he sent out, via his furtive messengers, for even older books and long lost scrolls, the works of eminent worthies from times long past, the works of great minds that had been forgotten, or who had lived in remote epochs that had been forgotten or never known to be. In the process he greatly increased his collection, and added to his general store of occult knowledge. Somewhere along the way he found the solution he sought, and he set out to implement it.

He removed her body from its sealed, airtight tomb, and carried it to his laboratory of sorcery, where he treated it with exotic chemicals and potions derived from herbs and minerals found only in the Earth's wilder and most dangerous locales. He prepared a great iron cauldron, which he filled with a soup composed of stranger solutions, and he heated the contents to a bubbling, steaming intensity. Then he cut up the corpse of his beloved into convenient fragments, and dropped them one by one into the noxious stew. At intervals, while he mixed the erupting, choking mess, he chanted obscure words, and drew in his own blood impossible geometrical signs on the stone floor, and read aloud long quotes from a certain ancient tome written in a language no man had spoken for eons. He boiled and he boiled, until the contents of the black pot distilled down to a thick, filthy, stinking, quivering ooze.

Bleek gathered up the congealed mass into a container of wrought brass, and he carried it to the forbidden chamber at the top of his tower, and there he deposited the ghastly slime upon a basalt altar. A new series of incantations, drawings, and readings commenced. He continued throughout the night, until just before morning the heavens opened, lightning danced upon the hill, the wind roared and the beasts of the woods howled.

It had happened. His grand, hopeless dream had been fulfilled. From that disgusting condensation Bleek the wizard had recovered the essence of the girl who had meant something to Bleek the man. That concentrated muck had captured the dwindling filaments of her personality, her sweetness, her devotion—her soul?—and restored them to vitality. Then Bleek the creator had given them shape, and fashioned for them with his hands a new form, a fresh body in which what was truly of her could survive and thrive. The woman of Jacob Bleek lived again.

How could anyone know of and confirm such a story? The chronicles say it is so, and they record the aftermath. They tell of the companion who lived with Bleek from this time, a personage of vaguely feminine appearance who dressed in the old clothing of the innkeeper's daughter, but who never again visited the village, nor suffered the townsfolk to come near. She always went about—according to those who glimpsed her at a distance—heavily dressed, and with her face obscured by a coarse veil. It is written that once a gang of young boys dared themselves to approach her, and that one of them gazed upon her unconcealed face, but the story goes on only to relate that he fell down dead on the spot from fright. One may speculate that Jacob Bleek was not moved by physical charms, and that in reviving her spiritual inner beauty, he had paid scant attention to outer loveliness.

Regardless, it is possible to conclude that Jacob Bleek and his wife lived happily ever after. In time they must have perished, both of them, for good, for this is a very old story, although even that apparent fact is presented as problematical. There are those who claim that Bleek still lives in his house of mystery on the shunned hill. That is difficult to credit, for it grants to him a span of life far beyond that of any wholesome mortal man. On the other hand, being categorical about a fellow like Bleek may not constitute the surest path of wisdom. Perhaps he and his lady love still live up there above the antique village. The only way to find out is to climb the hill and see, and no one has done that within the memory of those now living.

The City at the End of Time

In the olden days the great sorcerer Jacob Bleek, who would know all things in heaven and earth that ever had been or ever would be, who would conquer knowledge for his eternal glory and private satisfaction, made a mighty magic in the secret lower chamber of his shunned old house, and there he gazed through steaming mist and roiling vapors into a unique crystal, an uneven, geometrically confusing mass of rare element wrought by his own hands, and peering through the crystal he beheld a far marvel. There, at a distance infinite in space and time, he saw a bleak, blasted, lifeless plain of broken rock, a twilit plain beyond which low mountains aged by eternity rose shadowy in perpetual gloom. In the inky sky burned a staggering number of stars, thousands of them, of various colors and hues, each as bright as the Star of the Dog that he knew from the commonplace winter constellations. In the center of the plain loomed the Black Tower, a mighty edifice of iron, with a single sheer shaft rising into the murk, and a vast bulbous or domed chamber residing atop the spire. Ugly it was, harsh and painful to the eye, yet intriguing and alluring to a man such as Bleek, for no doorway graced its structural perfection of unity, no openings of any kind save that in the bulging cap which crowned it, where a single square window emitted a pale, weakly yellow, baleful light, a mysterious radiance thrown out into the world by the unknowable forces within.

Thrilled Bleek was to see this much, for he guessed—nay, deduced from his arcane studies—the Black Tower to exist beyond the wearisome sweep of time and matter, rather to stand at the center of all things, within and apart; raised not by the hand of man nor any other material entity, but rather by the great powers that underlie and control all existence: the Old Gods, the original and the eternal, as personified by Their boundless master Xenophor, "He Who Creates and Destroys," who lords over the universe and is the universe, the cosmic totality of all. The Black Tower was Their, was His, citadel encapsulated inside the attainable realms of being, and there Jacob Bleek would go, and experience wonders.

Never taking his eyes from the crystal of vision he made the proper obeisance, uttered the secret words, offered all that he could afford and more that he could not; damned himself a dozen times over, pausing only to laugh as he did so, then concluded the rites with imperious demand. As he did so the foul mist swirled afresh, the image in the crystal fading from view as the grim stone chamber disappeared around him. He found himself in terrifying, mind-stealing void, but he tarried there not long, for presently—in a moment, or an eon, or many ages—he came to full awareness of hard ground beneath his feet, and shattered rocks about him on a level surface, and dense gloom all around, and the fierce stars overhead, and the majestic sight of the Black Tower rising before him.

241

He had come to the place appointed; very well, but what should it signify? He did not approach the tower, choosing instead to circle it at a remove in order to confirm what he assumed, that no convenient doorway opened along the compass of its base. None did, therefore cause for approach was lacking. One did not stride up and knock at gates which did not exist. Therefore he lifted his gaze, staring into that solitary window so far above, a window which, he noted with strange pleasure, beckoned still from whatever direction he observed the structure. He saw nothing within that window—no faces or mock-faces peered down at him—saw nothing at all save the sickly, feeble glare that trickled over that unreachable sill. Upon that he focused, and though nothing changed to his eyes, a whisper crept into his mind. Within the deepest recesses of his mortal brain came a voice without words, a speech of impressions and hints and indications more true and intelligible than any common utterance of tongue. It spoke to him, seeking to draw him in, dangling ultimate insights like priceless baubles should he agree to enter as They would have him do so. He had only to bow down and agree, and it would be done; he would be translated into the tower, there ever to reside, there ever to know as They knew; but this Jacob Bleek refused, for he knew it would mean in addition more than the death of him. He denied, he pushed away that final prize, yet did so with sacred reverence, and having done so asked of a lesser boon, though still enormous.

The strange high light from the tower winked out. Bleek waited pensively in the grim darkness, then saw a new source of illumination gathering before him. An eerie greenish radiance developed, oozing up from the harsh ground, coagulating into a scintillating ball of cold, silent fire. A shape appeared within it, a suggestion of willowy form—human form—the image of a young and lovely woman with golden tresses cascading past her ivory throat, and bright eyes like diamond stars, and silky dress of antique or oddly foreign style. The green glow faded but did not die, instead radiating softly and steadily from the beautiful vision. She said, in a voice like rare music:

"Jacob Bleek, mage extraordinaire of your world and time, the Great Ones have heard, and They grant thy request. Fain would They take thee unto Themselves, but this thou would put by, so the lesser shall be given as it pleases thee. All thoughts are known to Them. Thou would penetrate the wall of eons, gaze upon the final, the ultimate glories of your kind and your cosmos. Come, then, with me as thy appointed guide, and behold marvels of the final days. Is this as thou would wish?"

He said it was, and she cried a mighty word that no mortal could ever speak, and the scene vanished, all sight of tower and terrain and woman disappeared, and then he gazed down from an aerial vantage upon another place, a dark orb mysterious to him, from which one discrete, circular source of light gleamed. He realized that he hovered in the outer spaces above a dark world, one lit by no sun, in a vast, cold universe devoid of stars. In every direction his disembodied presence observed total blackness, save from a single round spot far below his invisible self. The musical voice of the woman spoke from nowhere into his ear: "This is the culmination at the end of time. Let us stride amidst that glory."

Darkness obscured his vision. After a moment, marked by no sense of falling or motion, he stood in the heart of an incredible vista. A realm of pure artifice confronted him. Above him, stretching to distant horizons, hung the interior of a mighty metallic dome, well lit by curious lamps hanging from that stupendously vast ceiling, lamps that never flickered, only burned with unwinking white light. Bleek deduced that he stood within the solitary circular light he had seen from the void. Impressive enough that was—for how could the sweat of human labor ever have raised that roof?—yet what lay inside must dominate his thoughts and catch his breath with awe. The amazing dome shielded, from the ravages of eternal night, a titanic city of dazzling light and frenetic activity.

"Is it not wondrous, Jacob Bleek?" asked the woman at his side. He had not noticed her until she spoke. She took him by the hand. "Are not the fruits of the ages magnificent beyond thy most astounding dreams? This is the eventuality of thy kind, thy people, men and minds like thy own, fashioning and delving to the brink of ultimate attainment. Observe, investigate, and be happy with thy legacy, for this is the destiny of all for which thou has striven. I leave thee to it, but I shall not wander far. When thou hold my hand again, then may thou return to thy own time and place." And with those words she was gone.

Bleek heeded not her absence. He had come to the scene of mankind's triumph, the city at the end of time, a deathless metropolis which held at bay (perhaps forever, he mused joyously) the implacable forces of entropy which would have annihilated a more feeble race. It thrilled him that his folk should have achieved this, that studied brilliance and the lust for knowledge should combine, in accordance with his fondest fantasies, to defy even the remorseless cruelties of blind fate, which ever operated to sweep away accomplishment and life. Bleek's descendants had chosen, even as he, not to bow down and admit defeat before the innate hostility of the universe, but had struggled without pause, without flagging, until they conquered the forces of death and decay which smote man and his makings from the elder times. And what an accomplishment they achieved, a marvel without peer through all the ages!

The city moved and flashed and beamed with vibrant life. Across the artificial sky strange gleaming machines buzzed and swooped like insects, darted like lightning, cruised imperiously like stately ships. Around the unending array of spires, minarets, soaring spikes of metal and glass swept encircling balconies and ledges, sky-flung roadways on which cruised or raced weird conveyances, metal carts without horses that drove faster than eagles could fly, others like trains of wagons joined together, inching quietly and surely up and down the planes without any hint of propulsion. He had never beheld a landscape so alive, yet one without any evidence of what made it work. His keen eyes sought the masters of these mechanisms, beheld them not. Bleek could only suppose that the drivers of these rolling or flying carriages were housed within the metal bodies, gauging their courses through unseen windows.

He stood in the center of a square plaza perhaps a quarter mile across, its surface an unbroken, unlined mass of firm metal which might have been fine steel, perhaps something grander. It resembled a public square, but no denizens were about at the moment. Strange buildings, low, rectangular edifices of windowless metal, brooded around the deserted perimeter, buildings without doors or windows but many lights, flashing on and off at intervals, creating patterns which meant nothing to him. Narrow lanes passed betwixt the structures. Beyond rose the stupendous towers of the city, rank after rank fading into distance. It was a big place, this city, and he would see it all, converse with its wise men, mingle with its blessed inhabitants. Such stories they could tell him!

Bleek set forth, choosing a direction at random, making for a particular dagger of gold which knifed the air, glittering prettily, between two solemn towers of gray metal. Toward this he strode because it amused him, because he must begin somewhere, and the gold spire pleased his eye. He entered the relatively shaded passageway leading that way, with the odd buildings at each side. Or were they machines? No one emerged to greet him or ask his business, nor were there any portals for them to do so. Were these ubiquitous structures artifactual? It might be that they, in some manner currently beyond his ken, performed service to the wonders about him. In the past he had speculated about such possibilities.

Before him his quick ears detected an amalgamation of sounds which quickened his pace, for he desired to meet those who produced the noise. He chuckled when he pondered the difficulties of introducing himself, explaining his presence. Yet these people must be all wise; they would know, they would understand.

The passage opened onto a smaller square, this one strung with metallic wires drawn tautly overhead, strands of coppery hue along which hummed pulses of red light. Through the air among the wires unusual rays of intensely blue light danced and flared back and forth, emitting at times a sound like the crackling of electricity, at periodic occasions a powerful droning which oppressed the ear. These were the sounds he had heard. He brightened when a metal carriage whined into view from an enclosed passage, advancing gracefully on several metallic rollers. It moved purposefully to a spot beneath a humming strand, and a skinny, segmented metal arm rose from a hatch to fiddle with the wire. The points of contact twinkled blue and white. Then the squat conveyance began rolling away into another tunnel. Bleek leaped forth, striving to attract the attention of the occupant or occupants, to no avail. The thing vanished around the corner without heeding him in any way.

He consoled himself by concluding that these people, so accustomed to marvels in their daily life, would not be overly intrigued by his obscure appearance in their midst. They were used to stranger wonders. He left the open space, threading his way along a corridor framed by larger slab-sided structures, emerged onto a shelf overlooking a metal gorge hundreds of rods across. At his feet the path ended abruptly at a yawning brink, from which he could look down into shadowy depths where moving lights glistened and throbbing sounds welled. He threw himself full length at the edge of the gulf, for it dropped without slope at least a mile, and he imagined more. So this city plunged down in subterranean majesty as its towers rose, level upon level. Bleek could hazard no surmise as to its full extent.

From the lower murk ascended a series of transparent, glassy bubbles, large shimmering orbs that caught and reflected the multi-colored lights. What they were he did not know, but within one of them he spied a definite human figure. At last he was to be acknowledged. A closer view told true: it was the woman, beckoning to him and laughing. As she drifted by she called to him, saying, "Thou seem forlorn and lonely in the midst of the great city. Continue thy delving, that thou may learn more and know all. The revelations to come are many and instructive." She passed beyond the rim of the gulf, lost to sight, laughing again.

It struck Bleek that he should find the inhabitants within the towers which rose like the spires of fairy castles. There they could live in splendor, and there he would treat with them, learn their ways and gain their thoughts on the past and present, for all secrets must be open to them. He recalled the golden spire, which he had lost in the maze, moved through another passage in what ought to be the requisite direction, glimpsed it and its framing towers looming above a wall of blank, humming buildings. A broad avenue of sorts spread before his path and led him immediately to his destination. Sure enough, a round open doorway gaped at the base of the spire. He strode to it, peeked inside, found the interior well lighted, entered. No one was there, but the place more resembled living quarters than anything he had seen so far. There were chambers connected by a central hall—rooms approached by doors that opened as if by magic—all constructed of metal and glass and other elements he could not identify, with counters filled with lights, knobs, levels. Such ornamentation crowded the walls as well. In one room he actually found something like a chair, in which he sat before an array of esoteric devices. He tinkered with the mechanisms, got results. An empty portion of the wall suddenly flared into life, revealed to him an image of the city as seen from a point near the top of the sky dome. It made for an excellent map. Bleek experimented with what he now knew for controls, causing the image to expand, shrink, or change. He saw much that was fantastic and beautiful, much mysterious. This marvelous instrument allowed him to search distant regions for signs of his fellow men. He undertook this goal, devoting considerable time to the task, without success. Eventually he wearied of this, chose to ascend into the upper reaches of the spire.

This proved a simple matter, though he sought in vain for a staircase. In time he discovered a tiny, drab chamber which upon entering immediately began carrying him upward. Bleek was amazed by this moving room. There were no controls on the walls, which mystified him, until he spoke to himself aloud, at which time he discovered that the odd conveyance responded to speech. His specific words meant nothing to the machine (for such it obviously was, like so much else in the city), but trial and error determined which basic vocal sounds made it start, stop, proceed up or down. For a while it was a shaky ride. He got off at certain floors, examined the desolate contents. Dwellings certain of the chambers undoubtedly were—he goggled at what passed for furniture among these folk in the twilight of the universe—but all were vacant, impossibly clean, none containing a single item nor any evidence connoting current or recent occupancy. He could not credit this, cursed his ignorance, moved on in his exploration. In the end Bleek bowed to the transport device, which seemed to have some intent of its own, let it carry him to the highest level at the slender peak.

He stepped out onto an isolated balcony, one not connected to the spire's encircling ramp, and gazed out over the busy vista of lights and machines. He peered down, clutching the railing, observed the woman standing on an out-jutting ledge directly below. She cried, "Where are thy people, Jacob Bleek? Do they hide from you? Have they mastered concealment in addition to aught else? 'Tis a pity, for much they could tell. Over eons without number they dreamed of taming death, of extending themselves, individually and racially, in perpetuity. Against all odds they labored, in the waning days of time, to fabricate this city which should endure as they, so long as the universe should last. Out there, in the cold, dark beyond, all has returned to the void from which it sprang. The stars have burned out, their ashes blown away by the breath of the Old Ones; the planets, all save this, have crumbled to dust; even light and time falter, grow sluggish, expire. Yet the city still lives, perhaps will do so though a thousand eternities die. Is it not magnificent? Is not the soul a paltry price, to gain in return the pure knowledge of this? The Black Tower stands invitingly, but thou would rather hear thy truths from the mighty among men. Go to them, Jacob Bleek, seek them, for all time is thine. No need for thee to sleep, or drink, or eat; go, search, investigate until no hiding place remains. Then call for me. My hand is warm."

THE CITY AT THE END OF TIME

Bleek searched. No pangs of hunger slowed him, no bodily cravings weakened his flesh. He continued until it was his mind that cried for mercy. He looked everywhere, through mystic lifetimes, without finding what he sought. Every room, every burg finally opened to him, yet never did he behold the masters of the city. He learned the ways of the moving vehicles, forced them to halt, broke into them, found artifice, amazing contrivance, but that only. He learned how records could be revealed and read, studied them, learned only of mechanical cleverness. He descended into weird regions beneath the city, delving leagues below the surface, uncovered eventually the mighty storehouses of energy, drawn from the earth's core, which powered the city and gave it life. It was a faux life though, a life of preconceived motion and mindless effort, a life granted to machines which had been erected in a long ago age to serve the builders, the masters of the city who dreamed of eternity.

And they were gone. The life man had breathed into his machines he had not, perhaps could not, retain for himself. The city lived, but the masters had departed forever, suffering the fate of all men before them when at last their knowledge, their charms, their ceaseless struggles could no longer hold at bay the murderous forces of cosmic death. They had failed, as had all the great and glorious minds who grasped at forever and sought to break it to their will. Knowledge entire availed them not; in the end they too died like dogs, the city lingering as their splendid tomb.

Bleek quailed at this realization, and sobbed piteously to himself, for he sought no less than had they, and with lesser means. If the city, that sterile mausoleum, be their culmination—the conclusion of their story, of every tale that had ever been written—then what scope of success remained to him? Was not he, the questing man of a forgotten past, merely a meaningless footnote in the ancient war against nothingness, one more who had striven, fated to face doom?

At the last he did cry out, and the lovely vision of the woman came serenely to him. "Time it is that thou came home," said she. "Those who sent me know of thee, Jacob Bleek, and would take thee unto Themselves. Encompassed within Them is entirety, the all of all. Journey with me to the Black Tower, where all care, worry, and useless struggle fade as dost thy dregs of flesh and mind. Accept the oneness of imperishable oblivion."

To this Bleek said nay. Soothe They might the pain in his soul, which knew such horrors, but never could They satisfy the longings of his mind. He demanded return to his own place and time. The beautiful woman sneered and spat at him a grotesque word, at which she vanished, and in another instant the city blinked out of view, and Bleek felt himself falling, tumbling head over heels, roughly buffeted by angry forces, and then he found himself standing in his familiarly grim chamber of magic, with smoking retorts on the oaken table, and a grinning skull staring from the mantel.

THE JOURNEY OF JACOB BLEEK

The odyssey was over. Bleek had seen the despicable future, learned much, guessed more. All in all, he assured himself, as he came to ponder his experience, it had been an edifying journey, one providing a deal of wisdom and food for subtle speculation. So that was the time to come as the Gods conceived it? Very well, he knew now the tribulations he must confront. Though the Great Ones—though Xenophor Himself—strove against him, he would face the ordeal, overcome all opposition. If only the Gods could decree the future, then he would make himself like Them, and with Their power remake the universe to suit his own demands. This outcome he would pen in the book of destiny.

Notable facts concerning the author:

A degreed anthropologist, wilderness enthusiast, and photographer who makes his home in Arizona, Jeffery Scott Sims is a writer of fantastic and weird fiction. He is the creator of popular characters such as Professor Anton Vorchek, investigator of strange mysteries; Sterk Fontaine, self-serving dabbler in the supernatural; Jacob Bleek, the obsessively questing medieval wizard; and the combative and colorful heroes of ancient Dyrezan.

His publications include the collections *Science and Sorcery, Science and Sorcery II, Science and Sorcery III*, and *Eerie Arizona*; plus many dozen short stories of the bizarre and the macabre. A number of these tales are set in the exotic and mysterious wilds of Arizona, or in imaginary lands of far times and places, ranging from forgotten eras to the distant future.

The author maintains a literary web site, *The Weird Writings of Jeffery Scott Sims*, which in addition to providing useful information on his works also offers an ever growing collection of entertaining essays devoted to unique or unusual topics related to the weird tale. This material may be freely accessed at https://jefferyscottsims.webs.com/index.html